Praise for MARIO ACEVEDO and the bloody good adventures of FELIX GOMEZ, UNDEAD PRIVATE EYE

"Deliciously unique. A smooth combination of Anne Rice and Michael Connelly, with a generous portion of Dave Barry. Loaded with thrills, sex, violence, and laughs."

J.A. Konrath, author of *Bloody Mary*

"My built-in garlic factor usually puts me off vampire books, but Mario Acevedo has come up with such a fascinating character—Iraq war veteran Felix Gomez, who is a private detective as well as a vampire—that I was won over."

Chicago Tribune

"Raymond Chandler
L.A. like this wh
vampires fight cri
during lunch break
never been meaner—
a high-speed, well-crafted romp through the forests of the night."

Booklist

"[Acevedo] manages to update vampire lore in clever and imaginative ways."

El Paso Times

"Acevedo's work is part hard-boiled private eye, part soft-core erotica, and part pure humor."

Statesman Journal (OR)

By Mario Acevedo

The Adventures of Felix Gomez

WEREWOLF SMACKDOWN
JAILBAIT ZOMBIE
THE UNDEAD KAMA SUTRA
X-RATED BLOODSUCKERS
THE NYMPHOS OF ROCKY FLATS

MARIO ACEVEDO

An Imprint of Harper Collins*Publishers*

This book is a work of fiction. The characters, incidents, and dialogue are drawn from the author's imagination and are not to be construed as real. Any resemblance to actual events or persons, living or dead, is entirely coincidental.

EOS
An Imprint of HarperCollinsPublishers
10 East 53rd Street
New York, New York 10022-5299

Cover art by Will Staehle
ISBN 978-0-06-156720-9
www.eosbooks.com

First Eos paperback printing: December 2010
First Eos trade paperback printing: March 2010

Printed in the U.S.A.

10 9 8 7 6 5 4 3 2 1

To the Rocky Mountain Fiction Writers,
thanks for the leg up

Acknowledgments

SINCERE THANKS to HarperCollins, specifically my publisher at Eos, Liate Stehlik; my editor, Diana Gill; her assistant, Will Hinton; marketing manager Jean Marie Kelly; publicist Gregory Shutack; and online marketing manager Shawn Nicholls. Also, much thanks to my agent, Scott Hoffman, and staff at Folio Literary Management, LLC. I couldn't have gotten this far without my critique group: Jeanne Stein, Sandy Maren, Terry Wright, Tamra Monahan, Warren Hammond, and Margie and Tom Lawson. To those in the rah-rah section: Lighthouse Writers Workshop, Mystery Writers of America, El Centro Su Teatro, the Chicano Humanities and Arts Council, and the League of Reluctant Adults. Rebel Sinclair and Mark Jones of Black Cat Tours, thanks for showing me the high and low in Charleston, South Carolina. To Dr. Roberto Cantú, of California State University, Los Angeles, for putting up with my weirdness. And a shout-out to Manuel Ramos, Jennifer Mosquera, Eric Jaenike, and Eric Matelski. I can't forget the support from my sons, Alex and Emil, and family, especially my sister, Sylvia.

WEREWOLF Smackdown

CHAPTER 1

FELIX, I want him dead." Eric Bourbon held up a severed head. The head belonged to a Caucasian man in his early thirties. By the musky taint of the cadaver reek, the victim had been more than a man—he was a werewolf in human form. A *were*.

The eyelids were hooded, the cleanly shaven jaw slack, the pale lips opened slightly, the waxy complexion bleached from the loss of blood. The neck was a ragged stump that had been gnawed off the shoulders. A diamond earring glittered in the left earlobe.

I said, "He looks pretty dead to me."

"Not him." Bourbon dropped the head into a large Tupperware bowl on his desk and wiped his hand with a kerchief. He shuffled photos from a manila file folder and pointed to the top photo. "Him. His name is Randolph Calhoun," Bourbon explained in a melodious Southern drawl, the inflection equally polite and condescending.

As I took the photos, he dropped the kerchief over the

severed head, fit the lid back on the bowl, and worked the edges to seal in the freshness. He opened a desk drawer and pulled out a can of room deodorizer.

I sat back in my chair to avoid getting misted with the scent of spring meadow and studied the ink-jet photos of Calhoun. Bourbon dumped the room deodorizer back into the drawer.

Calhoun sported a helmet of black hair with graying temples. Dapper whether in boating clothes or a tux, but with his wrinkles and slack jowls, he looked like the has-been love interest in a soap opera. His physique varied from trim to paunchy. I arranged the photos in the order from slim to heavy and noticed the accumulating wrinkles and gray hair that accompanied his weight gain. The pictures had been taken at social events, always with people huddling close to absorb the warmth of his charismatic smile.

"Is he one of you?" By that I meant werewolf.

Bourbon grinned in acknowledgment, radiating a hungry, predatory demeanor. His eyes shone with a wolfish glint from pink, wrinkled sockets. When I first saw them, I'd thought of sphincters.

I have seen werewolves before. As long as they stayed out of my way, I stayed out of theirs. I never bothered mentioning them for the same reason I never said anything about skunks or cockroaches.

Bourbon dressed like a *were* used to spending money, most certainly someone else's. He wore a trim white shirt with blue pinstripes and monogrammed cuffs. The shirt creased sharply over the angles of his athletic torso. A silk tie complemented his shirt and gold jewelry. His blond hair, short on the sides, was separated with a razor-neat part.

We sat in his office on the third floor of a commercial building on Broad Street in Charleston, South Carolina. A sky of azure blue filled the one picture window.

The walls displayed his J.D. from the University of South Carolina. A framed illustration from the weekly *City Pages* showed Eric Bourbon, attorney-at-law, leering above a cartoon map of the Charleston peninsula. I'd done my homework on him and was familiar with the article. (But my homework wasn't thorough enough. I'd missed his being a werewolf until I walked past his *were* bodyguards out in the hall.) The newspaper had slammed Bourbon for having the opportunistic scruples of a pickpocket. His reply: "You don't get in the legal business to make friends."

I'd come here thinking this would be a case of straightforward PI work. I wanted nothing that had to do with my previous assignments involving the paranormal, both the successes and the screwups. No alien conspiracies. No political intrigue on behalf of the Araneum—Latin for "spiderweb"—the worldwide secret network of vampires. No supernatural hoodoo. Two thousand just to hear Bourbon pitch his case. No refunds. Strictly gumshoe hustling for money.

But I was wrong.

Bourbon hadn't sought me out because I was from out of town and off the local radar. He wanted a special detective. A vampire detective. Me.

Why?

I returned to one photo in Calhoun's file, that of a buff young brunette sheathed in a paint-thin green dress with a plunging neckline. She clung to Calhoun's left arm, the one that had a prosthetic with metal claws instead of a hand.

I turned the photo around for Bourbon to examine. "Full moon comes around, how does a three-legged werewolf mount his harem of *were*-bitches?"

His lips quivered as he fought back a snarl. Bourbon paid for my time; the sarcasm was gratis.

I asked, "What about Calhoun's arm?" If werewolves were like their natural wild brethren, they kept a strict hierarchy. Any weakness would be challenged. That the disfigured Calhoun was able to keep his place at the front of the chow line, accompanied by a fine specimen like the one in this photo, meant he was definitely one badass.

Bourbon folded his hands on the desktop and kneaded his fingers. "He's an Iraq war hero like you. Held the rank of commander in the Navy Seabees. A roadside bomb chewed him up. Lucky son of a bitch lived, unfortunately."

"Was he a werewolf at the time?" Getting medical treatment could've revealed his shape-shifter nature.

"He was," Bourbon answered, "and the *weres* over there kept his identity hidden."

We vampires had similar arrangements for protecting the Great Secret, the existence of the supernatural world. What protected us vampires—and werewolves, too—from being discovered by humans was their belief that we supernaturals were nothing but myth. After I was turned in Iraq, a vampire colonel in the field hospital made sure no one found out what I'd been turned into.

So Calhoun was a fellow veteran of our time in the sandbox. If we met, our shared experience was worth a nod, maybe a drink and a couple of war stories, but nothing more.

I was here from Denver on Bourbon's dime, so I owed him my attention. He wanted my services as a private detective. So far I didn't know much about the case except for the final payout: fifty thousand dollars. Cash. I might be an undead bloodsucker, but I like money. Especially big steaming piles of it.

I pointed to the head in the Tupperware. "What does this have to do with Mr. Where's-My-Body?"

"He worked for me."

"Let me guess," I said. "Calhoun killed this guy."

"Had him killed. Same thing."

I asked, "What about the police?"

"If I wanted to involve the police, why would I ask for you?"

"Then this business with Calhoun is about revenge?"

"I wish it was that simple," Bourbon replied. "How much do you know about us?"

I again pointed to the head. "You mean him and you? Not much. Except he's dead and you like keeping his head as a souvenir."

"I meant werewolves. Though you and I are both supernatural, we live in different cultures. Unlike *you* vampires, relationships among us are very important."

I put an equally dismissive spin in my reply. "Important enough for you guys to murder each other? Please don't invite me to any family reunions."

Bourbon gave me a you're-a-shit-for-brains smile. "Our relationships can get complicated. I'll try to explain them in a way you might be able to understand. Among us, groups of *were* families belong to a pack. These packs form clans. Six clans make up our Lowcountry Territory, which is bounded by Savannah, Augusta, Columbia, up the coast to Wilmington, with Charleston in the center."

"Sounds too organized for me."

"Of course," Bourbon said with a sneer. "You have that rabble you call the Araneum and all that"—he gave a weak wave—"hocus-pocus undead stuff."

I wasn't surprised he knew about the Araneum despite our rules to keep quiet. Supernaturals share more among themselves than they ought to.

"The Araneum is a social club. Far different from true family." He clenched a fist. "The closeness of blood ties."

Blood ties. What bullshit. He ought to put that *mierda* on a greeting card. "How does that family coziness figure into your infamous blood feuds? Isn't that how you determine your standing from *were*-cub to clan chief?"

"Not clan chief. Clan alpha." He scratched the back of his hand. The closer it got to a full moon, the more werewolves itched like they couldn't wait to morph out of their human skins.

He glanced at his fingers and held them still. "We've had more killings." Bourbon nodded toward the photos. "Calhoun's scheming to take over the territory."

"Calhoun is a clan alpha?" The mystery of why I was here cleared a bit. "If he's killed one of yours, that means—"

"I'm also a clan alpha," Bourbon interrupted, looking surprised that it had taken me this long to understand.

"Of rival clans?" I replied. "Assuming Calhoun is such a threat to your order, how come you don't take care of this yourselves? Why not call the clans together and discuss this problem around a can of Alpo?"

Bourbon's eyes narrowed. I expected his ears to lie flat against his skull. He began scratching the back of one hand and then clasped them together.

"Because first we have to choose a new alpha of the territory."

"What happened to the previous one?"

"She was killed in a plane crash."

"So you and Calhoun are scrambling to be the top boss?"

"I wouldn't have said it that way, but you are correct."

"Now what do you do? Keep killing one another's *weres* until one of you cries uncle?"

"There is a process for selecting the new alpha of the territory." Bourbon unclasped his hands. "Calhoun is the favored choice. He is the current alpha of the Magnolia Clan and was the protégé of the late top alpha."

I thought about the werewolves' reputation for ruthless domination over one another. "Any chance Calhoun caused the plane crash?"

"He did have the most to gain by her death. But as much as I'd love to see him get blamed for it, no. I don't see how he could. It was an accident."

My gaze went back to Bourbon's eyes. They still looked like sphincters. He also had much to gain by the top alpha's death.

"Did you?"

"Of course not."

Even if he had, would he admit it? I had to hear his denial.

He clasped his hands again. The action reminded me of a nervous tic. "If anyone deserves to be the alpha of the territory, it is I."

"How does that concern me?"

"An outsider, a vampire, takes him out—"

"You're asking me to kill Randolph Calhoun? An alpha werewolf?"

"Yes."

CHAPTER 2

I WAS BROUGHT to Charleston to murder a werewolf? I raised my hands. "Whoa, whoa, hold on to your leash. There's one big problem. You asked me here to do an investigation, not an assassination. I'm no thug."

Bourbon shrugged. "You're a vampire, what's the difference?"

No surprise that Bourbon had the same low opinion of vampires that I had of werewolves. To Bourbon, we vampires were scumbag indiscriminate killers who didn't need much of an excuse to fang as long as we got to lap fresh blood. And to me, werewolves were oversize, barely housebroken mutts.

Bourbon tilted his head like a dog trying to figure me out. "I don't understand. You get some money, we get some peace, everyone wins."

"There's an uneasy truce between your kind and mine," I

said. "We both share the same fear—being outed and hunted to extermination by humans."

Bourbon unfolded his hands and laid them on the desktop. He kept his eyes steady on me.

I explained, "This truce"—more of a thin promise that we'd each stick to our side of the supernatural realm—"is what keeps the violence from blowing out of control between us. I kill a werewolf, especially an alpha like Calhoun, then my existence wouldn't be worth one penny. If werewolves didn't get me, the Araneum would for screwing up the peace. You're looking for a fall guy and it's not me."

"Surely we can come to an agreement. Something we keep between ourselves."

I gave him a forceful, "No."

Bourbon paused and scratched along his collar like he was digging for a tick. "Is this about money?"

I laughed. "For half the money you offered me, you should have dozens of triggermen eager to collect. No one answered the call. They know the score." I raised an eyebrow. *Correct*?

Bourbon's silence was my answer. I was right.

"Kill Calhoun and . . ." I made a slash motion across my throat.

Bourbon steepled his fingers and looked through me, brooding.

His desk phone rang. His eyes cut to the caller ID display. He put one hand on the receiver and pointed to the door with the other. "We'll keep in touch."

"Why bother?" I got up to leave. "You've already got my answer."

I expected Bourbon to frown. Instead, a tiny smile tweaked the corners of his mouth.

I didn't like the expression. "Anything else you want to tell me?"

"Like I said, we'll keep in touch."

I went out and let the door close behind me. His receptionist—human—gave me the stink eye as I made my way out of the office.

I passed two *were* bodyguards. One was dressed as a janitor and he sat in a chair with a bucket between his boots. A towel covered the bucket. What was in the bucket? A Beretta submachine gun? Hand grenades?

The other *were* stood behind a coffee cart. She stiffened warily and slid her hand beneath the urn marked DECAF. The urn probably hid a Luger.

I rode the tiny, antique elevator to the ground floor. Once I was on the sidewalk, a humid spring warmth warned of hot, soupy days ahead.

I'd taken Bourbon's deposit money. With the case dead in its cradle, I could bum around Charleston for a couple of days before heading home. Besides, I was curious about the charms of the local Southern belles.

But like it or not, I had been drawn into this murderous conspiracy between Calhoun and Bourbon. Calhoun might learn of the offer and try to calm his worries by taking me out. And now that I'd refused Bourbon, he might want to cover his tracks by shutting me up . . . permanently. In any case, the dangerous information inside my head had put me in the center of the bull's-eye. So forget Charleston. Better that I return home ASAP.

I walked back toward the Atlas Mortuary, my digs here in the city. I'd found the place in the classified listings of *The Hollow Fang*, the online newsletter for vampires and their aficionados.

Charleston was a surprisingly compact grid of historic buildings—mansions, row houses, churches, slave auction markets, brothels—crammed into the tip of a narrow peninsula bounded by the Ashley River to the west, the Cooper River to the east, and pointing toward the Atlantic Ocean to the south. But outside the boundaries of the lower peninsula, Charleston and its suburbs offered the same sprawl you'd find in Atlanta or Tallahassee.

The Atlas Mortuary was a few blocks away, and rather than waste time figuring my way around in a car, plus trying to find parking, I'd walked to get my bearings and check out the scenery. I followed the reverse course I'd taken to Bourbon's office, crossed a cobblestone road dating from colonial times, and continued along a sidewalk shaded by magnolias and cottonwoods.

The Carolina sun warmed my face. During my years as a vampire, I'd become expert in applying sunblock and makeup that allowed me to keep a daylight schedule. Yet I remained mindful to avoid the dawn, as the rays of the morning sun could burn through the thickest of makeup and incinerate any careless undead bloodsucker.

When I passed the parking garage near Church and Horlebeck, the hairs on the back of my hands and neck stood on end. My fingertips and ears tingled. My sixth sense, the braiding of sight, sound, smell, touch, and taste, heightened by supernatural awareness, rang my internal alarm.

I swept my gaze around me.

Nothing.

What caught my sixth sense?

A shadow grew around my feet.

I cast no shadow.

I looked up.

Something large fell from the roof of the parking garage. Something red, blue, and green.

A giant crab.

CHAPTER 3

THE GIANT crab tumbled straight for me.

I dove forward at vampire speed.

The crab smashed onto the concrete right where I'd been walking. It didn't go *splat* but shattered into pieces. Shards spun through the air and ricocheted across the sidewalk in a spray of iridescent colors.

I sprang off the sidewalk. The last of the pieces skittered around me.

The broken shell of a crab sculpture lay in the gutter. Fiberglass littered the area like shrapnel. A wiring harness connected several loose pieces.

I picked up something the size and shape of a doorknob. It was the end of an eyestalk with a recessed socket for a lightbulb. The fiberglass was a quarter of an inch thick, smooth on the outside and rough-textured on the inside. The piece had heft to it. I guessed the complete sculpture had originally been ten feet across at the widest and certainly weighed enough to have broken my skull and neck.

The crab had been airbrushed in gaudy shades of red, green, and blue lacquer. I tried to imagine the original purpose of the sculpture and decided it must have been for the marquee of a restaurant.

I palmed the fiberglass eyestalk and looked up to the roof of the parking garage. Hopefully whoever was responsible for dropping the crab was staring down. If for nothing else, to check his or her aim.

No one looked.

An elderly couple stepped toward me from across the street. Tourists for sure, judging by their baggy, casual clothing. She carried a lime-green tote bag and wore a wide-brimmed straw hat. His greasy and tattered ball cap read BREWERS.

"Damn, you move fast," the old woman said. Her accent was from the upper Midwest.

"Having a crab fall on you will do that," I answered.

The old man rolled his shoulders, adjusted his cap, and said to her, "I used to move like that." He shared the Midwestern accent.

"In your dreams." Her lips twisted in scorn. "If that was you instead of him, you'd be wearing that crustacean instead of that stupid cap of yours."

"Nothing wrong with my cap." He adjusted it again.

More people clustered around us in a parade of astonished moon faces.

I gazed up to the roof again. "Better see who's up there."

"If you find the careless sons of bitches"—the old woman gave her tote bag a hearty swing—"bring 'em down here and I'll beat their asses good."

The old man looked to the roof. "I'm sure they're trembling in fear."

I started for the closest stairwell up the garage. Once out of sight, I sprinted to the fourth level. I gripped the fiberglass eyestalk. Whoever had dropped the crab, I'd make them eat this. At the top, I kicked the steel door and pounced into the open, certain that I'd catch the crab droppers by surprise.

Brilliant sunshine lit an expanse of dirty concrete. The rooftop level looked as big and flat as the deck of an aircraft carrier. I stepped out of the stairwell, a brick-and-steel structure that jutted above the pavement. Cars were scattered across the parking spaces. The view was a cluttered landscape of tall leafy trees, church steeples, and square buildings.

To my left, an open trailer had been backed up to the wall at the spot where the crab had fallen. The sides of the trailer were made of metal sheets crudely welded together. Lengths of frayed nylon rope lay on the trailer where the crab statue must have been tied down to a cradle of two-by-fours.

A waist-high double railing topped the garage wall. The crab hadn't slid from the trailer and off the roof—the trailer bed was too low. The crab would have had to be lifted and tipped over the railing.

I peered down the wall. The crowd numbered about fifty people. Large pieces of the crab lay in the street, blocking traffic.

Maybe the trailer had been backed hard against the wall and the crab got tossed by accident?

Just as I was walking below, and I didn't hear the sculpture bang against the railing?

This was no accident.

I had been returning to the mortuary along the same path I'd taken to Eric Bourbon's office. I'd been followed and ambushed. Served me right for being complacent.

I imagined my obituary in *The Hollow Fang*: DENVER VAMPIRE DETECTIVE CAKED BY A CRAB IN CHARLESTON.

Whoever did this had a sense of humor. Hope they wouldn't mind my chuckles when I worked them over with my talons and a crowbar.

There wasn't a license plate attached to the trailer. Even if I found the owner, I'd bet the trailer had been stolen.

I hadn't noticed anyone leaving. If the crab droppers had escaped on foot, they must've disappeared through one of the other stairwells at the far ends of the garage.

I caught the whiff of something out of place.

I closed my eyes, breathed deep, and sifted through the layered scents.

Gasoline.

Motor oil.

Beyond that, the faint odor of a corpse in a crypt.

The smell of the undead.

The undead like me.

A vampire.

Here?

What else did I sense?

Vibrations from vehicles rolling though the garage trembled through the bottoms of my feet. My sixth sense sizzled with a warning. I felt another vibration, of rushing feet, moving toward me.

I opened my eyes and jerked to the side.

A vampire, talons extended, lunged from behind the staircase I'd come up. His mouth gaped wide, fangs aiming for my throat.

I pivoted, leaned back, and swatted his talons aside. As he passed by, I stabbed his neck with the broken end of the eyestalk.

He clutched his neck, howled in pain, and stumbled forward. But he caught himself and whirled around. He tore the eyestalk free and tossed it aside. Blood spurted from the wound and drenched his coat. The red gush of vampire blood oxidized into a spray of brown confetti that disintegrated into ash and smoke.

He was gaunt and looked about thirty in blunt-tooth years. His dark hair was gelled into a faux hawk. He wore black over black, down to his socks and buckled shoes, in the clichéd Goth fashion of the unimaginative newly turned.

We faced off. He leaped at me in a *Matrix*-style tornado of slicing talons and wild kung-fu kicks that I easily batted aside. A clumsy attack. Downright insulting.

And a diversion. A second vampire appeared to my left from behind a Dodge Durango. He was also dressed in a black Goth outfit and attacked with a spear. Sunlight glistened off the shiny metal point. Silver.

Even a touch of silver would burn like red-hot steel. I backtracked to buy time. The dropping of the crab must've been Kill Felix Plan A. Two vampires against one was Plan B.

Both vampires advanced at an angle, certain I couldn't defend against a simultaneous attack from two sides.

The vampire with the spear had blond hair matted into spiky points so it looked like he was wearing the pelt of a yellow hedgehog. He jabbed at my arms and legs to keep me on the defensive. The other vampire flexed his taloned fingers. I saw the moves clearly and distinctly, but as we moved at vampire speed, humans would've seen only a blurry cloud of arms and legs.

I faked a punch at him, knowing it would expose my left side. Spiky-hair vampire saw his chance and stabbed for my ribs. I snatched the spear just below the point.

The first vampire jumped for me. I lashed out with my right arm and socked him in the jaw. His head snapped backward and he staggered as if his ankles had turned to rubber.

I yanked on the spear, and as I expected, spiky-hair vampire yanked back. So I pushed the spear as a countermove against his momentum and caught him by surprise. The butt of the spear smacked his chest.

The blow stunned him and his grasp on the spear weakened. I pulled the spear free, twirled it around to whack him on the head, and left him stumbling.

The first vampire recovered and sprang for me. I hesitated for a split second, gauged the swing, and swatted the spear against his belly.

Crunch. Pieces of a cell phone fell from under his coat. He doubled over and dropped to his hands and knees.

Spiky Hair had caught his balance. He rushed at me with hands clawing for my face.

I held the spear at the ready like a bayonet. With a quick parry to the left and right, I knocked his hands aside and skewered him through the sternum. I pushed hard. The spear point poked out his back.

He clutched the shaft. His expression broke in pain and anguish. Blood spurted from the wound and drenched his shirt. The crimson drops turned into brown flakes, then ash and smoke.

I let go of the spear. He fell backward and the spear point protruding from his back clanked against the concrete. He squirmed while his face contorted hideously. Smoke plumed from his wound. In a few moments, he'd be nothing but dust and a bad smell.

The first vampire was back on his feet and danced around like a boxer.

I said, "Give it up. Let's talk."

He ran his tongue over the points of his fangs. "There's no talking. Only dying. You."

"How about your friend?" I pointed to Spiky Hair, who writhed and belched smoke. "Wanna join him?"

The first vampire raised both arms, stood on one leg, and folded the other leg before him. Heaven help him, he was assuming the crane pose.

I relaxed my arms. "Listen, Karate Kid, spare yourself. Quit fooling around and talk to me. Who put you up to this?"

The vampire squinted in angry concentration. His arms and body quivered in the effort of keeping still.

I circled around him. He made tiny ridiculous hops to keep me centered. Suddenly he jumped and snapped one leg at me.

I leaned to the side as his kick slashed where I'd been. I stung him with a couple of slaps, then popped him hard on the mouth. His lips burst into pulp. His head reeled back and I followed with a swipe of my talons across his chest.

His shredded coat and shirt fell open, exposing naked, translucent skin. The fierce Carolina sun immediately fried his unprotected body. Smoke curled from the bubbling flesh. He yelped and beat his chest as if trying to put out a fire.

Jackass. "We can talk or I can watch you burn."

His eyes bulged from the agony.

"It's an easy choice," I said.

I expected him to surrender. But the pain seemed to have filled him with determination and he sprang at me once more.

I swiveled on my feet, hip-checked him, and snagged his hair in one hand. With my other hand, I grasped the seat of his trousers and aimed his trajectory for the trailer.

I wanted to bash his face against the metal side and end the fight with him in decent enough shape to answer my questions.

But he jerked his legs, his feet finding purchase on the concrete, and gave himself a boost through the air.

I pulled against him a little too hard. Instead of smacking the trailer, his head swung over the ragged edge of the side.

The metal sliced across his throat like a serrated blade. His shoulders struck the trailer while his head continued in an arc, the spinal cord severing with a crisp snap.

His head spun into the bed of the trailer and landed with a hard thump. The stump of his neck was a circle of raw meat. Blood gushed from his head and shoulders, the red gouts turning into streams of brown flakes. I let go of his pants and let his body drop to the concrete.

His skin crinkled and cracked, destroying any protection sunblock and makeup might have provided for his flesh. He was gone; might as well let the sun finish him off. I stuck the toe of my shoe under his shoulder and flipped him over. Sunlight fell across the naked skin on his torso. His head and body began to smolder. Now I had two dead vampires.

They deserved this, the stupid bastards, but still, I recoiled in horror as nature reclaimed them with her pitiless fury.

Smoke rose from their skins, from inside their shirts, and from around their heads. In seconds, their clothes deflated as the flesh and bones of their bodies crumbled into gray ash.

A sudden breeze tossed their clothes. The ashes swirled and mingled into a dust devil. Soon there was nothing left of the vampires but gray smudges and empty clothes.

Sunblock protected me, but the sight of their immolation filled me with a dread of my own vulnerability.

I stared at the piles of clothes.

Who were they?

Why had they attacked me?

Were they acting alone or with someone else?

I searched the pockets of the first vampire. I found change, a set of keys, and loose dollar bills. I patted his coat and trousers and poured the remaining ash out of his shoes before feeling inside. Nothing else.

I turned to spiky-hair vampire, finding more change, a key ring, and a wad of cash bound with a rubber band around a couple of business cards.

I wiped the ash from my fingers. I undid the roll of money and counted twenties and hundreds—a thousand forty total—which I pocketed.

I examined the business cards. One belonged to Eric Bourbon.

Not much of a surprise. The werewolf couldn't have been more oily if he bathed in 30-weight. At least with this clue, I knew where to direct my questions.

I read the second card.

A chill of astonishment screwed through me. My *kundalini noir*—a coil of supernatural energy that animates my body instead of a pulsing heart—felt suddenly unbalanced, like I was skittering on ice. My mind tumbled in incredulity.

Quiz me for a thousand years and I would've never guessed the name on the card.

That of a former lover.

Someone who had once saved me.

Wendy Teagarden.

CHAPTER 4

I STOOD ON the rooftop level of the garage, the empty clothes of the dead vampires gathered about my feet. I held the business card with Wendy's name.

My mind stalled on the question. What the hell?

I'd come to Charleston hoping for a break from my past. Now here's Wendy.

Was she in trouble? My *kundalini noir* sank into my belly, heavy and sickened.

Wendy is a dryad. We had met when I arrived in Denver years ago, a new vampire, struggling with my undead nature and the guilt of my turning, and I'd refused to drink human blood. That weakened my powers, and I was almost snuffed out after being wounded by vampire hunters. Wendy fed me her blood and that rescued me from oblivion to plant me firmly in the world of the undead.

Strong. Healthy. Dangerous.

I pictured her sweet face, her smooth skin and beautiful

freckles, those curls of exquisite red hair. And that grade A rump.

Wendy was the first supernatural I'd ever slept with, a forest sprite who loved pot and had flowers growing magically from her hair. The sex was more than supernatural—it was amazing and raunchy and left me floating on a euphoric buzz of satisfaction.

Our brief time together had ended when the Araneum sent her to Indianapolis. We parted on good terms and managed one last quickie behind a gas station on the way to the airport.

After that? Well, absence doesn't always make the heart grow fonder: out of sight, out of mind. And now we were in the same city.

I kicked at the vampire's clothes. Ash puffed from the folds. What was he doing with Wendy's business card?

Hopefully, this was a different Wendy Teagarden.

The card listed her name, a business name—Pirate Coast Tours—a phone number with the local 843 prefix, and a Web address.

I pulled out my cell phone and tried the number.

The phone rang twice, then a message began: "Thank you for calling Pirate Coast Tours. Your call is important to us. We're either closed or on another call . . ." Yada, yada.

Irritated, I snapped my cell phone closed.

Why did the vampire have her business card? Was she a victim?

The thought rang through me like the ominous peal of a distant bell.

What about Eric Bourbon? What was his connection?

A moment ago I'd been certain I was pinched between rival factions of werewolves. Now I had vampires after me.

Why?

Who knew I was in Charleston? Only Bourbon.

I flipped the business cards to read the backs. Wendy's was blank. But a name had been scrawled across Bourbon's card.

I had to think about the name for a second before it registered. When I realized who the name belonged to, the sensation was like a cold hand clasping my throat.

Julius Paxton.

It could only mean Julius Paxton, another vampire who had once tried to kill me.

CHAPTER 5

JULIUS PAXTON. Formerly a deputy chief in the Los Angeles Police Department.

And formerly the undead henchman of another renegade vampire, the head of the Los Angeles *nidus*, Latin for "nest." That vampire sought to break away from the Araneum. He and Paxton wanted to reveal the Great Secret and partner with humans to form a new society, according to them the next step in the evolution of civilization. Despite their pretensions to create a better world, the foundation of that new society was poured from the blood of both humans and vampires.

The Araneum had sent several enforcers to L.A. to bring the renegades to justice. All these enforcers had disappeared. Then the Araneum sent me.

Julius Paxton had been the leader's muscle. Despite his efforts to assassinate me, I managed to destroy the cabal of renegades and stake the leader. Once their little empire had collapsed, Paxton ran away to save his ass. I caught up to him, but he proved tough and gave me the slip. But he didn't get completely away. A psycho human who was part of the conspiracy had run him over and almost killed me. When I returned to the scene to get Paxton, he had disappeared.

That had been years ago. Now Paxton was back from the sewer he had sunk into? To get me? And was he working with Bourbon?

Whatever that scumbag Bourbon knew about Wendy, Paxton, and this attack, I'd use my vampire mojo to yank the truth out of him.

I picked at the remains of the cell phone that had fallen from the first vampire. Too bad the phone was in pieces, I could've read the directory for clues.

I tucked the business cards into my shirt pocket.

Now to get rid of the vampires' clothing. First I broke the spear into pieces. Standing upwind to keep the remaining ashes from smudging me, I bundled the clothes around the fiberglass eyestalk from the crab and the pieces of the spear.

I glanced over the railing. Two police cruisers blocked the street on either side of the broken crab sculpture. A crowd lingered on the sidewalk, taking photos and pointing at the fiberglass remains and up the garage to show where the sculpture had fallen over the railing.

I pulled my head back. Better leave before someone came up. I ran down a stairwell at the other side of the garage to avoid the gawkers and the cops. On the way to Bourbon's office, I tossed the bundle into a Dumpster. Setting fire to the clothes might draw attention, so I walked away.

Once at Bourbon's address, I took the elevator up to his office and removed my contacts. Wearing contacts masked my vampire eyes but at the cost of preventing me from using hypnosis or seeing auras.

Every living creature emits a psychic aura. What's useful about seeing auras is that each psychic envelope is as expressive and unique as a face. The color of an aura corresponds to the chakra where the owner's psychic awareness resides. Human awareness seldom rises above the lowest chakra—material concern—so their auras are red. Vampire awareness, like that of most other supernaturals, resides at the next level—connection of the physical world to the spiritual—and our auras are orange.

Werewolves? Their awareness bounces between the first and second chakras.

Vampire hypnosis didn't work on other supernaturals, but it might on werewolves. They were practically human except for the occasional need to grow fur and lift one leg to pee.

When the elevator door opened, the two *were* bodyguards were at their stations, janitor by his bucket, the coffee lady behind the cart. Their auras glowed suspiciously, red with flames of orange. They hadn't expected to see me again so soon. I didn't bother using hypnosis on them. I'd wait for Bourbon.

"Call your boss," I said. "Tell him I'm back." I proceeded to his office.

His receptionist waited for me by her desk. She stood with her arms crossed. Her aura covered her like a cloak of red syrup. Resentment at my return made a prickly fuzz grow from the penumbra of her aura.

I looked through the window into Bourbon's private office. He and another man were hunched over documents on a table. The second man wore a fitted shirt and dress trousers. He had neatly trimmed red hair and long sideburns that followed the line of his jaw.

I gave the receptionist a hard gaze. Her irises dilated into a pair of blue O-rings. Her aura flashed as my hypnotic power surged into her. Feathers of anxiety fanned from her aura, then retracted, and the shroud of her psychic penumbra glistened smooth. She froze in place, her shoulders slumped forward, her eyes vacant. Besides paralyzing her, the hypnosis would erase the memory of my visit.

I stepped around her and banged open the door to Bourbon's office. The air stank of werewolf musk. Hadn't they heard of cologne?

Bourbon and his guest's auras flared with annoyance, then anger. Neon-orange tendrils lashed from their red penumbras. They snarled and squared their shoulders.

I gave Bourbon my most focused glare, one strong enough to zap a platoon of marines.

He scowled. "What's with the goo-goo eyes, bat-breath?"
Okay, hypnosis didn't work.

I pitched Bourbon's business card on the table. "Explain this, hair bag."

He picked up the card. "The hell you talking about?"

The other *were* pushed his shirt cuffs back. He had the muscular physique of a pro hockey player. The hair on the back of his hands thickened. His fingernails extended into claws.

My talons sprang out.

Bourbon growled. "Not now." He pointed to the other *were*. "Sean, wait for me outside."

Sean grimaced angrily and shifted weight from foot to foot.

"Go," Bourbon insisted.

Sean morphed back into human form and jerked the door open to leave the room. The door snicked closed. I saw him through the window when he startled the receptionist, who broke out of her trance. She glanced about, confused, then joined Sean to glower like they wanted to see me tossed headfirst onto the street.

"Who's your goon?" I asked.

"Sean Moultier is the alpha of my favorite pack. My number one assistant." Bourbon read the business card. His aura grew thorns of irritation. "What's this about?"

"Two vampires attacked me."

"So?"

"I found that card on one of them."

Bourbon's mouth tightened in annoyance.

I said, "Turn the card around."

He flipped the card over and read the name. "Julius Paxton? This somebody I'm supposed to know?"

"You tell me."

The thorns of his aura glowed orange like fire.

His eyes twitched. "You're reading my aura, aren't you?"

"So what if I am?"

"Let me give you a little insight into werewolf-vampire etiquette. You want to talk, put on your contacts."

"And if I don't?"

"Then you can talk to yourself. Meanwhile I got things to do."

I'd come here to bust his chops, and he'd just slapped me on the wrist. All right, I'd play his game if it kept him talking. Pissed that I'd let him gain the advantage, I put my contacts back in.

He walked to his chair and sat. "And because you found my business card, you think I know something?"

"That's why I'm here."

He offered a chair. I remained standing.

He picked up the card again and reread the back. "Who is this Julius Paxton?"

"If it's the guy I'm thinking about, he's a vampire. A real vicious one."

"Was he one of the vampires who attacked you?"

"Not today. But I'm convinced he had a hand in it."

"You and this Julius Paxton have a history?"

"We go back. What puzzles me is, why is he here? The last time I saw him was in Los Angeles."

Bourbon laid the card on the desk. "What happened during the attack today?"

"Those vampires dropped a giant crab from the top of the public garage on Horlebeck."

One corner of Bourbon's lips twitched in amusement. "What kind of crab?"

"Fiberglass."

"I meant: rock, blue?"

The question made my neck stiffen. "Forget the goddamn crab. What matters was that it was huge, and the vampires pushed it off the garage to squash me against the sidewalk." I explained about the trailer and the vampire ambush.

"What about Julius Paxton?"

"That's my question," I replied. "What about him? Did those vampires work for him?"

Bourbon pulled a Montblanc fountain pen from his shirt pocket. He scribbled notes across a pad on his desk as he mumbled. "Huge. Fiberglass. Crab. Julius. Paxton."

He turned his attention to me. "What happened to the vampires?"

"I killed them."

"Did you question them first?"

"That was the idea, but neither cooperated. Happens," I said. "There's more. You know Wendy Teagarden?"

A tiny smile crossed his lips. He capped his pen. "Why do you ask?"

He knew Wendy. "Just answer the question."

Bourbon put his elbows on the desk, gripped the pen in both hands, and leaned toward me. "Mr. Gomez, you need to tone down the antagonism. If you want my help, then we must proceed on a more amicable footing."

He motioned again that I sit.

I took the chair and smiled, not because he'd won but because I was looking forward to smashing his face. "All right. Could you please tell what you know about Wendy Teagarden?"

He clipped the pen to his shirt pocket and grinned: *That's better.* I expected him to reach across the desk and pat me on the head. If he did, I'd bite him.

"Met her once," he said. "About a month ago. The party of a mutual friend. She's a professional tour guide. I know she's a supernatural. A dryad."

"Where is she?"

"It's tourist season, so she should be working. Try asking one of the tour companies."

"Is she all right?"

"I have no reason to think otherwise." Bourbon's eyes gave a quizzical glint. "Why are you asking?"

"I also found this on the vampire." I pulled the Pirate Coast Tours business card out of my pocket. "It's got her name."

Bourbon cupped his chin and dropped his gaze. Was he thinking of Wendy . . . or himself?

"You think she's in danger?" I asked.

"I don't know. But if she's a friend of yours . . ." He brought his eyes back up and they were filled with foreboding.

"I did my best to keep your visit with me under wraps, but Randolph Calhoun's *weres* have got sharp eyes and sharper ears. They'll want to know why you're here. Calhoun may see you and me as in bed together. Rhetorically speaking."

"I've thought of that. But I'm not getting mixed up in this business between you and Calhoun."

"Might be too late for that. Think someone, this Paxton character for example, dropping a crab on you was coincidence?"

"'Course not." Whoever put those vampires up to the hit was hoping for an easy mark. Somebody had gone to a lot of trouble setting up the trailer and crab on the garage. I had been more than a target of opportunity. They knew I was in town. Who had they worked for? Why come after me? I was sure there would be a next time.

"What are you going to do?" Bourbon asked. "Leave Charleston?"

"You kidding? Someone tried to flatten my ass and I want to know why. I'm not leaving until I get answers."

Bourbon's expression turned sly. I knew he was about to tell me something I didn't want to hear.

"Seems to me, Mr. Gomez, that despite your earlier refusal of my offer, you and I are working together."

CHAPTER 6

ERIC BOURBON let the wily expression ease from his face and his eyes softened with empathy.

I didn't buy into his act. He was gloating behind that facade, smug that he'd talked me into his corner.

What did he know about the assassination attempt on me? My questions about him, other werewolves, the vampires I'd killed, and Julius Paxton thickened into muck.

"Don't look so hurt, Mr. Gomez, werewolves and vampires have cooperated before."

"When?"

Bourbon sat straight in his chair. "That truce you referred to earlier comes from that cooperation. The truce started during the reign of Suleiman the Magnificent. You know who he was?"

"The head of the Ottomans. A sultan who had most of Europe shitting their pants."

Bourbon quirked his head to one side and smiled. "A vulgar interpretation but accurate. During the last Crusades, the Christian and Muslim armies crisscrossing the Balkans almost captured some of our ancestors. Just before Suleiman became caliph, *weres* and vampires negotiated a truce and approached him with this deal: We will help your conquest if you repress the truth of the supernatural world. Shape-shifters and the undead served as Janissaries." Bourbon paused to make sure I followed.

I nodded impatiently. "They were the sultan's secret army. Spies, scouts, assassins. I watch the History Channel."

"Very good," Bourbon congratulated me in his offhand way. "Their service explains Suleiman's prowess as politician and commander. Unfortunately, that was the last time *weres* and vampires have worked together as equals, but the truce has held."

"For the most part," I replied. "I can think of a half-dozen violations, of vampires and werewolves going fang to fang. The 1894 Amazon River riots in Rio de Janeiro. The 1913 wharf brawls in Seattle. The 1955 mountain mayhem in Bern, Switzerland. The 1971 urban rumble in . . ."

Bourbon made a halt signal with his hand. "I get your point."

I added, "The Araneum pulled out all the stops to keep mention of that supernatural violence from humans."

"As did the clan and pack alphas."

"But as far as cooperating with you," I said, "I'm not interested in Calhoun. I'm only interested in finding Wendy and making sure she's okay. After that, finding out who's after me and why."

"You may discover Calhoun is interested in you."

"I'll take my chances. Too bad I didn't bring a gun."

Bourbon slid his chair to the side and opened a desk drawer. "I can help you there. If you're not picky."

His sudden generosity startled me.

He laid an unusual-looking pistol on the desktop. The weapon had a matte-green finish and soft curves, unlike the hard machined lines of a typical firearm, and looked like it had been regurgitated from a Frankenstein Venus flytrap.

"What's that?" I asked.

"A Vektor nine-millimeter. South African."

Very cool. I reached for the pistol. "Thanks."

Bourbon pulled the Vektor out of reach. "That is mine. Here is yours." He lifted a revolver from the drawer and pushed it across the desktop to me. The gun was a .38 Special with a stubby barrel and a minuscule grip. It looked like a Smith & Wesson snub-nose. Once upon a time, this type of pistol was the favorite of plainclothes cops.

I picked up the gun. It wasn't a real S&W but a cheap copy, a vintage Saturday night special.

Old school.

Rust had formed where the bluing had worn off along the barrel, frame, and cylinder. The plastic grips were cracked and loose. I opened the five-shot cylinder and it fell into my hand.

Make that *real* old school.

"Might need a little TLC," he said.

"Might need to get chucked off a bridge," I replied. "This is a piece of junk. Don't you have something that's a little more intimidating? A BB gun? Slingshot and marbles?"

"I said you couldn't be picky."

"Yeah, there's nothing to worry about. I pull this out to defend myself and my enemies will die laughing." I put the revolver back together and clicked the cylinder into place. "I need to shop for a pistol that's worth carrying."

Bourbon cocked a thumb out his window, to the north. "Try America Street on the other side of the Neck."

"The Neck?"

"The peninsula north of Spring Street. Separates Charleston proper from the rest of the dirty world."

"What kind of a place is America Street?"

"In the daytime, it's like the bad part of Metropolis. After dark, it's Gotham City. In other words, ghetto."

I couldn't walk downtown Charleston without someone trying to kill me. What would happen if I went to America Street?

Bourbon dropped a Ziploc bag that rattled on the desktop. "Here's your ammunition."

I took the bag and counted about two dozen rounds. Some had nickel cartridge shells, the rest were brass. Most of the shells were tarnished and mangy with verdigris. A few bullets were factory hollow points, others had lopsided lead-slug home loads.

He handed a paper bag with the logo of a sandwich shop. "I wouldn't advise carrying in plain sight."

I dropped the snub-nose and Ziploc into the bag.

Bourbon folded his hands on the desk. "You got a gun. You got bullets. Now what?"

"Like I told you, find out who's after me and why."

"How are you going to do that?"

"I'm a detective, remember? I have methods."

"What methods?" he asked.

"Harsh methods. I've already killed twice today, and it's barely past noon."

His eyes shifted from me, not much, but enough to signal that my answer had jostled his thinking like a speed bump.

"I better get started." I cupped the paper bag with the revolver inside and stood.

Bourbon withdrew his hands from the desk. "The sooner the better." His eyes gave a red lupine shine, and they betrayed the doubts I'd put into his head.

I looked into the receptionist's foyer. She was busy at her desk. Sean Moultier was gone.

As I turned to leave, a spray can went *fsst* behind me. I looked to see what Bourbon was doing.

He aimed the room deodorizer at the chair I'd just vacated. "Don't take this wrong"—he wrinkled his nose—"but you vampires stink."

CHAPTER 7

I LEFT BOURBON'S office, passed his bodyguards, and got into the elevator. I was holding the sandwich bag that contained the revolver and Ziploc of ammo he'd given me. No sense in carrying an unloaded gun, especially as I'd already been the target of one assassination attempt today.

I reached into the bag and pulled out the revolver. I selected five of the least crappy-looking cartridges from the Ziploc and loaded the snub-nose. Since I was up against werewolves—and vampires as well—I needed silver bullets instead of these lead slugs. And a pistol that inspired more confidence than this knockoff relic.

I dropped the snub-nose into the right leg pocket of my cargo pants. I stepped from the elevator and went out the front door of the building onto Broad Street.

What next?

Find Wendy.

Make sure she's okay. Learn how, or if, she's mixed up in this mess between the werewolf clans and the vampire assassins that I'd killed. Bourbon knew Wendy. That was enough to convince me that she was in danger.

The second thing I'd do was contact the Araneum. Let them know there's trouble brewing among the werewolves. A fight between clan alphas could spill over into our side of the supernatural realm. And tell them about Julius Paxton. I was convinced this was the same Paxton I'd gunned for in Los Angeles. Back then he didn't seem the type to forgive and forget. I doubted that in the meantime he'd answered an altar call and found Jesus.

If Paxton wanted me, I wasn't hard to find. He could've attacked me in Denver. Then what prevented him? What about Charleston encouraged this attack?

And Wendy? I wondered how she'd greet me. A big sloppy kiss would be nice. Maybe we could play house while I was in town.

Her business card didn't show an address. I would check the Internet when I returned to the mortuary. To orient myself, I pulled out a tourist map of Charleston from my back pocket. Dozens of ads for local attractions crowded the margins of the map, but only one caught my eye: Pirate Coast Tours.

The tour companies were clustered around the intersection of State and Market streets. I'd start there.

A black Mercedes limo glided to the curb and halted at the corner in front of me. A man in a dark gray suit climbed out of the front passenger door. He had a bull neck and shoulders wide as an ox yoke. He popped the rear door, held it open, and stared at me.

His expression brimmed with guarded hostility. I couldn't decide if that look was meant for me to keep my distance or to say that we had pending business.

His eyes flicked to my right, a tell that someone was coming up on that side.

I started to turn. I got the whiff of garlic and stiffened, frozen by the disgusting odor.

A hand swung from behind me and to my left. The tell had been a diversion. The hand moved at supernatural speed and clamped a cloth over my mouth and nose. The cloth brought the revolting stench of more garlic. My guts seized and I was overcome by the need to retch.

Another hand clasped the back of my head and kept the cloth tight against my face.

The poisonous vapor of the garlic twisted through me. Nausea sucked the strength from my body. I slapped at the hand over my face like a sick kitten. The world swirled before me.

Two large hands clenched my upper arms, their grips strong as iron. In a blur of motion, I was pushed into the limo and fell across a cushioned seat.

A gruff voice barked, “Don’t make trouble, asshole. Understand?”

The garlic odor kept me weak and nauseated. Everything around me was a dizzying smear of colors. I could barely sit upright, let alone fight. I nodded.

The cloth was lifted from my face. Cool, soothing air washed up my nose, into my mouth, and down my throat.

A hazy apparition of a woman, wearing a brown business suit—short jacket, slacks, white blouse—folded herself in front of me. The door beside us slammed shut. Someone climbed into the front seat—someone heavy enough to make the limo rock in place—and the front door thumped closed. The door locks clicked, sealing me inside.

My *kundalini noir* withdrew into an anxious ball. My shoulders, neck, and back stiffened in panic.

Who were these people? Supernaturals? What did they want? Since they had used garlic to subdue me, they knew I was a vampire. A sickening lump grew in my throat. They could’ve done worse than jam me into this car. Maybe the garlic treatment was only a start.

The woman extended her arm and offered a white object. With my eyes still blurry and my head wobbling in dizziness, I couldn’t tell what she held. It smelled like lemon.

I snatched the object. It was a cloth, soaked with lemon juice. I pressed the cloth over my face and breathed deep.

The refreshing aroma washed away the nausea and loosened the knots in my body. When I lowered the cloth, I caught another strange whiff. A musky aroma filling the interior of the limo.

Werewolf.

My shoulders and neck tightened again.

The woman before me came into sharp focus. She sat on a jump seat unfolded from the back of the partition between our compartment and the front of the limo. She was a stocky, muscular brunette with the unwavering, alert gaze of a watchdog. Her lips parted to show impressive fangs. Coarse hair grew from the back of her hands as she started the process of morphing from human to werewolf.

She pointed a bizarre pistol. The black metal gun had brass fittings and a sleek tapered barrel. A glass vial jutted from the top of the pistol. A vaccination gun, but loaded with what drug?

I stared at the vial until I could make out the label: *Oil of garlic*. Concentrated.

I was so fucked.

My *kundalini noir* recoiled. My guts loosened at the thought of garlic oil dissolving my flesh and turning me into a bag of vampire *menudo*.

Two more *weres* sat up front, the driver and the guy in the gray suit who had distracted me. He draped a thick arm over the partition. He scratched the mat of fur growing from his wrist to his knuckles.

Go *ahead*, his fanged snarl taunted, *try me*.

Someone to my left stirred. I wasn't alone on the backseat.

An older man wearing a finely tailored suit lounged beside me on the leather upholstery.

"Welcome, Mr. Gomez," he said in a relaxed Southern drawl. "I'm looking forward to telling my side of this story."

In his dark, almost black suit, he seemed to melt into the inky interior of the limo. I blinked a couple of times before I recognized him.

Randolph Calhoun.

The werewolf that Bourbon wanted me to kill.

CHAPTER 8

I SAT IN the back of the limo, me against four *weres*. The two goons up front. Calhoun next to me. And don't forget the hairy bitch with the garlic-oil vaccination gun.

Not quite the worst-case scenario but pretty damn close.

Calhoun waited patiently, as if he expected me to thank him for the ride. His suit rippled over his body like liquid cloth. The cut of his jacket and the design of his shirt and tie were fashionably understated, but even so, they made Bourbon's expensive clothes seem bargain basement.

Calhoun's thick hair looked sculpted rather than combed. His platinum-gray eyes seemed to float in their deep sockets as if sheltered from the cares of the world by money and privilege. He looked heavier than he had in any of the photos Bourbon had showed me. The beginnings of a double chin clung to his jaw. He looked well fed and prosperous.

Then he raised his left arm.

The three claws of his prosthesis glimmered surreally. He

rested this arm on his lap. The claws protruded from slots in a steel knob that extended from inside the starched cuff of his shirt.

I wasn't curious about his prosthesis. It was enough that I knew Calhoun had lost his arm in Iraq. I had war wounds of my own, on the inside. I didn't want to talk about mine, and I was sure Calhoun didn't want to talk about his. Besides, all the theatrics with his goons and the garlic weren't so we could snuggle and reminisce about our time working for Uncle Sugar.

Calhoun needed information from me. When he got it, then what? I slipped my hand into my cargo pocket and touched the sandwich bag. If there was trouble, I could rip it open and grab the snub-nose. The pistol wasn't much for range, but within the confines of the limo, it should do enough damage. The female *were* holding the vaccination gun would get the first .38 slug between her eyes.

The *were* up front, the biggest of these supernatural mutts, dropped his gaze to my hand in the cargo pocket. He frowned and curled his right upper lip to show me a long curved fang.

I withdrew my talons, pulled my hand from the pocket, and showed him my empty palm.

The *were*'s fang retracted. He smirked and said, "Same plan, Mr. Calhoun?"

Calhoun replied yes. The *were* turned around and tapped the driver on the shoulder. The Mercedes glided from the curb.

I asked, "Where are we going?"

Calhoun answered, "Someplace so you can get a broader perspective of our situation here." His voice was cool as a mint julep.

"Meaning where exactly?"

"My office in Mount Pleasant. On the other side of the river. I'd like to talk to you about Mr. Eric Bourbon."

Mister? These Southern werewolves were polite, even as they schemed to kill one another.

The limo turned left and headed north up East Bay Street. We passed a horse-drawn carriage loaded with tourists. I thought of Wendy working as a tour guide, and my eyes panned the carriage in the hope of seeing her.

Calhoun asked, "What did Bourbon tell you?"

I brought my attention back to him. "That's between him and me."

Calhoun's eyes gave a malicious red sparkle, like the trace of light on the edge of a crimson blade. "Let me be a little more direct. What did Bourbon propose to you?"

I've done dumb things in my career, but I wasn't stupid. If I told the truth—that Bourbon wanted me to kill Calhoun—I'd bet that female werewolf would pump me with garlic oil.

"Privileged info. I can't tell you."

"What if I made a counteroffer?"

"Keep your money. Buy what's-her-name"—I pointed to the *were*-bitch—"a personality."

She gave me the finger.

Calhoun moved uncomfortably and spewed a vibe of frustration.

I felt the vibe. If he ordered an attack, getting the revolver would take too long. I'd go after the female *were*'s throat with my talons and then decapitate Calhoun.

He must have sensed my tension. He signaled her by raising his good arm and wagging his fingers. She flicked a button on the vaccination gun and dropped it into a purse by her feet. Her muscles slimmed, becoming more feminine. The hair on her hands turned into wisps and disappeared, leaving behind tanned naked skin. Almost human. I could handle human.

"If it makes you feel any better," I said, "I'll throw you a bone. Whatever Bourbon offered, I turned him down."

The throw-you-a-bone comment made Calhoun tighten his brow in offense. "Are you leaving Charleston?"

"I was," I answered. "But I've changed my mind now that someone's tried to kill me. I need to find out who and why." I recited the details about the crab, the vampires, and the business card belonging to Bourbon. I wanted to prime Calhoun before I asked about Wendy and Paxton.

Calhoun's gaze flitted about my face as he read every twitch and nuance for extra meaning.

When I paused, he said, "I don't understand. You're here because Bourbon wanted to hire you. Now you tell me he had something to do with the attack on you."

"Let's not jump ahead of ourselves. I asked him and he denied it."

"You believe him?"

"Let me get the facts. Then I'll tell you what I believe."

"If Bourbon wanted to attack you, why use vampires?"

"Maybe there's no werewolf up to the task."

Calhoun suppressed a laugh. He glanced at the female *were*. She grinned and shook her head.

He said, "Too bad you had to kill the vampires."

"Yeah, I'm real torn up about those morons." I waited a beat before mentioning, "I found another business card."

He perked his eyebrows.

"Wendy Teagarden."

CHAPTER 9

CALHOUN LET his eyebrows settle and his expression became flat and opaque. He was hiding something about Wendy.

Our limo passed a restaurant with people sitting under umbrellas on a patio.

"You know her?" I asked.

"We're friends." His eyes turned curious. "How do you know her?"

"We're friends."

Calhoun gave an amused nod. "You're surprised she's here?"

"I am. Haven't seen her in years."

"She's doing well," Calhoun said without my prompting. "By her standards."

"What's that mean?"

He chuckled. "It means Wendy is being Wendy. She does things her way."

I understood. However Wendy earned her keep, she was always a free spirit.

"But we're here to talk about Bourbon," Calhoun said, "not Wendy." He raised his prosthesis to display his claws. "He and I are equivalent alphas within our respective clans."

"And you're both here in Charleston?"

"This city is the symbolic center of werewolves in North America. Neither one of us will cede ownership to the other. Given the snug confines of Charleston, it was inevitable that he and I would clash when our clans maneuvered for dominance."

"When you say 'clash,' do you mean killing one another's werewolves?"

Calhoun restrained a smile. "Such as one with a missing head?"

"Actually it was missing the body."

"Regrettable. He killed one of my *weres* and I had to respond. It's a matter of honor. Is it my problem that his boss is a mangy son of a bitch?" Calhoun paused. "And I mean that in the best possible way."

He kept quiet, a cue that I was supposed to laugh. I didn't. "How you *weres* handle your affairs, I don't care."

"I might tell you something to make you care." His claws flexed and relaxed. "Miss Inga Latrall." Calhoun said the name with exaggerated reverence.

Inga Latrall? The name rang dimly. I paged through my memory. Maybe she was big news here, but all I remembered was a brief mention of her. NPR maybe. Or an Internet news feed. "She was a high-powered local socialite, right? Died recently? Plane crash?"

"High-powered local socialite?" Calhoun huffed like this was an insult. "That label diminishes her significant business and philanthropic accomplishments."

More details came to me. Latrall was the guru queen of self-improvement. Tony Robbins and Suze Orman went to her for advice.

I remembered Bourbon mentioning the death of the territory alpha. Which prompted me to ask, "Was Latrall—"

"Miss Latrall," Calhoun corrected.

"—a werewolf?"

"A very remarkable *were*. She was our alpha."

My *kundalini noir* knotted in amazement. What would the media have said if they learned that this celebrated font of advice and touchy-feely wisdom had been a top werewolf?

Before I could say anything else, Calhoun added, "She didn't just die. She was murdered when her airplane crashed off Seabrook Island."

"Bourbon told me it had been an accident. Why do you say murdered?"

A malicious glint returned to his eyes. "Because of my position as the chief executive of operations for Latrall Worldwide Holdings."

Which had made him her go-to man—make that go-to *were*.

The limo got on the highway ramp for the bridge going east over the Cooper River.

"Miss Latrall's unfortunate plane trip was the opportunity," Calhoun said. "Let me explain the motive. A year ago, Eric Bourbon took on a client, a developer from Myrtle Beach. They approached Miss Latrall with an offer for a partnership to develop portions of her estate. Miss Latrall said the Lowcountry had enough strip malls and gated communities. What was needed was more pristine land. After she refused their offer, Bourbon's client floated the idea of using eminent domain to take her property, but Miss Latrall had the connections, and more important the money, to scuttle those plans."

The comments about the Lowcountry compelled me to look out my window and down from the bridge. Soft, luscious humps of the Carolina shoreline faded into the humid haze about the Cooper River. I agreed with Latrall: keep the landscape.

"Bourbon's failure to deliver the deal cost him reputation and money." Calhoun opened the claws of his prosthesis and made it rotate. "Now here's the sinister twist. If he got Latrall out of the way, his legal business could again pursue its case against her estate. And his supernatural ambitions would be satisfied when he took over Latrall's *were* dominion, the Lowcountry Territory."

I saw what Calhoun was getting at. "You're telling me Bourbon killed Miss Latrall?"

"I have no proof. It's a serious allegation, especially on the werewolf side. Miss Latrall was much beloved and any *were*, even a clan alpha, would face the wrath of werewolf justice if it was murder."

"Bourbon told me it was an accident."

"Miss Latrall's airplane crashed into the Atlantic shortly after it took off. The investigation was inconclusive. The wreckage showed no signs of unexplained structural failure, no sabotage. There were no radio transmissions of distress. The airplane simply dropped from the sky."

I asked, "What about the black box recorder?"

"Those are only required for commercial aircraft. Miss Latrall was in her private jet."

"You're not buying it was an accident?"

"If you knew Eric Bourbon, neither would you."

"He told me you had as much to gain from her death as he did."

Calhoun grimaced as if the comment had wounded him. "Miss Latrall's death is a tragedy I cannot undo. The best way I can honor her legacy is to dutifully manage her estate, though I could never take her place."

"What about the issue of the new territory alpha?"

"Bourbon's problem was that his plan backfired. After Miss Latrall's death, he thought he could bully the other clan alphas into joining him."

"But they chose you instead?"

Calhoun nodded and tried not to smile.

"What kind of arm-twisting did you do?"

"I prefer to call it gentle persuasion."

The limo reached the other end of the bridge. The highway forked and we passed a golf course. The limo followed West Coleman Boulevard, made a right onto a deserted road, and halted for a blinking red light on a temporary stop sign.

My ears tingled. Danger.

I put one hand on the upholstery beside me and the other on the window. My left hand felt the engine's purr through the seat. My right hand felt cool glass.

Now my ears and my right fingertips buzzed in alarm.

Lots of danger.

From outside.

To my right, a cargo truck barreled at us from a side street.

I yelled a warning. I pushed away from the door and shoved myself against Calhoun.

The limo driver accelerated.

Time slowed.

We moved inches while the truck moved in feet. The front of the truck followed us like a charging buffalo. The chrome grille with the Freightliner logo filled the limo's window.

My insides contracted and my shoulders hunched in preparation for the impact.

The truck rammed us broadside with a monstrous crunch.

CHAPTER 10

THE TRUCK smashed into the Mercedes.

I bounced against Calhoun.

The right doors and panels of the limo telescoped into the cabin. Glass sprayed across the interior. The female *were* was thrown from her jump seat and knocked against us like a bag of sharp sticks.

The limo swerved across the pavement and stopped. Calhoun lay beside me, his mouth clutching for breath. The female *were* sprawled over us, her eyes empty, her open mouth dripping blood.

I groped for the door lock, released it, and pushed the door open. Calhoun and I spilled onto the road, piled against the side of the limo, followed by her corpse.

Gears meshing, the truck's engine bellowed, and it bulled forward to give the Mercedes another bash. The limo was shoved across the pavement and pushed us along. The two goons trapped in the limo howled in panic.

I shoved the female *were* off my shoulder—she was as dead as a cold steak—and slid my legs from under Calhoun. The Mercedes shook as the truck's front tires clawed over the wreckage. The roof of the limo collapsed. The sheet metal buckled around my shoulders.

Any second now, the truck would grind us into the asphalt. I hadn't come to Charleston to be roadkill. But I didn't have time to free myself and get away.

Vampiric strength charged my body. I locked my legs and heaved against the limo.

The truck's engine grunted as its rear tires spun against the asphalt. The odor of burned rubber thickened the air. More meshing of gears and the driver gunned the engine.

The Mercedes pressed against me and metal folded over me like a giant hand. I planted my heels in a crack in the pavement. My legs quivered in the effort of holding back the truck.

I clenched my teeth and pushed my shoulders into the limo. My *kundalini noir* hardened into a bar of steel.

The truck's engine grunted.

I grunted.

The *weres* trapped in the limo howled louder.

My legs trembled. My heels pressed divots into the asphalt. The pain felt like I had the whole world crushing my lower back.

My vision dimmed from the strain.

My *kundalini noir* flexed and pushed through my psychic column like a piston of energy. The exertion boiled into anger.

I was angry at the driver of the truck, at Freightliner for making the truck, at Calhoun for putting me here, at the werewolves for their damn howling, and most of all, at myself for thinking that going mano a mano against a three-ton diesel truck was a good idea.

The truck climbed farther onto the limo and put more weight against me. My knees weakened. The anger transformed into fear. The truck was winning.

My *kundalini noir* flexed again. My legs locked strong.

I heaved again.

The truck kept coming.

I had power for one more shove. I heaved once more.

The engine stalled. The truck rolled backward and its front tires slammed the pavement. The weight lifted and my spine straightened.

I'd won.

Some victory—tell it to my back.

My legs collapsed and my side of the limo crashed to the ground. I tore the sheet metal away from my shoulders.

Calhoun lay by my feet.

Now for my counterattack.

But I couldn't move my legs. My lower back had cramped solid as concrete. Pain shot from my hips through my legs.

The doors of the truck banged open. They were coming to finish us off.

I rolled onto my belly. I dragged my legs behind me as I crawled alongside the limo to the rear bumper. Reaching into my cargo pocket, I tore the bag open and grasped the snub-nose.

The driver of the truck vaulted over the limo's trunk and landed beside me. Hair had sprouted along his jaws and around his ears. His nose had darkened and turned into a doggie's snout.

Werewolf.

He gave a fanged scowl and aimed a sawed-off shotgun at me. He let loose with both barrels.

Ignoring my pain, I sprang from the ground.

Buckshot pinged against the limo.

The werewolf broke the shotgun open—the spent shells twirled in the air—and reached into his shirt pocket for fresh ammo.

I dove at him. He swung at me with the butt of the shotgun, but I deflected the blow with my arm. I grabbed his belt, pulled tight against his waist, and jammed the revolver into his gut. I'd make him eat all five bullets belly-buster style.

The *were*'s eyes clamped shut in terror.

I worked the trigger. The revolver went *click, click, click.*

Damn.

Click. Click.

Useless piece-of-crap pistol.

The werewolf opened his eyes. They crinkled in amusement. "You lose, vampire."

CHAPTER 11

THE WEREWOLF'S leer turned into a deep, pissed-off scowl, and he tried to knee my crotch. I put the snub-nose to better use by slamming it against his kneecap. He doubled forward, making it easy for me to smack the pistol against his chin.

His teeth clacked together as his face scrunched in pain. He dropped the shotgun and his legs folded. I held him upright to smack him again.

A deafening blast slapped the back of my head. My muscles locked up in fear.

The werewolf shook in my grip. A rope of blood looped from his chest. I hopped back and let the blood splash beyond my shoes.

Calhoun's *were* bodyguard held a humongous Desert Eagle .50 AE pistol. Smoke curled from the muzzle. A spent thumb-size cartridge pinged on the asphalt. He stood where he'd crawled from the driver's door of the limo. His suit and shirt hung in bloody tatters from his muscular chest and arms like he'd been worked over by an industrial cheese grater. Blood seeped around the glass bits stuck to his face.

Beside him, the limo driver clutched the twisted remains of the door and pulled himself to his feet.

I let my werewolf drop. Smoke curled from the hole sizzling in his chest. He'd been shot with a silver bullet.

His body crumpled to the ground next to Calhoun and the dead female *were*. Calhoun extended his leg to push the attacker's corpse away as if it could contaminate him.

Calhoun's bodyguard shifted aim to his left and fired again. The bullet cracked into the truck. Something—or someone—plopped to the asphalt.

I stepped around the rear of the limo and looked at the truck. The passenger door was open, a bullet hole the diameter of a nickel in the center. The other werewolf lay on the road, blood pooling around his torso and smoke feathering from his shirt.

The *were* bodyguard gazed at his victim. He grinned and nodded to himself. Satisfied by his marksmanship, he stuffed his big pistol into a shoulder holster and brushed the glass from his face.

The fight was over. My blood quit churning with adrenaline. My *kundalini noir* relaxed. Pain returned to my lower back. I leaned against the limo to ease the discomfort. I was immortal, had superpowers, yet at this moment, I'd kill for ibuprofen.

My guts simmered from a low burn of anger. Screw these werewolves for dragging me into their bullshit.

The driver helped Calhoun to his feet. Calhoun shrugged him off. He used his prosthesis to straighten his tie and his good hand to smooth his hair.

The bodyguard nudged his shoe against the dead werewolf's chest. "One of Bourbon's pups?"

Calhoun massaged his right thigh and stood with his feet astride the corpse's head. "I'm sure of it, Dan." Judging by the contempt on his face, I thought he was going to unzip and pee on the dead werewolf. "Take him out of my sight."

Dan the bodyguard grasped the werewolf by the ankles and dragged him around the limo.

Calhoun limped to the female *were* and knelt beside her. He snapped his fingers at the driver, who returned to the limo.

The driver rummaged through the remains of the front seat. He came out with a gray metal box bearing the markings of a first-aid kit. After unsnapping the two clasps on the lid, he opened the box and withdrew three stubby cardboard tubes.

Calhoun said, "Give one to Felix."

The driver handed me a tube and took the rest to Dan.

The tube was waxy cardboard with a short red cellophane ribbon dangling from one end. The tube had FRAGILE stenciled along its length but no indications of its contents.

Calhoun beckoned me. He stroked the female *were*'s hair. Blood seeped through her clothes. Her nose shrank into a wrinkled black knob. The hair on her face and arms grew dense with a speed that mimicked time-lapse photography. Her hands curled into gnarled paws with her fingertips growing long and yellow. Must be werewolf rigor mortis.

Calhoun said, "Open the tube."

She was beyond the help of first aid, no matter what was in the tube. Better fast-forward to last rites.

I tugged on the ribbon, unwinding it until the paper cap fell off one end. I upturned the tube over my other hand. A black rubber bulb the size of a miniature bottle of liquor slid out. An olive-green plastic nipple jutted from one end of the bulb. This . . . bulb thing was in new condition but appeared to be a vintage medical device.

Calhoun unbuttoned the female *were*'s blouse. He spread the blouse to expose her sternum and the soft mounds of her breasts swelling from a white brassiere. A brown fuzz covered her skin.

The blouse flapped across her chest. He used his prosthesis to fold the blouse open, but it kept sliding closed. Frustrated, he said, "Little help."

I was going to ask, *You mean, give you a hand?* but decided against it.

I took a knee beside him and held the blouse open. Her skin was cool, the hair on her chest fine as lint.

Calhoun ran a fingertip along her sternum until he found a gap in her rib cage. "Right here. Insert the needle and pump the bulb three times."

I pulled the plastic nipple from the bulb and exposed a syringe needle. I steadied the needle over the spot on her sternum, then pushed the syringe until the needle disappeared into her flesh. There was no reaction.

I squeezed the bulb until it collapsed with a soft crush. That was one pump. I released the bulb and gave it two more squeezes. I withdrew the syringe. A drop of blood clung to the needle's tip and a second tiny drop welled from the puncture.

Calhoun sighed and put his weight on his heels. I stuck the plastic nipple back on the needle and returned the bulb to the cardboard tube.

The *were*'s skin turned a shade lighter. The change in color was due to the fuzz on her chest curling and fading. The hair on her face and hands shriveled and dropped like dust. Her nose lost its black color and grew back into its previous shape. Her fingernails shrank and her hands returned to human proportions.

I shook the tube. "What's the serum?"

"A distillation of a potion made from herbs and the dissolved shell of the Moroccan hirsute beetle." Calhoun stared at her. "Destroys the werewolf enzymes. As far as anyone can detect, she was always an ordinary human, even at the molecular level."

Though she was dead, there was more dignity in this ceremony than in the ways we vampires got rid of supernatural evidence: roasting our dearly departed under the sun and vacuuming the ash.

Calhoun caressed her cheeks with the back of his hand.

"Who was she?" I asked.

"A faithful servant. A dutiful messenger." He closed her eyelids and stood awkwardly by bracing his prosthesis against one knee. "A clan sister."

He said this with reverence. Why did these werewolves harp on clan allegiances? I saw it simply as one more excuse to kill each other.

Dan the bodyguard came back holding a cell phone. "Sergeant Kessler's on the way."

"What does that mean?" I asked. "Cops? The army?"

"Kessler's one of us in the Charleston police. She'll make sure to cover this up." Calhoun motioned to the wrecked limo, the truck with the smashed grille, and all the debris around us. Werewolves had to hide their supernatural tracks same as us vampires.

Calhoun tapped my shoulder. "Thanks."

"Can't say I welcomed the opportunity." I palmed the revolver, grateful that I had gotten some use from its metal bulk.

Calhoun's gaze followed the pistol. "You had that gun the whole time?"

"Yeah. Should've searched me." I dropped the gun back into my cargo pocket. "But no worries. Did as much good as carrying a rock."

The limo driver collected the cardboard tube from me. "We recycle," he explained.

Calhoun and I trod through the pieces of wrecked car over to the truck. The other two werewolves, now in human form, had been stretched out beside each other.

Calhoun addressed his bodyguard. "Any ID?"

Dan said, "Driver's licenses," and recited a couple of names. "Both are from outside the territory." He and Calhoun went back and forth discussing what pack and clan they might have been from. They agreed these werewolves had to have been freelancing for Bourbon.

A patrol car zoomed up the road, emergency lights flashing but without a siren. The patrol car skidded beside us.

A female police officer opened the front passenger's door and got out. She projected a have-no-fear, I'm-in-charge demeanor. She had an attractive face, though her wide bottom showed a career cruising too many doughnut shops.

The driver, another cop, climbed out. He hustled to the middle of the street. A passing car slowed to gawk. He waved: *Move along.*

The female cop asked, "You okay, Mr. Calhoun?"

"Yes, considering." He brushed dirt from his trousers. "Make sure this incident stays quiet."

"As always." She saluted, turned, and busied herself talking to the bodyguard and the limo driver.

An unmarked car, red and blue lights flashing from inside the grille, halted next to Calhoun.

The driver, wearing ordinary civilian clothes but with a badge clipped to his belt, scrambled out of the car like he was late for duty. He opened a rear door. Calhoun started to get in and motioned for me to join him.

"Where are we going?" I asked.

He answered, "Our original destination. My office."

An ambulance circled and parked beside the truck. Two men—*weres*?—climbed out of the back with a gurney. A third passenger carried a stack of orange traffic cones and a push broom. He arranged the cones around the wreckage and began to sweep the debris.

No one took pictures. No one wrote anything down.

I thought of the *were*'s head in Bourbon's office. Bourbon had mentioned he didn't want the police involved in the killings among werewolves. This attack had to have been his attempt at revenge and therefore kept off the official records.

I got into the police car, and we proceeded to Royal Avenue. Dense, mature trees shaded tidy houses behind white picket fences. Pure Norman Rockwell in the land of Lowcountry werewolves.

The driver twisted his mirror to scan the backseat. He squinted at where he should've seen me but couldn't. He glanced over his shoulder to make sure I was still in the car. I waved at him. He must not have had much experience with vampires.

Calhoun took a cell phone out of his coat's inside pocket. He made calls as he massaged his thigh with the curved side of one claw of his prosthesis. He spoke in crisp phrases, replying with variations of "Yeah. Yeah. Get on it. No. That's your job."

He closed up the phone and slipped it back into his pocket. He stretched his leg, his face pinched in discomfort.

I said, "Tell me what you know about Julius Paxton."

Calhoun's face went, *Huh?* He asked, "Who?"

I explained my history with Paxton. I included the details about the vampire attack and that I had found his name on the back of Bourbon's card. I finished by saying, "Maybe that attack that just happened wasn't against you, but me."

Calhoun kept massaging his thigh. "An interesting assumption, but I assure you, those werewolves were after me."

We made a couple of turns. The neighborhood stopped abruptly at a sign that said PRIVATE ROAD. NO TRESPASSING.

The road narrowed to a single asphalt lane that wound under a canopy of elm and maple trees and through a gap in a boxwood hedge as thick and imposing as a concrete wall.

The road circled before an enormous mansion of pink stucco iced with white trim. Hickory and beech trees hugged the front of the edifice. The foliage was a lush green, as if it had been planted with freshly printed money.

I asked, "What's this place?"

Calhoun answered, "My office."

A man and a woman in green polo shirts and khaki shorts stood beside the road. *Weres*, no doubt.

They had radios clipped to their shirts and hunting rifles slung over their shoulders.

The *were* cop driving the police car looked for me in the rearview window. His eyes hunted back and forth until he asked, "Know anything about guns?"

"More than I should. I've been shot a few times."

He grunted, like I'd beaten him to the punch line. But he continued, "Those are .458 Winchesters. The African Safari model. They can take down anything with one shot. Elephants. Cape buffalo. Hippos. And we got 'em loaded with silver bullets."

"What're you expecting?" I asked. "Really fat werewolves?"

The *were* cop's smile filled the rearview mirror. "No. Smart-ass vampires."

CHAPTER 12

WE PASSED the two guards. The female *were* crouched to peer through the rear window of the police car. We locked eyes for an instant. She squinted and cupped a radio mike to her mouth.

"What kind of a reception are you planning?" I clenched my fists to hide my growing talons. Being among werewolves was like walking a tightrope over a pit of . . . well, werewolves.

Calhoun looked over his shoulder back toward the guards. "We have to be ready for anything. If you behave yourself," he joked, "you've got nothing to worry about."

I was surrounded by werewolves; I had plenty to worry about.

Our police car followed the road circling to the mansion. A half-dozen other cars—expensive sedans and SUVs—crowded the pavement along the shoulder.

The road curved under the roof of a tall porte cochere. An attendant in a powder-blue chambray shirt and navy blue shorts waited by a massive bronze door with beveled glass inserts. When our car halted, the attendant sprang for the rear door like a nervous terrier.

He yanked the door open and I gave a quick sniff. Definitely *were*. In fact, the mansion smelled like a kennel. A very clean kennel, but still, you had better love your dogs.

The attendant held a surprised look and stood aside for me to climb out. Ignoring me, he helped Calhoun.

Blood dotted Calhoun's shirt collar. He moved stiffly, as if during the ride his injuries from the crash had time to settle into aches.

The *were* cop got out of the car and joined them, grasping Calhoun's good arm. Calhoun pulled loose with a snarl. He rolled his shoulders, as though to shrug off both the help and his pain. His posture strengthened and he limped to the entrance door. "Detective Simone, thank you. Give Sergeant Kessler my thanks as well."

The detective nodded and got back into his car.

The attendant stepped beside Calhoun and opened the door. I followed them into a foyer with a vaulted ceiling and a chandelier as big around as a grand piano. We continued through the foyer to a set of French doors.

Calhoun whispered to his attendant, who in turn said to me over his shoulder, "Mr. Calhoun will rejoin you shortly."

We were separating? Was Calhoun's invitation the bait for a trap?

Calhoun went through the French doors. The attendant lingered behind to say, "Please, wait for Mr. Calhoun on the terrace."

Of course, a place this classy had a terrace. Not a mere deck or a backyard.

The attendant motioned that I go to the right. They weren't giving me much of a choice, so I went as directed and made my way through the mansion.

I passed under arched door frames separating cavernous rooms, each with a lumberyard's worth of wainscoting, picture rails, and crown molding. Every ceiling was an example of exquisite plaster relief. An interior designer must have been handed a blank check and told to cram the mansion with whatever looked expensive: porcelain figurines, statues, paintings of antebellum maidens with dogs and horses, furniture that must have boasted historical pedigrees (or were good fakes).

But nothing showed that someone lived here. No framed snapshots. No magazines or papers casually strewn about. No socks on the floor. The rooms looked as sterile as a bank lobby.

The air carried a scent of fruit and flower potpourri. Didn't hide the wolf musk, only now the place smelled like a girlie poodle.

So far, no hint of trouble. To make sure, I stopped beside a heavy wooden credenza and laid the palm of my left hand on the top.

Over the years, I've learned how to better exploit my sixth sense. Hasn't kept me from getting smacked around on occasion, but it gives the comforting illusion that I'm ahead of the bad guys.

I kept still and focused on the tiny vibrations that whispered through the credenza. I listened. I analyzed. I linked faint noises to the vibrations and formed images in my head.

Someone walking on hard heels over a tile floor. Quick steps. Female.

Water running. Water turned off—the spigot closing with a squish—and a muted thud from the water hammer effect in the pipes.

The purr of a laser printer.

No threatening clicks like a gun being cocked.

No feet creeping over carpet.

No knife sliding out of a sheath.

I closed my eyes and inhaled deeply.

No poisons. No telltale adrenaline surges.

I swept my sixth sense around me like a radar beam. My intuition would further link my senses and draw new pictures.

But nothing new. Nothing suspicious. Only that pervasive werewolf smell that reminded me in bold highlights that I was here as a bit player in the struggle between Bourbon and Calhoun.

Yet I had to relax. Concentrating too hard would make my brain cramp. I continued my walk through the mansion and ended in a room in the northwest corner. Sunlight streamed through tall multipaned windows and yet another set of French doors on the back wall.

I grasped the brass handle of one door—it was unlocked—and stepped onto the terrace.

Colored pennants along the perimeter of the terrace flapped lazily in the breeze. A banner hung from a pole next to the doors. The banner showed a crescent moon rising above a howling wolf superimposed over a palm tree.

I breathed the aroma of moist, fertile soil. Fluffy clouds paraded across the sky. The sunlit landscape shimmered in hues bright as fresh watercolors.

The terrace was made of hexagonal slabs of terra-cotta flagstone bordered with concrete planters and benches. The terrace looked over a garden that sloped to a lawn the size of a football field. An S-76 helicopter, sleek as a torpedo, sat on a concrete pad in the center of the lawn. A man in a blue flight suit stood beside the open cargo door of the helicopter.

A path of square paving stones snaked from a porch on my left at the opposite side of the house. The stones led to the helicopter pad and continued through a line of magnolia and cypress trees that separated the lawn from a flat muddy beach. The path ended at a long, narrow pier extending from the beach into Charleston Harbor. Speedboats and a yacht, a sixty-footer I guessed, were moored to the pier.

Something bothered me.

Everything seemed new. Not brand-new, but the mansion and grounds looked recent, unlike similar buildings in Charleston that dated back centuries.

Along the northern boundary, a wall of dense shrubs and trees masked the view of the neighbors and, in turn, kept them from looking in. I got the impression that Calhoun and his patroness, the late Inga Latrall, despite her promise to keep the Lowcountry pristine, didn't hesitate at bulldozing the locals out of the way and carving out a place for this mansion.

What the werewolves wanted, they took.

CHAPTER 13

ONE OF the French doors at the back of the mansion opened. Calhoun came onto the terrace, alone. He wore a white terrycloth bathrobe over black nylon track pants with his white socked feet tucked into shower clogs. The left sleeve of the robe was pinned to his shoulder, and it made him look unbalanced and incomplete. I wondered how much he missed his arm.

His hair was slicked back and raked with comb marks. His cheeks and nose looked red and irritated, as if he'd scrubbed his face with a scouring pad. A gold chain necklace lay across the gray athletic shirt peeking between the lapels of the robe.

How long had he been gone? Fifteen minutes? Considering he'd been tossed about in a car wreck, he appeared fresh and full of vigor.

Calhoun extended his right arm and gave a toothy smile so perfect it looked Photoshopped. He smelled of bay rum and tea-tree oil. "It's belated, but thanks for saving me."

We shook hands. His grip was feverishly warm. Maybe *weres* ran hot while we vampires ran cold.

"Your bodyguard Dan and his big gun did the saving. You need to thank him."

Calhoun noticed my glance at his empty sleeve. He said, "It's getting cleaned and adjusted."

"Don't you have a spare?" I figured he'd have a closet full of bionic arms.

"I do, but switching prosthetics is like trying on a new pair of stiff shoes."

I swept my hand across the view along the back of the mansion. "Fancy office."

"Actually, my office is at the other end of the mansion."

"Let me guess," I said, making sure to emphasize the *Miss* when I continued, "this was Miss Latrall's house."

"One of her many holdings. It's corporate headquarters and was her private residence."

"You also live here?"

"I have a suite for when I have to sleep over."

Sleep over for what? Pajama parties?

He answered like he'd sensed my questions. "Late-night meetings. Receptions."

The helicopter's engine started with a groan and interrupted Calhoun. The rotor blades began to spin. The blades turned faster and faster and the helicopter let out a high-pitched whine.

A golf cart trundled down the path from the house to the helicopter pad. A man in the uniform of the house staff drove. The woman passenger clasped her hand over the scarf on her head. The cart halted just outside the arc of the main rotor blades. The man in the flight suit helped the woman passenger from the cart to the helicopter. She wore goggle-like sunglasses, a loose blouse over a tank top, and Capri pants. As she climbed aboard, I recognized the overtoned figure and the teardrop face drawn to a severe chin.

"Is that Madonna?"

Calhoun nodded, unimpressed that I'd mentioned it. "Here to attend a private remembrance for Miss Latrall, her mentor."

Madonna climbed into the S-76. The crewman followed her aboard and slid the door closed. The whine of the engine and the beat of the rotor blades echoed against us. The helicopter lifted to a hover, blowing a circle of grass and dust from the concrete pad. The tricycle gear retracted and the helicopter zoomed in the direction of the harbor, darting through the air like a shark through water. The golf cart circled and returned to the mansion.

I asked, "Any other celebrities?"

"Not today. Earlier in the week we had Deepak Chopra, John Malkovich, and Diablo Cody."

"You're mixing rather cozily with humans. I'm sure you're taking precautions at keeping the Great Secret."

"We do. Miss Latrall had many admirers, and none of them had a clue about us."

"What's with the 'Miss' anyway? Some corny Southern mannerism?"

"Corny? To you maybe. Simply my way of paying homage to her. I owe her much, and it's my duty to make sure her wishes are respected even after her death."

A conscience. Or pretending to have one. I had no doubts that however Calhoun took care of Latrall's estate, he'd wind up standing tall on a big pile of moolah.

A compelling reason for Bourbon to hate him.

"I understand your allegiance to her, but what was Bourbon's? What kept him from taking his clan and going renegade while she was alive?"

"Bourbon rose through the ranks of the Palmetto Clan when Miss Latrall was the territory alpha. Every *were* in every clan was beholden to her." He pointed to the banner with the howling wolf. "That was her standard, the Lowcountry Territory."

"Now she's dead."

Calhoun repeated, "Now she's dead."

"You brought me here to broaden my understanding of your situation."

He motioned across Charleston Harbor. The water was a swath of turquoise green dappled with silver. "See that speck on the water?"

"I see lots of specks."

"The dark spot in the middle of the entrance to the harbor," he said. "Fort Sumter."

I noted, "Where the Civil War began."

"There was nothing civil about it. The War Between the States, if you please."

"What are you getting at?"

"The animosity between myself and Bourbon is one crack of a much larger fissure in the werewolf community." He groped absently in front of himself as if searching for his missing prosthesis. He reached across his chest and touched his robe's empty sleeve. "Sides are being drawn among werewolves."

"Among werewolves," I noted. "That sounds like your business. I'm here with you because hopefully you can help me learn why a couple of vampires tried to kill me this morning. That in turn has something to do with a good friend who I'm certain is also in trouble."

"Wendy?" he asked.

I nodded.

He scratched his neck. "Let me explain what's ultimately at stake." His voice dropped to a somber whisper. "Beyond my and Bourbon's ambitions and the fate of Miss Latrall's property. Perhaps that will shed light on why all of us are in danger."

CHAPTER 14

CALHOUN TURNED his back to me and walked to the edge of the terrace. "You must help me prevent an enormous catastrophe."

I asked, "What kind of catastrophe?"

"A war." He turned around to face me. "A war that would betray the Great Secret."

A shiver radiated from my *kundalini noir.*

If the Great Secret was revealed, the repercussions would surge through society like the blast wave of an atom bomb. Humans would have to contend with the existence of the undead, shape-shifters, and all the fantastic paranormal creatures. The overlap of the psychic world with the natural one. Magic was real. The foundations for science, religion, and philosophy would collapse. And in that chaos, humans would have a tangible excuse for all of civilization's evils: us supernaturals.

Calhoun looked at me and the despair I felt was mapped

on his face. "This is my fear." His voice was dour. "We may come to terms with humans, but in the meantime, they will turn on us like they have done to the Neanderthals and the biblical giants. Humans will tolerate our existence only after we've been reduced to pitiful numbers, if they allowed us to exist at all. Imprisonment in zoos, fiendish experiments in cages, and mass graves loom in our future."

His eyes hooked mine. "I know what you are, Mr. Gomez. An enforcer. It is your job to protect the Great Secret. A vampire gets compromised—put in jail or hospitalized by humans—it's up to vampires like you to either rescue . . . or destroy."

Calhoun didn't mention the other circumstances when I'd been called to action. Such as to locate and eliminate renegades like Paxton. Or zombies who attack humans without regard for the consequences to the supernatural world. For that reason, in a previous assignment, I had wiped out an army of zombies and their creator.

Werewolves safeguard the Great Secret for the same reason as vampires: a mistrust of humans. But *weres* are prone to mass violence on a scale that would attract the attention of blunt-tooth society.

The Araneum can't police the werewolves. One-on-one, a vampire can handle a *were*. But they fight in packs. Werewolves would also resent our meddling in their affairs even if the intent was to prevent compromising the Great Secret. The implication would be that *weres* weren't competent enough to take care of themselves.

In the event of a werewolf war, the Araneum would pull back and protect the vampire world. Standing order: Do not interfere in the affairs of werewolves.

Nevertheless, I felt like my feet were in a pan of water set on a stove. Moment by moment, the water was getting hotter.

"A war starts, doesn't Eric Bourbon have as much to lose as you do?"

"That's what this is about. Blackmail. First, Bourbon murdered Miss Latrall. When he realized I'd be chosen over him, he instigated a campaign to fan the discontent werewolves have about safeguarding the Great Secret."

"What discontent?"

"Living with humans. The need to hide our true selves. The need to compromise. A compromise that grows more oppressive as humans become more numerous and sophisticated. A belief that it's a matter of time before we supernaturals are 'outed.' "

Calhoun's words lay heavy in my mind. "A lot of vampires feel the same way."

His brow furrowed. "Many werewolves say the time to reveal the Great Secret is now, on our terms. Start with a preemptive strike on the human centers of power. Economic. Cultural. Political. Military."

"Forgetting," I replied, "that all this time we supernaturals have lived with the belief that humans fear us because we're evil. If we reveal ourselves and attack, then we'll have justified that fear."

"Exactly," Calhoun said, as if hitting a nail. "Humans would counterattack and we'd have total war. A war you vampires won't be able to sit out for long. Some bloodsuckers would join us werewolves. The humans would learn how to fight us all."

"If you werewolves want to start a war that could reveal the Great Secret, you're on your own. It's not my job to keep you guys holding hands and singing 'Kumbaya.' "

That was the Araneum's party line. The fear was that a war could pull vampires into whatever mess the werewolves created. Foreboding made my mouth go dry.

I needed a drink and paused at the liquor table on the terrace. I put my hands on a bottle of Bombay Sapphire and raised an eyebrow. *May I?*

Calhoun said, "Make it two."

I scooped ice from a bucket and into two old-fashioned glasses. "Since the cops seem to be in your hip pocket, why don't you have them take care of Bourbon?"

Calhoun smiled politely and shook his head. "*Weres* in the police represent many packs and both of our clans. They must remain neutral at all times. Werewolf presence on the force simplifies keeping the supernatural world hidden from humans."

"Won't make any difference if there's a war."

"True. But if the police act against a clan alpha, it would only aggravate the situation."

"Why don't you and the other clan alphas gang up on Bourbon and take him out? After all, he killed Miss Latrall."

"Which I can't prove. Besides, werewolf combat at the clan level is the same as war."

I made gin and tonics and offered Calhoun his drink. We clinked glasses and mumbled, "Cheers." *Here's mud in your face.*

I made a sweeping gesture across the terrace and the mansion. "I can see why Bourbon has his furry little heart set on this place." I took a sip. The drink tasted too cold and mellow. Not enough of a kick. Needed a blood chaser. "Now, what do you want from me?"

"Help me prevent his war," Calhoun said. "Meanwhile, I'll do what I can to find Paxton."

"Back up. I'll find Paxton on my own. But there is only one way I see to prevent your war. Kill Bourbon, which I won't do."

"There is another way. Find proof that Bourbon caused Miss Latrall's airplane to crash. Bring that proof to me and I'll make sure Bourbon gets the werewolf justice he deserves. I'd reward you well."

"I've already said I don't want your money. Besides, how do you want me to help? I haven't gotten the red carpet since I've been here. I'm no werewolf. I don't like being around you guys any more than you like being around me."

"You won't be inconvenienced for long." The statement was heavy with sarcasm.

"I don't follow."

Calhoun set his drink on the table, raised his hand, and spread his fingers. "Four days, Mr. Gomez. Four days is all we have before this"—he swept his arm across the panorama—"is destroyed."

"Why four days?"

He scratched his neck again. "Because in four days it will be the most dangerous time for us werewolves."

"Why's that?"

"The full moon."

CHAPTER 15

I'VE SEEN Lon Chaney Jr.," I said. "I get the whole full-moon-and-you-guys-go-feral routine."

Calhoun raised his hand to signal that I listen. "Unlike the movies, we can control the shape-shifting. But this full moon is special. We will convene Le Cercle de Sang et Crocs. It means—"

"The circle of blood and . . . crocs?" I interrupted. "Crocs, like the shoes?"

"No, crocs is French for 'fangs.' "

Circle of Blood and Fangs. They got points for drama.

"It's the council that chooses the new alpha of the territory," he explained. "The selection of a new top alpha is a big occasion. While only pack and clan alphas of the territory may vote, werewolves from all over the country come to witness the ceremony."

"And this Cercle has to occur during the full moon?"

"It's tradition and it's when our werewolf personas are at their strongest."

"Once your circle thing makes its pronouncement, then what's the problem?"

"Bourbon may not submit to the decision of Le Cercle."

"You say that as if you've been chosen."

Calhoun didn't correct me.

"What if the vote goes the other way?"

"I will abide by the decision of Le Cercle." He said this like he had to.

I asked, "If Bourbon is threatening war, then why not strip him of his power and boot him from the territory?"

"There is a process for that as well," Calhoun answered. "We can banish him. That means no clan. No pack. No family. Hell for social creatures like us."

"I get the impression Bourbon wouldn't accept banishment."

"Not without causing a war."

"And if Bourbon doesn't submit to the pronouncement of this Circle of Blood and Fangs or shoes or whatever, then what?"

"Anarchy."

"What about the werewolves in Bourbon's clan? Is their loyalty to him or to the territory alpha?"

"Bourbon wouldn't challenge the authority of Le Cercle unless his werewolves are behind him."

"Those *weres* who ambushed us," I asked, "they came from another clan?"

Calhoun nodded. "Sympathizers from outside the territory. Bourbon recruits them to encourage others to challenge clan and pack authority."

"Why is this seditionist spirit focused here in Charleston?"

"Because werewolf clans from all over the country are looking to us as an example. If we break apart, we can expect *were* hierarchy to crumble. But if we hold together"—Calhoun made a fist—"then we'll avoid disaster."

"I've noticed that everyone in Charleston thinks highly of themselves. What makes this place so important?"

"We're a symbol. We're the first community of werewolves to settle in America."

"Weren't there indigenous werewolves?" I asked, annoyed by the typical *gringo* attitude that overlooked everyone else. "What about the Spanish? Their settlements predate those of the English."

"Don't get me wrong," Calhoun said. "Our conquest of this land was as rapacious as that of the humans. The indigenous alphas were replaced."

"Replaced? Or murdered?"

"Past is past, Mr. Gomez. My ancestors mated with the surviving families and absorbed their bloodlines. There are a few indigenous wolf packs here and there. Up in Maine, there's even a Nordic pack that stayed intact after the Vikings left."

"One big happy family, aren't you?" I said.

"I wish it were," Calhoun replied. "A rebellion in Charleston will initiate the breakdown of werewolf structure below the pack level. That's why this Cercle is so important. If hierarchy and territorial control cannot be maintained, then every werewolf in the Lowcountry could go feral. They would attack regardless of species. Chaos would spread from territory to territory, clan to clan, pack to pack, werewolf to human."

Calhoun gazed at me. "And werewolf to vampire. The coming full moon could be the last we'll see in peace."

Once again, he raised his hand and spread his fingers. "Four days, Mr. Gomez. Four days."

CHAPTER 16

FOUR DAYS to werewolf Armageddon.

Werewolves at war with each other. Add humans. How long before we vampires get drawn into the disaster?

The consequences of that scenario spun around me. Total interspecies warfare. Death and misery would bury us all.

I looked from the terrace and across the harbor to Charleston. Where was the Araneum? And the local *nidus*, what were they doing?

"It's happened before," Calhoun said, as if to underline the grimness of what he'd just explained. "During the War Between the States, at the battle for Vicksburg, an interclan fight for werewolf dominance took place along the Mississippi River. If you examine the history books, that battle was noted for a preponderance of night casualties. Soldiers from both sides claimed to have witnessed savage night stalkers raiding their outposts. The few survivors babbled incoherently about men torn to pieces. The mutilated remains prompted ugly reprisals."

"All because of werewolves?"

"Yes. Fortunately, the chaos of the battle was enough to mask our numbers."

"But this time," I said, "there is no war for you to hide this scale of *were*-on-*were* violence."

"Now you understand my worries." Calhoun stirred abruptly. He pulled a cell phone from the pocket of his robe and glanced at the display. He opened the phone and tapped the keypad.

"If you don't mind"—he turned to the French doors at the back of the mansion—"I've made arrangements for your return to the city. You're staying at the Atlas Mortuary on King Street, yes?"

The question pricked like a needle. "How do you know?"

"Please," he said, as if my question had insulted him, "it's my job to stay informed."

"Meaning you have *weres* that can alert you of everything?"

"Not everything. Today's incident on the way here was proof of that. I look forward to your help."

"Which you're not getting."

"But I've explained the situation."

"Which I understand. But I'm not getting involved for two reasons. One, I'm not going to be your proxy in the fight between you and Bourbon. And two, the Araneum has a rule about vampires meddling in werewolf business."

"But the war?"

"I fear the Araneum more than I do a werewolf war."

Calhoun stood quiet for a moment and opened one of the French doors. I couldn't read him. The *were* was a master at cloaking his emotions.

His attendant waited in the room. Calhoun took my hand and gave a lukewarm shake. "Thank you for your time, Mr. Gomez."

The attendant waved that I accompany him. Calhoun stayed behind and remained framed by the doorway, as if boxed in by his circumstances.

I was taken to the foyer, where a woman waited for me. She was tall with swirls of brunette hair falling to her shoulders. She gave an easy, sunny smile that was a relief from the gloom obsessing Calhoun. The tight cut of her white strapless dress showed off every delectable curve. An inviting line started at her high-heeled mule pumps and went up one slit on the side of her dress.

All that tanned skin made her eyes seem an intense electric blue. Full lips parted to show teeth as shiny and precisely aligned as pearls on a necklace. I had seen her in another photo, back in Bourbon's office, one in which she was arm in prosthesis with Calhoun.

She introduced herself. "Angela Cyclone." She wore lots of jewelry, gold and diamonds, including a tennis bracelet.

A very beautiful woman. A sniff added the caveat: *Were.*

I replied with my name, then asked, "Are you a cyclone before or after you shift into a werewolf?"

"Vampire, I'm *always* a cyclone."

The difference between us pulled at me like we were opposite ends of magnets. Which surprised me. Never thought I'd be attracted to a *were*, even one as pretty as her.

She guided me out of the foyer to a black Maserati GranTurismo sports coupe in the porte cochere. "Hop in."

"With a name like Cyclone, does Calhoun trust you to drive these wheels?"

"He trusts me with you," she replied.

"You work for him?"

"I'm on his staff."

"He must pay very well, judging by this car."

"Since you asked, the car was a gift."

I wouldn't doubt it. Calhoun acted like he had the money to dole out cars like they were party favors.

"For?"

"An acknowledgment of my loyalty. Not that he needs to buy it."

"What's your job?"

"I do whatever he asks, but my formal job is as his expert on Lycanthrope Law."

"Is there such a thing?"

"Can be very complicated."

"You went to law school? Or was it through correspondence?"

Her eyes narrowed as if she debated whether I was curious or sarcastic. "It's informal. There's a lot of reading and discussion. Most of what we do is set by precedent."

We got in and buckled up. She started the engine. We eased from under the porte cochere and veered around a line of big SUVs.

I'd never been in a Maserati and admired the leather-and-wood interior. "Makes quite an entrance."

"And an exit." She mashed the gas pedal, and the coupe shot forward, fast enough to press me into the seat. We slalomed through the estate gates and pounced onto the public road, the Maserati as sure-footed as a leopard.

She asked, "You don't have much experience with werewolves, do you?"

The question set off an alarm. My ears tingled. "Are you asking for you, or are you asking for Calhoun?"

"Are you always this paranoid?"

"Only when I'm around werewolves."

"I'm curious about the vampire detective from Colorado."

"How come everyone knows so much about me? Did someone post my visit on craigslist?"

"Maybe that's a good thing," she answered. "It's a big rock that makes a big splash."

"It's a big rock that sinks straight to the bottom." Angela was far too easy on the eyes and I had to be careful not to let my guard down. It wasn't a coincidence that she was my ride back to Charleston. "Did Calhoun put you up to this?"

"He asked me to give you a ride."

"Knowing that we'd talk?"

"If you say something I think is important, I'm obligated to tell Mr. Calhoun."

"Thanks," I said.

"For what?"

"For being honest."

The expensive car, the way Angela drove it, her toned body, extroverted expression, and no-nonsense manner reminded me of my vampire friend Carmen Arellano.

Carmen was deep in space, a prisoner of alien gangsters.

I had no way to free her—hell, I had no idea where she was other than "up there."

But Angela was taller, her frame less compact, a smaller bust, her pretty face a long rectangle with a chevron of a chin.

We reached Coleman Boulevard, close to the scene where I'd been ambushed with Calhoun. I put my sixth sense on maximum alert to scan the traffic and the landscape. I detected nothing. Being among werewolves was like shadowboxing, only sometimes the shadows hit back.

Angela slowed enough so that we merely passed cars instead of whipping around them. "I have something else I want to discuss with you. Off-the-record."

There was no such thing as off-the-record. But if she wanted to talk, I was ready to listen. "Go ahead."

"It's this trouble between the clans."

I asked, "The war?"

Sadness clouded her eyes. "I don't understand why this is happening. There is always this tension between the alphas, but conflict has a benefit. Keeps the juices flowing, the strongest pushing their clans forward. Now this ridiculous competition between Calhoun and Bourbon threatens to tear everything apart."

Angela's candor surprised me. Maybe she'd said this as a trick to build empathy and get me to talk more freely. I gave a quick look around the interior to see if I was being recorded. A useless gesture, as any recording device would be well hidden.

I asked, "What about Inga Latrall?"

"She was a beautiful woman," Angela replied. "An extraordinary *were*."

"You think Bourbon killed her?"

"If he did, it was a big mistake and a bigger crime. Calhoun used the opportunity to rally the other clans to back him. If Bourbon had killed Latrall, assuming he did and we had proof, then even his own clan would turn against him."

We got to the bridge over the Cooper River and Angela slowed down to an almost legal speed.

She adjusted her posture. The hem of her dress inched

above her knees, which gave me a great view of her calves as she worked the floor pedals.

The highway merged onto the I-26. We took an exit east and wound up on King Street. She was driving toward the mortuary when I said, "Drop me off down the street."

"Oh?"

"I have errands."

"Do these errands involve someone?" Her voice sounded conspiratorial and teasing.

"You say that like you already know."

"Wendy?"

These werewolves must be tapping my brain.

Angela grinned. "Calhoun told me."

"You know her?"

"We've never met, but I know who she is." Angela stopped at the corner of Hasell Street.

When I reached for the door handle, she put her hand on my shoulder. "We'll see each other again?" My white lie about an errand and Wendy didn't seem to bother her.

I smiled, said, "Hope so," and got out. The Maserati pulled from the curb and turned west. I did mean that I hoped to see Angela again. I liked her, but she was a distant second place behind Wendy.

I went south a couple blocks to Market. Four touring carriages waited in line on State Street. None of the tour guides at the reins looked like Wendy.

The barn for Pirate Coast Tours sat at the closest corner. I went into the office. A woman in a white polo shirt with the company name and logo stood beside a desk. The phone on her desk was ringing and a row of red buttons flashed. She had a knee propped on a chair and spoke with forced restraint into the cordless receiver. She raised a finger to signal *give me a minute* while she responded to whoever was giving her an earful.

When there was a break in the conversation, she clutched the receiver to her chest. "Whattayawant?"

"Wendy Teagarden?"

She put the receiver back to her cheek and winged a thumb toward the stable.

I left the office and went to the stable. A man was waiting for a horse to finish drinking from a salvaged kitchen sink mounted to a post.

"Seen Wendy?" I asked.

The man nodded toward a big-ass pale gray horse—a Clydesdale or Percheron—that stood with its big ass aimed at us.

A short, stocky woman in the company uniform, white polo over khaki shorts, brushed the shoulder of the horse.

She had a freckled perky nose and soft features that made her face seem plump in contrast to Angela's sharply angled face. A ponytail of red hair dangled from the back of her cap.

Wendy Teagraden.

Here. Alive. Safe.

My *kundalini noir* twitched in anticipation of holding her again. I fought to keep my smile from broadening too much. I wondered about taking out my contacts so I could witness how her aura would blaze upon seeing me. Her aura was green, as her psychic awareness resided at the fourth chakra, compassion.

My feet crunched through the straw spread over the floor.

Wendy held her brush still and looked over.

Her eyes, brilliant as emeralds, opened in shock. "What are you doing here?"

CHAPTER 17

WENDY STARED at me, her expression one of cool, unpleasant surprise.

That coolness chilled my anticipation and my *kundalini noir* became still.

"It's great to see you, too," I said.

She recovered and gave a weak smile. "Felix, you look good."

The horse sensed her discomfort and gave a nervous whinny. It shifted one hind leg. I backed away in case the horse was about to kick.

Wendy stroked the horse's head and cooed. She grasped the bridle and led the horse into the closest stall. She removed the bridle and hung it from a nail on a post. The horse lifted its head, holding it in profile to me, and stared with one eye. A subtitle for its expression might have been: *Back off. I don't like you.*

"What does your horse have against vampires?"

"Nothing. He loves everybody. Human or supernatural. Just not you."

"What did I do to him?"

She said, "Maybe he's reacting to a vibe."

"Must be yours."

Wendy didn't reply. She made sure the stall was locked and turned briskly toward the office. "I gotta clock out. Wait for me outside."

Her words sounded stale. I told myself, Don't take it personally, maybe she's had a crappy day. After not hearing from me for years, what did I expect? That she'd drop whatever was in her hands and jump my bones?

I stood at the corner. Wendy came out of the barn. She stamped her trail runners on the pavement to clean off the mud and horseshit.

I accompanied her across the street to a little Ford coupe parked on a dirt lot. The back of the car was covered with bumper stickers.

REUNITE GONDWANALAND.

WHY ARE DUMB ANIMALS SMARTER THAN MOST PEOPLE?

ALL WHO WANDER MAY BE TOO STONED TO MAKE IT HOME.

She unlocked the front passenger's door. She repositioned a box stuffed with magazines and bags of birdseed from the front passenger's seat to the back. The interior smelled like dirt, hay, and marijuana.

"You carrying weed?"

"Was. Smoked it all." The tension returned to her voice. She pulled a garment bag from the floor between the front and backseats.

My eyes lingered on the bag.

Wendy said, "Change of clothes." Her clipped tone told me not to press for an explanation.

I pushed aside thoughts of sex and romance. Long ago, Wendy had been kidnapped and tortured because of me, and she almost lost her life. I had been wounded during our escape and she had sliced her arm with a piece of glass to save me with an offering of her blood. Since learning she was here, I had recalled the sweetness of our past relationship, but I couldn't ignore that much of what we had shared was also trial and trauma.

"Let's talk. Come on." She said this with a little more warmth and it gave me hope that we might hit it off again.

We returned to the barn across the street and approached a wooden stairway that rose to a second floor above the office. She led me up the steps.

When we reached the landing outside a door, I stood close as she pulled keys from her pocket. The weave of her many scents—perspiration, pheromones, perfumed soap, shampoo—brought back memories of lying next to her. I thought about putting my arms around her but knew better.

Wendy unlocked the door. We entered a studio apartment: one room in front, a small kitchen along the back, and a bathroom at the right rear corner.

The furniture—a sagging couch, a battered coffee table, and mismatched chairs—looked like thrift-store castoffs. Empty pizza cartons, paper cups, and bags of fast food overflowed from a trash can. Discarded computer equipment and boxes of file folders were heaped along one wall below a window.

I asked, "This your apartment?"

She laid the garment bag over an arm of the couch. "Not this dump. It's a place to store crap for business and crash after work." She plopped on the couch and untied her boots with jerky, agitated movements.

I said, "It's been a while we haven't seen each other."

"I know."

"I missed you."

She slipped out of her boots and peeled off her socks. "Yeah, I missed you, too. We missed each other so much we kinda forgot to stay in touch."

She placed her feet on the coffee table, closed her eyes, and leaned against the back of the couch. Each moment of silence made the wall between us grow taller and thicker.

"Maybe this isn't such a good idea," I said, uncomfortable and awkward. "We could try again another time."

"No, there are things we have to discuss. Have a seat."

I took the chair closest to the coffee table. "You act like there's a problem with me being here."

Wendy stared at the ceiling. "It's that you, of all vampires, shouldn't be in Charleston."

"Why not?"

"Let me tell you why I'm here." Her eyes cut to me. "I'm a spy."

CHAPTER 18

SPY? That revelation whipped through me like I'd taken a sharp turn, and it left me unsteady and dizzy.

"Working for who?"

"The Araneum." Wendy kept her voice low.

Araneum. A clammy sensation trickled down the back of my neck like cold, runny mud. "Why am I not supposed to be here?"

"I've been told. About Carmen. About the girl from the San Luis Valley."

The words were a knife dragged across my belly. I feared my anxieties and regrets would spill to the floor. Carmen was the vampire—make that friend, lover, confidante—that I'd let get captured by the aliens.

The girl from the San Luis Valley was Phaedra, and she had caused me much heartache, a major accomplishment given that I had no heart. Phaedra had honed her clairvoyant powers into a psychic weapon. She could scramble my brain with a blast of mental mojo. If that's not freaky enough, then add zombies, the undead scum that collects in the drain trap of the supernatural world.

I'd gone to destroy the zombies, but their reanimator had kidnapped Phaedra in order to make her his immortal love slave. In the fight to rescue her, she'd almost gotten killed. I saved Phaedra by doing the very thing I swore I'd never do: turn her into a vampire. Now Phaedra is on the lam as a teenage undead bloodsucker, defying the Araneum, and biding her time until she causes who knows what new mayhem.

Yeah, I had two big black marks on my permanent record.

Wendy said, "I remember Carmen. Never thought you two would connect."

The comment felt like a tug against a scab. "Why? I wasn't her type?"

"You have a penis. That made you her type. I meant if she's prime rib, you're hamburger."

"Thanks. I like to think that I was at least good hamburger."

"On occasion." Wendy let a smile trick across her lips before her expression turned somber. "Do you know where Carmen is?"

"So far away the Hubble Telescope couldn't find her."

"Are you getting her back?"

I replied, "Planning on it."

"How?"

"Haven't a clue."

"What about the girl? Phaedra?"

"Right now she's not my problem." The memories of Carmen and Phaedra curdled in my throat like a lump of bile. "What did the Araneum do? Hand over my file?"

"They know about our past relationship. I was told in case I ran into you, as a precaution. This is a dangerous time for the supernatural world."

"As in werewolves?"

Wendy looked up at me, with beautiful eyes like discs of green glass, eyes that should be smoldering with passion instead of burdened with intrigue. "What do you know?"

"More than I'd like," I said. "I've met the two rival clan alphas."

Wendy nodded. She knew who I had meant.

"I was worried the Araneum wasn't aware of the werewolf troubles and the danger to vampires. But since you're here, the Araneum does know." I tried to sound relieved.

I told her I'd come to Charleston because Bourbon wanted to hire me to kill Calhoun. I explained that I had refused. I left out the vampire attack for now and went straight to my ride in Calhoun's limousine and the ambush in Mount Pleasant. I added that I'd refused Calhoun's offer to find proof that Bourbon had caused Latrall's plane to crash.

Wendy said, "I've heard that rumor."

"Which brings me to why I came looking for you," I said. "I wanted to make sure you are okay."

"Well, I am. Thanks for your belated concern. How did you know I was here?"

I gave her quick details about the vampire attack. I described the crab, and her lips curled with a twitch of humor. But when I mentioned finding her business card on one of the dead vampires, her mouth formed a cold, flat line.

I asked, "Did you know those vampires?"

"No."

"What about one named Julius Paxton?"

Another "No."

"That's a good thing," I said and related his story.

"Two vampires came after you?" Wendy asked. "Wasn't one of them Paxton?"

"No. I found his name on the back of Bourbon's card. After the attack, I went back to Bourbon's office, but he claims he's never heard of Paxton."

She stared at the floor and, after a moment of contemplation, looked up. "I'll ask the Araneum what they know about Paxton. See if he's got anything to do with either Bourbon or Calhoun. I'll get back in touch when I get information. Meanwhile, go back to Denver and wait."

My *kundalini noir* tightened in defiance. "I'm not going anywhere until I find out who's after me and why. Somebody wants to drop a crab on me, there's a price."

"Like that macho talk has saved your ass before."

"What's saved my ass is confronting my enemies, not hiding from them." I stood from the chair. "I'm also staying because you might be in danger."

Wendy snapped at me, "I don't need you to protect me."

"You don't? Until I mentioned Paxton and his vampires, you had no idea they existed."

"Okay, thanks. But we'll all be better off if you left Charleston."

"I'll decide what's best for me. Paxton has a score to settle. There's a reason he waited until I came here. I need to find out why and finish this business between us."

I expected a volley of spite, but Wendy's face softened as she let the antagonism drain from her expression.

"God, you're predictable."

"If that means dealing with assholes who're trying to kill me, then call me predictable. Now you tell me, since when are you a spy?"

"Since long before you became a vampire."

From my time with Wendy, I'd pieced together an episodic history of her life and guessed she was three-hundred-plus years old. But I knew better than to ask her age. Even dryads have their vanity.

"What do you hope to accomplish?"

"Prevent a disaster," she replied. "Stop a war between Bourbon and Calhoun. If I can't do that, then help the Araneum make plans in case the situation between the werewolves explodes."

She read her wristwatch and picked up the garment bag from the couch. "I need to get ready. Help yourself to the fridge." She disappeared into the bathroom and closed the door.

I wasn't thirsty, though a drink of type A-positive would've helped my mood. I checked the fridge and, as expected, there wasn't any blood available.

The sound of water spraying in a tub came from the bathroom. At one time I would've taken off my clothes and surprised her. But not today.

The Araneum was keeping its distance from werewolves. Good. I needed to do the same thing, except I knew that somehow Paxton and Bourbon worked together. How had they met? If Paxton was after me to settle a score, what was in it for Bourbon?

Spigots in the bathroom squeaked and the water stopped splashing. I heard a blow-dryer. After several minutes, the door opened and Wendy emerged. She'd changed from her tour-guide clothes into a tight low-cut, knee-length dress, the quintessential little black number. The dark fabric of her skirt made her muscular legs look succulent. Her hair hung in luscious, tempting curls. She padded barefoot and carried the garment bag rolled under one arm. She bent behind the couch and came back up with a small red vinyl purse and a pair of heeled sandals.

"You look great," I said without much enthusiasm. "What's the occasion?" *Obviously not me.*

"I'm meeting my contact."

"You changed into that dress to meet a contact?" I sounded whiny, and shut up. More questions lurched into my head, but I didn't want to appear like I was prying. Dressed like she was, I knew how she gathered intel: pillow talk.

She fastened her sandals and stood straight to adjust her dress. I'd forgotten how alluring Wendy could be. This reminded me of times back when, watching her get ready for the day. Now she was preening for someone else and I felt like I was at the vet waiting to get neutered.

A cell phone chimed. She plucked a phone from her purse. She glanced at the screen and put the phone away.

I wanted to ask the obvious. Her date?

Why bother? It was over between us. Long over. I wasn't even horny. There wasn't even the slap of rejection. Let her go.

But it hurt.

Wendy motioned that we should leave. After she locked up, we descended the stairs to the curb and her heels clipped along the wooden steps.

"It was good to see you. Really." She rose on tiptoes and gave my cheek a light pass of her lips.

We stood in the deepening twilight of the evening. Would've seemed magical, if not for the barn smell and the fact she was waiting for someone else. The manure stink seemed appropriate.

A car rounded the corner from East Bay Street and slowed as it approached. A black Mercedes. Identical to Calhoun's limo.

CHAPTER 19

THE LIMO stopped. Wendy trotted to the rear door. Jealousy singed me.

The door opened. I strained to see inside, trying to catch a glimpse of Calhoun. But Wendy was in and the door slammed closed before I had a chance to see.

The limo pulled away. The driver beeped.

I waved, but what I wanted to say was *Up yours.*

The Mercedes continued west. The taillights flickered and the limo turned north and disappeared.

I needed to cool off. I remembered passing a bar close to here and walked in that direction through an alley. I turned the corner and ended beside a battered entrance door. The sign above read: BIG JACK'S SALOON.

Inside, a wooden bar ran the length of the tavern. The bar was so old it looked like it had been shot at with muskets. Water stains, darts, and garlands of bras decorated the ceiling. College team pennants and a frayed Confederate flag hung from the altar of booze behind the bar.

Most other places in Charleston made an effort to present the refined side of Southern living. Not Big Jack's. Every town needs a dive. In this part of Charleston, Big Jack's must have been it.

What had to be a phalanx of the neighborhood lushes guarded their stools around the bar and talked extra loud like this was a gathering of the hard of hearing. A blond barback hustled drinks.

The smell of hootch tugged at my thirst. The barback leaned against the shelves of bottles and tapped the butt of a Marlboro against a fingernail. "Whatcha need?" She sounded like a ref yelling during the middle of a game.

I forced myself through the crowd around the bar. "A manhattan."

The barback quit tapping the Marlboro. "Do you know where you are?" She pushed away from the wall of booze. "You want a froufrou drink, Charleston's got plenty of joints for you and your silk panties."

"Since when is a manhattan a froufrou drink?"

"Anything with more than three ingredients is froufrou. And that includes ice."

"All right," I replied, "gimme a beer."

She squinted. "You get ditched?"

"Why do you ask?"

"If your face sagged any lower, I could use it to mop the floor." She made a whiskey on the rocks. "You need stronger medicine than beer."

"Thanks." I stayed at the bar and worked on the drink.

The barback attended to the customers and pummeled them all with the same snarkiness she'd given to me. She moved with confidence, clearly enjoying herself as the mistress of ceremonies. She leaned behind the bar and made crunching noises as she dug into ice. "Where you from?"

"Denver."

"Never been there. You been to Missoula?"

"Nope," I answered.

"So you and me got something in common. We've both been places the other hasn't."

I got what she was going for. I gave her my name and she replied in turn, "Charly. With a *y*."

No supernatural vibe. Purely human.

She kept digging into the ice. A couple of chatty girls made their way behind the bar. They clocked in and traded gossip with Charly.

I plowed through a couple more whiskeys. Many of the regulars began to leave—curfew at the halfway house?

When one of the other girls said last call, Charly clocked out and counted bills from the main register. She folded the bills into a fringed leather purse and came from behind the bar. "Gimme a sec." She went to the ladies' room.

She returned, wrinkling her nose, and her pupils were dilated to the diameter of dimes.

I gave a sniff.

There was that delectable cat-piss odor. Cocaine.

She asked, "Where you staying?"

Charly wanted to keep me company. She moved fast, and I wondered if she might be a setup by werewolves. Once we were alone, I'd use hypnosis to discern her intentions.

She repeated, "So, where you staying?"

I couldn't say Atlas Mortuary without freaking her out, unless she was the freaky type. After getting curbed by Wendy, I needed the distraction of getting freaky.

"A boutique hotel. Not far. On King Street."

She rubbed her nostrils like she had the sniffles. "King Street? Where?"

Didn't figure she knew the city so well. "It's a small bed-and-breakfast. A friend owns it."

She shrugged, satisfied. Once we stepped outside, she lit a Marlboro. "Where's your ride?"

"I walked. Like I said, the hotel's not far. Where's your car?"

"Needs work. A friend . . . a girlfriend gave me a lift."

I started through the alley. From there, it was another four blocks to King Street. By then, I hoped to have figured Charly out enough to see if she was up for party time in the mortuary.

She said, "Things must be different in Denver, 'cause in this neighborhood, at this time of night, we don't take short-cuts through alleys."

I smiled. For us vampires, alleys were great hangouts. "We're almost at Market Street. It's okay."

She tossed the Marlboro, grasped my hand, and pulled close.

Not to worry, we were safe.

My earlobes tingled. My fingertips buzzed.

We were not safe.

Not safe at all.

A musky odor curled at me.

Wolf.

No, werewolf.

In the shadows at the far end of alley, two pairs of red eyes burned like embers.

Correction. Were*wolves*.

CHAPTER 20

I PUT MYSELF between Charly and the werewolves.

They came hulking from behind a Dumpster, two brawny-shouldered, furry shapes, halfway between man and animal. Smart and treacherous as a human, cunning and brave as a wolf. Add to that deadly combination, supernatural speed and strength.

"What the hell?" Charly turned to me, one eyebrow canted in question. "Your friends? What are they practicing for? Halloween?"

I grasped her wrist and pulled her behind me. "We should be so lucky."

One werewolf was my height. He wore a pocket protector in his shirt pocket. The logo on the plastic flap read *Super-Tek IT Solutions*. Werewolf software engineer?

"Look what we have here," he said. "A bloodsucker and his gal pal."

"Bloodsucker?" Charly asked. "What the fuck?"

Werewolf engineer's buddy was tall and thick like a couple of barrels stacked on each other. He spread his arms and went, "Eeee. Eeee. I'm a bat."

"What are they doing?" Charly asked.

"Being assholes." I raised my hand and pointed to the left. "Listen, fellas, why don't I go this way. You go that way." I pointed right. "And we'll—"

"How about we stay here and tear your ass apart?" the tall *were* said.

They lowered into a crouch, paws extended, snarling mouths exposing long fangs. Bulging muscles showed in shirts stretched over hairy torsos.

"Damn good costumes," Charly said. "They look professional."

The werewolves advanced, their pointed ears pressed flat. Werewolf Engineer scratched his neck.

Just my luck, run into a couple of werewolves spoiling for trouble before the full moon. If they attacked, to keep the odds close to even, I had to sprout my talons and fangs.

What about Charly? Once I revealed my vampire self and the fight started, she'd know this wasn't a prank.

I pushed her away. "Get going. Now."

She panned the werewolves, then back to me. "What? You're serious, right? These clowns in doggie clothes are going to jump you?" She fumbled in her purse and pulled out a cell phone. "Screw this. I'm calling the cops."

I slapped the phone from her hand. "No cops." The phone smashed into the ground. I didn't know which kind of cop, human or werewolf, would show up.

"My phone," she screeched.

The two werewolves spread out to attack in opposite directions. Heavy lupine musk clouded the air. They flexed their claws.

The tall *were* pushed Charly aside. She yelped. Blood trickled from scratches on her forearm. She frowned, not in pain, but anger. "You douche bag."

The werewolf kept his eyes on me.

I had the werewolf engineer to my left and the tall were to the right. If I was by myself, I'd do the smart thing. Take off running. But I couldn't leave Charly to face these furry brutes alone.

Chapter 21

TWO WEREWOLVES against one vampire.

Me.

I needed more than talons and fangs: I needed a weapon. All I had was the next-to-useless revolver.

Charly smeared the blood oozing from the scratch on her arm. She scowled at the tall werewolf and cocked her leg. "I'm talking to you, dog breath." She kicked him in the butt.

His ears sprang up and his eyes popped in alarm. He snarled and whirled about. Both werewolves glowered at Charly. I still had my contacts in, so I couldn't read their auras. No problem, as I could glean their confusion in spite of their half-man, half-wolf faces.

I reached into my cargo pocket and got the pistol. I leveled it at the bigger threat, the tall werewolf. When I cocked the hammer, both werewolves faced me.

The werewolf engineer sneered. "What are you going to do with that popgun?"

Tall *Were* squinted at the revolver's cylinder. "I don't see silver bullets."

The werewolf engineer gave his claws a slow and dramatic swipe through the air. "You might get one shot. Go ahead. Take it." He looked at his partner with an expression that said, *Get a load of this chump.*

"Okay." I flicked my wrist and threw the revolver just as the werewolf engineer turned back to me. The gun bounced off the top of his head. His eyes pinched shut and his head reared back.

The pistol arced upward and dropped against the pavement.

Bang.

I flinched. The gun worked. Maybe I should've shot him.

The tall werewolf yelped and dropped. Blood stained his shin. He clutched his leg and moaned as he rolled on the ground.

I went to vampire mode, talons and fangs full out.

Charly caught sight of my face. Her eyes lit up like I'd hooked her up to a car battery. She let out a siren-loud scream, her face reddening, until the last of her breath wheezed from her lips. She backed up to the closest wall and slid down until her bottom settled into the weeds and trash.

The werewolf engineer wiped his scalp and glanced at the blood on his paw.

Tall *Were* kept moaning.

Werewolf Engineer glared at me. "I hate vampires." He reached for the tall werewolf and grabbed an arm. "Enough. Man up already."

The tall *were* struggled to his feet, clearly in pain and embarrassed. He put weight on his injured leg and grimaced.

The werewolf engineer flexed his arms and shoulders. "Okay, bloodsucker, you took your best shot. Now get ready to feel the love."

Tall *Were* limped to his side. With every step, he walked a little stronger.

I extended my talons and fangs to combat length. We were about to trade a lot of pain.

"That's enough." The gruff voice came from down the alley. A man approached, dressed in a dark suit and an open shirt with no tie. Under the alley lights, his hair and side-burns shone like copper wire.

Sean Moultier, the werewolf from Bourbon's office. The time I'd been with him before, he looked like he wanted to trash me. Bad. With three against one, this was his chance.

I retreated, certain that if I was to survive this encounter, I'd have to exit. Now.

Sean remained in human form. He stepped between the other *weres* and grabbed their shoulders. He addressed the werewolf engineer. "Jerry, back off."

Werewolf Engineer pointed to the blood-soaked trouser of the tall *were*. "We got a score to settle."

Sean grasped Jerry by the snout. "I don't like to repeat myself." He lowered his voice. "Now go."

Both werewolves relaxed their arms. Their claws and fangs retracted.

Sean gave a quick nod to the side. The two of them re-treated down the alley, the tall werewolf limping.

I studied Sean, not sure what he was up to. "Did Bourbon send you guys?"

"No, they acted on their own," he answered. "Trying to score points."

His candor confused me. I thought my scalp would've made a great trophy. "Why'd you stop the fight?"

"I have my reasons, Detective."

Detective? Was Sean being cute? Or was he getting at something? He didn't seem like the cute type.

"I owe you. Thanks."

"What happened here stays between you and me." He stepped close and leaned menacingly. "Got it?"

"Got it," I replied, confused.

Sean backtracked warily in the direction the other *weres* had taken. When he slipped into the shadows, he turned and disappeared into the gloom.

An undertow of intrigue between Sean and Bourbon swirled around me, unseen yet dangerous. Sean was Bour-bon's number one *were*; what game was he playing?

My fangs and talons shrank. I was back to looking as hu-man as ever.

I picked up the snub-nose and checked the cylinder. All the cartridges had been dinged by the hammer. Each remaining bullet had been a dud, yet might still go off, as the first one had. I emptied the cylinder into my hand. I didn't want the cartridges to go off again and this time hit me. I slid the empty revolver into my cargo pocket and dropped the cartridges into the trash in a nearby Dumpster.

Charly's eyes looked as red and watery as stewed tomatoes. Her cheeks had lost color. Her blond hair jutted like clumps of broken straw. Blood clotted the scratch on her arm. Trash and dead leaves clung to her clothes. Even though she'd missed most of the fight, she had a dragged-through-the-alley look.

She dug into her purse. She pulled out a slender glass vial, twisted the cap off, and dumped white powder into her open hand. After staring at the powder as if in prayer, she jammed her palm against her nose and made a loud snort.

She brought her hand down. "Oh, man. Rehab never warned me about this."

I'd left the saloon hoping for fun and games with Charly. Now, thanks to the werewolves—another reason to hate the hairy mutts—I had to ditch Charly and make her forget what she'd seen.

I flicked the contacts from my eyes. Her aura burned like a lit match.

"Charly, I gotta explain something." I stood above her.

CHAPTER 22

CHARLY KEPT her face down and ran a hand through her hair, now stringy with perspiration.

I tapped her boot with my shoe.

She snorted into her hand again and raised her head. White powder dusted her nostrils.

When our gazes met, her irises screwed open.

I knelt and grasped her shoulders. *Relax.* My fangs grew. I nudged her head aside with mine and put my lips to her neck. Adrenaline, tobacco, alcohol, and cocaine tainted her smell.

My fangs punctured her skin. The warm delicious blood flooded my mouth. I gave her a dose of pleasure enzymes. Her pheromones scented the air like I'd brushed against a fragrant blossom.

I added a good measure of the amnesia-causing enzymes. She'd forget everything from the time she had kicked the tall werewolf in the ass until now.

I swallowed another mouthful of her blood. The heavy

copper taste caressed my tongue. The warm liquid flowed down my throat like the most delicious of soups. Dizzy with pleasure, I lost my balance but caught myself before tumbling over.

Charly leaned to the side. I wiped the tiny drops of blood dribbling from my fang marks on her neck. By morning she'd have no souvenirs other than a blank spot in her memory.

I couldn't take her with me. Better that I leave her here. I was sure Charly had woken up in stranger places.

I pulled her behind a Dumpster and left her stretched out over a bed of flattened cardboard boxes. Should anyone find her, what's she going to say? *I saw a fight between werewolves and a vampire. And by the way, don't pay attention to my drug problem.*

She had been scratched by a werewolf. Did that mean she'd turn into one?

With Charly and my appetite taken care of, I decided I'd had enough excitement for my first day in Charleston. Better get to bed, thankfully a coffin, and get ready for tomorrow.

I didn't trust that the werewolves had given up. Sean might have changed his mind. They knew the city better than I did, and I didn't want to blunder into a trap.

Werewolves can't levitate, but I can. I took a couple of quick steps and leaped. My momentum carried me to the closest roof, a detached garage beside the alley. I set down quiet as a shadow and glided along on light feet, keeping my speed so I could spring off the roof and sail over the street to the top of the next house.

I crossed the city, levitating from rooftop to rooftop. Cars and trucks cruised below me, the drivers and passengers wrapped in shimmering auras. Every aura was red, meaning only humans were braving the darkness—no werewolves, vampires, or other supernaturals.

I halted across the street from the Atlas Mortuary. Streetlights illuminated the front of the pale yellow building. The coast was clear, so I jumped over the street and landed on the building next door—a print shop. Pines and mossy oaks marked the property boundary. The trees created deep pockets of shadow, and other than the telltale auras of foraging possums, mice, and raccoons, nothing else lurked in the night.

I glided to a dark niche close to the side door of the mortuary. After pausing for a moment to see if the way was clear, I went to the door and punched in the access code. I entered the mortuary so quietly that a cat could've asked me for lessons.

A light down the hall was on. I swept my psychic awareness like a ray. Someone was in the kitchen. I smelled herbal tea brewing—Tension Tamer. No hint of danger.

Lemuel Cohen waited in the kitchen, where he leaned against the counter. A small fluorescent lamp under the cabinets illuminated the room with a dim glow. A red aura hugged him like the calm flames of a hearth. Human.

Lemuel was one of the few exceptions to the rule that only "chalices" are permitted to live with the knowledge of the supernatural world. Chalices are humans who offer their blood in exchange for the thrill of serving vampires. But the cost of those kicks is silence about the supernatural world, under penalty of death.

Though he wasn't a chalice, Lemuel had our trust. He owned the mortuary, which allowed him to operate a bed-and-breakfast for vampires. He offered the newest coffins and, equally important, privacy. We vampires could relax without troweling on the makeup or risking encounters with nosy humans. Room service was provided by a chalice he had on call.

His face resembled a ball of old chocolate, dusted white across his cheeks and under his lips, and deep brown around his eyes and nose. He wore a bathrobe cinched over pajamas. Scuffed leather slippers covered his feet. Vapor steamed from an electric teapot on the counter beside him. He sipped from a mug in his hand.

We nodded to one another in salutation. I kept from zapping him.

"Who you waiting for?" I asked.

"You." He yawned. His aura stayed even, so he wasn't lying. "Wanted to make sure you're all right."

"How'd you know I'd be coming in now?"

"Hang around you types long enough, you learn things." He glanced at the wall clock. "It's a couple of hours before sunrise. Wasn't hard to figure out." He pointed to the teapot and the refrigerator. "Help yourself. I got goat's blood."

"Thanks." I grabbed a cup from the counter and filled it halfway with the herbal tea. The goat's blood was in pint jars in a door shelf of the fridge. Each jar was labeled with a date scribbled on a strip of masking tape. I topped off the cup with the freshest blood. The tea-and-blood combination went down warm and agreeable.

"Lemuel, what do you know about the local werewolves?"

"I keep my ear to the ground, but I am busy enough taking care of you vampires."

I brought up Calhoun and Bourbon. Lemuel said he knew who they were and added, "They stick to their side of the supernatural, and I stick to ours."

"How safe do you feel?"

"Pretty damn safe considering my best clients are vampires."

I gave him the big picture, starting with Bourbon's offer, the vampire attack, werewolf ambush number one, Paxton, my visit with Calhoun, Wendy, and werewolf ambush number two. I trusted Lemuel as much as I could any human, but I kept from him that Wendy was a spy.

Lemuel sipped from his mug, and when I was done, he went to the teapot and got a refill. "You've been a busy man. How long have you been in town?"

"Since yesterday."

"I haven't had that much excitement since I've been back from 'Nam."

"Well, I heard Charleston was a happening place. I would've preferred to have been disappointed."

"And you're worried about Wendy?"

"I'm also worried about you."

"Me?" Lemuel chuckled. "I'm minding my own business."

"Paxton comes after me, he's certain to run over anyone else in his way."

"Does the Araneum know?"

"I'll send them an update. Let me use your computer."

Lemuel put down his mug. I followed him to his office. He kept the lights off, but no matter, as I could see with vampire vision. It was a simple workspace. A desk and furniture probably bought on sale at Office Depot. Piles of paper crowding a keyboard and a flat-screen monitor.

I got on his computer and logged onto the antiquarian booksellers Web site, the Sagging Bookshelf. I searched for a first edition of *The Van Helsing Encyclopedia of Urban Canines*. I clicked on a picture of the cover. This was a secret procedure to indicate I had information about werewolves. A comment box appeared, and I wrote a brief summary about the attacks and Julius Paxton.

When I clicked the send button, the words turned into strings of cuneiform letters, which jumbled up and fused into one black blob. The comment box disappeared, replaced by the words: *Thank You! Your business is appreciated.*

Now to wait for a reply, usually a message delivered by crow. I felt more at ease now that I had alerted the Araneum. I had just me to worry about. And Wendy. And Lemuel.

After I shut off his computer, he took me to the coffin prep room. The place smelled of contractor's glue and polyurethane. Lemuel turned on the light and adjusted the brightness to keep it low and soothing.

My luggage sat beneath a wooden bench. My casket, a Model Norteck 3000 (cherry finish; bronze—not brass—fixtures; silk lining; with custom connections for my iPod and a charger for my cell phone), rested on the bench.

Lemuel patted my shoulder. "Good night. What's left of it." He turned off the light and closed the door.

Darkness surrounded me like a welcome blanket. The smells grew sharper, the sounds more pronounced. Lemuel's slippers scuffed the floor as he shuffled to his quarters at the other side of the building.

I opened my overnighter and changed into my sleeping clothes: black sweat cutoffs and a Chicago Cubs T-shirt. I connected my iPod and cell phone and climbed into the coffin. The silk lining felt cool against the back of my legs. I put my earbuds in and scrolled through my playlist to select tracks featuring Jeff Beck.

I pulled the lid over me. Sleeping in a coffin helped restore my psychic balance. Living out in the sun and keeping to a daylight schedule wore us vampires out.

I was glad the werewolves had interrupted my time with Charly. I didn't want her; I wanted Wendy.

Where was she?

With Calhoun. I fought the image of them wrapped around each other, though I was sure there had been plenty of that.

What about Angela? Was her teasing sincere, or a way to get me to talk?

Sleep pulled me away. I dreamed of wild women banging on guitars, beating drums, and wailing like horny banshees. They shed clothes at the start of every song in a musical version of strip poker. I was in the audience wondering which of these party girls was my door prize.

The drummer started missing her rhythm. The beat sounded like rocks tumbling in a clothes dryer. When I was about to complain, I realized that it wasn't her drumming but someone knocking on the casket lid. Unfortunately, the music and the naked ladies vanished like wisps of smoke in a breeze.

I opened my eyes, pushed the casket open, and sat up.

Lemuel stood beside the table. He was dressed in his mortician's garb—cheap black suit, white shirt, and a polyester tie decorated with a pattern that was someplace between vintage ugly and hand-me-down hideous.

"You got a visitor," he said.

I blinked, bleary and a little groggy. "Who?"

"Me," said the visitor at the door. In stepped Eric Bourbon.

CHAPTER 23

BOURBON, THE treacherous bastard.

I sat up in the coffin, fangs and talons out, ready to strike. Ready to kill.

Orange stripes of alarm zigzagged through Bourbon's red aura. "Whoa, whoa, Count Chocula, settle down."

Lemuel stepped between us. "Felix, if Mr. Bourbon had come here looking for trouble, would I have let him get this close without warning you?"

I tamped down my anger. "What do you need from me?"

Bourbon said, "I want to talk. You saw Calhoun, and I have to undo his bullshit."

I let my talons and fangs retract. "Okay. Gimme a couple minutes to get ready."

Bourbon and Lemuel left the room.

I changed out of my cutoffs and T-shirt, shaved, put on the makeup, and got dressed. Since *weres* get cranky about vampires reading their auras, I put my contacts in as well.

Bourbon waited at the small circular table in the kitchen.

I took a seat opposite him. "How did you find me?"

"Please, you're in my town. You want to keep secrets, don't come to Charleston." He said this in that lyrical Southern accent, like he was reading poetry when he was really giving me the backhand.

The forearms of his suit rested on the edge of the table. He remained perched on the front of his chair as if trying his best not to dirty himself with anything in the mortuary. I'm sure werewolves are like vampires in that personalities don't change much when they cross the boundary from the normal to the supernatural world. Assholes are still assholes.

I warmed myself with coffee mixed with goat's blood. Bourbon's nostrils fluttered when I had uncapped the jar of blood. I asked, "You want some?"

He shook his head, acting embarrassed, like I'd caught him enjoying a guilty pleasure. He idly scratched the back of one hand.

I said, "Considering that yesterday your werewolves tried to kill Calhoun and me, you got some balls coming around."

"Those werewolves didn't answer to me."

"If those werewolves didn't work for you, then who?"

"Freelancers."

"Acting on whose behalf?"

Bourbon cleared his throat. "Did you ever think that werewolves from outside of Charleston have their own reasons to make trouble?"

"Calhoun told me how things work in your big happy hairy family." My gaze drilled into Bourbon. "You didn't answer my question. Who did those werewolves work for?"

"I've already told you. Not me."

I was going to ask about last night and the two werewolves who had tried to get me outside of Big Jack's. But I remembered Sean had said to keep the matter between us.

I took the revolver out of my pocket and laid it on the table. "Another thing—what about this piece of crap?"

"Why are you complaining? You knew it was junk to begin with."

Fair enough. I put the revolver back in my pocket. "You came to talk. Get started."

He got up from the table. "I need to show you. Let's go for a ride."

Bourbon and I went out the front of the mortuary. His car, a BMW 530i—I know because Bourbon told me three times—was parked across two spaces. Asshole.

A crow sat on the edge of the roof of the mortuary. The Araneum used the birds as messengers. I hesitated a moment, waiting to see if the crow approached. It stayed on the roof, watched Bourbon and me get into the BMW, then flew away.

Bourbon started the car and we proceeded from the driveway. Down the street, a black H2 Hummer pulled in front of us. With its boxy lines and narrow tinted windows, the H2 looked like a bunker on wheels. Behind us, a couple of piranha-like Ducati crotch rockets closed on our rear bumper. The riders wore identical mesh racing jackets and had boom mikes attached to their helmets. The Hummer and Ducatis kept in formation with our BMW. Bourbon acted like he'd expected them.

"Who's the company?" I asked

"My security detail."

I extended my talons. "If this is a double cross, these are the last things you'll see."

"Whatever. Now pull in your nails before you scratch the upholstery."

I let my talons retract but kept myself primed for trouble. "Calhoun told me about Inga Latrall and the circumstances of her death. He points the finger at you."

Bourbon scowled like the taste in his mouth had gone rancid. "Ask yourself this, Mr. Private Detective, who's in the better position as a result of her death? I had my disagreements with Miss Latrall, but who's got his paws on her estate and her money?"

"Are you saying Calhoun was responsible for the crash?"

"I'd like to say that, but I have no proof. And neither does he. Remember, Felix, you're dealing with werewolves. We talk family and loyalty, but we get ahead by ripping each other's throats."

Like Bourbon had said earlier, he wanted to undo Calhoun's bullshit. Problem was, I didn't know what was bullshit or what was truth.

We drove through downtown Charleston and paused along Legare Street. The Hummer and Ducatis stayed close. "Take a look at that."

I didn't know what I was supposed to be looking at. I saw Colonial row houses and bungalows. Lush vegetation—bushes, flowers, magnolias—framed the homes in the vibrant colors of springtime.

"This"—Bourbon gestured—"is what every upscale community aspires to be. Charleston."

Lemuel had warned me about this conceit. SOB. South of Broad Street. The center of the universe. The top of the pecking order. And of course, SOB meant "son of a bitch" as well.

Technically, Lemuel said he himself was a SNOB, Slightly North of Broad Street, because of his address. Usually that would've meant he was in close orbit to the center of the universe. But Lemuel was black. His business catered to the African-American community largely ignored by those more worried about guarding their place on the Charleston social register.

Bourbon continued down the street and ran his mouth about the preeminence of Charleston above all American cities. I never imagined a werewolf to be so enamored with anything other than a rawhide bone to gnaw on.

We turned on Lenwood Boulevard and pulled into a driveway beside an antebellum home. The house was the largest on the block—I knew Bourbon wouldn't settle for anything smaller than a castle—and he kept his running commentary on the real estate (little about the history and much on the costs).

"Buying the house is the easy part," he said. "You move here, you're moving into the oldest and proudest neighborhood in the United States. But there's a price for owning a piece of history. Keeping your place from falling apart is like raising the *Titanic*. And changing so much as one screw in an electrical outlet requires approval by a review board."

The more Bourbon complained, the more a touch of pride crept into his voice. The bother of having so much money and property.

We stopped in front of an iron fence. The Hummer halted at the next corner. The Ducati motorcycles paused behind us on opposite sides of the street. Bourbon pulled out his cell phone, and his thumb danced on the keypad. The fence gate rolled to one side. We drove into a carport overgrown with vines and parked next to a Prius.

Bourbon led me inside, past a dining room, the house sumptuously decorated like it was the subject of a feature in *Southern Living*. A woman greeted us in the front parlor and introduced herself as Lori.

I gave a sniff. Pure human. She was a late-twenty-something blonde wearing what a fashion catalog would call gardening casual: jeans, a loose blouse, and plastic clogs. Her eyes brightened when she greeted Bourbon.

He let Lori kiss his cheek, acting as if this show of affection was a duty. After he pulled away, she still beamed, oblivious that the attraction was one way.

Bourbon ordered, "Bring me a scotch and soda."

Lori smiled at me. Her eyebrows arched inquisitively.

I said, "Manhattan."

Bourbon continued through the room. "We'll be on the piazza."

The piazza was the long porch on the south side of his house. When Bourbon opened the door, a crow flew off the railing, circled a tree in his yard, and landed on a branch.

Bourbon took no notice of the bird, but I did. Was the crow spying on us?

We looked over an English-style garden in his front yard. Down the street, White Point Gardens sprawled across the southern tip of the peninsula. A steady breeze pushed a pair of sailing schooners through the harbor. The view alone was worth a million dollars.

The Hummer was still at the corner, but the motorcycles were gone.

Two groundskeepers strolled the perimeter of the yard,

not doing any work other than looking around. Both had small leaf blowers slung over their shoulders in the manner of guards carrying submachine guns.

"They are my *chevaux-de-frise*." Bourbon pointed to tangled masses of points and barbs atop sections of the fence. "Before the invention of barbed wire, the owners put those up to discourage slaves from climbing the fences during uprisings. My groundskeepers' leaf blowers hide rapid-fire shotguns, a much better deterrent."

Lori brought our drinks. She let her gaze linger on Bourbon's face and didn't bother to hide her infatuation. When she left, he stared at her trim bottom, showing the extent of his interest in her.

"Girlfriend?" I asked.

"Simply the help."

"Does she know that?"

Bourbon smirked as he brought his scotch and soda to his lips.

"She know you're a *were*?"

"Certainly." He leaned against the railing of the piazza. "We have a relationship with humans in the know. We have to. You vampires have—"

"Chalices. What are your humans called?"

He sipped. "People. Servants. The help. We don't need a special name." Again with the Southern dismissal. "And we don't feed on our help as you do." More of his Southern backhand.

His attitude got to me and I was ready to leave. "You brought me here to show me something. What?"

Bourbon extended a finger toward the ships in the distance. "They're bringing werewolves from outside the territory for Le Cercle de Sang et Crocs. Hundreds of werewolves. Calhoun mentioned that to you, right?"

CHAPTER 24

BOURBON POINTED to the sailing ships in the harbor. "The one with the striped spinnaker, that's *Carlita's Cujo*, from Miami. The other one is the *Rin Tin Tin* from Baltimore. They've got a long-standing feud. *Were* discipline breaks down and . . ."

"It's war. Yeah, I know." I sniffed my drink, suspicious of poisons. Smelled okay. I gave it a taste. Damn good manhattan. The real crime would be ruining this cocktail.

I looked back to the schooners. "How many boats are you expecting?"

"Dozens."

"Why sailing ships?"

"Ostensibly, it's a tall-ship festival. The city welcomes the business." He sipped from his scotch and soda.

"Is this what you brought me out here to see?"

"I wanted you to comprehend the stakes in this battle between Calhoun and me."

"I'm already aware of them. Calhoun said that if you're

not chosen alpha of the territory, you'd risk war. I want to hear that from you. Don't you owe your clan and the other werewolves something other than catastrophe?"

Bourbon's expression turned sour. "You say that like I should live with Calhoun as my alpha. Did you ask him if he would accept submission to me?"

"A war starts, you could lose everything."

"I'd keep my honor."

"It would be more than a war between werewolves. You'd destroy the Great Secret."

"Maybe the Great Secret has outlived its usefulness."

"For you werewolves, perhaps."

"Maybe for you vampires as well." The threat of his words pressed against me like the barrel of a gun.

"What about your Lycanthrope Law?" I asked. "Once Le Cercle makes its decision, that's the end of the discussion, right?"

Bourbon acted amused that I'd been smart enough to mention this. "Are you a legal expert?"

"I know enough to understand that this war of yours will be a disaster."

"You want to prevent the war, kill Calhoun."

"How about I kill you?"

Bourbon spread his arms and presented his chest. "Go ahead. You know what will happen."

I should kill the egomaniacal bastard, right here, right now. But Bourbon had too high a profile. I kill him and it would knock down a different row of dominoes.

He rattled the ice in his empty glass. He asked if I wanted another drink. I said no. He'd said his piece, now it was my turn.

"I saw Wendy," I said.

Bourbon shrugged. "And?"

"She's doing okay, and I want her to stay that way."

"Why are you telling me? Why not Calhoun? He's the werewolf she's banging." Bourbon grinned, as if to add, The *joke is on you.*

I pushed the comment deep until I could no longer taste its bitterness. "No matter, as long as she stays safe. I've told you before. Something bad happens to her, you're the first I'm coming to see."

"You made that clear."

"The same goes for Lemuel Cohen."

"Lemuel hangs around vampires, not werewolves. Anything bad happens to him, you should start with your fellow bloodsuckers." Bourbon pulled his weight off the railing. "Anything else?"

"Have you heard from Paxton?"

Irritation flashed through Bourbon's eyes. "No. I'm not expecting to, and if I do, I'll let you know. Wasn't that our agreement?"

He whisked his cell phone from his belt, pressed a button, and said, "Lori." He clicked the phone back onto his belt. "Thank you for your time. Can't say it was a pleasure."

Lori appeared at the door to the piazza.

He told her, "Mr. Gomez needs a ride."

He was trusting to allow his gardener and domestic booty to be alone with me. The ride back to the mortuary would give me the opportunity to chat her up and get information.

As I stepped off the piazza, Bourbon hailed me. "Felix. None of this." He pointed to his eyes, meaning no hypnosis.

He wasn't that trusting.

Lori and I left in the Prius. Lori was cordial yet cool. The best indication that she didn't want to talk was the radio turned up loud. The groundskeepers flanked the driveway as we rolled off the property. The Hummer followed us for a block, then turned away.

I stayed alert. I'd been a day in Charleston and already there'd been three attempts on my skin. That's one attack every eight hours. I peeked at my watch. I was past due.

CHAPTER 25

LORI LET me out in front of the Atlas Mortuary.

Lemuel was attending to a middle-aged couple in the front room, showing them casket options on the flat screen mounted on the wall as he scrolled through an Internet catalog. He flicked his eyes from his customers to me. *I'm busy.*

I mouthed, *Let's talk*, and pointed down the hall.

He sighed, annoyed by my interruption. He handed the couple some brochures and swatches of lining samples. He excused himself and followed me.

I waited in his office. Lemuel came in and closed the door.

I said, "I need a gun."

He acted like I'd poked him with a stick. "What for?"

"Why does anyone need a gun?"

"When?"

"Today. Tonight by the latest."

Lemuel chuckled, amused like he was about to watch me get hit by a cream pie.

I asked, “What’s so funny?”

“Then you need to see the king.”

“Elvis?”

“No. A real king. King Gullah.”

CHAPTER 26

I ASKED, "AND who is King Gullah?"

Lemuel went to his desk. "One of y'all."

I wasn't sure what he was getting at, so I guessed, "A vampire?"

"The head of both the Charleston *nidus* and the local—how do I put this? Street entrepreneurs."

"He's a crook?"

"As are most of our politicians."

Street entrepreneur? "He's a gangster?"

Lemuel nodded.

"A gangster vampire?"

Lemuel reached for the telephone on his desk. "Let me make a call and see what I can arrange."

"You've got pull?"

"He owes me. Our relationship started when he came to me and asked, 'If I can deliver eight bodies this month, would you give me a discount?' "

"And you said yes?"

"Of course I did. But I learned to be careful what I said around the King. One time I griped that business was slow, and the next day I was called to make two funeral arrangements. Hit-and-runs according to the po-leece."

Lemuel made the call and spoke when someone on the line answered. "Rooster, this is Lemuel. I need some of the King's time."

Lemuel stared at the wall and listened.

"Today would be great."

I whispered, "Tell him I need a gun. A forty-five would be ideal."

Lemuel cupped the receiver. "It's not wise to discuss those details over the phone."

He turned his attention back to the call. He perked up—nodding—and said, "That'll do. Later, brother." He hung up and addressed me. "Rooster's going to confirm with the King. He'll call back in a few with the where and the when."

"Who's Rooster?"

"An assistant to the King. You'll see."

Someone knocked on the door and opened it without prompting. A young African-American woman stood at the threshold. In her white-and-pink blouse and matching shorts, she looked like a sorority girl on spring break, all smiles and bubbly personality. Except for the scarf tied around her neck. She was either going for the retro-'70s look or she was a chalice.

Lemuel said, "This is my intern, Shantayla."

"Intern?" I asked. "In the funeral business?"

She pulled at the scarf. "Actually, I don't do much for the funeral part of anything."

I introduced myself and offered my hand.

We shook politely. Her fingers were long and sported elegantly manicured fingernails.

Lemuel said, "Shantayla will help you stay occupied until I hear from the King."

"Occupied how?"

Lemuel smiled. "If you don't know the answer by now, it's about time you went back to school."

Shantayla kept the door open. Lemuel returned to his customers while I followed her to one of the mourning rooms. The room had two couches, an armchair, and a credenza. Pictures of Jesus Christ in a decidedly darkened hue—Tootsie Roll brown—hung from the walls. Shantayla turned a plastic sign around on the front of the door.

The sign read: GRIEF COUNSELING. DO NOT DISTURB.

She shut the door and pushed the button lock on the knob. She removed the scarf, folded it on the credenza, and slipped out of her shoes. Her pink toenails matched her fingernails.

I felt uncomfortable, even a little creepy, that Lemuel had offered his intern as my afternoon snack. "Lemuel do this often?"

"Do what?" Shantayla asked.

"Set you up with out-of-town vampires." I removed my contacts.

Her aura simmered. "It was my decision. He asked and I said yes. Why, there something about you I need to know? Are you some kind of Rocky Mountain pervert?"

Only if I get the chance. I kept my hypnotic power in check. I showed her my fangs and talons.

Shantayla nodded, more out of politeness than from being impressed. She sat on the couch and patted the cushion next to her.

I retracted my talons but kept my fangs extended.

She unfastened the top buttons of her blouse. The collar spread and I got a good view of her bra and the tops of her breasts.

I sat next to her and clasped her waist. She relaxed against the back of the sofa and turned her head to expose her neck. Her enticing smell—mountain-berry shampoo, Satan's Kiss cologne, and the gathering pheromones—caressed my nose. Hunger made my stomach ache and my teeth itch.

Shantayla was too much woman to appreciate just by fanging. I ran my hands up her torso.

"Hey, hey," she protested, and pulled away. "No funny stuff." She raised a hand, palm toward me. "Strictly fanging. Besides . . ." She turned her hand around and wiggled her ring finger. She wore a diamond engagement ring. "I'm getting married."

"Okay," I said, and readjusted my hold on her. "Lucky guy." I didn't understand chalices. Fanging could be a lot more intimate than any sexual fooling around.

Shantayla pressed her throat against my face and whispered, "*Bon appétit.*"

CHAPTER 27

LEMUEL KNOCKED on the door and announced himself. He said King Gullah would meet me at two-thirty. My watch said it was five after two. Not much time.

Shantayla lay on the couch, snoring. I'd covered her with a small white blanket I'd found in one of the drawers in the credenza. Her bare legs and arms looked like ribbons of caramel extruded from under a marshmallow topping.

As I left the room, Lemuel peeked over my shoulder at Shantayla. Whether out of avuncular concern or to sneak a glance at her fine body, I couldn't tell. He shut the door behind us and twisted the knob to make sure it was locked.

"Some girl," I said. "I'm definitely going to look at hiring an intern." But one less strict about saving herself for her fiancé.

Lemuel slapped my shoulder as if he were a coach and I'd done well for the team. "How you feel?"

"Great. Why?"

"Just wanted you to be in top form when you meet King Gullah. You need to make a good impression."

"Where am I meeting him?"

"Place called Tom Tom's Barber Shop." Lemuel gave directions. The address was on Nassau north of Spring Street. "I wouldn't show up empty-handed. A bottle of good whiskey would tell him you're a straight-up guy."

"Where's the closest liquor store?"

"We don't have liquor stores in Charleston."

"Then where am I—"

"They're called package stores around here. On the way to Tom Tom's, you'll pass a Piggly Wiggly. Keep going until you see Short Billy's. Stop there."

"Any particular brand?"

"Nothing cheap. But he doesn't like single-malt scotch, so stick to the major labels. Johnnie Walker. Crown Royal. Wild Turkey."

Lemuel nudged me to the side door. "Better beat feet. The King doesn't like to be kept waiting."

For an extra twenty bucks a day, Lemuel let me drive his Mercury Sable. Still had the sticker from the used-car lot and enough miles on the odometer for a trip to the moon. The Mercury was behind the mortuary, parked next to a hearse and an older Cadillac limo.

When I stopped at Short Billy's, I noticed a black kid sitting in a blue Ford Escape parked near the corner. He wore mirrored sunglasses and tried to look tough despite drawing short nervous puffs from a cigarette. The engine was running and that made me suspicious that he was driving the getaway car for a robbery.

When he panned the Mercury, then me, and suddenly tossed aside the cigarette, it was obvious he wasn't casing the store but waiting for me.

What troubled me was the timing of the kid's appearance. Lemuel had told me to stop by Short Billy's and I found that somebody was waiting. Was Lemuel working a deal behind my back with King Gullah?

I acted like I hadn't noticed Super Fly junior. I went into the package store, bought a bottle of Wild Turkey, and paused by the front door. I could go around the back of the store and surprise the kid by coming from the opposite direction.

When I looked outside, his Ford was pulling from the corner. I surveyed the street and the surrounding neighborhood. At the intersection, a white Escalade rolled to the curb.

Another watcher.

The clerk cleared his throat. "Something wrong, mister?"

I turned from the door.

The clerk set a battered ax handle on the counter. The business end was wrapped in barbed wire. The suspicious set of his eyes and his tense posture told me to take my problems off the premises.

Fair enough. There wasn't anything outside I couldn't take care of.

I returned to my car and continued to Tom Tom's. The white Escalade let a couple of cars pass and followed me.

The economic standing of the residents dropped with every block going north from downtown Charleston. Many of the houses were two-story wooden structures with crooked piazzas and balconies. Scabs of flaking paint marred the walls. The railings and warped stairs showed the grimy mange of rot. Weeds, trash, and stained sheets of broken plywood littered the driveways and alleys.

The barbershop occupied the middle of a three-store front on a corner lot. A weather-beaten sign reading *Tom Tom's* in red script hung over the entrance. I parked between a rust-eaten Chrysler minivan and a showroom-new Lincoln Navigator.

Prices and services had been painted across the window of the shop. Faded posters of haircut styles, grooming products, and Obama for President were taped to the inside of the glass.

I got out of the Mercury. A crow sat on the corner lamppost. The third crow I'd seen today. Maybe I hadn't noticed if crows were common around here. I got suspicious that the Araneum was keeping tabs on me.

I approached the shop and looked through the window.

An older man with a graying 'fro and a white smock sat in one of the two barber chairs. He joked with a couple of men lounging in plastic chairs along the opposite wall.

The white Escalade halted across the street. The windows rolled down halfway, enough for the occupants to watch me but not low enough for my gaze to penetrate the gloom of the interior.

With the bag of whiskey in my arm, I pushed open the barbershop door. A buzzer made an irritating chirp. All three men became quiet and serious. The friendly warmth in the room became hostile and ice-cold.

CHAPTER 28

I ENTERED THE barbershop.

The two men on the plastic chairs were in their early thirties. One wore a blue uniform with the patches of a heating-and-air-conditioning repair service. The other had a blue-and-orange Charlotte basketball jersey and gold necklace chains. In each of his earlobes was a diamond the size of a pea.

The place smelled of skin bracer and cologne. Nothing from cadavers—meaning the undead—or werewolf musk. Only humans here. Except me.

The barber uncrossed his legs and placed a Styrofoam box piled with chicken bones on the counter behind him. "May I help you?"

The other two men acted relaxed to show that I wasn't a threat, but if they had been cats, they'd be hissing and arching their backs.

"I'm here to meet King Gullah."

The barber said, "Ain't no one here by that name."

Jerk me around. Thanks. "Lemuel Cohen sent me." I hoped this would improve my welcome.

The barber gave a frosty smile. "I know Lemuel. So?" He motioned about the shop. "As you can see, there's just us. No King Gullah. Unless he's invisible."

The other two chuckled and slapped one another.

I should give these three comedians a lesson in vampire kung fu, but I was here to stop trouble, not add to it. Better that I return to the mortuary and ask Lemuel to give me straight answers.

"Pardon me." I backed out the door.

The three began to joke, at my expense no doubt.

The crow was still on the lamppost, watching.

A black kid in a baggy T-shirt and sagging cargo pants walked across the sidewalk toward me. Once we made eye contact, he veered toward the street and waved that I follow. He stopped by the curb.

Another black guy emerged from the Escalade at the corner. He wore a doo-rag, chains, and a checkered shirt that showed the outline of a pistol in his waistband. Gangsta.

A Chevy turned the corner. It was a big Impala with wheels as big as those on a Conestoga wagon. The Chevy was emerald green with gold metallic panels on the hood and sides. On the quarter panel behind the front wheel was the number 25. Took a moment to understand the numbers meant these wheels were twenty-five-inchers. *Mine are bigger.* A ghetto version of public dick measuring.

A second white Escalade followed. I couldn't see through any of the tinted windows.

My *kundalini noir* compressed. My ears and fingertips tingled an alarm. Did these gangsters know I was a vampire? If they worked for King Gullah, they should.

The Impala slowed and passed close, but I couldn't see through the darkened windows. The Impala and the Escalade picked up speed and continued.

The gangster in the checkered shirt answered a cell phone. He whistled and waved me toward him. He opened the door of the Escalade.

As I crossed the road I spied a white Crown Vic parked at

the next corner. Its windows weren't tinted and I could see two men in the front seat. Cops in an unmarked car.

The gangster sent out an undead vibe. Now close, I made out a faint trace of cadaver smell. Vampire. His makeup was expertly applied, but foundation showed within the folds of his ears—always a tricky spot to cover.

Made sense that at least one of King Gullah's henchmen was undead. But this vampire family was decidedly dysfunctional, and if needed, I wouldn't hesitate turning this fanged gangbanger into ash.

Another gangster—a teen kid—sat in the third row of the SUV. Lots of bling. He cradled a TEC-9, a cheap submachine, the original ghetto blaster.

The vampire gangster took the bag of whiskey from me. He peeked into the bag and gave it back. He cocked his thumb to the Escalade, meaning *climb in.* The kid with the TEC-9 would be sitting right behind me.

I said to the vampire gangster, "Tell your little buddy to put away the gun."

The kid asked, "Or else what, motherfucker?"

"Or else I take that gun and shove it up your ass."

He tensed up and his nostrils flared in anger. His index finger stretched over the trigger.

In another second he'd be learning how to walk with that TEC-9 lodged deep in his rectum.

The vampire said, "Ease up, TL."

The kid scowled, his lips curling to show his grille: a mouthful of rhinestones and white gold.

The vampire raised his voice. "I said, ease up."

TL pursed his lips and put the gun aside.

I said, "Remove the magazine."

TL slapped the TEC-9 and jerked out the magazine.

I climbed into the Escalade. The interior smelled of pine air freshener, gun oil, and testosterone. I scooted against the far door and set the bag with the whiskey in my lap.

The vampire sat next to me and closed the door. He gathered his shirt about his waist to show a large pistol.

The driver glanced back. "Hey, TL. You okay back there? I got some Midol in case your period is bothering you again."

The front passenger and the vampire laughed.

TL said, "Fuck y'all."

We trailed after the Impala and the other Escalade. The driver turned up a rap tune. Loud. With more bass than a barrage of howitzers. Something by 50 Cent. Or Two-Bits. Shiny Penny. What the hell did I know about rap music?

The gangsters mouthed the words. In a display of vigilance, the front passenger panned his gaze from side to side. I know he had seen the unmarked police car but didn't act concerned.

These gangsters snuck wary glances at me, which was okay, as I didn't trust them. I mentally rehearsed a counterattack, just in case. I would decapitate my biggest threat, the vampire gangster, take his gun, and bail out the door.

The other gangsters in the SUV weren't vampires. They didn't act like chalices either. None of them wore collars or bandannas around their necks marking them as blood supply. Maybe they were in an undead apprenticeship program.

We turned right, straight for a few blocks, then a left on America Street.

Charleston ghetto central.

I tightened up.

The white Crown Vic still tailed us.

We cruised past government projects with wash on the line and big plastic toys on the lawn. Our parade halted in front of a small house, white stucco surrounded by a weedy yard with a slack chain-link fence.

The vampire gangster got out and motioned that I join him. TL crawled out from his seat in the Escalade and hustled to the driver's door of the Impala. The other gangsters dismounted. One crossed the street and stood sentry. Another took a position behind our Escalade. A third stood in front of the lead Cadillac.

The vampire and two other gangsters (human, I was sure) waited beside the Impala. TL popped open the driver's door and stood to the side like an aide-de-camp. The scene had the drama of the entourage for an African warlord.

An older black man, with a complexion the color and texture of tarnished, nut-brown leather, emerged from the Impala. Broad ears jutted from under a cylindrical skullcap, honey-colored leather on top with kente cloth around the crown. Oversize sunglasses in plastic chrome frames sat on his chiseled nose. He sported a dashiki of ocher material covered in white swirls with gold trim along the sleeves and collar opening. His legs were draped in loose white trousers, and he wore cordovan loafers.

Stretched to full height, he wasn't any taller that I was, though he projected a regal bearing. Like a king.

Who else could this be but King Gullah?

He paused to study TL. The sunglasses covered Gullah's eyes but couldn't hide the depth of his scowl.

"Where's the ammo for your weapon?"

TL shifted his feet and rubbed his hands across the empty magazine well of the TEC-9. His eyes widened and he was no longer a street tough but a frightened kid ditching school. He swung the muzzle of the TEC-9 to the Escalade. "I . . . I . . . must have left it back in the—"

Gullah slapped TL's head. "You're not here because I like looking at you. You're my guard. Someone jumps me, what are you going to do? Stare them down with those frog eyeballs of yours?"

Gullah addressed the vampire gangster. "Rooster. Take his gun away and give this boy something he can handle. Start with a box for shoeshine."

Two young black women—each about twenty pounds past voluptuous and well into chunky—came out of the house. They wore matching low-cut vests and hot pants in metallic red. Both had scarves tied around their necks. Chalices.

They carried a length of slate-blue cloth and wove the cloth through a wire trellis that arced over the front door.

The ceremony with the guards I understood. But the meaning of the blue cloth mystified me.

Gullah strode for the house. The guards formed a cordon around him, two in front, two at his heels. One of the women held the door open and the other touched Gullah's shoulder and pecked his cheek.

Rooster tapped my arm and motioned that I go in. Down the block, the men in the unmarked police car watched.

I wanted to take out my contacts, but with Rooster and King Gullah being vampires, I couldn't chance it. If I did, I'd be signaling that I didn't trust them. Which I didn't, but I couldn't afford to advertise my suspicions.

I quickened my sixth sense. My ears gave a slight tingle, but that was more from my nervousness than any threat.

Rooster closed the door behind us. We were in a small living room and the pea-green walls made the space shrink. Not so much cozy as claustrophobic.

Gullah sat in an Aeron executive chair centered on a Persian rug with a border of that slate-blue color.

I asked, "What's with the blue cloth?"

"The color's haint blue," he replied. "Keeps the haints, the boo hags, our local ghosts away."

"Why blue?"

"Haints confuse the cloth for water. They won't cross it because they think they'll drown."

"Does it work?"

"You see any haints?"

Rooster handed him a cane with a crystal knob. One of the women draped a stole of golden silk on Gullah's shoulders. He remained impassive, allowing the woman to complete her ritual. He placed the cane across his lap like a scepter and let the other woman remove his glasses.

After all the ritual, I expected a dramatic unveiling of his eyes. But they were an ordinary set of peepers with contacts. The whites yellowed. Deep wrinkles crowded the rim of his orbits. An old man's eyes.

He pointed to one of the leather ottomans arranged before him. I took the middle seat. I pulled the whiskey from the bag and rose from the ottoman to offer the bottle to Gullah.

He grinned. "Lemuel told you to bring this?"

"He said it would be a good idea. A tribute to your hospitality."

I waited in mid-crouch and held the bottle for Gullah to accept. All he had to do was lean forward or signal me to get closer.

He remained relaxed. One of the gangsters took the bottle from me and handed it to Gullah.

He grasped the bottle and gave it back to the gangster as if what was important was that King Gullah had anointed it with his touch. He motioned that I sit.

I said, "You know there's an unmarked police car down the street."

Gullah sighed. "It's the end of the month. Time for my insurance premium." He clicked his fingers. One of the women left the room and returned with a cash box. She held it open for Gullah. He fingered a stack of hundreds, counted out a pad—I'd say fifty bills—and handed it to one of the human gangsters. He fit the money into an envelope and slipped the envelope into a box of Little Debbie snack cakes. He tucked the box under his arm and disappeared through the kitchen.

Gullah crossed his legs. He tapped the cane against the bottom of one shoe. "Rooster, privacy if you please."

Rooster faced the others. Without a word to command them, they left through a door into the adjacent kitchen. Rooster stood in the kitchen, pulled a pocket door from the wall, and slid it across the threshold.

Once we were alone, Gullah said, "Felix Gomez."

"Lemuel told you my name?"

"No. I had to learn about you on my own. A vampire comes visiting a *nidus*, it's only common courtesy to pay respects to the head vampire. You didn't, which makes me curious about you and your business."

I wasn't aware of this protocol. Must be another of these arcane Southern customs.

"My business here? I'm a private detective. I came to speak to a prospective client."

"And who would this prospective client be?" Gullah knew. He was batting me around the way a cat does a ball of yarn.

"Eric Bourbon."

"And what did Eric Bourbon want?" Gullah kept the beat of his cane against his shoe.

I didn't like being toyed with like this. "Before I answer that, with you being the head vampire, could you tell me about Julius Paxton?"

CHAPTER 29

GULLAH STOPPED tapping the cane. "Who the hell is he?"

I started by telling him of the crab attack by the vampires. Gullah smiled at first—why was the idea of killing me with a giant fiberglass crab so goddamn funny?—but as I talked about Paxton, he gripped the cane hard, his knuckles showing like a row of rusted bolts. I read the anger in his unease. If he had been colluding with Paxton, then my presence meant the attack had failed. If that was the case, why did he let me get this close? No, he didn't like learning that another vampire was running amok in his fiefdom.

Gullah chewed his lower lip. He held the cane upright and tapped the tip against the rug.

His gaze softened, and he held the cane still. "It embarrasses me to admit this, but I know nothing about the attack or Paxton." He pointed the cane at me. "But as the *nidus* leader, I'll look into it. Now tell me about your business with Eric Bourbon."

If I mentioned Bourbon's desire to have me kill Randolph Calhoun, would this revelation work to my advantage or sink me further in this mess?

Gullah recognized my hesitation. "You want information, you give information."

Good point. I decided to start with the worst of the news. "You know there's a pending war between the werewolves?"

"The Araneum told me."

All this time I'd been floundering in a vacuum and yet Gullah knew the situation. I said, "If trouble explodes, we vampires could get sucked into it."

"I'm the king, no one's going to mess with me. There's a war, I tell you exactly what I'm going to do."

"What's that?"

"Enjoy the festivities. I'm going to pull a chair on the roof of this house and watch those mongrels tear themselves to pieces. Have me a bombardment party."

"A what?"

"During the blockade of Charleston Harbor, when the Union navy shelled the city, folks would picnic and take in the poor displays of gunnery." Gullah leaned forward. "I've been the head of this *nidus* for close to seventy-five years. I've learned that the key to survival as a vampire, as a black man, is to lay low when trouble comes. After it passes, then I stand tall when I can take care of things on my terms. What do you know of the Gullah?"

I shrugged. "Nothing."

"The first Gullah were the African slaves who built the Lowcountry." He swung the cane. "You see plenty of statues and plaques commemorating this white guy and that white guy as building this place. But it was the Gullah who dug the trenches, laid the foundations, toted brick and lumber on their backs. Charleston became a port of wealth because of the slave trade."

"That the reason you've taken the name of King Gullah?" I asked.

"Not entirely." He rubbed the crystal knob of his cane. "It's my homage to Gullah Jack. Two hundred years ago he organized a revolt, intending to hit the white man hard and taking this land for our own. But Gullah Jack underestimated the wiliness of white folk and the timidity of his own people. They lost their nerve and sold him out. Gullah Jack and his crew were captured and executed."

Gullah's eyes narrowed. "I'm never going to make that mistake. I'd slit the throat of my brother if it bought me an extra day."

"You sound like a werewolf. What about my throat?"

"Do I have to worry about you?"

I said, "No," but I meant, *It depends.* "And you've been the head gangster since then?"

Gullah laughed. "Oh no. It's only recently that the opportunity presented itself that I take my place as the head of the economically disenfranchised. Especially during this recession. Duty called. Consider me a working philanthropist."

"What kind of philanthropy?"

Gullah gave a wide smile, both too wide and too smug. "A lucrative one."

"If there's a war between the werewolves, how much longer would you get to enjoy this 'lucrative philanthropy'?"

Gullah chuckled. "Are you worried about my financial well-being?"

"Do I look like I give a rat's ass?"

Gullah's smile deepened. "Then we understand each other."

"Fair enough," I replied. "Let me find out who's trying to kill me and why. I'm sure the werewolves and this attempt on my life are related."

"Why's that?"

"I was brought to Charleston because of Paxton. I'm certain of it. And there's more. I'm worried about Wendy Teagarden."

"Yeah, I know who she is. That hippie dryad working on Market Street."

"You've met her?"

"No. She likes keeping company with the werewolves."

Calhoun in particular. If Gullah knew she was working for the Araneum, he would've said so. But he didn't, so he probably didn't know she was a spy.

He asked, "What do you need from me?"

"A gun."

Gullah nodded pensively. He banged his cane on the floor and yelled, "Rooster."

Nothing.

More yelling and banging of the cane.

Still nothing.

Gullah huffed and slid in the chair to pull a cell phone from his trousers. He hit a few buttons and put the phone away.

Rooster pulled the pocket door open and stuck his head through the gap.

Gullah ordered, "Send Yo-Yo in here."

Rooster hollered over his shoulder. "Yo-Yo." Footsteps approached. The front passenger of the other Escalade entered. Rooster closed the door and watched us.

Yo-Yo the gangster was short and wiry, with a bony head, and ears that stuck out like radar dish antennae. Tattoos covered his arms. His earlobes were decorated with rhinestone earrings in the shape of pistols. His baggy jeans were embroidered with *Broad River Posse* down the leg seams.

"Broad River?" I asked. "That some musical group?"

"No, fool," Yo-Yo replied, "it's the state pen."

"Handy way to advertise your credentials."

Gullah cleared his throat to draw the conversation to himself. "Mr. Gomez, so you know, I am a law-abiding citizen, honest as a councilman." He beckoned for Yo-Yo to come close. "On the other hand, my man here is as dishonest as a councilman."

"I'm curious," I said. "Yo-Yo?"

"'Cause the man keeps sending me away, and I keep coming back." Yo-Yo sat on the ottoman next to mine. He smelled of fried okra, Velveeta cheese . . . and undead cadaver. One of us.

He rested his elbows on his lap and relaxed, cocky as a rich frat boy. "So what you want?"

"I need a gun." In a deliberate motion, I pulled the snubnose from my pocket. "Something better than this."

I opened the cylinder to show it was empty and held the revolver by the barrel.

Yo-Yo took the gun, his face scrunched in disdain, and laid it on the carpet between his Nikes. He wiped his fingers against a trouser leg. "What are you looking for?"

"A handgun. Three fifty-seven. Nine-millimeter. Forty-five."

Gullah said, "Show him your inventory."

In the movies, at this point, the gun broker brings a metal valise. He opens the valise and reveals several handguns nestled in black foam. I'd touch the selection, choosing a couple and inspecting the barrels and chambers with a macho racket of slides yanked back and slammed home.

Here, Yo-Yo dug into his jeans and took out an iPhone. "How much you rollin'?"

I had to think a moment to understand. Did he mean how much was I going to pay? "You mean money?"

"Yeah, money."

Gullah interrupted, "Show him what you got."

Yo-Yo mumbled, "Jus' so long as you ain't jacking me with bullshit." His index finger danced across the screen. He brought up an array of thumbnail photographs. "Here's what I got in stock. All in new or in gently used condition." He touched one picture and it grew into a side view of a semi-auto pistol.

"Colt Double Eagle. Forty-five." He touched the screen. The picture turned into a short video of the gun firing. He touched the screen again and brought back the thumbnail photos. He selected another pistol. "Here's a nine-millimeter. Taurus PT92."

We spent several minutes going through his cyber inventory. I preferred the old-fashioned way.

"Springfield Panther. Browning Hi Power. Mauser 90DA."

I liked the Browning. "How do I get the gun?"

"We're like Domino's," Gullah replied. "We deliver."

Yo-Yo quoted seven Benjamins. I opened my wallet. I'd only brought three hundred bucks. I showed him the money. "Could you carry the difference until you deliver the gun?"

Yo-Yo's dark face hardened in annoyance. He looked at Gullah, who frowned at me.

Yo-Yo said, "You either got the money or you don't."

"What have you got for this?" I handed him the three hundred dollars.

Yo-Yo took the money, played with his iPhone, and showed me a picture of a large revolver. "Webley Mark V."

After my experience with the snub-nose, I wanted something more modern. But at least a Webley had the reputation for being as reliable as a hammer.

"Ammo?"

"No problem." Yo-Yo put the iPhone away.

I added, "Silver bullets."

Gullah asked, "Who's on your shit list? Vampires? Or werewolves?"

"Depends on who's in front of me when I pull the trigger."

Gullah tipped his head toward the door. Yo-Yo got up and left.

I asked, "What about your gang? I noticed that other than Rooster and Yo-Yo, the rest aren't undead or chalices."

Gullah answered, "I've fudged the rules regarding who knows who and what I am."

"Fudge the rules too much and the Araneum might not like it."

"Fuck the Araneum. I'm the King. What are they going to do?"

"You're not worried about one of your crew turning snitch?"

"If you're in the life, you talk, you die. Besides, the *weres* among the cops have their own interests in keeping supernatural matters within the supernatural."

"When do I get my pistol?"

"Yo-Yo is putting the order in as we speak. You'll get it before nightfall."

I asked, "Where's the gun now?"

"Safely stored under military lock and key."

I was sure Gullah was kidding and let the comment pass. "Any refunds if I don't like the gun?"

"You get store credit."

He thumped the cane on the floor. Rooster went out the

kitchen. Gullah stood and swung the cane at the front door. "I have to tend to business."

We traded insincere good-byes. Rooster waited for me outside. Two of the other gangsters stood by an Escalade. The unmarked car with the cops had left.

Rooster and his crew drove me back to Tom Tom's Barber Shop, where I got Lemuel's Mercury. The crow on the lamp-post was gone.

I'd hoped Yo-Yo hadn't stiffed me about the gun. I hated to think that any trouble between Gullah's gang and me would be over something as trivial as three hundred dollars.

It was middle of the afternoon, and as I slowed to enter the driveway into the mortuary, my sixth sense rang the alarm.

Someone hustled up to the Mercury from the right side. The passenger's front door jerked open.

Wendy slid in.

"Don't stop," she said. "Keep driving."

CHAPTER 30

I RUSHED HERE from work to catch you." Wendy buckled the seat belt over her tour-guide uniform. She was breathing hard and smoothing hair from her brow.

I did a quick look around, then accelerated from the mortuary. My sixth sense eased from a tremble to a hum. I didn't spot anything unusual but remained wary.

"Why didn't you call?" I tried not to sound annoyed. "I would've picked you up."

"You didn't give me your number."

She hadn't asked for it, either. But I had to let go of my resentment and pay attention to what she had to say. "What's going on?"

"I feel bad about yesterday. I was a bitch to surprise you about my seeing Calhoun."

"You're a spy. If I can't handle it, that's my problem."

She gave directions toward Broad Street.

"Where are we going?" I asked.

"My house. I live on the other side of the river."

Anticipation ratcheted tight. I didn't know what she had planned, if anything, but that wall of indifference from yesterday was gone. "Any particular reason we need to go there?"

"We're caught between two clans of werewolves about to go at each other's throats. We have to be careful where we talk."

Broad Street merged into Lockwood Drive. We passed by the city marina heading for the bridge over the Ashley River.

I was glad Wendy was here, that she trusted me, yet I couldn't forget that hollow, abandoned feeling when she had left me to go running for Calhoun's limousine.

"Does Calhoun know you're working for the Araneum?"

"I hope not. That's the"—she made air quotes—"spy part of why I'm in Charleston."

"Yesterday he saw you with me. He's not suspicious?"

"He knows you and I are friends. You told him. And he knows that you've been very protective of me. Says you've been talking like an old boyfriend who won't let go."

"I'll work on that. What about you and Calhoun? If you're hooking up with him, I think as a honcho alpha, he should be able to protect you."

"Hooking up?"

"Sleeping with him. Isn't that how the Araneum told you to get information?"

Wendy pivoted in her seat and glowered. The freckles on her creamy skin became brown dots the color of hot coffee. "I was told to gather information, yes. I slept with Calhoun because I wanted to."

Her scathing tone told me I had jumped a line it was not my business to cross. I let go of the steering wheel for an instant to make a t with my hands. *Time-out.*

"I'm not judging you," I said. "If it sounded that way, forgive me." I was going to add: *You're doing your job. It's for the greater good.* And so on, but it would've sounded patronizing. So I chose the best course I could under these circumstance. I kept my mouth shut.

Wendy's freckles cooled to caramel-colored dots. "Thanks. This is a tough assignment. I'm having problems choosing between being true to myself and doing what I have to do." Her left hand strayed across the console and clasped my wrist with a touch that asked for understanding.

"Meaning?"

"Sure, I sleep with Calhoun. He has his charms. Doesn't mean I don't use the opportunity to get him to talk." Wendy pulled herself close and rested her head on my shoulder. "Afterward I feel like a fraud and a whore."

"Then stop. Tell the Araneum you're quitting."

"A job gets difficult, you don't run away."

"How long do you intend to stick around?"

"Until the threat of war between the clans has passed." Wendy rubbed her head against my shoulder. A tender gesture but not at all amorous. I felt more like a big brother than an ex-lover.

I swallowed and acknowledged the truth. I wanted to think we could start down that path we had taken together years ago. But that hope was naive. Wendy and I were settling into being close friends. For now, that would have to be enough.

Wendy sat straight and told me to turn off the highway. I signaled right and slowed behind a Volvo sedan. Traffic halted and waited for the light to change.

"What's the Araneum doing with the information you give them?"

"Hedging their bets. If war breaks out between the *were* clans, the Araneum will sit tight and wait for the dust to settle."

"What are the chances this war will spread into the human world?"

"Quite high," she replied. "That's why I'm here."

"What were you asked to find out?"

"The disposition of the clans. Numbers. Locations. Intentions. What the military calls the order of battle. Hundreds of *weres* are converging on Charleston."

"I saw. Bourbon took me to his place and pointed out the sailing ships bringing them."

The light turned green, and I got on a wide road next to the parking lot of a strip mall. Wendy said to continue straight.

She grew quiet, and in her silence, she seemed especially small, as if shrunken by her worries.

I asked, "And Calhoun?"

"For my part, I try to help him keep a cool head. After yesterday's ambush, he wanted to strike back at Bourbon. I talked him out of it. I told him to wait."

"For what?"

"The selection by Le Cercle de Sang et Crocs."

"What if the vote goes against him?"

"It won't."

Wendy sounded confident.

I asked, "The fix is in?"

Wendy gave her head a slight shake. "I don't know if the fix is in or not, but right now most *weres* think the choice is between the status quo and anarchy."

"That's how I see it."

Wendy countered, "Some argue we've reached the limits of that status quo, and the real choice is between survival and annihilation. According to them, the situation isn't going to get any better. There are too many humans and they're becoming too sophisticated. Better to strike the humans first than wait for things to go bad."

"You strike first and things just don't go bad, they get worse." Horrific images—houses exploding into flames, sobbing women holding lifeless children, vampires hacked to pieces and disintegrating into ash—flashed through my mind like painful bursts of light. I let those images recede and grasped for optimistic thoughts. "But should we worry? Sounds like Calhoun has the numbers to maintain control over the werewolves."

"Unless Bourbon convinces enough *weres* from other clans to follow him. He only needs to stage an insurrection. That would provoke the war."

"Don't you have potions? Make everyone all lubby-dubby."

"Not for werewolves. Not for this kind of madness."

We arrived in the suburb of Ashley Forest and entered a wooded neighborhood of twisting streets. Wendy told me to park in the driveway of a modest brick home nestled between sweet gum trees and tall pines. A rainbow of coneflowers, goldenrod, and begonias blossomed from clay pots lining the porch and front steps.

Wendy got out. I followed. She pulled keys from a pocket in her shorts and unlocked the front door.

When she pushed the door in, a brass bell jangled at the top of the entrance. Immediately, the cawing of crows—must have been a hundred of them—roared through the house.

"What's with the crows?" I shouted.

"I keep the local roost."

"For the Araneum?"

"Who else? The crows come here for R and R. Charleston's a nice place for them to visit." As a dryad, Wendy had special empathy with animals. I could never get used to her trading gossip with the neighborhood fauna by cooing, clucking, and meowing.

A rich, humid scent rolled past us, a heavy hothouse smell of moist loam and fertile plants that brought memories of her house back in Denver.

There was a hallway to the left, a kitchen in front of us, and a small dining room to the right. Potted plants sat on almost every horizontal surface and still more hung from macramé slings. There was so much green the interior looked like it had been hacked out of the jungle. From down the hall came that squawking of crows, as if the birds were in the middle of a riot.

Wendy pointed to a stuffed armchair beside the dining table. "Wait for me." She lowered the blinds in the front room, then proceeded down the hall and disappeared into the room at the farthest end. The crows began to quiet until all I heard was her making weird bird whistles.

I brushed aside the curtain of leaves and vines from spider plants, creeping Jennies, and sweet potatoes that draped around the chair and sat.

Something moved along the leaves above my shoulder. A sliver of green crept across the leaf of a sweet potato vine and stopped. A praying mantis, about two inches long. The triangular head swiveled left and right. It extended one barbed foreleg to groom the hooks with its mandibles.

I sensed more movement. Dozens of praying mantises crawled along the leaves and vines. Large mantises as big as my index finger, small mantises with green-and-white bands to match the leaves of the spider plants, skinny brown ones, wide gray ones with skins the texture of tree bark emerged from the foliage.

More praying mantises crawled up the sides of my chair. Some looked like walking flower petals, fantastic twisted shapes in white, yellow, or pink. Must be Wendy's welcoming committee.

They scurried over my arms. Their tiny feet tickled. Others dropped from the vines and clung to my shirt.

Having so many bugs skitter over my body should've repulsed me, but I'm a vampire. I sleep in crypts, so I've gotten used to the occasional creepy critter. Besides, as a boy, I liked praying mantises and had kept a few as pets. I would feed them flies and black widows.

The mantises advanced without hesitation, though a careless move by me could squash bunches of them into crunchy goo. I kept still, as curious about them as I'm sure they were about me. They grasped onto one another, and after a minute, I had heavy ropes of mantises circling my neck and shoulders and crisscrossing the front of my chest.

The mass of insects seemed to tighten, and I got worried about their intentions. Even by supernatural standards, this was weird.

CHAPTER 31

WENDY CAME back down the hall. She walked in her socks, having taken off her boots, and yanked the tail of her white polo shirt out from her cargo shorts.

When she noticed the hundreds of mantises looped over my shoulders, around my neck, and across my chest, she halted and gasped. "Oh no." She let go a faint whistle that turned into a series of clicks.

The mantises leaped into the air, forming a buzzing cloud of green with blurs of brown, gray, and the amazing flower colors. The whirring shapes disappeared into the plants. The leaves quivered for an instant, and the room went quiet.

I remained on the armchair, dumbfounded by the bizarre sight that had come and gone like a hallucination.

"Sorry," said Wendy. "They get a little protective."

"I was in danger?"

"They could've crushed you like the coils of an anaconda. Others would've gone after your eyes, your nose, down your pants, up your—"

"I get it." My butt sphincter clenched at the thought. "If you need protection, why not get a pit bull?"

"Praying mantises are more vicious."

Wendy used her ankle to hook one of the chairs belonging to the dining table and turned it around. She sat and examined me. I could see the weight of concern in her eyes. "Calhoun is very interested in you."

"You're supposed to be grilling him about the werewolves. How did I come up?"

"You're a wild card. He hasn't decided where your loyalties lie."

"I thought I made that clear when I talked to him. My loyalties are to me. And I have loyalties to you, to keep you safe. The werewolves are none of my business."

"Calhoun asked me to convince you to help him."

"How are you going to do that?"

Wendy chuckled. "I'm not going to try."

"Good. Did you ask about Paxton?"

"Calhoun told me the same thing he told you. He'd never heard of him until you mentioned his name."

"You believe that?"

"I haven't found a reason not to."

Because you sleep with him? A worm of jealousy gnawed at my *kundalini noir.* "What's Calhoun like?"

"Interesting."

"But he's a werewolf."

"There's an intensity to *weres* I find stimulating. Unlike you and me, they're not immortal, so they squeeze pleasure out of every moment."

"As opposed to us boring vampires?"

Wendy bit her lower lip and waited to answer. "Vampires are only boring when they ask stupid questions. That *were* intensity comes from their sense of mortality, which tightens their family bonds. Something you vampires don't have."

"We have chalices."

"C'mon, that's hardly close. Despite a few exceptions, you vampires regard chalices as a cross between pets and milk cows. That can't compare with family. The trust. The dropping of pretenses and establishing real intimacy."

"You sound like Oprah." I was joking, but inside, I chafed. I understood what Wendy was getting at. Both vampires and werewolves are turned from human, and at that instant, they must pull away from their natural family.

She said, "You vampires go at it alone, while werewolves have packs, new families to bond with and share their lives."

"Those tight families haven't prevented them from killing each other."

Wendy gave a sarcastic grin. "As if vampires are a bunch of Quakers." Her expression turned curious. "You haven't yet outlived your human family. Ever think of them?"

I'd rather think of werewolves. That chafing from earlier heated to a burn.

When I told my older sister, Elvira, that I'd joined the army, she yanked off one shoe and threw it at me. "*Cabrón*," she had yelled. "You've been to college. How many of our relatives have to die in stupid wars?"

I ducked and the shoe whizzed past my ear. "But there's no war."

Elvira took off her other shoe. "Just you wait. There will be." She threw that one and it also missed. "At least tell me you're going to learn a trade. Construction? Computers?"

"A trade?" I puffed up my chest. "No, I'm going to be in the infantry."

Her purse smacked me across the face.

Elvira was right. There was 9/11 and then the war in Iraq. Since I was in the Third Infantry Division, I had an automatic RSVP to attend.

But the chief source of the estrangement between my sister and me came after I'd been turned into a vampire. I was sent home a wounded veteran in the protective custody of the Araneum. I kept to myself as I started my new existence as one of the undead. After nearly a year of silence, Elvira found me—only she was not so silent.

"*Cabrón*," she had yelled over the phone. "I knew you joining the army would bring us nothing but heartache. Where have you been?"

"Working. Are you calling for money?"

"We don't need money. We need you to come home."

What could I have said? *Sorry, I'm a vampire.*

I hung up the phone.

Elvira never called back.

Yeah, I know about family.

I'd let the acrimony simmer. Elvira had a way of whipping me with guilt despite our years and miles of separation.

"We've kept apart," I said. "What about you, Wendy? Weren't you born a supernatural? Where is your family?"

"After a hundred years, it was time to leave the roost. Besides, do you see me as a stay-at-home kind of girl?"

"Hardly. I see you riding on the back of life's motorcycle."

She scowled playfully. "Like hell. I don't ride bitch. I'm up front with my hand on the throttle."

Something clattered in the kitchen. I sat up, surprised. Wendy raised a hand for me to remain where I was. My sixth sense gave no alarm, and if there had been an intruder, I'm sure that army of trained mantises would've sprung from the plants and strangled the unlucky bastard.

A crow limped onto the kitchen counter.

Wendy explained, "There's an entrance in the window by the sink."

Normally, messenger crows are shiny and sleek. This bird had the appearance of a frazzled dust mop. Broken feathers jutted in dull, frayed clumps from its head and body. Its normally beady and luminous eyes looked like buttons made of charred wood.

The crow staggered across the countertop, a small white container dragging from its leg.

Wendy rushed from her seat to the bird. "What the hell happened?"

I bolted from my chair and joined her.

The crow fell to its side, chest contracting in rapid spasms.

Wendy cooed and clucked and stroked the black head. The crow closed its eyes and rubbed its beak against her hand. The bird flexed one leg and the object wired to the shank—a plastic 35mm film can—clattered against the countertop. Blood smeared the inside of the translucent container.

I've seen crows carry the Araneum's messages only in capsules the size of my little finger and made of filigreed platinum and gold. Why use this film can?

"Take that off," Wendy ordered, her voice sharp with distress. She caressed the crow's body and cooed and clucked some more. The bird replied with a soft cackle.

Baling wire held the film can to the crow's leg. I extended a talon and cut the wire. The film can fell into my hand. A length of cellophane tape secured the cap. I slit the tape and pulled the cap off.

An odor puffed out. The Araneum wrote their messages on parchment made from the skin of condemned vampires and it stank of rancid meat. But this odor had a freshly spoiled smell, like hamburger that had been left out too long. What remained inside the can was not a folded piece of desiccated vampire hide but a scroll of recently flayed skin, slimy with blood.

I got lost in my questions. Who had sent this? Why? Where did the skin come from?

Wendy remained focused on the crow. She ran her hand across its body. The bird's breathing slowed to a shallow diminishing cadence. Wendy's eyes seemed to melt into tears.

I used my talon to pull the skin from the can. I unrolled the swatch, bloody side against my palm. It opened to the size of a playing card. The sender was familiar with the Araneum's message procedure, so I expected to see a note written on the skin.

I wasn't disappointed.

The handwriting was not neat calligraphy but a crooked, angular scrawl.

Felix,

I will kill you.

Paxton

CHAPTER 32

IF I were still human, the breath would've shriveled in my lungs and my heart would've stopped.

But I drew no breath. My heart had stopped long ago. Instead, my *kundalini noir* compressed from the weight of astonishment and dread.

Paxton was alive. And he was after me.

I stared at the message, astounded, speechless. I returned to my chair and sank into the cushions.

I reread the message. I examined the letters. They were black marks singed into the dermis as if the author had written them with a soldering iron.

Paxton wanted to get my attention and he'd succeeded with ghoulish precision.

If this swatch was untreated vampire skin, it should've crumbled to dust by now. The Araneum used a special process to preserve undead skin as parchment.

I sniffed the skin. Definitely human. I pitied the donor.

It was no big deal that I held a piece of flayed human skin

in my hand. Hell, I could've chewed it like gum. Remember, I am a vampire.

The swatch had crooked sides like it had been carved freehand. Other than the burned letters, there were no other marks. No tattoos. No scars. No freckles. No zits.

I offered the skin to Wendy to examine. But she remained busy with the crow. Wendy laid her hand on its chest. She closed her eyes and mouthed words. A prayer? Tears squeezed from her eyelids and trickled over her cheeks.

I didn't like the pesky birds. They never brought good news. Still, this crow deserved better.

"My condolences, Wendy."

She lifted a kitchen towel from a hook on the wall behind her. She wiped her tears and spread the towel on the counter. Wendy laid the crow in the center of the towel. "She was part of the flock I had sent on reconnaissance to find information on Paxton and the werewolves."

"I've seen crows around town. They were your birds?"

"Might have been. Did you ask them?"

"Not all of us are Dr. Dolittle."

Wendy wrapped the towel around the crow. "She was the first to return and she comes back poisoned."

"How do you know?"

"She complained her blood felt like fire."

"Who did this to her?"

"She never said." Wendy wiped another tear. "Poor thing was in too much pain."

I held the piece of skin. "Take a look—"

Wendy waved to cut me off. "Not now." She sniffed.

"That's what I'm getting at," I said. "Paxton. Look." I angled the skin so she could read it.

Wendy's gaze latched onto the swatch. Her tears evaporated. "What the hell is that?"

"Human skin. Paxton copied how the Araneum sends messages. He must've captured the bird and attached the film can."

Wendy nodded, concerned, angry. "He gave her just enough poison to make sure she'd deliver the message."

"How did Paxton know I was here?"

"Maybe he doesn't. He could've told her to find you. That's the crows' job." Wendy ground her teeth and her cheeks turned danger red. "What's that asshole up to?"

"His idea of a mind fuck."

Wendy rubbed her temples. "It's working."

On me, too. I imagined Paxton looming in the unknown, invisible, powerful, as menacing as a bomb about to drop from the sky. I felt cold. Naked. Isolated.

Wendy leaned against the wall. Her face mirrored my apprehension. Fear should've pulled us together. But instead it lodged between us, another wedge forcing us apart.

Her eyes flicked at me and then away. In that fleeting glance, I read that she blamed me for her anguish.

I said, "Look, I'm sorry . . ."

Her eyes cut to the swatch. "Throw that in the disposal and wash up."

"We might want to keep it as evidence."

"Does this look like *CSI*?" Wendy pushed from the wall.

I went to the sink and rinsed the piece of skin and the blood from my hand. I ran the disposal and the skin disappeared with a slurp.

Wendy asked, "When was the last time you contacted the Araneum?"

"Last night." I washed and dried my hands. "I gave them an update about the werewolves."

"Any reply?"

"Not yet."

Her cell phone chimed. She pulled it out of a cargo pocket of her shorts. She read the screen and slipped the phone back into her pocket.

"You don't want to hear this, but that was Calhoun." She tried to keep her tone light.

"Another date?" There was no point in being jealous.

"Like you said, it's how I do my job."

"Mind if I wait until Calhoun shows up? I'm worried about what Paxton might do."

"It would be better if you didn't stay. I can take care of

myself." Wendy went to the front door and grasped the knob.

We exchanged bittersweet glances. I found it hard to move.

Wendy opened the door and positioned her body behind it. She peeked around the edge. "I'll see you soon. Maybe tomorrow." She didn't try for a kiss or a hug. We may have stood close enough to touch, but it felt like we were a thousand miles apart.

"Tomorrow for sure." I lurched out the door. The dead bolt clicked.

Whatever we had was over. I had no soul, so what part of me felt like it had just died?

I stood on the porch, drenched in misery and self-pity, my guard down. At this moment I'd be the perfect target.

Wendy had a job to do. So did I.

Find Paxton.

I drove back to Charleston. I kept my head and awareness on a swivel, like a fighter pilot cruising above enemy territory. Trouble could strike at any time, from any direction.

Bourbon and Paxton were connected. They had to be.

Bourbon. Damn werewolves. The less I had to do with them, the better. I wouldn't let any of them get close to me.

I arrived at the Atlas Mortuary. A luxury coupe was parked in the back lot by the hearse.

Angela Cyclone's Maserati.

CHAPTER 33

I ENTERED THE mortuary extra quietlike. Just in case. I hadn't expected Angela. Being in Charleston made me feel like I was wearing crosshairs for a hat. My sixth sense detected nothing unusual.

I found Angela in Lemuel's office, both of them drinking coffee. He was behind his desk, feet propped by his computer monitor. She was in the chair in front of him. Angela sat crooked, looking over one shoulder at the door, meaning that she expected me despite my stealth. Had to be that werewolf hearing.

Lemuel took his feet off the desk and stood to greet me.

Angela had a smile waiting for me. After the ache of leaving Wendy, I found Angela's warmth both welcome and disconcerting.

The neckline of her red dress was cut extra low. She wore a fresh set of expensive spangles and different open-toed pumps with tall heels. I got the impression that Angela was the kind of woman (and *were*) who would consider any heel less than three inches as too casual. She was dressed to make heads turn and keep eyes locked on her.

After I had told myself I didn't want to get close to a werewolf, Angela was making me eat my words.

Lemuel's phone chimed: "I Heard It Through the Grapevine." He snatched the phone off his belt and flicked it open. He stared at the screen and slid the phone back into its holster on his belt. "Gotta run, kiddos."

He patted my shoulder. "Hold down the fort." He glanced knowingly from Angela to me. "If there's any hanky-panky, please keep it at a tolerable level. Felix, don't tear this place up and make me regret my hospitality." He left Angela and me alone.

The hanky-panky comment hung in the air like a piece of awkward. Wendy and I were kaput, she was getting ready for a date with Calhoun, and I wasn't up for the rebound. Not with Angela. Not with anyone else.

I broke the silence when I asked, "Did Calhoun send you?"

"No, I'm here on my own. To see you."

I liked the reply. But I was among werewolves and wasn't about to be duped by a femme fatale, no matter how friendly or desirable.

"Is that a problem?" The cheeriness in her face disappeared. She stood and reached for her purse. "Maybe I misread you earlier. I should go."

No, she hadn't misread me. This funk I was in made me talk like a jerk. I was about to tell Angela, *Stay*, but as a werewolf, she'd find that insulting, I was sure. "Don't go. I appreciate you coming to see me."

I gestured that she sit down again. "Please." I leaned against the front of Lemuel's desk.

She crossed her legs and my gaze traced along the inside curve of one calf to her ankle.

I drummed my fingers along the edge of the desk mainly to break focus and redirect my thoughts. "I saw Bourbon again. I'm not optimistic about peace among you werewolves."

Angela's face turned solemn. She looked much prettier with a smile.

"You could leave Charleston," I suggested.

Her cheeks flushed and her brow knit like I'd insulted her. "Leave my family? My pack? And go where? At what cost? Werewolves are part of a family. We are each links in the chain holding the packs and clans together."

"Chain? Meaning you can never leave?"

"You make it sound like a prison, which it's not."

"Suppose you're not happy? Can you switch clans? Divorce your pack?"

"You can, but only when it's done with the blessing of the appropriate alphas. I'm not going to be a rogue. A loner. One of those who've been banished."

"There's a lot I don't understand about werewolves. Does this visit to see me violate a rule in your Lycanthrope Law about your fraternizing with the undead?"

The smile finally returned to Angela's face. "Don't worry, Felix. You're legal."

"What do you want from me?"

"I'm not looking to put another notch on my bedpost." She shrugged demurely—an act, I was sure. "Both Calhoun and Bourbon are keen on keeping an eye on you. I've never seen them so concerned with a vampire and I want to see if you're worth the attention."

"I'll try not to disappoint."

Wendy was with Calhoun. Angela was with me. I liked the symmetry.

She turned her head in the direction of the front door and perked her ears in a decidedly canine manner.

The doorbell rang.

My sixth sense had not detected a thing. Her *were* hearing was damn sharp.

The bell rang again. And again.

With Lemuel gone, I had to answer the door. My sixth sense gathered clues. The shifting of feet. The faint patter of a human heart. But no danger. No trouble.

I hesitated at the door, wondering if I should use the peephole. But what was I? An old maid or a vampire? A flush of embarrassment heated my face.

Angela came around me and jerked open the door. She

didn't act afraid. My talons remained on a hair trigger, ready to extend.

A young man in a uniform—black military shirt over gray trousers—waited on the porch. He stiffened to attention. He was ruddy-faced, with reddish-blond hair clipped close to his scalp. He wore a tentlike garrison cap that matched the gray of his pants. Both of his shoes shone like obsidian mirrors. A cadet. From the Citadel nearby.

He held a box in one arm and used his free hand to snatch the cap off his head. "I have a package for Mr. F. Gomez."

"If the *F* means Felix, that would be me."

He pushed the box into my hands. It had a heft like it contained a brick.

Now that he'd completed his mission, the cadet replaced his cap and did an about-face off the porch. He double-timed to a waiting Hyundai sedan, driven by someone also in cadet uniform. The car backed away and turned north.

I closed the door. Angela peeked over my shoulder.

I held the box to her nose. "Let's test your *were* powers. Smell anything? Explosives?"

She wrinkled her nose. "That's no bomb."

I gave the box a sniff. Gun oil. I grinned. "You're right."

I extended a talon and cut the shipping tape. The box held a smaller carton and this one, in turn, under wads of newspaper, contained the Webley I'd ordered.

Gullah wasn't kidding when he said this pistol had been stored under military lock and key. Seems Yo-Yo's inventory was kept in an arms room at the Citadel.

In the corner of the carton I found a second smaller box. I put my fingers around it and sensed a warmth, like what I'm sure plutonium felt like.

I slid the box open.

Silver bullets.

Eighteen of them. Big fat ones. .455 caliber.

We returned to Lemuel's office with the carton. I grasped the Webley and worked the mechanism. The pistol was made of blackened steel and seemed as solid as an engine block.

"You really need that?" Angela asked.

"Unfortunately I do. Someone's trying to kill me and I need my questions answered." I pointed the Webley at a trash can in the corner. "Consider this gun a conversation starter."

"With who?" she asked.

I told her about Paxton and the vampires I'd killed. Like the others I'd related the story to, she smiled when I described the crab attack.

"You've got vampires after you? And werewolves?"

I picked up the box of silver bullets. "That's why I bought these."

CHAPTER 34

ANGELA CAST her eyes downward. A firmness settled around her mouth.

I put the box of silver bullets on the desk, next to the pistol. "You don't like guns?"

Her gaze lifted. "You have a right to defend yourself."

"I'm way past defending. I'm on the offense."

I wanted to impress her with the dramatic punch of what I'd said. Instead, her ears quirked and she turned away.

I put my sixth sense on alert. Nothing.

The lock of the side door clicked. Lemuel announced himself. Loud. Like he didn't want to surprise us.

He came into the office carrying a package of powdered mini-doughnuts. "You guys still dressed? I made all that damn noise so I wouldn't catch you buck naked in the middle of business. Damn if you two aren't taking a long time to know each other." Lemuel opened the center drawer of his desk and took out a small white bottle of pills which he rattled. "Felix, you need Viagra or something?"

My *kundalini noir* twitched. The pills were aspirin, but he'd made his point. Angela twisted her lips together to keep from chuckling.

Lemuel dropped the bottle in the drawer and closed it. He looked at the pistol. "I see you've been shopping with the King. What did you pay?"

"Three hundred bucks."

"That all?" Lemuel shook his head. "I won't get much of a finder's fee." He paced behind his desk and turned on the computer. He sat and tore open the package of doughnuts. "You guys can hang around as long as you don't bother me."

In other words, *scram*.

Angela retrieved her purse from where she'd left it on a filing cabinet. I gathered the pistol and ammo.

She took a set of keys from the purse. "Can you sing?"

The question puzzled me. "I can belt out a tune when I have to."

"Good. I want you to impress me."

I got my knapsack and put the revolver and ammo inside. We drove her Maserati south to downtown Charleston. We parked. Angela told me it would be best to leave the pistol in the car.

"We're safe," she assured me. "A gun wouldn't do you much good anyway. You'll see."

I shoved the knapsack and gun under my seat.

We walked to a place called the Blind Tiger Club. The sign above the door showed a tiger with shiny circles over its eyes like a pair of mirrored sunglasses.

"Creepy name," I said.

"Comes from Prohibition days," Angela explained. "They couldn't sell liquor, but if you bought tickets to a blind tiger fight, you'd get complimentary drinks. Then the management would announce that the blind tiger was sick and you could buy tickets for tomorrow's bout. Some people bought tickets for years and never saw one blind tiger fight."

"Imagine that. In straitlaced Charleston."

A crow squawked. It peeked over the blind tiger sign. Had to be one of Wendy's recon birds.

Around the front door, I caught the smell of canine musk. Werewolves.

I grasped Angela's arm. "Is this a trap?"

She stroked my hand. "Trust me, will you? With so many werewolves coming into the city, the pack alphas called for a parley. Everyone chill. Enjoy the city before we convene Le Cercle." She led me inside. "This place has been designated a sanctuary. Even you are safe."

The interior of the Blind Tiger showed its history: wood darkened by the passing decades, brass edges worn smooth, and a ground-in taint of old tobacco smoke. Rock music blared from a back room. The manager hustled the few human customers out the door, telling them the Blind Tiger was closing early for a private party.

A black curtain had been hung across the threshold between the front dining area and the back room. The canine scent was strong, practically an odor, and the room smelled like the arena for a dog show.

A sign had been taped to the wall beside the curtain.

PACK AND CLAN ALPHAS
WELCOME TO WICKED CHARLESTON
SEND TEXT MESSAGE
TO THE LATRALL ESTATE
FOR INFO ON
TOMORROW'S WEREWOLF COSTUME BALL

I turned to Angela. "Werewolf Costume Ball?"

"Another activity in the parley. Calhoun arranged the ball to keep the alphas happily distracted."

We passed through the curtain.

Everyone was in human form, but by the smell, there was no denying they were all *weres*. Dozens of them. Angela had been right; my one pistol wouldn't intimidate this crowd.

Tables and chairs faced a big flat-screen TV. Four werewolves were in front of the TV; three stood, and the fourth sat behind a small drum kit. Two of the standing *weres* played plastic guitars; the other swayed and sang into a mike. Animated musicians performed on the TV while colored lights scrolled down the center of the screen.

The speakers blasted Creedence Clearwater Revival's "Bad Moon Rising."

The *weres* played Rock Band. Werewolf Rock Band.

Angela shouted into my ear. "Check out the graphics."

The animated characters were cartoons of werewolves.

"Those two"—she pointed to a pair of Asian *weres* sitting up front and bobbing their heads to the music—"hacked the game code to change the play list and make the musicians into werewolves."

Angela led us to a table. "You going to sing?"

"Not until I get my voice box lubricated."

An hour later I was on my fourth bronx cocktail. And on the rhythm guitar and deep into Rock Band. By using vampire speed, I was able to keep track of the colored dots on the screen and press the appropriate buttons on the guitar. We jammed to Kiss's "Detroit Rock City." I played the guitar because a dopey-eyed *were* who looked like the offspring of Pee-wee Herman and a basset hound wouldn't let me sing. He kept failing at the vocals, and we ended in third place.

Not good enough.

On the next song, basset-hound *were* returned to do vocals.

"No way," I said. "You sank us last time."

Basset Hound tipped a beer to his lips and shrugged me off. "Who asked you, bat-dude? Go suck a vein." He grabbed his crotch. "Better yet, suck this."

My talons wanted to spring out. I laid the guitar on the floor. Maybe eighty werewolves crowded the room. And one of me. All those drinks puffed up my courage and I thought I could live with the odds.

"You're the one who sucks!" the werewolf on drums yelled at basset-hound *were*. "Quit being an asshole so we can win."

"Like hell, dude. He's a party-crashing vampire. Who invited him?"

"I did." Angela stepped from behind me and motioned with her finger.

Basset Hound grinned like he was expecting a proposition. He stepped close and she whispered in his ear. He nodded enthusiastically. She whispered something else. The grin faded. He quit nodding. The grin turned into a flat line. The flat line turned into a scowl. His face darkened with humiliation. He handed the microphone to me.

"What did you tell him?" I asked Angela.

"I said I was going to shave his nuts and paint them fluorescent pink. Here. In front of everybody. For insulting my guest."

"And he believed you?"

"He better. I did it to his brother."

Tough girl. That's why I liked her.

I got the microphone while Angela got on the rhythm base.

At this stage of the contest, we were all at expert level. The colored dots were going to come at us like tracer bullets from a machine gun. But vampire speed wouldn't help at vocals. You either sang or you croaked.

Our cartoon doubles flexed and primped on the screen while the game console scrolled to the next song.

"Werewolves of London," by Warren Zevon.

The *weres* in the room howled in delight. They punched each other and bared their fangs.

A voice cried above the din. "A vampire is singing lead."

Someone else picked up the cry of protest.

"No vamp."

"No bloodsucker."

A vampire singing this tune must be like Che Guevara wailing "The Star-Spangled Banner."

"We have to sing," Angela shouted to a judge. "We get docked for refusing a song."

The two judges brought their heads close and chatted. After a moment, one raised his hand and jumped on his table.

"Shut your steak holes and listen. The rules say nothing

about a vampire or whatever"—the "whatever" sounded like he was referring to something you'd scoop from a lawn—"singing any song from the playlist. So the contest goes."

The audience booed. Someone threw a cup of popcorn. A beer bottle smashed on the ceiling.

We started the song. Until now, the audience had followed along. This time it was just us four onstage and me singing. Alone.

I didn't have any problems with the start of the song, not even when a second bottle broke against the rafters and showered me with beer.

But when I got to the chorus, the "Ah-wuuu, werewolves of London," I had all but the stick-up-their-asses diehards singing along. By the start of the second stanza, even they couldn't resist joining in. This was their anthem.

Werewolves jumped on the tables. The air shook with howls that started low in their throats and grew into roaring bellows. The singing, the reverb from the speakers, the thick aroma of canine musk and pheromones, the pounding of paws and the stamping of feet—my sixth sense was on overload. My ears and fingertips buzzed in excitement.

Me, vampire, the leader of the werewolf band. I hopped in the air and floated to the closest table, where I danced, microphone in hand.

The colored dots sped down the screen like streaks of lightning. Angela and the other player moved their fingers on the guitars in a blur like hummingbird wings. The drummer beat the skins and worked the pedals in a feverish spasm until the song ended.

Our score: 100 percent.

We had won.

The band cheered. I cheered.

Our cartoon doppelgängers vogued and pumped their animated paws in triumph. I floated down from the table, eager to claim my place as equal in Rock Band to these werewolves.

I clipped the microphone to its stand. Angela warmed me with her smile and wrapped an arm around my waist.

My sixth sense reverberated, probably from all the excitement.

Maybe vampires and *weres* could be friends.

My head rocked from a blow to the back of my neck. Pain spiked through my backbone. My eyes blanked out. I stumbled into chairs and werewolves.

CHAPTER 35

I LAY ON a dirty wooden floor, not sure of where I was or how I got here. A distant voice called through the chaos of pain in my head.

"You've had your fun, bloodsucker. Not get the hell out."

Faces whirled around me as blurry smears. Second by second, the faces came into focus. I was in the Blind Tiger Club. Playing Rock Band with werewolves.

Slowly, strength returned to my legs.

My *kundalini noir* went into battle mode.

I bolted upright and whirled around, talons and fangs at the ready. My attacker was Jerry, the werewolf engineer from the other night, at the rumble outside Big Jack's Saloon.

I grinned. "Back for more, hair bag?"

His right paw swiped at my face. I caught his wrist and got ready to rip his paw off when he wrenched free.

Two more *weres* stood by his side. Other *weres* pushed chairs and tables to make more room.

One of the Rock Band judges stepped between the *weres* and me. “No fighting. This is sanctuary.”

Jerry shouted. “Fuck sanctuary.” He pumped a clawed fist. “The Palmetto Clan rules.”

Other *weres* jumped to their feet and chanted, “Palmetto rules. Palmetto rules.”

These werewolves were no longer directing their ire at me but at the crowd. *Weres* kicked over chairs and readied their claws. Someone punched the judge and he staggered into a table, knocking glasses of beer to the floor.

“Magnolia Clan,” a *were* yelled. “Band together.”

“Hickory Clan,” another shouted. “By the bar.”

Werewolves clustered back-to-back and waited for others to declare themselves friend or foe.

Angela grabbed Jerry’s shirt. “Stop this. Honor the parley.”

He pushed her away. “Fight or get out.”

My talons sprouted and my fangs got ready. I advanced on Jerry.

Werewolves blocked my way. “This ain’t your fight, bloodsucker. Get the hell out.”

A new chant started. “Dog pile. Dog pile.”

Bottles crashed against the ceiling and walls, spraying us with beer and glass. Werewolves climbed on tables and jumped into the crowd.

We were seconds away from mosh pit to riot.

A shriek echoed over the pandemonium. A police whistle. Cops, rather *were* cops, rushed into the room, swinging big hairy arms and truncheons.

Rather than bring the peace, the whistle acted like a signal. Suddenly every werewolf was biting and throwing punches.

Angela held her shoes in one hand. She clasped my wrist and tugged me toward the door. She cleared a path through the mob with a flurry of barefoot karate kicks.

A werewolf staggered atop a table, his clothes ripped, blood streaming from his head, his right arm bent and cradled before him. He shouted, “Palmetto Clan rules.”

More cops bulldozed into the room. As they crossed the threshold, each morphed from human form to werewolf.

Angela and I made it to the front dining area. A line of cops, as humans, kept the curious from entering the club. The cops let us out.

We walked away, relieved like we'd made it off a capsized boat.

Angela said, "Sorry about what happened. It was supposed to be a party."

"I learned something. Didn't realize werewolves could be violent."

Angela leaned against me and put her shoes back on. She smoothed her dress. "That was mild. Tempers are running hot. We need to keep even a bar fight from turning into the first skirmish of a war."

"That was clever of you using the loophole to keep me playing Rock Band," I said. "Arguing that the rule didn't exclude vampires."

"I know the importance of nuances."

"Even so, I better stay clear of werewolves. I hate to rely on nuances to save my ass. You saw how they used me as an excuse to make trouble."

"All werewolves?" Angela cocked an eyebrow.

"Maybe I could handle one."

"Sounds like a challenge." She unlocked the Maserati. "Let's find out."

We got into the car.

"What's this going to do to your reputation?"

"I'm a werewolf. I'm *supposed* to have a bad reputation." She gripped the steering wheel and gunned the engine. "Let's go. I'm curious to see how bad my reputation can get."

Chapter 36

We drove east over the Ashley River, then south to Centerville. Angela explained that we were on James Island, miles away from Charleston.

A waxing moon followed us across the night sky. The luminous circle was almost complete. The time for Le Cercle de Sang et Crocs drew closer. Werewolves couldn't behave themselves at a party; what would they do when all the territory clans got together?

"When the moon is full," I asked, "do all of you turn into wolves?"

"We can resist the impulse. But it's hard. We may not be pleasant company, as you've seen."

"So it's like a mass interspecies PMS?"

"I wouldn't put it that way."

"I always figured wolves as northern animals," I said. "How do you *weres* put up with the heat and the humidity?"

"You're thinking of gray or timber wolves," she answered. "Many of us, like me, are red wolves, indigenous to the

South. We're used to the climate. There's also the Mexican or desert wolf."

As she talked, I loaded the Webley with silver bullets. I snapped the frame closed. The other twelve rounds remained in the carton. After tonight's trouble, I kept the Webley on my lap, just in case.

"Are you stuck living here? I mean, if you're a red werewolf, what's to keep you from living in Idaho?"

"Nothing. Different types of werewolves live in different types of climate. Besides, most of the time, we're in human form and we take advantage of air-conditioning and central heating."

"How do you become a werewolf anyway?" I asked. "A bite?" I thought about Charly in the alley of Big Jack's. "A scratch?"

"If your mom is a *were*, you can be born as one. If you're turned from human to *were*, the first turning has to come from a special werewolf bite. Here." She rubbed her left clavicle. "Or here." She touched the bottom of her nape. "Otherwise, we'd be up to our chins in werewolves. What about you vampires?"

"You fang somebody and feed them their blood."

"How?"

"With a kiss."

Angela grimaced. "Yuck. You vampires can't do anything without blood." She eased off the gas and we slowed to ninety.

"How were you turned?" Hopefully it didn't involve Calhoun or Bourbon. I was certain making werewolves from humans was an intimate undertaking like vampire fanging.

"Someone who's since moved on," she answered. "Leave it at that."

We were past the suburbs, at a spot where the highway connected low islands surrounded by sloughs of water.

"That's the Folly River." Angela flicked the high beams. "Up ahead is Folly Island."

The highway cut through a series of intersections and ended against, ironically enough, considering we were in the Deep South, Arctic Avenue.

The intersection overlooked the beach and the long pier jutting into the Atlantic Ocean. Angela turned right and we continued south. Arctic Avenue curved into Ashley. The neighborhood was mostly cottages, with a sprinkling of upscale beach houses, two-story homes with big windows on the top floor and a carport underneath. The few shops were closed for the evening.

Angela pulled beside a small bungalow near the end of the road. She parked on a narrow driveway paved with gravel and seashells.

We got out but she didn't make the offer that we go inside the house. I carried the Webley tucked into my waistband.

She had me follow her into the backyard. Bushes grew into a U around the yard and shielded us from view by the neighbors.

Angela slipped out of her shoes and stood barefoot on the grass.

My *kundalini noir* quickened.

She acted relaxed. "You vampires can shift into animals, right?"

"We can."

"Bats?"

I answered, "Not all of us."

"What do you shift into?"

"A wolf."

"What a coincidence. I like wolves. Do you need anything special to shift?"

"Like a full moon? No."

"Can you shift," she asked, "for me?"

"Any particular reason?" I asked.

She reached behind her back and unzipped her dress. "Curiosity. I'll show you mine if you show me yours."

CHAPTER 37

ANGELA WIGGLED her shoulders, and the dress slipped down her torso. With a shimmy of her hips, the dress fell around her ankles.

I removed my contacts and stored them in their plastic case.

Angela's aura surrounded her like a veil of yellow light. Orange blobs swirled through the glow, the blobs breaking apart and re-forming like the hot wax in a lava lamp. A human aura I was expert at reading. A *were*? Different language.

Angela straightened her back and stood tall, her body toned, her abdomen a series of smooth ripples, her black bra and matching thong panties drawing attention to what they concealed.

Her aura brightened. The orange blobs broke into small circles that floated in her psychic envelope like cartoony polka dots.

Angela hooked her thumbs under the shoulder straps of her bra. "This is all you get until you play along."

I unbuttoned my shirt and stripped to my tank top.

She said, "More."

I took the shirt and tank off. The sea breeze caressed my skin.

Angela nodded, confirming that she was pleased. She pulled the bra strap off her shoulders and reached around to undo the clasp.

The bra released. Her breasts—firm, round—pointed from her chest.

With those preliminaries over, we were soon naked. Her aura sizzled. The orange polka dots separated into thousands of tiny bubbles that effervesced within her penumbra.

She approached. Her gaze slid from my eyes to my chest and lower. Those eyes came back to mine and they beamed with approval.

An invisible cloud of pheromones swirled around her. The scent and her body and her smile and her beckoning eyes sent my *kundalini noir* pulsing with desire.

She put one arm on my shoulder and drew close, stopping when our bodies were about to touch. Her free hand clasped my neck and she pulled me close, her mouth open, her eyes sliding shut.

Our lips touched. An electric lust sparked through me.

I reached to take her in my arms. She pushed away. "Later." She motioned to my clothes. "Bring them." She turned away and collected her clothes and keys.

We stored our clothing and my pistol in the Maserati. She beeped the locks and hid the keys among the roots of the bushes.

Angela faced me. The orange spots had become a mass of tiny points and surged through her aura like hot foam.

Her shoulders hunched. Her legs twisted. She bent forward in a stoop. Her ears grew long and pointed. Thick hair darkened her body until she was covered in fur.

Angela was a beautiful woman, and for me, her change into a werewolf was not at all grotesque, simply different and fascinating.

Her hands reached for the ground. Her fingernails curled

into claws. By the time her hands reached the grass, they had grown into paws.

Her eyes locked on me. They glinted red as rubies lit by fire.

The shifting was done. Angela Cyclone was more than a werewolf. She was a supernatural wolf.

Her tail wagged. She sat on her haunches.

My turn.

Her transmutation had been quick and looked painless. I wish mine were as easy.

I chose a spot on the grass and lay down on my side. Angela trotted over so she could keep eye contact.

I summoned the transmutation.

My *kundalini noir* jolted in pain like I'd run myself through with a sword. My back arched. My vision dimmed to black. Smells disappeared. The outside world faded and I sensed nothing but the agony within me.

My bones twisted and bent into new shapes. My face felt like a hook was tugging at the front of my skull. Fire churned though my veins. Needles of pain tore at my flesh as fur emerged from naked skin. A new pain yanked at the bottom of my back, where a tail elongated from my spine.

I forced a breath, hoping the fresh air would soak up the pain. Smells flooded my nose. Rich smells. Complex smells. Inviting smells.

I opened my eyes. Breath by breath, the pain receded.

I drew my legs close and rolled to my belly. My *kundalini noir* burned strong. I pushed myself upright.

Angela circled me, her tail held high like a flag, her lupine bitch scent as irresistible as a gush of arterial blood. Her aura clung to her fur-covered body.

I darted for her. She bounded away, escaping through a gap in the brush.

She ran through the next yard, leaped over a fence, through another yard, and onto an open field facing the river. She ran nimbly, her feet racing across the ground, the leaves and grass whispering beneath her soft paws.

I chased after her.

Lights illuminated the shoreline, the buildings, and the deserted boat docks.

Angela and I galloped, our footsteps silent as the sea breeze. We were a pair of shadows racing through the broken darkness.

We ran along the edge of the sandy beaches. Angela veered into a clump of bushes and disappeared. I lost even her aura. I slowed to track her scent.

Something nipped my haunches. I whirled around.

Angela bounded away, her tail knotting into a playful curl, and circled north, our original direction.

Together we tore through the sea grass, breaking the stalks, the scent collecting on our fur.

The world was a torrent of scents—the humid beach, nesting gulls, the decay of the mudflats from across the water, fish and crab rotting along the shore. Wet sand squished under our paws and moist earth spattered against our bellies. Lamps from human dwellings striped the night with light and shadow.

We headed back in the direction of Angela's home. Dogs broke into yapping howls, warning the island that wolves prowled the neighborhood. Not to worry, humans didn't understand canine.

The closer we got to her house, the more we slowed our gait. We slunk through the shadows, using our noses to guide us from fresh human and dog scents.

We stopped in the brush close to the roads—listening, sniffing, then darting across when we were certain no one suspected our presence.

Angela led me through a path in the pines and scrub to her house. Again, we stopped and watched. Listened. Sniffed.

We entered her backyard. Angela circled to face me. Orange dots swirled through her aura like bubbles in boiling water. Her glowing eyes gazed into mine. The playfulness was gone, replaced by anticipation.

She ruffled the hackles of her neck and slowly approached me, her eyes never leaving mine.

We stood wet nose to wet nose. She stretched her neck and rubbed the tip of her snout against mine.

My *kundalini noir* buzzed like I'd swallowed a hive of horny bees.

I raised my head to let her sniff my throat. Nip my skin.

She strutted beside me, leaning into me so her shoulder scrubbed against my shoulder, my ribs, my haunches.

I raised my tail. She raised hers.

The fragrance of her sex dug into my nostrils, the smell so overwhelming, so intoxicating, that I started to buck my hips and wanted nothing more than to lose myself in her pleasure. I closed my eyes to focus on her aroma.

Angela walked around my other side, again rubbing against me until her rear brushed along my snout. She turned before me and lowered her chest to the ground. Her ears splayed flat.

Her eyes stared at me.

Her ears stood up. She raised her head and looked past me. Thorns formed on the penumbra of her aura.

She growled and sprang beside me.

I spun around, my lust frustrated.

Something black whooshed in front of Angela. Something with wings, something bigger than me.

A bat.

A giant bat.

Large fangs glistened in its mouth.

Not a bat but a vampire.

Angela leaped at him.

A blade flashed in the vampire's hand. Angela snapped her jaws, yelped, and staggered to one side. A dagger tumbled to the gravel.

My *kundalini noir* burned like fire. I lunged for the vampire, my teeth bared, my jaws ready to rip him to pieces.

I moved fast.

But the vampire moved faster. He jumped straight up. His wings unfolded and beat the air with a mechanical hiss.

I snapped the empty air under his boots.

He sailed to the roof of Angela's house, where he cocked his legs, jumped again, and continued to the next house. He repeated his motions, reaching higher with each jump until he soared over the river, back in the direction of Charleston.

Who was he?

I turned to Angela. Her limp favored her right hind leg. I smelled blood. Hers.

The knife lay on the gravel and crushed seashells. I brought my nose close to the blade to sniff the scent of the vampire. The metal put off a heat.

Silver.

Deadly to both Angela and me.

I'd had my back to the vampire when he'd attacked. Was he after me? Or Angela? Or us both?

Birds called.

Birds?

I looked to the east.

A thin line of blue stained the black horizon.

Dawn approached.

Angela was wounded, and my most feared enemy was on the way.

The morning sun and its deadly rays.

Chapter 38

I RUBBED ANTISEPTIC balm into the wound on Angela's right calf.

We were back in human form, on a queen-size bed in the small bedroom of her cottage. I couldn't apply first aid in wolf form. As I wasn't a veterinarian, Angela had to change into human form as well. I could treat women, not wolves.

The windows of the bedroom faced south and west, away from the rising sun. Blinds covered the windows. The slats of the blinds glowed from the morning light. But I was safe.

Angela lay on her back with the bedsheet covering her torso and thighs. She had tucked the top of the sheet under her armpits. I sat beside her, dressed only in my trousers, and cradled her wounded leg across my lap.

The gash on her leg was as long as my index finger and deep enough to bleed profusely. I'd closed the wound with strips of cloth medical tape. The wound had scabbed over and flesh grew where the lips of the wound touched. Werewolves healed fast, though not as fast as vampires.

She studied the wound. "Think it's going to scar?"

"Pretty sure of it."

She dropped her head against the pillow. "Damn."

I said, "Scars add character."

"Men don't mind showing character. Women hate it."

After we'd transmutated to human form, I retrieved our clothes and my pistol from Angela's Maserati. I had bandaged her wound with my tank top and supported her as she limped inside. I had hoped that the evening would end with our naked bodies rubbing against each other, but not this time, thanks to the bat-wing vampire.

The mud and sand had sloughed off the fur during the transmutation, but dirt caked our feet and hands, and grass stained our flanks. We had showered together. My attention was on getting her clean and tending to her wound rather than play. Unfortunately.

The vampire's dagger lay where I'd placed it on the nightstand.

"Any idea who this guy was?" Angela reached for the dagger.

I had given it thought and, not surprisingly, drawn a blank. "Has to be related to Paxton and the two vampires who came after me with the crab."

She inspected the dagger. It looked new but resembled a war-surplus trench knife: stacked-leather grip, steel hilt, a thick blade with deep blood grooves. What made this dagger a custom job were the sharp silver edge and the reinforcing steel spine. This dagger was made to kill vampires and werewolves.

Angela passed the dagger from hand to hand, careful not to touch the silver. "Was he after you or me? Or both?"

"Me, I'm sure of that," I said. "He showed up when I had my back to him. While I was preoccupied with you, he intended to run me through."

"And me?" She waved the dagger back and forth.

"I'm sure he didn't mean to leave a witness."

"What was that flying suit he wore?" she asked. "When I first saw him, I thought he was a giant bat. Or a dragon. Even a devil."

"Interesting disguise. Stealthy. A human sees him, they won't believe their eyes."

"Seems a lot of trouble to make him fly."

"The suit didn't make him fly. It aided his powers of levitation. Basically it let him take longer and longer hops through the air."

"Any idea on how to find out where he got it?"

"No, but I know where to start asking. You know King Gullah?"

"Only by name." Angela rested the dagger on the nightstand. "Do you think he's in on it?"

"I doubt it. Gullah is a shady character, but he wouldn't bother with a bat-wing contraption. I'll talk to him because he might know somebody who knows somebody."

"When you find the bat-wing guy, call me. I want to work on his complexion with my claws." Angela tossed a tube of aloe vera lotion. "Until then, make yourself useful. If we can't have sex, at least get busy with this." She flexed her calf where it rested on my lap.

"What do I get out of this?"

"My gratitude."

"That all? After I saved you from that vampire?"

Angela raised her foot and pressed it against the bottom of my chin. "Like hell. I saved you."

I grasped her ankle and held her leg still on my lap. "Okay, rubbing your leg is privilege enough."

She rubbed her toes against my belly. "You'll never get anywhere with a werewolf if you give up so easy."

"The worst mistake any human, any vampire, any supernatural can make," I said, "is to underestimate me."

She brought her other leg from under the bedsheet and propped her left ankle on my shoulder. "Felix, don't make promises you can't deliver."

I ran my hand down her leg and cupped the bedsheet in the gap at the top of her thighs. "Don't worry, when you're ready, I'll deliver."

She lifted her leg off my shoulder. Her face became veiled in melancholy. I wasn't sure what had brought the change in mood, so I stayed quiet.

"Lie beside me." She raised her head so I could slide my arm along the pillow. Her neck felt pleasantly warm.

Angela's eyes tightened and relaxed to the anxious cadence of her thoughts. "How are things between you and Wendy?"

The question surprised me. "They're not."

Angela rolled onto her side, facing me, and traced a finger along my ribs. Her touch caused a hot tingle. She laid her hand flat on my chest. Her skin contrasted with mine, tanned and warm versus translucent and cool.

"Your body looks like it belongs in a science lab."

"Humans would think the same thing," I replied. "That's why we have the Great Secret."

Angela pulled her hand away. "Does it bother you she's with Calhoun?" We were back to Wendy.

"I'm over it." Or at least trying. "Why are you asking? You jealous about Wendy and Calhoun?"

"I'm pretending that I'm not."

"What's the arrangement between you and him?"

"Sexually? Werewolves are polyamorous. We like to fuck as much as we like to fight."

"Calhoun gets his pick?"

"Being an alpha has its perks as well as its headaches."

The silence returned.

"I need to warn you about Calhoun," she said.

More silence.

"He comes across as the voice of reason and understanding, but he can be as ruthless as Bourbon. Trust me, if the situation was reversed, with Bourbon as the presumptive top alpha and Calhoun out in the cold, he'd be rattling the cages for war."

Angela lifted her head and pushed my arm free. The melancholy got deeper. "After Inga Latrall's death, I was shocked at how fast Calhoun rallied the other clan alphas behind him."

"You're not suspicious he had something to do with her accident?"

"Calhoun is ruthless, not stupid. He wouldn't risk it. A top alpha like her dies so suddenly, it shakes up the hierarchy.

Pack and clan alphas start maneuvering for turf. They cut deals like the Mafia. Bourbon wasn't as good at it as Calhoun."

I thought about Sean Moultier, Bourbon's number one pack alpha. What was he keeping from his boss? Had Sean cut a deal with Calhoun?

Angela glanced at the clock on the nightstand. Time was ten after eight. "We better get going."

I looked at the blinds to confirm that it was safe to go out into the sunlight. Before we went anywhere, I had to apply the sunblock foundation and makeup that I'd brought in my knapsack.

Once properly covered and dressed, I joined Angela in the kitchen. She had put on a blue dress and poured coffee into plastic to-go cups. I was hungry, though sadly, I hadn't brought blood.

We drove back into Charleston. I thought of the city and its surroundings as a resort. So I was surprised, naively of course, by the crush of morning traffic clogging the bridges. Everywhere you went, people had jobs and appointments.

We finally made it over the Scarborough Bridge, passed the city marina, turned onto Rutledge Avenue. It was after nine; Lemuel should be at work. I was looking forward to a snooze in my casket.

We drove by the dry cleaners south of the mortuary. There were no cars parked along the curb in front. As far as I remembered, there were no memorial services scheduled for the day, so the place should be quiet.

A white Ford coupe was parked in the mortuary's driveway by the front door. Wendy's car.

What did she want this early in the morning? Why was she here? Didn't she go out last night with Calhoun? I'm showing up with Angela and I imagined the drama. My guts knotted.

Angela made no comment about Wendy's car. Maybe she didn't recognize it.

My ears buzzed. My fingertips started a faint quiver.

Danger.

Wendy's presence shouldn't cause this kind of alarm. I

concentrated on my sixth sense. What was the problem?

I couldn't pick out any one stimulus. The clues remained vague and out of reach. A smell? A sound? The pressure of a lurking gaze?

I panned the neighborhood with a fast scan.

Someone was watching.

Angela turned onto the mortuary driveway.

My sixth sense bundled into a hunch, and that hunch tripped the red alert in my head. The buzzing in my ears was loud as a shriek.

"Back up," I shouted.

Angela touched the brakes and stared at me, her face lit up with confusion.

"Don't stop," I shouted. "Back up. Now. Now."

Angela put the Maserati in reverse and craned her head around to look out the rear window. "What's the matter?"

"Give it gas."

She mashed the accelerator, and the Maserati shot out backward from the driveway.

I jerked the steering wheel and we swerved into the street.

"Keep going," I shouted. The alarm in my head was screaming. I straightened the steering wheel and we tore away from the mortuary.

A gigantic blast rocked the Maserati.

CHAPTER 39

THE ROOF of the mortuary broke apart into flames and smoke. Fire blew out the front door and shattered windows. A tongue of flame reached from the building and engulfed Wendy's coupe. A fireball swelled over the car and twisted into the air.

Dust and smoke slapped the Maserati's windshield. Glass and debris showered the street. Car alarms blared in a chorus announcing disaster.

Everything happened so fast I could only watch in disbelief.

Shock and fright washed over me. But I was safe. So was Angela.

There was an instant of relief; then the fright surged back, stronger, concentrated, toxic. Not simply fright but terror.

What about Wendy? Lemuel? The intern, Shantayla?

Halfway down the street, I shouted, "Stop."

The Maserati slammed to a halt.

I bolted from the car screaming their names.

The front of the mortuary collapsed into a pile of broken bricks. I ran past Wendy's burning Ford and the smoldering debris—wood framing, parts of a desk, shattered caskets, embalming supplies—that littered the sidewalk and the front lawn.

My *kundalini noir* trembled in desperation. My mouth dried. I had to tear into the building and search for survivors.

In the back lot, dust and pieces of bricks covered the hearse and the limo. The Mercury's windshield was broken, its dented hood and roof piled with dust and pieces of brick.

I could think only of Wendy. I grabbed the lid of a coffin and used it to pry open a break in the mortuary wall and enter the inferno.

Fire singed my face and hands. Luckily, I didn't have to breathe and that kept the flames from torching my lungs. My vision glazed over from the heat, and I navigated the fire as though looking through wavy, distorted glass. I discarded my contacts but that didn't help.

Who could have done this? Was this attack meant for me?

I found a charred lump heaped in the corner where Lemuel's office had been.

Wendy? Lemuel?

If this was a body, there was no aura. The life was gone. Flames spurted from the blackened, crooked limbs and the roasted torso.

Fire whirled around me. Hurriedly, I kicked at one of the twisted smoking stumps to turn the body over so I could get an ID.

Not Wendy. Please, not Wendy.

The body rolled over. A smoldering tie curled across the front of the chest. Lemuel.

Another charred body rested under his. The fire had burned off the blouse and bra. A woman. No aura. Also dead.

Lemuel had thrown himself over her in a vain gesture of valor. Wendy? Shantayla?

My *kundalini noir* seized in cold dread, a chill so strong it made me forget the fire.

The head and hands had shrunk into black lumps. Something glittered on what had been a finger. A ring. A big engagement ring.

Shantayla.

Shameful relief chased away the dread.

Heat and smoke roared around me. I shielded my face and crouched to hop between gaps in the fire.

I followed an open trail between the flames toward the back of the building and reached the coffin prep room. I kicked the door open.

Superheated air blasted me. I dropped to my knees and crawled over the hot floor.

Over to my left, a faint green glow. An aura.

Wendy.

CHAPTER 40

WENDY LAY under a pile of debris. Her aura glowed; she was still alive.

The ceiling groaned. Embers rained through the smoke. The roof was about to collapse.

I scrambled toward her. I flung aside the debris covering her body. I cradled her head. Her eyes were closed and her skin, blouse, and jeans stained with black smudges.

The ceiling groaned again. Another warning. Perhaps my last.

I didn't know if Wendy had any broken bones or internal injuries, but I had to get her out now.

I scooped her in my arms and stood. Where was the exit? I couldn't escape back through the hellish heat of the mortuary.

There was a door at the opposite side of the room. I held Wendy tight and ran toward it. At the last second, I spun around and smashed backward against the door.

The metal door held firm. Wendy bounced in my arms. I

beat against the door. The dead bolt and hinges squealed in protest.

More embers showered me. The smoke was thick as paste. I gave the door another bash with my shoulder blades.

The door swung loose and clanged to the concrete sidewalk. Smoke whooshed past me. I staggered outside into fresh air.

We were on the south side of the mortuary. I laid Wendy on a patch of grass alongside the driveway. Acrid smoke clung to our bodies.

She settled on the ground, limp. Her aura trembled like a weak, meager flame.

But she was alive.

A set of keys had fallen from her jeans pocket. I scooped them up and stuffed them into my trouser pocket. I would return the keys later.

I settled next to her. My *kundalini noir* relaxed. Why was she here? To see me? For what reason?

The screams of fire engines and police cars echoed through the neighborhood. Bystanders congregated in the street. Their red auras blazed with awe, curiosity, and fear.

Someone grabbed my shoulder.

Angela. Her face was taut with dread. Her red aura roiled with orange spots of alarm.

"Are you okay?"

I tried to talk. Smoke puffed out my mouth and nostrils. I tasted scorched wood and plastic.

At last the words came. "I'm fine."

Angela knelt beside Wendy and released a sigh heavy with distress. "Why was she here?"

"To see me, I think."

"What for?"

"I don't know."

Cops and firefighters rushed about us. Too late to do anything except keep the fire from spreading to the surrounding houses.

Lemuel was dead.

Shantayla was dead.

Wendy had barely survived.

Guilt and sorrow pushed the strength out of my body.

I slid my hand across Wendy's temple to her forehead. I felt for a pulse, a twitch of her eyes, a tiny spasm of life.

Nothing.

But her aura glowed, so she was still alive.

Angela got to her feet. "I'll get help."

Exhausted, I closed my eyes. I breathed deep, the remaining smoke circulated in my lungs, and I exhaled the malignant odor of fire and destruction.

Someone tapped my shoulder.

Angela again. She motioned that I get up.

A police officer came toward us from the line of patrol cars on the street. It was Sergeant Kessler, the *were* who had arrived when Calhoun and I had been ambushed over in Mount Pleasant.

Things moved around me in a slow drama like the world had been drenched in thick syrup. Shouts and the blare of sirens sounded distant and muted. Firefighters pulled hoses and aimed streams of water. Police in safety vests held the onlookers back. Emergency cars and trucks crowded the street, their light bars flashing red and blue in frantic, spastic fits.

Kessler grasped my arm and pulled me aside for a couple of EMTs to hustle past. She flicked open a pair of sunglasses and handed them to me.

I looked at the glasses in confusion, then realized—of course, to hide my eyes.

I brought the glasses close to my face and hesitated. The EMTs set their bags down and attended to Wendy. Her aura still shone green. I put the glasses on and the tinted lenses made her aura vanish.

One of the EMTs examined her eyes and face. The other unbuttoned Wendy's blouse.

The first EMT fit an air bag mask over Wendy's mouth and nose. The other EMT readied a syringe and gave Wendy an injection in the arm. They took a box from their bag, unwrapped wires, and attached them with sticky pads to Wendy's chest and arm. The screen on the box lit up and showed her vital signs scrolling across a grid.

I felt panic. Wendy was a dryad. If she was taken to a hospital, the doctors would discover her supernatural identity.

I started for the EMTs. Kessler grabbed my arm.

I blurted, the words slurring from my mouth, "You can't take her. Not to a hospital."

Kessler shouted in my ear, but her words sounded faint, like they'd come over a faulty telephone connection. "She'll be with family. The Secret is safe."

I struggled to get away, but Kessler held tight.

Wendy would be taken care of.

The Great Secret was safe.

I'd done all that I could. Fatigue enveloped me and my knees weakened.

Another EMT pushed a gurney to Wendy. The three EMTs slid her onto a backboard, which they placed on the gurney, and covered her with a blanket. They pushed her away, ignoring an ambulance, and trotted down the street.

The cops parted the line of bystanders for the EMTs to pass. Where were they going?

Kessler pulled me along. Angela grasped my arm and jogged beside us.

We passed the Maserati.

There was a note stuck under the wiper on my side.

Who had taken the time to leave a note? I halted, jostling Kessler and Angela. I pulled loose of their arms and approached the Maserati.

I snatched the note.

It was an index card, blank on the front.

I flipped the card over.

Words had been scrawled in blue ink.

They read:

Felix.

You still owe me. Next time.

Paxton

CHAPTER 41

I'D JUST crawled out of an inferno, my breath still tasted of smoke, and yet the chill of terror made me shiver. The mortuary explosion was no accident; it had been arson and murder.

I reread the note, thinking I had hallucinated the message.

I rubbed my thumb along the card stock and left a gray smudge across the words.

The fear became rage.

Paxton. I could feel the tendons of his neck breaking under my grip.

I removed my sunglasses and jerked my gaze about the neighborhood, searching for anything suspicious.

Werewolf. Vampire. Human.

A telltale aura glowing in the shadows. A pair of eyes glittering from a dark window. A reflection on the lens of a telescope. A silhouette where one shouldn't be.

Nothing. Only the mobs of people drawn to the burning mortuary.

Angela came up to me. "What's wrong?" Her question sounded loud. My hearing was back to normal. She retreated abruptly. I realized my talons were out.

I pushed the anger down and forced my talons to retract. My fangs were out as well and I drew them in.

I showed her the card. She looked back at the fire, then to Wendy on the gurney. "What does this mean?"

"It means there's going to be a next time. Paxton will strike again." I stepped back. "Get away. I don't want you close."

"And I should be scared?" Angela showed her fangs. Her nose darkened. "Don't forget that I'm a werewolf. Your enemies should be scared of me."

CHAPTER 42

THE EMTS pushed Wendy and the gurney to the end of the street. Cop cars blocked the intersection.

The drumming of rotor blades reverberated over the neighborhood. A shadow passed over us. Something sleek vanished behind the trees.

Angela morphed back into human shape before anyone noticed. She and Kessler grabbed my shoulders and led me to the EMTs.

A helicopter banked over the neighborhood, then leveled and descended toward the intersection. Wheels and struts extended from the trim fuselage.

The helicopter slowed, came to a high hover, and inched its way to the middle of the intersection. The rotor blast swirled dust and trash. The EMTs grasped the loose ends of the blanket covering Wendy. The police clasped their hands over their caps and turned their backs to the wind.

I recognized the helicopter. It was an S-76, identical to the one I'd seen at Latrall's estate.

The helicopter wheels touched the asphalt. The struts compressed as the S-76 settled to the ground. There was a change in pitch to the rotor blades and the wind stopped slapping around us. The cargo door on the fuselage slid open. A crew member in a blue flight suit and headset hopped out. He waved to the EMTs.

Heads bowed, the EMTs raced the gurney to the cargo door.

Kessler pulled the radio mike from her shoulder loop. She covered her mouth to isolate the helicopter noise. She hooked the mike back on the loop and patted my arm. "You go," she shouted. "You know Wendy best. She'll need you by her side."

Angela kissed my cheek. "Take care of her."

I shouted, "Why don't you come along?"

Kessler shook her head. "They can only take one extra passenger."

The EMTs lifted the backboard into the helicopter. The crewman fixed the backboard in place along the cargo floor. A second aircrew member, this one a female medical tech judging by the red crosses and colored patches on her flight suit, took the monitoring equipment and positioned it alongside Wendy. The med tech and EMTs put their heads together for a quick discussion.

The EMTs hustled their gurney away from the helicopter. The crewman waved at me from the open door.

I sprinted with my head low. The last time I'd run to a helicopter like this was in Iraq. The emotions flooded back. Excitement. Anticipation. Fear.

I hauled myself into the compartment. Wendy rested across the middle of the deck, her head toward the cockpit. A pair of straps kept the blanket tight around her torso and legs.

I was directed to the left side of the floor. The crewman shut the door and joined the med tech on the right.

The rotor blades renewed their loud drumming. The helicopter became light on its wheels and floated upward.

We rose above the rooftops and the trees. Cars and people shrank to the size of toys and miniature dolls.

The air-bag mask on Wendy's face trembled from the vibration. Wisps of her hair flicked across her brow.

Her complexion had a frightful anemic pallor. She looked fragile, close to the edge of death.

The med tech wore a bulky headset and big safety glasses. I couldn't read her expression as she studied Wendy's vital signs on the monitor.

I peeked over the rims of my sunglasses. Wendy's green aura simmered like the weak flame of a gas burner set on low.

I checked the crew's auras. The med tech and the pilot had the red-and-orange psychic envelopes of werewolves. The crewman and the copilot were human.

We passed over the wharves. Tall ships cut through the harbor. More werewolves.

I slipped my hand under the blanket and found Wendy's right hand. I interlaced my fingers in hers. Her touch was abnormally cool.

I remembered when I'd done this before.

In the early days of our invasion of Iraq, my M2 Bradley Fighting Vehicle had run over a 152mm howitzer shell buried in the road. The Bradley weighed thirty tons and had been tossed onto its side like a cardboard box. The blast had sheared the armored skirt, the track, and wheels from the right side of the hull.

That's what I was told. At the time I'd been hunkered inside the hull, perched on a seat and commiserating about the filth, the discomfort, the lack of hot chow when . . .

I woke up lying on my side, buried under equipment, my ears ringing, a horrific pain pounding through my skull, smoke burning my nose and mouth.

The rear hatch of the Bradley was flung open. The sudden light blinded me. O'Brien and Washington scrambled in and grabbed the straps of my load-bearing equipment. They dragged me through the dirt to the side of the road. Soldiers ran beside us, yelling that the Bradley was about to catch fire.

The warmth and sounds of the world receded from me. I

became very cold. One of my squad members was laid next to me. It was Specialist Price, who looked wasted and pale despite the fact that he was a muscle head and blacker than Miles Davis.

A UH-60 landed beside us. Dust blasted my face and I had to tell myself to close my eyes. I took a seat on the left side of the cargo compartment, next to Price. The medics had him juiced up and an IV dangled from a bag hooked to a strut.

We took off and I looked down on the squalor of Karbala.

Price had seemed so frail. I thought that if I touched him, some of my life force would travel into him. I gripped his fingers. They were cold as Popsicles.

I concentrated on pushing my energy through my hand into his. I'd keep Price alive with unrelenting willpower.

I prayed. *Don't let him die.*

The UH-60 started its descent to the MASH landing pad.

Price's fingers curled against mine.

He was alive.

I rubbed Wendy's fingers. I concentrated on pushing my energy into her. I had kept Price alive, and back then I was only a human. Now, as a vampire, I had more power, more awareness of my psychic energy. I would keep Wendy alive.

I put my other hand on her forehead. The more of me that touched her, the more power I could transmit from my body into hers.

The med tech pushed my hand off Wendy's forehead. The woman frowned, admonishing me not to touch.

I kept my other hand hidden under the blanket.

I closed my eyes and concentrated.

Death would not win.

The helicopter banked to the right.

Death would not win.

The med tech shifted. She talked with great animation into her headset and scribbled on a notepad. Even through the lenses of her safety glasses, I could see a sheen creep over her eyes. She pushed a finger under the safety glasses to blot away the tears.

My *kundalini noir* pulsed. A dull spark of dread ran up my spine.

The med tech switched off the monitor and disconnected the wires. She removed the air-bag mask, reached for the blanket, and pulled it over Wendy's face.

The med tech looked at me and shook her head.

I gripped Wendy's hand and sought for a signal, a twitch, anything that would say the medic was wrong.

Wendy's fingers remained cold and limp.

I let go.

Bitter pain cut through me and filled me with sadness.

I wanted something to blow away this pain and sorrow. I wanted something to let the light of hope shine through, but there was only the blackness and that pain and that sorrow.

And rage. Volcanic rage that could tear a mountain apart.

My fingers shook. My talons sprang out and I clutched at the air.

I looked out the window back to Charleston. Bile and wrath tore at my insides. I'd raze the city, demolish everything, punish the innocent and guilty alike to avenge Wendy. Charleston had survived two wars, a siege, an earthquake, a pirate invasion, and slave uprisings.

But the city wouldn't survive me.

CHAPTER 43

THE HELICOPTER had landed on Latrall's estate and Wendy's body had been taken off. The waiting medical staff didn't have much to do except certify her death.

I had asked about the protocol regarding her remains. One of the *were* doctors, a guy with a European accent I couldn't place, explained that since Wendy was a dryad, a wood nymph, she was to be returned to the forest around the Pilica River of her native Poland.

Wendy was Polish? Death reveals many secrets while it buries others. I had figured by her red hair and complexion that she was Irish. Wendy Teagarden was only one of the many names she'd used over the centuries.

I was given a change of clothes and bathed to scrub away the stink of smoke and failure. King Gullah had arrived with an assortment of contact lenses and, like any good vampire, a makeup kit.

He sat beside me in the back of one of his Escalades. We

were on the way to Wendy's house to cleanse the premises of any supernatural evidence.

Gullah did me the favor of not talking much. Sade whispered on the stereo. A gentle rain pattered against the roof and windows. We rode in haunted silence back over the Cooper River, crossed Charleston at the Neck, and continued over the Ashley River into the suburb of Ashley Forest. Rooster followed us in the other Escalade.

The rain let up and left a shroud of gray haze clinging to the trees. A sheriff's patrol car waited at the curb of Wendy's home. I wondered if this meant trouble, with Gullah and his gang being criminals. But Gullah gave no hint of being worried.

A deputy sheriff stood by the front door on the porch. All the drapes and blinds had been drawn over the windows. The blossoms on the porch had wilted and their fallen petals circled the flowerpots. Wendy's house looked somber and forlorn as if in mourning.

Our Escalades halted behind the deputy's car. Gullah's gang jumped out and made no attempt to hide the fact they were armed. We climbed the short concrete steps onto the porch. Unlike yesterday, there was no ceremony with a blue haint cloth.

The deputy waited. A peek without my contacts confirmed he was a *were*. When we got close, he gave a casual salute to Gullah, who nodded in reply. Supernatural professional courtesy.

The deputy unlocked the door. A locksmith tag hung from the key. The cawing of crows sounded from inside the house.

Gullah let Yo-Yo enter first.

I remembered Wendy's guard force of praying mantises. "Careful when you go in."

Yo-Yo curled his lips and showed his fangs. He pulled his shirt up and back for access to the Glock inside his waistband. His teeth and gun were no match for the army of mantises, but before I could warn him, he and Gullah had gone in. I followed.

The house smelled musty.

A crunch came from under Yo-Yo's shoes. He lifted one foot. "What the fuck?"

Hundreds of praying mantises littered the floor. Still more dropped from the wilting vines laced across the walls. Most of the mantises were stiff and looked brittle. A few crept along in the final throes of dying.

I asked. "What happened?"

"This didn't grow on its own." Gullah pointed to the mass of plants—now yellowing and shriveling—and the carpet of dead mantises. "Wendy died and took the magic with her."

Yo-Yo swung his hand through the spider plants and ivy hanging from the macramé planters. The leaves and vines broke apart like old paper. "If you're going to grow something, then it oughta be some crunk weed, not all these houseplants. You can't smoke this shit." He stepped around the piles of dead mantises. "And all these fucking bugs. What's up with this? The chick liked animals so much, why didn't she get a cat or a dog? Maybe a goldfish."

Dozens of crows squawked from their roost in the back room.

I surveyed the interior, the hall to my left, the kitchen in front of us, the living room to the right. A sense of wrong screwed through me as we violated Wendy's private world.

I brushed the leaves and mantis carcasses off the armchair. I sat, weary of the loss. Weary of death.

I told Gullah about the note Paxton had sent, the one written on a swatch of human skin. Gullah and Rooster stared, equally fascinated and disgusted.

Gullah asked, "How does this happen to you? Crazy shit like that never happens to me."

He tapped my shoulder. "We got work to do." He fished a chrome cigarette case from his pocket. He opened the case. Instead of cigarettes, there was a tuning fork clipped to the inside.

Gullah removed the tuning fork. It looked to be made of brushed steel with brass inserts along the tines. A sapphire knob decorated the stem.

He flicked a talon against the tines and the fork emitted a

low whine. Gullah held the fork up and waved it slowly about the room. The sapphire knob began to glow.

Gullah handed the tuning fork to me. "You do it."

"What's this for?"

"Locates the Araneum's property."

"How does it work?"

"Move it around. You'll figure it out."

The stem was cool and vibrated faintly. Gullah gave the tines another flick. The stem vibrated harder and tickled my fingers.

I held the tuning fork up and moved it left to right. The light in the knob brightened or dimmed as the whine grew louder or softer. I kept the tuning fork at a point where the knob shone brightest and the whine sounded loudest, like a finger rubbed around the rim of a crystal goblet.

I got it. When the knob shone bright and the whine was loud, I was getting warm. Dim and soft, I was getting cold. The tuning fork was a homing device.

I advanced through the front room—dead mantises crackling under my feet like autumn leaves—and adjusted my steps to follow a path that kept the knob glowing bright and the whine singing.

The tuning fork pointed to the doors of a credenza against the wall in the dining room. Gullah opened the doors and pulled out a cardboard shoe box that he let drop to the floor. The box clanged from empty message capsules, the Araneum standard type, made of filigreed platinum and yellow gold, about the size of a little finger. These were the capsules that were clipped to the legs of the messenger crows.

I waved the tuning fork over the credenza. The box was all it found.

Gullah busied himself digging through the box. "Keep looking about the room."

I waved the fork and followed its lead to a table against the far wall.

The fork pointed to a leather-bound book tucked within a pile of mystery novels and copies of *Vanity Fair*, *Yoga Journal*, and *Blueboy* magazines. Wendy had eclectic literary tastes.

When I took the book from the pile, the tuning fork began to whine loud and the sapphire knob became bright as a halogen bulb.

"Hey, Rooster," I called out, "come take this." I gave him the tuning fork.

Gullah said to Rooster, "Go search the rest of the house. Bring what you find."

The book was the size of a hardback textbook. Bits of leather flaked from the cracked and wrinkled cover.

I opened the book, delicately, afraid the pages and binding would crumble in my hands. I glimpsed these words written in script on the title page:

The Endtimes Volume III
The Rapture
A Calendar and Index of Signs
Uncorrected Advance Copy

A shriek loud as a fire alarm echoed in the house. Rooster yelled from across the room. "What the fuck you doing?" He held the tuning fork with both hands. The sapphire knob pulsed like a strobe.

I shut the book and the shriek faded back to its previous whine. The knob dimmed.

"Somebody doesn't want you reading that," Gullah said.

I held the book. Astonished. Awed. Afraid that it might validate biblical prophecy. "The Rapture. You know what this means?"

"It means we bloodsuckers are fucked. What else is new? When Jesus Christ, Allah, the Buddha, L. Ron Hubbard—whoever the hell is upstairs—starts plucking souls, you think we're invited to the party?" Gullah gave an impatient wave. "Bring that book over here."

With great care, I handed him the book. Gullah tossed the book into the box with the message capsules.

Rooster came from the hall. He carried a pillowcase lumpy with bulky objects. "I got everything."

Gullah pointed to the box. Rooster shook the pillowcase over the box and dumped out two ancient-looking scrolls, a

Tibetan prayer wheel, various clockwork devices made of brass and steel, and an English–House Cat language dictionary.

Rooster said, "I also brought this stuff from her desk. It ain't Araneum property, but we oughta make it destroyed." He tossed items from his pocket: a diary, a plastic bag with seeds in it, folders, and a handful of computer thumb drives.

Rooster dropped the empty pillowcase and the tuning fork into the box. Gullah sorted the items so everything fit close together. He said, "Go get the stuff."

Rooster turned and left the house through the front door.

"What stuff?" I thought we were collecting Wendy's things to take with us, but it seemed Gullah had another plan.

Yo-Yo came from a back room at the end of the hall. I noticed that the crows had long since gotten quiet. Had Yo-Yo killed them?

First one crow, then a second, a third, a half dozen, more crows, maybe forty, strutted into the hall. They moved behind Yo-Yo like a shimmering black pool.

He looked over his shoulder at the crows and then to Gullah and me. "Ain't this some freaky-ass shit?"

Rooster opened the front door from the outside. He carried a package the size of a ten-pound bag of cement. His eyebrows perked up in surprise when he saw the advance of the crows.

He held the door open for the flock to march past him. When they crossed the threshold, each bird launched itself into the air and flew off.

One crow broke ranks and walked to me, ignoring the mantises around its feet. It stopped and we exchanged glances. The crow lowered its head, shook it, turned away, and joined his comrades.

"You know that bird?" Gullah asked.

"I'm not sure. They all look alike."

When the last crow had flown off, Rooster closed the door. He brought the bag to us.

"Dump it on that," Gullah ordered.

Rooster extended a talon and sliced the bag open. He

tipped the bag over the box. A gray powder spilled out, the odor metallic and acid.

Gullah crouched and shook the box so the powder filtered deep into the crevices between the items inside.

"What's that?" I asked.

"Thermite powder," he answered, standing.

Thermite powder is an incendiary agent made with aluminum and magnesium. Other than a direct nuclear blast, there is no better way to destroy anything made of metal.

Rooster reached under his shirt and pulled out an olive green cylinder he had hooked into his waistband. The cylinder was a hand grenade, slightly larger than a beer can, with a yellow band across the middle and stenciled letters that read SMOKE WP BURSTING TYPE.

WP. White phosphorus. In the army we called it Willy Peter.

The plan was to set the grenade in the box and initiate the thermite burn.

"Why are you going to destroy this?" I asked.

"Property of the Araneum. Their orders. But am I going to destroy this? No, that honor is yours."

Gullah pointed and Rooster handed me the grenade.

The grenade was heavy and felt like it contained concentrated evil. "Why me?"

"Because you knew Wendy better than any one of us," Gullah said. "Burning her house to the ground will mean more to you."

CHAPTER 44

I LOOKED ABOUT the rooms, at the plants, the mounds of dead mantises, and the few pictures on the wall. Everything carried the presence of Wendy. To destroy the house was to destroy part of her.

But she was dead.

What was left behind was nothing but the flotsam everyone leaves on the deserted shore of their lives.

Gullah was right. Torching Wendy's possessions would mean the most to me. I thought about dropping her key ring into the box, but it was the only memento I had of hers. I kept the keys in my pocket.

Every acquaintance we make is a joy and a curse. The time Wendy and I shared was the joy.

I gripped the grenade's safety lever and pulled the pin.

This was the curse.

The aching good-bye. First on the helicopter when she died. Now again as I was about to incinerate her property and belongings.

A heavy sadness pressed upon my shoulders. A sadness that underlined how powerless I was over circumstance.

I checked to see that the front door remained open. I shoved the grenade into the box and released the safety lever.

By the time the lever had pinged loose from the fuse, I was sprinting out the door at vampire speed.

Yo-Yo, Rooster, and Gullah were on the lawn. Yo-Yo counted, "Three. Four. Five."

The grenade exploded with a *whump*. The walls of the house shook. The front window shattered. A fist of dense white smoke punched through the window frame. More white smoke leaked from the front door, from the other windows, and from under the eaves.

"Damn," Yo-Yo cried out. "I got dibs next time we use one of those motherfuckers."

The deputy sheriff used his radio to call the fire department.

The white phosphorus and the thermite would melt the Araneum's secrets into unrecognizable slag. Wendy's house and possessions would be gone forever, just as she was.

The sheriff was here to add the veneer of authority.

Everything was under control.

Almost.

Something bothered me. Actually, a lot bothered me.

I asked Gullah, "What do you know about a vampire wearing a bat-wing costume?"

"What do you mean?"

I explained the attack on Angela and me.

Yo-Yo interrupted. "You were with Angela Cyclone?"

"Yeah. So?"

"Man, that is some fine trim."

"I never got to trim anything." I described the bat-winged vampire. "I'm sure he's working with Paxton."

Gullah chuckled derisively. "Anything else? Is Godzilla on the way? An asteroid?"

"There is," I replied. "How was it you showed up with the grenade and the thermite?"

"We were going to torch the house. Standard procedure."

Gullah reached into his pocket and withdrew an Araneum message capsule. "I do have something to show you." He unscrewed the ruby-encrusted cap and shook the capsule's contents into his hand, a roll of vampire parchment that resembled yellowed onionskin.

He crumpled the parchment into a wad and opened his hand toward the sun. As soon as sunlight hit the parchment, it began to smolder.

Gullah tossed the parchment toward my feet. The wad sizzled, smoked, and exploded with a pop that turned into a ball of smoke. The odor of burned rancid meat stank up the air.

Rooster clasped his nose and winced.

"What did the note say?" I asked.

Gullah twisted the cap back on the capsule with the assertive force he would use to wring the head off a chicken's neck. "The note said, 'Find Paxton.' "

I nodded, reassured that we had the Araneum's attention. "Great. Let's get started."

"That's not all," Gullah explained. "The note also said, 'Stay out of the werewolves' affairs. Don't let them drag us into their war. Whatever the price.' And the Araneum listed your name."

CHAPTER 45

GULLAH PUT on his sunglasses as if to distance himself from what he'd just told me.

The Araneum considered me expendable in their effort to keep out of the werewolf war. I felt dizzy and scared like I was on the edge of a narrow cliff.

Yo-Yo and Rooster stood on opposite sides of Gullah. Both vampire goons let their hands dangle in such a way that they could grab their pistols in a hurry.

I raised my hands palms up to show I didn't want any more trouble. I'd had enough with the werewolves, the mysterious bat-wing vampire, and Paxton.

"There was more to the Araneum's note," Gullah said. "They wrote my name after yours." He jabbed his finger into my chest. "I'm not risking my ass for anyone. If these werewolves demand your head to keep the peace, I'll give it to them."

I pushed Gullah's finger back. "I'd like to hear that from the Araneum."

"You heard it from me. That's enough."

Rooster coughed, a warning. He and Yo-Yo straightened their backs and folded their hands over the pistols stuck in their waistbands.

A black Mercedes rolled stealthily to the opposite curb and stopped. Dan, Calhoun's *were* bodyguard, got out the rear door on the driver's side. He held the door open and looked at me.

Gullah said, "I need this guy like I need a turd in my salad."

Why had Calhoun shown up? To express his remorse over Wendy's death? I'm sure he wasn't going to leave without first talking to me. I started for the car.

Gullah grabbed my arm. "What are you doing?"

I shrugged him off. "He might have information *we* need."

I walked across the street and entered the limousine and its cocoon of chilled air. Calhoun wore a black suit. Tie. Gold cuff links. I slid next to him. The spice notes in his cologne overlaid the canine musk smell. Dan got up front next to the driver.

We drove from the neighborhood just as flames shot from the roof of Wendy's house. I didn't want to look.

We caught the highway back to Charleston and passed a convoy of fire trucks going in the opposite direction.

This ride better not be my one-way trip to a landfill. I flashed my talons. This ride would be a one-way trip for the both of us, if he betrayed me.

Calhoun made a face at my lack of couth. "I want to express my condolences about Wendy."

I acknowledged the comment with a wave of my fingers and waited for him to get to the meat of this conversation.

"But the show must go on," he said. "We have responsibilities. You and I don't have the luxury of stopping to weep."

I don't weep because vampires can't. I asked, "Who planted the bomb at the mortuary?"

Calhoun's eyes iced over. "The investigators said it might have been a gas explosion."

"It was a goddamn bomb."

"None of the casualties was a werewolf. What do you want me to do?" His voice was cold.

"But Wendy?"

"She is dead." Now his voice was ice cold. "I know why the Araneum brought her to Charleston. You want to know the best way to honor her? Promote her mission. Peace among us werewolves."

He faced me. "Let me tell you the lengths the Araneum will go to in order to protect its interests." His eyes glowed warily from the dark pocket of shadow under his brow.

"During the War Between the States, werewolves served on both sides. Living among humans tests our loyalties." Calhoun touched his prothesis, a memento of his patriotic sacrifice. As a supernatural, he could've found a way out of military service, but he didn't. He went to Iraq and fought alongside his sailors.

"During the blockade of Charleston," Calhoun explained, "the local *nidus* took advantage of the chaos to feed on soldiers and stragglers from both sides. Despite warnings from the Araneum to evacuate the city, these vampires remained and grew complacent on the easy pickings until they were trapped within the Union encirclement. These vampires threatened to reveal themselves if the Araneum didn't rescue them."

A ray of sunlight slashed through the window but did nothing to brighten Calhoun's grim narrative.

"The Araneum wouldn't risk loyal vampires to save these renegades. So it ordered the trapped vampires to assemble for passage through the Union line. But the Araneum cut a deal with werewolves serving on both sides. Southern *were* cavalrymen led the vampires from Charleston to Hell Hole Swamp. Once there, the *were* cavalry and Union werewolf infantry cut the renegade vampires down in a cross fire."

"How do you know this?"

"I'm a clan leader and a Southerner. I must know these things." Calhoun reached into a pocket inside his coat. He brought out a small leather pouch. The hide was worn yet supple. He undid the rawhide cinch and spread the pouch open in the palm of his hand, careful not to touch a pitted and tarnished metal lump. A silver minié ball. "The vampires were killed with these."

The lesson was clear. Don't fuck with the Araneum.

We arrived in Charleston. Calhoun's limo drove to a small hotel on the southern tip of the peninsula.

"Why are we here?" I asked.

"You need a place to stay. Don't worry about the bill, I'll take care of your expenses." There was little warmth in his voice.

The place was an elegant boutique hotel. A bellhop helped a middle-aged couple into a horse-drawn carriage. This looked like a good place to stay except that Calhoun had brought me here. No doubt he had his *were* and human servants staffing the hotel, with orders to keep tabs on me.

"Any particular reason you chose this hotel?"

"You can stay anywhere you want. How about a Motel 6?"

Didn't matter where I stayed in Charleston, the werewolves would find me. Might as well be comfortable.

I got out without thanking him. The limo drove off. I had no luggage, as I'd left my knapsack in Angela's Maserati.

The concierge, a slender woman in a trim maroon skirt and a blue blazer, greeted me. "This way, Mr. Gomez."

It would've been a wonder if she hadn't known my name.

The concierge led me to a suite on the second floor. Miraculously, my knapsack rested on the bed. French doors opened onto a balcony with a wrought-iron railing.

She handed a plastic room key card. "Anything else?"

"Any way you can turn back the clock to last week?"

"If I could do that, sir, I wouldn't be working here."

"How about a drink?" Considering it wasn't yet noon, I ordered a screwdriver. For the orange juice.

She nodded and dismissed herself.

I opened my knapsack, certain that it had been searched. The Webley revolver was right on top. The cylinder still loaded. The extra ammo tucked next to my shaving kit. All my belongings were here.

Never figured werewolves to be so considerate. I'd bet it was Angela who'd taken care of this.

A steady breeze beat the leaves of the magnolia trees against the balcony railing. Out in the harbor, four tall ships rocked in the chop.

Farther to the south, rounding Fort Sumter, approached yet another tall ship.

More werewolves. The prelude to war. To what end?

Wendy, Lemuel, and his intern chalice were dead, killed at the mortuary. I'd had three attempts on my life, two by vampires and one by werewolves. And consider the fight in the alley behind Big Jack's and the brawl at the Blind Tiger Club.

The Araneum's original plan at defusing the werewolf war had been lost with Wendy. Calhoun was right; there was no time to commiserate. I had a mission. Find Paxton. I had to be hard. I had to encase my feelings in armor.

I got the Webley from my knapsack. The cylinder felt warm from the silver bullets in their chambers.

Standing in the doorway to the balcony, I watched the ships bring in more werewolves. I thought of ways to sink them: attach mines to the hulls, sneak on board to plant bombs or open the bilge drains. That could kill hundreds of werewolves but make everything worse. I couldn't kill Bourbon. I couldn't kill Calhoun. I had no options other than to wait and hope.

My ears tingled. Someone was in the hall.

Feet scuffed the carpet outside my door. Someone knocked.

My ears quit tingling. No threat detected.

I stuck the revolver in the front of my trousers and opened the door.

A young woman in a hotel staff uniform held a silver tray with my cocktail.

I invited her in and pointed to the table beside the sofa. She set the tray on the table and didn't act bothered by the Webley. Maybe that a guest could pack a firearm was a perk of the hotel. My first whiff told me "human" and that she'd recently had a latte.

I had to assume she was one of Calhoun's spies.

Out of habit, I let my gaze go to the choicest spot on her

neck, the hollow between the larynx and the muscles of her throat. My nose hunted for natural smells masked by the artificial fragrance of her deodorant and perfume.

Her pheromones and a trace of perspiration teased my nose like the aroma from a hot grilled steak. My stomach rumbled.

The attendant moved to the door. "Anything else?"

I loved that question.

"Do you know anything about vampires?"

She undid the top button of her blouse. "Mostly that their feeding habits are different from werewolves."

"Good, because I'd like something to eat." I removed my contacts. "And information."

CHAPTER 46

THE WOMAN'S aura lit up like I'd cranked up the electricity to a lightbulb. Her pupils dilated and her mouth sagged open.

I pulled her toward me and nudged the door shut with my foot.

I towed her to the sofa, her feet dragging on the carpet. I undid her uniform blouse midway and exposed a white lace bra.

I wrapped my left arm around her waist and held her in a clinch like we were about to tango.

I ran my fangs across her throat, using the tips to explore the curves of her neck. I knew where to bite, but I wanted to prolong the anticipation. I studied her smells and guessed her blood as type A-positive.

She shuddered and her breath puffed against my cheek.

I pulled away from her to again make eye contact.

Her irises were thin rings of hazel around the circular

chasms of her dilated pupils. There were no barriers between her mind and mine.

I asked for her name, in case it sounded familiar. It didn't.

I asked, "Do you work for Randolph Calhoun?"

"Yes." She turned her head, offering more of her neck. She wanted to get fanged. Bad girl.

"How did you know I'm a vampire?"

"I was told."

Damn. My hunger faded. Only a chalice is allowed to live with that knowledge. Lemuel Cohen had been the exception. According to vampiric law, to protect the Great Secret, I had to convert her into a chalice, turn her into a vampire, or kill her.

But she didn't answer to me; she answered to Calhoun.

"What happens if you tell anyone about werewolves? Or that I'm a vampire?"

Tendrils lashed from her aura. The penumbra grew bumps of fear. "I can't. It's forbidden."

"What happens if you do?"

"I'd be judged."

"What happens at this judgment?"

"Nothing good." Her muscles tensed and the bumps on her aura broke apart into a rash of blisters. "You don't come back the same, if you come back at all."

So *weres* did enforce protecting the Great Secret. I decided that if the woman did run her mouth, Calhoun would take care of her.

My thoughts turned back to my hunger. I brushed my teeth against her neck.

My fangs found the spot as if by divination. I pressed my fangs into her flesh. I wanted her blood to seep into my mouth, not spurt in.

The first drops welled around my fangs. A-positive, rich with metallic tones. I tasted fish—salmon?—lime, asparagus, bay leaves, a good Sauvignon Blanc. A fleeting oily trace of hemp.

The blood was no longer an appetizer, I wanted a full meal. Now.

I clamped my fangs hard. The blood shot into my mouth. Warm. Heavy. Delicious.

I gulped one mouthful, then another.

The rich taste swooned through me like an orgasm.

I wanted more. I wanted her to share my pleasure.

I pumped enzymes into her. The woman gripped tight and pressed her neck against my mouth. A shudder ran though her shoulders. Her chest heaved against mine. One breath puffed from her nose against my face. A second breath. A third, and she went limp.

The puncture wounds on her neck were larger than they should've been. I'd been too rough and careless. My fangs had gone too deep. I lapped an extra dose of healing enzymes into the wounds. That would help, but she still needed time for the bite marks to heal.

My amnesia enzymes would erase most of what had happened. She might remember seeing the Webley. No problem, let her tell the *weres* and their human servants that I had a gun. One more reason to stay clear of me.

I laid her across the sofa and slid a cushion under her head. I rebuttoned her blouse and placed a tissue on her punctures to soak up the blood until the wounds scabbed over.

I wanted the taste of her type A-positive to linger on my palate, but I had to wash the remaining blood down my throat. I finished the screwdriver.

Her blood collected in my belly, a satisfying mass like a sixteen-ounce slab of prime rib. My eyelids grew heavy. My mind no longer spun with my concerns. The fatigue returned and I was glad for the opportunity to cast off my worries.

I needed a nap. A quick one would do.

I got the pistol and returned to the bedroom. The woman could sleep off the effects of my fanging in the front room. The sofa looked comfortable enough.

I locked the door, cinched the blinds and the curtains, and let the room grow dark. I went to the bed, tucked the revolver under the pillow, and lay down on the covers.

I meditated on the sensations of feeding on the woman. I kept looping through the memory of my fangs punching through her skin, the warm liquid filling my mouth, the drenching of meaty, coppery blood. Each cycle of the loop was like counting sheep.

The next thing I sensed was my name being called. I opened my eyes and saw the muzzle of the Webley pointed at my nose.

Angela Cyclone held the pistol. "Wake up, sleepyhead."

CHAPTER 47

THE WEBLEY pointed right at my face. A half-dozen silver slugs waited in the cylinder. My *kundalini noir* jumped right to self-preservation mode. I flung my arm in an arc to swat away the pistol.

Angela stepped out of harm's reach and moved to the foot of the bed. She tossed the pistol in the air and caught it by the barrel.

She laid the gun on the mattress. "Anyone else, and you'd be coughing up silver right now."

The door to the front room was open, but I'd left it locked. "How'd you get in?"

"Your lunch, that woman"—Angela cocked her head to the empty sofa—"let me in. She has a staff key."

I settled against the mattress. Angela was right. For the last three days, I'd been the center circle of someone's target. Angela was no assassin and yet I'd been careless enough that she'd gotten the drop on me.

"Thanks for the lesson." I slid off the bed and put on my shoes.

I parted the curtains. The day was in the last throes of twilight. I took my watch off the nightstand. The time was 8:47 P.M.

Angela held a plastic garment bag. "We've been invited to a party."

"Tonight?"

"It's a soiree for the alphas from the tall ships. Remember the sign for the Werewolf Costume Ball?"

"I'm going?" A ball? What to expect? Boozing. Wild dancing? The images flipped through my head in a kaleidoscope of writhing bodies.

One hitch. "Werewolves." I made a seesaw motion with my hand to indicate my ambivalence. "Any problem that I'm a vampire? The last time you invited me out, I was the guest of honor at a riot."

Her smile made a sly curve. "Not for what you have to do."

"What? Dance. Have fun? I'm all over that."

Angela studied my waist. "You're a thirty-two around the middle. Thirty-four inseam?"

"That's right. What's this about? How did you guess that?"

"I know plenty about men's pants."

"An expert, I'm sure. What have you got for me? A costume?" I sounded like a little kid at Halloween. "As what? The king of the carnal carnival? The dean of debauchery?"

"Whoa, pony," she said. "You might want to change your expectations."

"About what?"

She opened the plastic bag and dumped new clothes on the bed: a white shirt, black trousers, and a gray vest.

"Try waiter."

CHAPTER 48

THE COSTUME ball was in the Old City Jail, not far from my hotel. We could've walked but Angela wanted to drive.

"Standing, dancing, whatever in these heels"—she pointed to her stiletto mules—"I can handle. But walking, even for a *were*, no freaking way."

The jail was a three-story building made of stone. Two towers guarded the front. With typical Charleston pride, Angela explained that the jail had originally been built in 1802 and had served as a military prison during the War Between the States, then was rebuilt after the 1886 earthquake.

"Not surprising, considering its notorious history, that the jail is known for its ghosts."

"Should I be afraid?" I asked. "The place will be full of werewolves. Compared to them, what's a couple of ghosts?"

We turned off Magazine Street for the yard behind the jail. A man dressed all in black trotted up to the Maserati. Angela rolled down her window.

I sniffed to see what kind of a creature he was.

Were.

He pointed to a row of luxury cars and SUVs in the middle of the yard. "Park over there."

Angela eased the Maserati between a BMW sedan and a black Suburban.

She was dressed in an abbreviated black sheath dress that covered her body like a whisper. Beads dangled from the hem. Angela explained it was what flappers would've worn if they'd had access to spandex. She got out of the car and tossed a shawl of gauzy gold material over her bare shoulders.

My waiter's outfit was polyester dork wear with extra points for the black bow tie.

I tried various ways to hide the Webley on my person, sticking it in the front of my pants, the sides, the back. I ended up slicing the lining of the vest and slipped the pistol inside, where it would ride shoulder-holster style between my rib cage and left arm.

We were in historic Charleston, yet the neighborhood was decidedly downscale. Lots of apartments. All well kept but none particularly fancy. The curious aspect was that all the doors facing the jail were painted haint blue in a vote of unanimous confidence in their belief in ghosts.

I followed Angela to a flight of concrete steps and up to a back door.

Once inside, Angela introduced me to Elizabeth Piexotto, the caterer and a *were*. She was on the reverse slope of middle age, blond hair in a pageboy cut, with a figure appropriate for someone with a craving for dumplings, meatballs, and petits fours. Her outfit was made of black leather with a tiny gold apron and big, fringed epaulets decorated with black skulls and crossbones. She wore turned-down patent-leather boots and waved a serving fork like it was a saber.

Angela said she had to attend to guests and left me with the doughy pirate dominatrix. Piexotto wrinkled her nose and slapped the fork against the top of her boot. "A vampire. Good. You're strong and won't sample the appetizers."

She rapped the fork on a stack of ice blocks, twenty in total. "Take these to the third floor."

I asked, "Where are the ice tongs?"

"Use your talons."

I couldn't carry more than two blocks. It wasn't the weight, but I could use my talons on only one block at a time. They sank into the ice, and cold shivers ran up my forearms.

I climbed the iron stairs to the top floor. The stairs ended on a landing in a hall between large holding cells with floor-to-ceiling iron bars along the front. Each cell was about forty by forty feet in floor space. The doors of the cells were wide enough to let two men enter side by side and had a dome on the inside at shoulder height. The dome was made of iron bars and allowed a guard to stick his head in and look into the corners of the cell at his right and left. I'd never seen such a fixture before and I was impressed by the ingenuity of the builders. The walls, floors, and ceiling were lined with iron plates to keep the inmates from digging through the stone. This place must have been hell in the winter and summer.

Another waiter—a dreadfully cheery human—unpacked bottles of wine and hard liquor from a stack of boxes along one of the walls. He set the bottles on a table.

I dumped the blocks into a galvanized steel tub beside him.

The waiter stopped working. "You have to chop that up."

"I was only told to bring the ice. Piexotto didn't say anything about chopping."

He jabbed a thumb into his chest. "Well, I'm the head of the waitstaff, and I'm telling you"—he stuck his index finger at me—"to chop the ice. Okay? And then we'll all be happy." He cocked his head to one side—he had a rainbow tattoo on his neck—and his voice rose an octave. "Okay?"

He was a shorty in tight-fitting clothes, as if to show off his skinny arms and build. Had he worn a green costume, he'd be one of Santa's elves—one with a piercing fetish; this guy had a dozen rings in each ear. I wanted to take that "okay" and jam it back into his mouth.

I asked, "Why not get bags of ice cubes?"

"Miss Piexotto says drinks taste better with chopped ice."

"Where's the ice pick?"

The waiter shrugged. "Improvise."

I raised a middle finger and hyperextended the talon.

"Oh my," he said, impressed. He studied the talon like he was measuring it. "What kind of a werewolf are you?"

Not only was I hired help but this goofball couldn't even tell that I was a vampire. "The pissed-off kind." With my teeth clenched in frustration, I pounded the ice blocks and reduced them both to a mound of shards. My finger ached from the cold.

Human helpers stood on stepladders and taped garlands of crepe paper to the ceiling and around the iron cell bars. Other helpers lay thin cable along the edges of the floor and connected the cable to speakers hanging from the walls. Someone tapped a microphone and feedback hummed through the speakers.

Mr. Head-of-the-Waitstaff stood beside the tub of ice. "About done with the pounding?"

"Whattaya think?"

"I think"—he touched his chin and rolled his eyes, then pointed to the other holding cells—"that you have more work to do. Every tub needs ice. We're going to have a lot of thirsty guests."

Eighteen more blocks remained below. That meant nine more trips. I didn't want to make even one more.

I was downstairs when someone whispered.

The voice sounded spooky and female.

"Over here."

She called from a small door waist level in the vertical shaft beside the staircase. I opened the door.

A woman who looked like she was made of smoke crawled from the opening.

I gave a quick look to my right and left, as I expected others to cry out in terror. A man carrying a roll of speaker cable passed by, oblivious to her appearance.

I was the only one who saw her. "What are you?"

"A ghost, darling. This is Charleston."

CHAPTER 49

THE GHOST stepped to the floor. A bare foot stretched from under a full skirt with a large apron. Her clothing and features were in shades of gray. Wisps trailed from the edges of her body and clothes. She stood on the floor and looked as substantial as a puff of vapor.

She wore a bandanna knotted above her forehead, Aunt Jemima style. Her clothes looked backward rural. Her skirt bore patches and stitches. In her mortal life, she obviously didn't have money, and I made the leap that she'd been a slave. I studied her face to see if I detected distinctive African features. A flat brow with sharp temples. A delicate nose that sometimes looked pointed, then softened into a round knob. Wisps of hair that curled from under her bandanna into tendrils of ethereal smoke.

What little I'd read about Charleston was that white slave masters weren't shy about tapping into the brown sugar, so many slaves were mulatto, biracial in today's phrasing. Hell, I'm Chicano, a cross-border transplanted descendant of the

Mexicans, who didn't exist as a people until the Spaniards shagged the native women.

But with the shades of gray, I couldn't read her features accurately and figured if it was important, she'd tell me.

"That's a lot of ice to carry. Try this," she said, referring to the compartment in the shaft. "It's a dumbwaiter."

"Yeah, I get it," I said, "but why are you here?"

"Because this jail is haunted."

"So it needs ghosts?" I asked.

"Not just any ghost. A haint. A boo hag."

She appeared to be in her late twenties, and other than a complexion made of swirling smoke, she didn't seem like a specter.

"You don't look like a hag."

"How about now?" Her mouth yawned and stretched open, wider, wider still, her teeth separated by lengthening gaps, her entire tongue protruding in an obscene undulating mass, until her head popped inside out.

That frightened even me.

Then her head snapped back to normal.

I said, "Does make an impression."

She rubbed the corners of her mouth. "If you think crow's-feet makes you look old, imagine what *that* does to your face."

"Are you the only ghost here?"

"Oh no. This place has plenty of them. Levina Fisher has staked out a good spot for the party."

"Who is Levina?" I asked.

"She was an innkeeper who drugged, robbed, and murdered her guests. They hanged her here in 1820."

"And you are not Levina?" I asked.

"Oh my, no," the haint answered. "I'm Deliah Joules."

I gave her my name, then said, "You don't talk like a ghost from the nineteenth century."

Deliah gathered her skirt and hopped on a table right on top of a platter of hors d'oeuvres. Her butt sank over the oysters Rockefeller and meatballs with mint jelly. "Unlike the other ghosts here, I wasn't hanged or murdered. I was killed in 1966 on this very spot. By accident."

"How so?"

She touched a black junction box on the wall by the dumbwaiter. Her finger went through the box. "There used to be a light switch right here. I went to turn on the lights, forgetting that I was soaking wet from coming in from the rain." She made a flick motion with her finger. "Zap. No more Deliah Joules."

"Ouch," I said. "You got here in 1966? What's with the clothes?"

"We had costume parties back then. Had I known this was going to happen, I woulda worn a nicer dress."

A ghost. "Am I the only one who can see you?"

"For now. It takes energy to make myself visible. The more visible, the more energy it takes."

"Where does this energy come from? You eat?"

"I wish. I'd love a dish of macaroni and cheese. We get our energy from sleep. That's why catching us is so iffy. See us today and it might be a month before we're able to make another appearance."

"What about a physical manifestation?"

"You mean like touching or moving something? That's like sprinting a marathon. Need lots of energy for that."

"Ectoplasm?"

She raised both hands in a show of disgust. "Yuck. You don't want to know where that comes from. Definitely not my scene."

"Is it true about you haints being afraid of water?"

She chuffed like it was a stupid question.

I asked, "What about haint blue? That you ghosts can't cross a threshold painted haint blue."

"What do you think?"

"I dunno, that's why I'm asking."

She smiled. The ethereal smoke swirled like whirlpools around the dimples in her cheeks. "Sure, we can cross it. Just because we're ghosts doesn't mean we've gone stupid."

"So the haint blue doesn't do any good?"

"It does, from a marketing standpoint. Think about it. People get haunted by a ghost. They paint the doors or hang drapes of haint blue. We stop visiting. The superstition works, meaning we ghosts must be real."

"You get around much?"

"Depends by what you mean 'much'?"

"You know King Gullah?"

"Who doesn't?"

"What kind of a vampire is he?"

"A bloodsucker. Same as you."

"How do you know I'm a vampire?"

"You're not?" She perked an eyebrow. The motion tossed a spurt of supernatural vapor from her temple.

"What do you know of this trouble between the werewolf clans?"

"The war. I'm looking forward to it."

Her answer puzzled me. "In what way?"

"I need the company. Seems every ghost in Charleston does nothing but talk about the good old days. Pirate days. The Revolutionary War. Antebellum parties. Most of them call a stereo a gramophone, for God's sake. I can't wait for someone to teach me how to get on the Internet."

Deliah pressed her fingers on the table as if punching a keyboard. Trouble was, her fingers went right through the table.

"Can you dish some dirt on the guests?"

"Depends." She slid off the table and looked at the guests and waitstaff filing past in the hall. "Unfortunately, my neighborhood has got some really boring people. I mean, this *is* Charleston and the folks I haunt think sneaking an extra doughnut is naughty behavior."

I asked, "Think you can tip me off in case someone wants to make trouble?"

"What's in it for me?"

"What do you want?"

Deliah sighed. "That's the problem. I don't know. I could ask for the usual. A dinner out. A date. But"—she passed her hand through her middle—"it'd be pointless."

Piexotto strutted by. She glanced at the remaining blocks of ice and frowned for my benefit. "The party starts in a half hour." She stabbed theatrically with the fork. The phone on her belt chimed and she snatched it, responding to the call by complaining, "Are we ready? You kidding? Not with this help."

"Time to get back to work," I whispered to Deliah.

She showed me how to use the dumbwaiter. The elevator creaked up a few feet and creaked back down.

Piexotto stared at the dumbwaiter. "I thought it was broken." Deliah walked behind her.

I tapped the control switch. "I guess I fixed it."

"Good," Piexotto said. "Now finish taking the ice upstairs."

Deliah made herself swell until her body matched Piexotto's proportions and she mimicked the caterer's gestures. I chuckled and Piexotto turned around to see what I found amusing.

"Later, Felix," Deliah said. The wall behind her showed through as she became transparent and vanished.

"Well," Piexotto snapped, "are you going to stand there or get to work?"

I loaded the dumbwaiter with eight blocks and sent the elevator on its way. I rushed up the stairs and met the dumbwaiter on the top floor. I chopped the ice and stocked the tubs. As soon as I had finished putting away the last of the blocks, Piexotto ordered me to take an apparatus made of wooden shafts with pulleys and ropes to a cell on the top floor.

I helped a *were* in black overalls and a tool belt put the apparatus together like this was a project from IKEA. He explained it was a replica "crane of pain," a torture device that had been used in the jail.

The crane resembled the letter *H* with two ropes dangling from pulleys on the top supports. Another set of ropes connected to pulleys along the bottom. Each rope wound through a separate winch. The victim was stretched between the ends of the *H* to suffer not only from having his (or her—I was told women were also tortured) limbs wrenched to the breaking point but also from being whipped and burned.

The handyman *were* and I were on our knees adjusting the bottom pulleys when a young woman in glasses came up to us.

Sniff. *Were.*

She wore a Revolutionary War period dress with the bodice cut so low she was one hiccup away from indecent exposure. She pulled the hooks on the ends of the ropes dangling from the crane part. "Very nice. Is this for play or decoration?"

"It's for play." The *were* handyman pointed to a large toolbox by the foot of the crane. "We got lots of toys. Paddles. Cat-o'-nine-tails. Gags. Clamps . . ."

"Where do I sign up?" Her eyes were lit up like she was famished and looking at a menu. "I don't want to miss my turn."

The handyman replied, "Downstairs. Make sure you fill out a limits sheet. Don't forget your safe word."

When we had finished assembling the crane of pain, I returned downstairs. Piexotto put me to work helping other waitstaff bring in trays of food from a van parked outside the back door. We shuffled back and forth like garden ants.

Me, vampire enforcer, a wage slave. The indignity.

We scattered the trays on tables about the jail and set up chafing dishes.

Meanwhile, Angela was busy schmoozing with other *weres* in various costumes: the colonial period; blue, gray, or butternut uniforms from the War Between the States; pirates; and a few wearing speakeasy fashion.

I was put to work on the bottom floor. My job was carrying trays loaded with hors d'oeuvres. But the garlic shrimp appetizers put me off, and I traded places with a waitress who offered flutes of champagne. She and I crisscrossed through the crowds. I thought the *weres* would needle me about being a vampire serving them. But I was the hired help and all but invisible.

The one time I ran into Angela, she plucked a flute from my tray. She kept talking to three guests, a man and two women dressed like the crew from *Mutiny on the Bounty.*

A twinge of humiliation stung me when Angela acknowledged me with a curt thanks. But as I turned away, she pinched my left butt cheek and smiled from behind the champagne flute, like both of us were in on the same joke.

I'd like it better if she was serving booze and I was the one schmoozing and pinching butts.

Eric Bourbon approached in the uniform of a Revolutionary War officer, complete with a powdered wig. He waved dollar bills and shoved them in my shirt pocket. "Go fetch me a real drink and I'll make it worth your while. I'd like a scotch and soda."

Asshole. "What are you doing here? I thought you and Calhoun were enemies."

"We're engaged in a truce. Even I'm welcome. I was curious to see what kind of a party the lopsided bastard can throw." He adjusted his wig. "Now run along and get my drink."

Bourbon waved, abruptly forgetting about me, and joined a group of *weres* dressed like Cherokees.

I took Bourbon's money out of my pocket and jammed it in the tip jar on the wine table. I got another tray of champagne flutes and circulated through the jail.

When I was back on the ground floor, there was a swell of agitated voices from the front door. My ears tingled, alerting me of trouble.

I wove through the crowd toward the entrance. A heavy black curtain hung over the threshold between the hall and the foyer.

I recognized the voice on the other side of the curtain.

King Gullah.

CHAPTER 50

WE DIDN'T need King Gullah crashing the Werewolf Costume Ball.

I parted the curtain and slipped into the foyer of the jail.

Gullah stood with Rooster by his side. There was a second curtain blocking the view from the street.

A pirate, a princess in white satin and strands of pearls draped across her cleavage, and a portly guy in the costume of Benjamin Franklin confronted King Gullah.

He was barefoot and dressed in rags, clean, but patched and tattered. The only touches that revealed his esteemed position as king were his crystal-knobbed cane and a simple crown of wrought gold. Gullah wanted to advertise his slave roots and at the same time let everyone know that he was a player in the local supernatural aristocracy. Rooster wore the uniform of a Union soldier, specifically an officer in the 54th Infantry Regiment.

The pretend Franklin held himself an arm's distance from Gullah. "But, Mr. Gullah—"

"King Gullah," Rooster interrupted.

"Of course. King Gullah," the pretend Franklin corrected himself. "But this is a private party."

"So I see. But how can you have a ball, especially a costume ball, and not invite me?"

"Really, please, King Gullah. You need an invitation."

"How about this for an invitation?" Gullah snapped his fingers.

Rooster reached to the curtain behind him and held it open. Eight young women filed through the gap. All wore puffy black bonnets and loose black cloaks that billowed to the floor.

The first girl in line had skin the color of a roasted coffee bean. The next girl had a lighter hue, that of coffee with a splash of milk. Each girl had progressively lighter skin. The last girl had an alabaster complexion.

The girls formed a semicircle behind Gullah. As if on cue, each girl doffed her bonnet and undid the neck ribbons holding the cloaks in place.

The first girl, with her inky complexion, wore a gown of royal opulence. Pearls and diamonds sparkled in the mass of curls on her head.

The next girl wore a less fancy gown, one of a lady of the upper class.

The next girl wore the dress of a well-off shopkeeper.

And so each girl wore a costume on a lower rung of the period's economic scale. The ice blonde who was last in line wore a short dress of rags that matched Gullah's outfit. But instead of a crown, she had an iron collar and iron wrist manacles connected by a rusty chain.

"These young beauties are my invitation," Gullah said. "Unless you object."

The girls gathered around the pirate and the chubby Ben Franklin look-alike and whispered in their ears. The men stood straighter, excited by whatever the girls promised.

"Yes, yes," Franklin said. "We can come to an agreement.

I mean, there are only nine of you, right, you and these lovely women."

Gullah touched his crown. "Only us."

The pirate looked at Rooster.

Gullah explained. "My lieutenant will remain outside. To guard against party crashers."

The woman in the princess costume stamped a foot. "Wait a minute. Where's my man candy?"

Gullah said, "That would be me."

Princess rolled her eyes. "Oh, please."

"In that case, if you feel left out," he said, "my entourage is very accommodating." He nodded and three of the girls raised their hands. "Bisexual. Not man candy but still very tasty."

The girls circled the princess. One took her left arm, the other her right arm, and the remaining girl lifted the train of the dress.

Gullah motioned with his cane. "Party time."

They paraded past me, Gullah at the rear. He stopped and gave me a deprecating once-over. He snagged the lapel of my vest. "What the hell are you doing?"

"I'm undercover."

"Undercover, my ass. Every mutt in this place can sniff you out as a vampire."

"How about you?" I asked. "What about the Araneum's warning to stay away from the werewolves?"

"I'm applying a creative interpretation," he replied. "The warning shouldn't prohibit me from adding a touch of class to this shindig. Besides, I'm here and the Araneum is far away."

We filed back into the jail.

Music reverberated from the speakers. A reggae beat, something from Burning Spear. In one cell, a group of women danced, while other guests cheered and sang along.

My ears tingled. An alert.

Someone was making their move.

I stood against the wall. I put my sixth sense on maximum gain. I touched the outline of the Webley inside my vest.

The crowd parted. A dozen *weres* entered, in the costume of Royal Navy sailors circa the late 1700s. They brandished cutlasses but, instead of flintlock pistols, had modern semi-automatics shoved into their waist sashes.

They guarded another *were*—their commander, Randolph Calhoun.

CHAPTER 51

CALHOUN WAS dressed like a sea captain, in a long coat of light blue cloth, dark blue breeches, and a chapeau with gold fringes. His clawed prosthesis added to the authenticity of his uniform.

His date wore a red satin dress and her hair was done up like Marie Antoinette's. She carried the front of her skirt off the floor. Slippers covered in red rhinestones kicked from under the mass of petticoats dragging about her ankles.

A knot of disgust twisted in my belly. Wendy hadn't been dead a day and here was Calhoun getting ready to party.

But I hadn't done much mourning either.

I had work to do.

With the full moon and Le Cercle de Sang et Crocs approaching, Calhoun had his duties to perform even if they meant having to serve as toastmaster of this costume ball.

Someone called my name. A faint voice. I looked around.

Smoke drifted from a lantern to the floor. A breeze should've pushed the smoke across the room. But the smoke stayed in place and grew into the silhouette of a woman.

Deliah.

She straightened her clothes and adjusted the scarf on her head. She looked the same as before, a blurry image in light and dark gray shades. No one but me seemed to have noticed her.

"I'm here to make good on your promise," she said.

"About what?"

"About what I want in return for warning you."

Warning? I glanced around.

"About who? What?" I asked.

She raised a finger. "The information is going to cost you."

"What do you want?" I couldn't imagine what would be on a ghost's shopping list.

"What I haven't had in a long time."

My first thought was that she wanted to get laid. Would be an interesting experience, as I haven't yet done a ghost booty call. Didn't think it was possible.

"Ice cream," she replied. "Strawberry."

Ice cream? "No problem," I said, though I remained curious about spectral shagging. "I didn't know you could eat ice cream."

She sighed. "I can't."

"Then what are you going to do with ice cream?"

"Nothing. I'm going to watch you eat it. You're going to let me know what's it like."

"Is there a catch? Like I have to eat a thousand pounds? Or wrestle a fat lady in a tubful of the stuff?"

She shook her head. "No. No. Just eat it." She pantomimed spooning to her mouth. "Share with me. The taste. The sensations."

"How? By telling you?"

"No, there's a ghost technique."

"Which is?"

"You'll see."

I pointed to the boxes and cartons of catered food. "You'll have to wait. There's no ice cream here."

"I trust you," she said.

"You were going to warn me."

Deliah leaned into the hall. Guests walked through her. She pointed to a petite blonde carrying trays of pastries stacked on each other. The woman wore a white chef's coat and had her hair pulled into a bun.

Deliah said, "She's carrying a pistol."

My *kundalini noir* began a slight tingle. "How do you know?"

"I'm a ghost. When she was in one of the storerooms, she made a call on her cell phone and I heard your name. Then she checked the gun."

The tingle in my *kundalini noir* spread to my ears and fingertips. My gaze followed the woman and I took a deep sniff in her direction. She was human. As small as she was, I could handle her. "Anyone else?"

"I've told you enough," Deliah said. Another breeze whisked through the prep room. "Remember, strawberry ice cream." Her features distorted, smearing, fading, and she disappeared like vapor.

The blonde set the trays on a table. I wanted to take my contacts out. I could read her aura and zap her with hypnosis. She'd tell me what she was up to. But if I took my contacts out, I'd be alerting the werewolves that I didn't trust them.

I had to admit the woman was a cool prospect. She didn't act one bit nervous, the way a normal person would if they were scheming to commit murder, especially if their victim was a vampire.

Deliah had said the woman carried a gun. If the woman knew I was a vampire, then the gun was certainly loaded with silver bullets.

The woman pulled foil off the trays. She grasped one tray, and when she lifted it from the table, turned and glanced at me.

Her look lingered for a split second, and in that quick exchange of glances, I could read the recognition in her eyes. She knew who I was.

The woman turned away and started for the hall and up the stairs.

I let her go up a couple of steps and followed. We were alone.

My ears and fingertips buzzed.

Danger.

From where? From who?

Damn you, Deliah, if you knew more, why didn't you tell me?

My hands clenched to keep from showing my growing talons. My fangs itched within my gums.

My sixth sense blared like a radar warning display, lights flashing, alarms whooping.

I whirled around.

A brunette in a white chef's jacket raised a pistol, a handful of black metal and right angles. A Glock.

I unclenched my hands. My talons sprouted to full length.

Her face blanched in fright. Didn't expect the full vampiric monty, did she?

She retreated, hesitating, the pistol muzzle quivering.

In a second, I'd be on her, gouging flesh, ripping her throat.

A tray banged across my head.

I dropped to a crouch, astonished. A flurry of pastries cascaded over me.

The blonde had thrown the tray to distract me. But the other woman had her gun out. She was the priority.

Droplets sprayed against the back of my left ear and the nape of my neck.

Heavy, burning droplets.

Garlic oil.

I cringed.

The blonde aimed a vaccination gun loaded with garlic oil. Her face was wadded in cruel fury.

The garlic sizzled my skin.

Get rid of the pain.

Now.

I sprang back into the prep room. I snatched a bottle of champagne from an iced tub. I cracked the neck of the bottle against the corner of the wall.

Foam sprayed from the broken bottle. I dumped champagne over my head and neck and scrubbed the cold bubbly against my ear and the back of my neck.

The bottle exploded in my hand.

The brunette aimed her Glock. She jerked the trigger, the gun went *bang, bang, bang,* and bullets whizzed through the air. Cups and food flew off the tables. Bottles of champagne exploded. Gouts of foam splashed across the room.

The blonde scrambled beside her. She raised the vaccination pistol, her face grotesque with hate and determination. Garlic oil spurted from the muzzle.

I staggered backward. My gun. Get my gun and shoot back.

Another spurt of garlic oil arced by my face. Tiny droplets landed on my cheek and each burned like the sting of a scorpion.

Get away. Now. I turned and launched myself at a window at the back of the room. My hands clutched the grate of iron bars blocking my escape. I drew myself onto the stone windowsill like a trapped racoon.

The women sprinted after me. They slipped on the champagne pooling on the floor and fell over.

I grasped the iron bars and pulled. The grate twisted and groaned. The windowsill cracked. One side of the bars tore free of the stone in a puff of dust.

Panic tore at my nerves. Get away before you're dissolved into undead paste.

I gave the bars another heave. The grate folded and revealed a hole just big enough for me to slide through.

I pushed my head through the hole and yanked on the bars to pull myself outside. Garlic oil splashed against my left hand.

The pain was like pressing a hot iron against my fingers. I jerked my hand away and tucked it against my chest. I pulled with my right arm and tumbled outside.

I landed on muddy ground. Inside the jail, my attackers clambered for the window.

I rubbed the back of my left hand into the mud to wash away the garlic oil. The cool, moist soil soothed the burning.

I rose to my feet.

The women wouldn't give up so easily. They'd come after me.

Let them.

I'd be ready.

I scuttled up the outside wall.

Instead of following me out the window, the woman with the Glock ran out the back door. She halted on the stairs and looked around.

Where was her accomplice?

The blonde came out. The two bunched together. I could get them both with one attack. I needed them alive, so I kept my pistol tucked away.

I pushed from the wall and fell upon them, silent as an owl.

The women collapsed beneath me. I tumbled to the right and landed on the woman with the Glock.

The breath froze in her throat. Her cry sounded as if it had been muffled by ice.

I swatted the Glock from her hand. My talons slashed through her wrist. For an instant, the wounds looked like parallel scratches, then widened into red furrows. Blood gushed from the slash marks.

The woman screamed and rolled down the steps.

I grasped one of her lapels and pulled her off the ground.

Her face went pale from terror.

I needed information.

Now.

I removed my contacts and put them in their plastic case, which I slipped back into my pocket.

The woman's red aura flared like fire consuming burning tumbleweeds. She grasped my wrist with her left hand. Blood stained the right sleeve of her white chef's jacket.

The blonde picked herself up off the ground. The vaccination gun lay in pieces, surrounded by a dark, noxious puddle. She ran for the parking lot.

I turned back to the brunette. "Not much of a team player. Looks like you've been abandoned."

I pulled her close to fang her throat.

Blam.

The report of a gun cracked the night air.

The woman went "Uh." Her arms went limp and she sagged against me.

Dead.

CHAPTER 52

A FIGURE APPROACHED from around the front of the jail.

A red aura bubbling with orange spots.

Eric Bourbon.

I pulled my Webley and aimed it at him.

He stopped, acting surprised that I'd drawn my gun. He held his Vektor pistol at the ready. "No need for congratulations."

I propped the woman on my knee. A red spot blossomed between her shoulder blades.

My bewilderment morphed into anger. "You killed her."

"Thought I was doing you a favor. Sorry. Couldn't be helped." He tried to sound apologetic, but his tone remained smug.

I laid her on the steps, stunned by Bourbon's indifference. "The bullet could've gone through her and hit me."

"Doubtful," he answered. "It was a silver slug. I'm sure it barely made it through her spine."

I didn't feel sorry for her. A minute ago she had tried to kill me.

A Pontiac Grand Am tore out of the parking lot.

The blonde?

The Pontiac's lights were off, but there was no mistaking the turmoil of the woman's turbulent red aura.

I stepped from the stairs, moving carefully, my gaze cutting from Bourbon to the fleeing Pontiac.

Bourbon slipped the Vektor into a holster of his colonial officer's costume and backed away. He wore the conceit of a poker player who was folding while he still hoarded a pile of winnings. Why? Because he'd killed the brunette or because the blonde was getting away?

Satisfied that I'd put enough distance between Bourbon and me, I took off after the car. I couldn't blow my supernatural cover by racing after her in public. A vampire running at traffic speed would raise questions.

I took a running leap and levitated to the closest roof. I jammed the Webley back into my vest. As I scurried across the roof, my feet sounded no louder than the scamper of squirrels. I jumped from roof to roof, bouncing from balconies and sailing over the streets.

The Pontiac turned on its lights. It screeched through an intersection, sped north on East Bay Street, and zigzagged through traffic. Even on flat ground at an undead run, I wouldn't have been able to keep up.

I doubted the driver was aware that I was chasing her. Still, she pressed her advantage in speed.

If she turned onto the bridge for Mount Pleasant I'd lose her for sure. But she kept going north on East Bay Street. I tracked her going under the overpass.

The high fences surrounding the docks pressed at us from the right. The distance between me and her Pontiac kept growing. After another minute, it was all I could do to keep her distinctive aura in sight.

Miraculously, her brake lights lit up and she swerved right. Dust hung in the air where she'd looped onto the shoulder of a road leading into the docks along the Cooper River.

I slowed to a trot.

A traffic bar blocked access through a gate leading toward the warehouses. The adjacent lampposts bristled with security cameras.

Where had she gone?

I stopped in the shadows by the fence. Hopefully the surveillance cameras couldn't see me unless they had low-light amplification or thermal imaging.

I listened.

The throaty groan of diesel engines echoed from the docks.

To my left. A car engine. The Pontiac.

I noticed a section of the fence that sat on small wheels. A gate.

How had she passed through the gate? Did she have a code or a card, or had the guards allowed her through?

I backtracked along the outside of the fence and searched for a blind spot between the cameras.

I was sure the guards were on alert. The Pontiac had come barreling through here, and unless security was in a coma, no way could they have missed her.

I found a place to levitate over the fence and slithered across the top like a snake, to give the guards less to see.

Once on the other side, I heard the quiet rumble of the Pontiac's engine. Its tires ground against gravel.

The car was up ahead. The engine noise picked up an echo that meant the car was in an enclosed space like an open bay or a garage.

My talons and fangs extended. I crept between rows of warehouses, levitating on the gravel so I made no more sound than a spider.

A door rattled closed.

I sped up.

The sound got louder.

I rounded the corner.

A door was about to descend to the floor of an open bay. The Pontiac sat inside.

I lunged and dove through the gap. I slid on my belly and tucked myself under the rear bumper into a bubble of stink from the catalytic converter.

The bay door rattled to the floor and locked.

I peeked around the left rear wheel of the car.

The driver's door opened. The blonde stepped out. Her bun was coming apart and she pushed the loose strands back into place.

Her aura bubbled with turmoil. A fuzz of distress scintillated along her penumbra. Her partner was dead, but she had survived the night. Until now.

The car's lights flashed once and the door locks clicked. She started for a door on the wall in front of the car. Her back was to me.

I scanned the bay. We were alone. No obvious security cameras.

Perfect.

Chapter 53

I PUSHED FROM the floor and floated over the Pontiac, brushing against the car with a touch as light as a helium balloon. I used my fingers to pull myself along.

The woman approached the door. The only noises in the bay were the clicking sounds from the Pontiac's engine and the woman's shoes scuffing the concrete.

Once on the other side of the car, I landed silently in the plume of garlic smell trailing her.

Just as she was about to touch the doorknob, I grabbed one of her shoulders and spun her around.

Her aura lit in horror.

I used only enough hypnotism to keep her paralyzed, but I showed my fangs. I wanted her to understand the trouble she was in.

Her eyes locked on mine and opened wide. There was nothing between her thoughts and me but terror.

Her face drained of color. And I hadn't gotten around to tapping a vein.

The garlic odor came from her coat, the residue of the garlic that had splashed against her when the vaccination gun broke. I unbuttoned the coat and slipped it off her shoulders. She wore a black T-shirt.

In my mind's eye, I saw the charred remains of Lemuel and Shantayla the intern. I felt the heft of Wendy's body when I carried her out of the burning mortuary. The sorrow of her death tore at me with morbid claws.

I squeezed the woman's arms. My talons dimpled her skin. I wanted her to feel pain, but I didn't want to draw blood. Yet.

I stared into the deep, empty wells of her pupils. She'd have no choice but to tell me the truth.

"Who are you working for?"

The skin around her eyes gathered. Her lower lip trembled.

Her resistance was strong but would break.

I asked her again.

Her eyelids quivered. Her mouth parted.

But she said nothing.

I increased the power of my hypnosis.

"Who are you working for?"

She squirmed.

"Is it Bourbon? Paxton?"

She clenched her eyes shut. "I can't tell you."

My *kundalini noir* caught. *Can't tell me?*

Suddenly bewildered, I hesitated. She had no choice. Since when could a human resist hypnosis?

I squeezed my talons into her arms. "Open your eyes."

Her muscles rippled in a spasm of agony. Her eyes opened, void of everything but naked fear.

I gazed deep and upped the power.

She still wouldn't talk. Someone must have put a subconscious block in her mind.

But who? Another vampire?

I had to break through that block.

How?

Through more pain. Like the pain Wendy suffered in her final moments.

I pulled the woman toward me.

I opened my mouth to completely expose my fangs and add to the dread of my bite.

I couldn't deny the pleasure rising through me, the bloodlust that lives hidden inside each vampire. We cast no shadow on the outside, but the inner shadow—the black stain of our damnation—points to the void in our soul.

Every whimper from the woman stoked a satanic muse imploring me to find pain, harvest misery, make music of her suffering.

I inched close to a dangerous fault. Was I causing this torment in order to get information or was this about vengeance?

Her eyes begged me to stop.

STOP.

The word reverberated in my mind as if Wendy had said it.

A wave of shame pulsed through my *kundalini noir*. I'd gone too far. I had let hatred and the lust for revenge take hold of my . . .

Heart.

Though I had no heart, only a dead muscle in my chest, there remained a space, a yearning for a better Felix to remain good and honest and virtuous.

Me.

Virtuous.

I let the woman go.

She sagged to the floor like her bones had turned to jelly. She fell to her side, her complexion anemic with shock, her arms drawn to her chest. Tears rolled down her cheeks. She sobbed and sank against the concrete floor.

But I felt no pity. I'd dirtied myself enough with this foul business, and if she wanted to talk, that was up to her. I retreated behind a moat of disgust that grew wider and deeper with every second.

But the moat disappeared when she said:

"Paxton."

CHAPTER 54

THE NAME lanced me. "What did you say?"

She repeated, "Paxton."

My frustration fused into anticipation. "Is he here? In Charleston?"

She whispered, "Yes."

"Where?"

The woman raised her face, her eyes bloodshot and sunken in wet red depressions, her mouth distorted, sweat gathering in the hollows of her neck. Every feature of her face showed the agony of fear and despair.

"Tell me," I shouted, the hatred returning like a fever.

The bay door began to rattle.

Startled, I whirled around, the Webley out, my finger on the trigger.

The front door opened and I turned around again. Calhoun came in. His red-and-orange aura swirled in alarm. He had changed from his costume to a dark business suit.

Three werewolves entered with him, among them Dan,

his bodyguard. Hairy. Brutish. Brandishing claws. Large pistol carried at the ready.

The bay door kept rattling open. Five more *weres* ducked inside. More claws. More guns.

They circled around me.

Though I was outnumbered, I saw myself huge, powerful, eager to shed more blood. My talons itched for the chance to rip flesh. I glanced to the ceiling. It was of simple prefab metal construction. Easy to break through. I'd attack the werewolves at thunderbolt speed, cause as much damage as possible, and escape through the roof.

Their auras roiled in excitement.

This was going to be a very ugly fight.

Calhoun didn't appear to recognize the woman or give an indication that he cared about her. He raised a hand and walked between his werewolves and me. "Easy, Felix. We're here to help."

"How did you find me?"

"My boys followed the Pontiac."

Calhoun motioned to his eyes, indicating that I put my contacts back in.

When I did, he mumbled, "Thanks."

He turned his attention to the woman. "Is she one of the assassins?"

"Yeah. She told me she works for Julius Paxton."

Calhoun stepped close to her. "What else did she say?"

"Nothing. He put a psychic block on her subconscious."

Calhoun yanked her hair. "You ruined my party."

"She's gone through enough." I started for him.

Calhoun's *weres* aimed their guns. I stopped and raised my hands, my revolver dangling from my fingers.

"Give me time. I'll get her to talk."

"She answers to me." Calhoun let go of her hair and wiped his hand on his coat. "I want to know how she got into the costume ball. She couldn't have done it without help from a *were*. Who? Bourbon?"

A car halted outside the open bay door. A Maserati. The driver's window scrolled down. Angela peered out, looking distraught, haggard.

Calhoun said to me, "Angela will take you back to the hotel."

"I'm not ready to leave." I pointed to the woman. "She's got information I need."

"Felix," Calhoun hissed, "go. I'll take care of her."

His *were* goons snarled a collective threat.

The woman started to sob.

He guided me to the open bay door.

"We'll tell you what she says." Calhoun's nose darkened and his fangs started to show. "Don't concern yourself anymore."

The woman's sobs deepened.

The bay door started to rattle close. The woman let out a long mournful wail. The bay door shut and muffled her cry.

I got into the Maserati.

The woman had tried to kill me, she wouldn't talk about Paxton, I had every reason to want her to suffer. But I didn't. "What's going to happen to her?"

Angela glanced back to the bay door with a bit of sympathy. "She knows about werewolves and the supernatural world. What are your rules?"

"Since she's human, I'd probably have to kill her to protect the Great Secret."

"Probably?"

I didn't want to argue. I didn't want to talk. I just wanted to get away. The night had already caused me to do many brutal things.

We drove to the end of the warehouses and turned for the gate. A security guard waved us through. *Were*.

How could the woman have passed through the gate without security's knowledge?

Who did the guards work for? Calhoun or Bourbon?

I thought about the vampire who had attacked us on Folly Island with the bat-wing outfit. He wasn't Paxton. So who was he? How did Paxton manage to put the note on Angela's windshield so soon after blowing up the mortuary?

I rubbed the Webley as if it were a talisman that could answer my questions and protect me from danger.

We were back on East Bay Street, going south, before

Angela broke the silence. "When are you going after Paxton?"

"As soon as I find out where he is. I need to find a way to flush him out of his spider hole."

"And then?"

"Finish business I thought was settled years ago."

I'd escaped Paxton's trap. Again.

It was my turn to be the hunter.

CHAPTER 55

ANGELA HALTED her Maserati in front of the Washington Arms. I expected her to wish me luck, to kiss me, but she didn't.

"What's the problem?"

Angela kept her gaze on the ship lights in the harbor. "There's all this trouble around me and I'm doing nothing but sitting and watching." Her voice softened with regret. "I could have protected you at the party."

"Don't worry about it."

"I have to do something to stop the war." She spoke in a whisper, as if thinking aloud.

I asked, "How?"

She shook her head. "I don't know." She put the Maserati in drive. "I have to go."

I started to get out when she grasped my hand. Her eyes shone like molten copper in the darkness of the car's interior. "Be careful, Felix."

"You, too." I thought about giving her a kiss until she let go of my hand.

I shut the door and watched her drive off, hoping that nothing happened to her. I'd already lost Wendy.

Once in my hotel room, I shed the waiter outfit, showered, and changed into my clothes. Then I called King Gullah.

A woman answered.

I introduced myself.

She said, "It's late. The King is indisposed."

"Then undispose him," I replied.

"I'll pass the message along." She hung up.

So much for my vampiric authority.

The last twelve hours had been all go, go, go. Fatigue crept in like a fog, dulling my alertness. I needed a meal and I needed to rest.

Rest, hell. I needed a good sleep. In a coffin, but the bed would have to do.

But I wasn't satisfied with the security arrangements. Last time I'd nodded off, Angela had snuck in here. Good thing she was on my side.

I locked the doors and lodged chairs under the doorknobs. Not sophisticated, but the racket of someone breaking in should alert me.

My phone vibrated.

It was Gullah's woman. "Where are you?"

I told her.

"The King will see you there tomorrow." She hung up before I had the chance to ask what time.

Someone giggled in the room next door. I put my ear to the wall. A woman teased, talking dirty. A mousy-voiced man replied.

The time was a quarter to three in the morning. I admired her dedication if she was willing to attend to such an early sprouting of morning wood.

An idea lit in my mind. I could hide in their room.

I went to my balcony and studied the one next door. One side of their French doors was cracked open and the sounds of their bed talk drifted out.

I removed my contacts. The landscape was dotted with

dozens of red auras from the little animals prowling the grounds.

With my Webley safely tucked inside my waistband, I climbed the railing of my balcony and leaped for their side. I landed as delicately as a mosquito.

The woman muffled a squeal. The man grunted.

I parted the curtain that billowed between the doors.

Two red auras mashed together on the mattress. Fireworks of excitement sizzled through the glowing penumbras. The woman and man, naked and going at it.

When I was a new vampire, I would've hesitated at disturbing them. Now bothering them for blood was the same as taking eggs from under a hen. God made me a vampire. I drink blood. God made humans. They have blood. Besides, hypnosis and the amnesia enzymes allow my victims to keep their dignity.

I levitated and glided into the room.

"C'mon. C'mon," the man grunted.

"Sorry to disturb the barn dance," I said. "But I need to crash here."

The man looked at me. His aura exploded. He sat up fast and rolled off the bed.

The woman lifted her face from the pillow. The penumbra of her aura brightened in concern. "What's the matter? What's going on?"

Her head swiveled to me, her eyes wide as king-size marbles. I zapped her hard, enough to keep her quiet for a few moments.

Lover Boy squirmed on his back. He reminded me of a scrawny hairless cat. Tendrils of fright whipped from his aura in knots of writhing sparks.

I fanged him first, then her. I gave them plenty of amnesia and pleasure enzymes, enough that they'd have trouble remembering what they'd started, much less that I had visited. The gaps in their memory would be a pleasant hum. I slathered on the healing enzymes so that when they woke up, they couldn't find my fang marks with a magnifying glass.

I left Lover Boy on the floor. Let him think he'd fallen off the bed in the passion of the moment.

I locked all the doors and closed the curtains. When morning arrived, I didn't want to let in one tiny crack of sunlight.

I got undressed and crawled into bed with the woman, to feed and to nod off. Her naked body warmed me like a giant hot water bottle. I laid the Webley beside me, just in case.

At ten in the morning I woke up. The woman rested her head on my shoulder. She murmured softly. Lover Boy snored on the floor.

Tonight, Le Cercle de Sang et Crocs. I could feel the hands of a clock scraping inside of me. I was almost out of time. Still no Paxton. Still no resolution between Bourbon and Calhoun.

I climbed out of bed, wary of what the day would bring, in need of a shave and coffee. I got dressed and decided that since it was daylight and my makeup needed a touch-up, I'd return to my room via the hall.

My room door wouldn't open. Of course, I'd left a chair wedged under the knob. I wiggled the door back and forth until the chair clattered to the floor.

No one had entered but me.

Then I sniffed.

A cadaver odor.

Faint.

Plus dried roses.

Vampire. But it wasn't me.

My talons zipped from under my fingertips. I clasped my revolver. The silver bullets waited for their deadly call to action.

What did my sixth sense detect?

My closet door was open. I'd left it closed. My knapsack was on the floor, surrounded by its spilled contents.

I entered the room, stood to one side, and carefully shut the door.

I kept silent and listened. Water ran through a faucet in a distant room. Someone changed channels.

But my room was quiet. I was alone.

The French doors to the balcony were closed, as I'd left

them. But the curtain rod at the top of one of the doors was broken and the curtain hung crooked.

I peeked outside through the doors. I was certain the intruder had come through the balcony. A vampire could levitate and pull himself up on the trellises.

What would account for the broken curtain rod? One side looked like it had been wrenched from the door.

The end of the curtain rod was shaped like an arrowhead and something small and black was snagged on one of the barbs. I pulled the object free. A piece of stiff black fabric the size of my thumbnail. Nylon? Kevlar? The wood at the top of the door was marred with scratches.

I tried to imagine something that high scraping against the door and snagging the curtain rod.

Like what?

The mechanical bat wings of the vampire who had attacked Angela and me. Paxton's assistant? The wings had caught the curtain rod, torn them loose, and left this piece behind. Clumsy vampire, he might want to rethink his trade as an assassin.

He'd probably come to finish me off with another silver-edged knife. I stashed the black material in my pocket in case I'd need it as evidence.

I gathered my knapsack and contents from the floor and set them on the desk. I inventoried my belongings and stuffed them back in the knapsack. The violation of the break-in made everything I touched seem dirty and tainted. Nothing was missing, fortunately. No clue as to what Bat Wing had been looking for.

I sat and let my thoughts settle into a pile of spaghetti. Loose facts, conjectures, and lies twisted over one another in an endless, tangled mess.

A despondent mood crept over me. What could I have done to save Wendy? Maybe if I hadn't blinded myself with pride and had left Charleston at the beginning, she might still be alive.

I still had her keys. I pulled them from my pocket and placed them on the desk. I'd been so busy that I hadn't bothered to examine them even as I had changed clothes. What for? She was dead and all her property burned to cinders.

I studied each key. There was the ignition key to her Ford, several worn brass house keys, a steel Master Lock key, a roach clip (used), and the key fob, a pistachio-size orange quartz with a gold fitting that attached to the key ring. A band of gold circled the middle of the crystal. I hadn't noticed the capsule before when Wendy had used these keys.

I held the crystal to the light and saw a dark object inside the translucent capsule.

This capsule couldn't hold much. A couple of aspirins. Maybe enough hashish for one bowl.

If this crystal was supernatural in origin, why didn't I detect it with the tuning-fork locator when Gullah and I sanitized Wendy's house? Apparently, since we were looking for the Araneum's property, this didn't belong to them.

I gave the crystal a twist and it loosened about the gold band around the middle. For an instant I thought it might contain a fragment of vampire parchment. The crystal came apart. Smelled like nothing. No parchment.

A piece of gold foil slipped out and hit the desk with a distinct *ping*. The foil unfolded in the manner of a raft inflating, becoming a solid-looking ring of golden metal, about two inches in diameter and thick as a pencil.

I grasped the ring. It weighed more than it should, even if made of solid gold. I pinched the ring, expecting it to deform, but it remained hard as steel.

I studied the inscriptions along the flat sides of the circumference. Some kind of runes. No clue about the meaning.

This hoop of gold was too small to be a bracelet—for someone of regular human size, that is.

I set the ring on its rim to see if it would balance. The ring fell over with a crisp *ping*, louder than before. The *ping* lingered for a moment before trailing to silence.

I held the ring an inch off the desk and let it drop. It bounced and pinged louder, the sound as sharp as the crack of breaking glass that faded to a lingering hum. The ring fell over and wobbled in a circle to lie flat. The space inside the ring began to glow blue.

I sat up, amazed. The ring settled still, and the glow disappeared. What was this device?

I dropped the ring again; it slipped from my fingers and I put an inadvertent spin to its fall. The ring bounced, pinged louder than ever, and began to spin on its vertical axis. The space inside the ring again glowed blue. The *ping* modulated into a voice.

Wendy's.

CHAPTER 56

MY ROOM phone buzzed, bringing me out of my trance. I must have sat there an hour, mesmerized the entire time by Wendy's magical talking ring.

I now had proof that Bourbon had murdered Inga Latrall. Was this the reason Wendy had come to the Atlas Mortuary? To show me this ring?

The phone buzzed again. I picked up the receiver and answered.

The concierge confirmed that it was me and added, "You have guests arriving in the lobby. Please come down and receive them." She clicked off.

The only guest I expected was King Gullah. By "guests," I'm sure the concierge meant Gullah and his parade of gangsters.

I took the talking ring and slipped it into a front trouser pocket. The ring pressed against my thigh, heavy in weight and importance.

I stuck the Webley into my waistband and fluffed my shirt to hide the pistol.

When I got to the lobby, the two bellhops, the desk clerks, and the concierge were staring anxiously at the front door.

One of Gullah's sidekicks stood outside, eyes covered by sunglasses, hands clasped in front of him like a guard from the Nigerian secret service.

A white Escalade was parked at one end of the drive. Gullah's green and gold Impala cruised to the curb and halted. The second Escalade waited behind.

His two female chalices—still looking as well fed as before, in matching shocking-pink hot pants and tiny bikini tops—tottered to the hotel entrance on gold platform stilettos. They carried what I first thought were push brooms, then realized were frames, which they held upright before the door. They propped a haint blue cloth over the entrance. Gullah loved his hokey ceremonies.

The gangsters had dismounted from their Escalades and formed a cordon around the Impala. Yo-Yo opened the car door. Rooster stood beside him.

King Gullah unfolded himself from the Chevy. Instead of a skullcap, today he wore a straw porkpie hat. And rhinestone-studded sunglasses. Today's dashiki was red, printed with brown human figures of an African design. Rooster and Yo-Yo nodded in a salute of respect, as though Gullah had just arrived from another continent.

He strode for the hotel entrance, his bearing imperial, with Yo-Yo and Rooster trailing. Yo-Yo carried a cardboard box big enough for a six-pack.

Gullah tipped his head forward to walk under the haint blue cloth. Rooster stopped beside the girls. Yo-Yo continued after Gullah.

The concierge sidled close. She bleated, "Will there be trouble?"

"Not if you do what he says."

She wrung her hands and an anxious wheezing came out of her throat.

"Relax," I said. "He's a good tipper."

Gullah entered the lobby, his right hand outstretched like a politician after my vote. We shook hands.

I was eager to show him Wendy's talking ring but didn't want to return to my suite. Didn't feel safe. Too paranoid. That would be the obvious place for Gullah and me to meet.

I turned to the concierge. "Can we get some privacy?"

"We have a special room." She hurried us through the empty main dining room to the wooden paneling on the back wall. She pushed against one of the panels, and it sprang open like a door.

"Interesting," Gullah remarked.

"It's from the Prohibition days," she explained.

We entered a small room paneled in dark wood. Antique bureaus and cabinets crowded against the chairs surrounding a dinner table in the middle of the floor. Paintings of hunting dogs and sailing ships hung on the walls. The room smelled of whiskey and cigars and secret deals.

Gullah panned the room and mugged in approval. We took adjacent chairs at the table.

"Drinks, if you please," he said to the concierge. "I'll have a Crown Royal. Neat." He aimed the lenses of his sunglasses at me.

"I'd like a manhattan."

"And the Crown Royal he didn't order . . ." Gullah added, "bring it to me."

The concierge said, "Of course," and left.

Yo-Yo set the box on the table. Gullah signaled for him to leave. The door closed behind him.

Time for our secret deals.

CHAPTER 57

GULLAH REMOVED his sunglasses. His eyes shone with a red vampire glow. He opened the box. He pulled out two plastic straws, two bags of blood (type B-negative), and paper napkins. "Wasn't sure about the feeding arrangements in this hotel."

He offered a bag and straw. I thanked him. The bag was warm. I wasn't hungry, but a snack of human blood should help me stay calm. After my days of getting slammed around Charleston like I was in a pinball machine, Wendy had given me information I could use to get Paxton. But how?

Gullah fanged his bag and inserted a straw. I did the same thing. The blood had a stale taste. The donor ate too much processed food.

Gullah sucked on the blood. His expression remained as inscrutable as looking into a dark well. "It's your nickel. Bring me up to speed."

There was much to share. What had happened during the costume ball, how I forced one of the would-be assassins to reveal Paxton's presence in Charleston, the visit by the bat-wing vampire, and my discovery of Wendy's talking ring.

The room grew so quiet I could hear our watches tick. Gullah put his bag of blood on the table. He wiped his mouth with a napkin and left a crimson stain. "You're taking a long time to answer. You got that much to tell?"

"Where do I start?"

"With what's most important."

The ring. As soon as I showed him the ring, I knew everything about it would come gushing out. I reached for my pocket.

Gullah's eyes gave a look I didn't like. I remembered his words: *I'd slit the throat of my own brother if it bought me an extra day.* Gullah's pledge of survival had another name: treachery.

When I'd called Gullah last night, I couldn't wait to discuss a strategy to find Paxton. But the ring had changed that plan. The ring contained valuable information, information that might tempt Gullah, I now realized, to turn on me.

So I told him about the attack in the jail. I elaborated on the vaccination gun loaded with garlic.

Gullah said, "You can skip that. I've done heard all about it."

"Anybody mention the haint, Deliah?"

Gullah's facade of stoicism cracked. His mouth curled pleasantly. "You saw her?"

"She saved me." I told him what had happened.

"How is she doing?"

"She's still dead."

Someone knocked. Yo-Yo opened the door and entered with a tray. A manhattan for me, a pair of shot glasses with Crown Royal for Gullah. He set the drinks on the table and left. The door closed.

I put my bag of blood on the table. My lack of trust in Gullah had soured the taste and I'd lost my appetite and my thirst for the manhattan.

Gullah raised one of the shot glasses. "To survival."

"I'm interested in more than survival."

"I can see why you're such a dangerous vampire. You are more than an enforcer."

"How's that?"

"You're a crusader. A vampire on a mission. A vampire with a conscience."

He gestured with the shot glass. "Here's to crusades."

I raised the manhattan. "What are your crusades?"

"Other than keeping my black ass upright, aboveground, and in style"—Gullah emptied the shot glass in one gulp—"ridding the world of Crown Royal one drink at a time."

I toasted, "To crusades," and sipped my manhattan.

A plan came to me. The blond assassin knew Paxton. Calhoun said she'd needed help from a *were* to get into the costume ball. She was the link between Bourbon and Paxton. I knew exactly what to do with the ring. It would be valuable to Calhoun but even more so to Bourbon. I'd trade the ring for information on Paxton's whereabouts.

Gullah drank the second Crown Royal and I finished the manhattan. My mood was like that of a kamikaze pilot drinking his ceremonial sake before the final mission.

I told him about my interrogation of the blond would-be assassin from the costume ball. "She confessed that she worked for Paxton and that he is in Charleston."

Gullah grunted, pleased. He waited for more details.

"That's all I have. Paxton must've put a psychic block on her subconscious. Calhoun took her from me before I could get through."

Gullah looked about the room but his gaze was far away. "If Paxton's in Charleston, I'll find him."

"How?"

"How would you?"

I put my hand over my pocket and traced the outline of Wendy's talking ring.

"Are we done?" Gullah held his sunglasses in both hands.

"For now."

He slipped the sunglasses on. "Later, then."

He reached over his shoulder to the door and knocked. Yo-Yo opened the door.

Gullah said, "Mr. Gomez and I have concluded our business. Tell the crew to get ready to leave. Get one of the boys to police this." He motioned to the bags of blood, the straws, and the bloody napkins.

I followed Gullah out the room and through the lobby. I halted at the entrance.

The two gangster chalices held up the haint cloth on the other side of the threshold. As soon as Gullah cleared the cloth, he pulled a cigar from the pocket of his dashiki. He put it in his mouth and angled his head toward Yo-Yo.

The gangster flicked a butane lighter and lit the cigar. Without breaking stride, Gullah puffed. Rooster and the gangsters formed a square around him. One of the gangsters hustled ahead to hold the door open to the Chevy Impala.

Gullah got into the car. The girls folded the haint cloth and clip-clopped on their stiletto heels to the street. Together with the gangsters, they climbed into their respective Escalades. The convoy pulled away from the hotel curb and headed toward Ashley Avenue.

The concierge and the bellhops clustered around me. When Gullah's caravan cruised out of sight, the concierge released a grateful sigh. She raised an arm to wipe her brow and the armpit of her jacket was dark with perspiration. She held a binder clip of hundred-dollar bills. Gullah's tip.

Time to talk with Bourbon.

I called his office. His receptionist said he was gone for the day.

"Know where I could find him?" I asked.

"He went home. Something about . . . are you that guy from Colorado?" With every word in her question, I could hear the spite build in her voice. "The one who was here four days ago?"

I wasn't going to stoke her resentment and dodged the question by asking, "Something about what?"

"Why don't you go fuck yourself." The phone disconnected with a *click*.

Not the best example of Southern manners.

Bourbon lived a few blocks from the hotel and I could walk to his house in minutes. I took Lenwood Boulevard. Tourists wandered the sidewalks, strolling at a relaxed pace, reading guidebooks and taking pictures. Oblivious to the werewolf war that rumbled beneath their feet like a volcano about to explode.

I stopped beside a hedge where I could observe Bourbon's house unseen. I had to assume that the receptionist had warned him.

There was no one on the street. I slipped off my sunglasses and contacts. I didn't spy any sentries. No telltale auras in the windows.

I circled the block to approach the house from another direction. From this new perspective, I could scan the other side of the house. No guards masquerading as groundskeepers. No auras in the windows or lurking in the shadows of the house. Bourbon's BMW was in the carport. A couple of sedans and the H2 Hummer were in the driveway.

Who was he meeting?

Werewolves?

Paxton?

Or both?

Bile floated up my throat, a bitter scum that tasted of anger, treachery, and violence.

The wrought-iron gate of the driveway clattered open.

A Maserati turned into the driveway.

Angela?

CHAPTER 58

MY *KUNDALINI noir* about leaped out of my aura in astonishment.

Angela was in Calhoun's clan. What was she doing at Bourbon's house?

Her Maserati halted behind the Hummer. She got out. Her penumbra bristled with anxiety. She wore a platinum-colored dress, low back, thin shoulder straps. High heels as usual.

She climbed the steps of the piazza and rang the bell. The door opened, revealing the glimpse of another *were*'s aura. Angela went in and the door shut behind her.

Why was she here?

I found a place along the fence hidden from view by a magnolia tree. A quick look around to make sure no one watched, and I levitated over the fence between two sections topped with *chevaux-de-frise*.

Once on the other side, I picked my way to the house and climbed a drain spout to a balcony on the second floor.

The door had a window and no curtain. The room inside was a study, with a globe and a brass sextant atop a vintage rolltop desk, a brass telescope on an adjacent nightstand, a swiveling wooden armchair in front of the desk. The room appeared seldom used. The bric-a-brac was meant to look like faux heirlooms. Why have a past when you can buy history?

I put my hand on the window and rubbed my palm over bumpy imperfections in the antique glass. I forced my *kundalini noir* to remain still and rigid like an antenna.

I collected vibrations transmitted through the glass. A jumble of voices. Footsteps on wooden floors. Footsteps muffled by carpet.

I couldn't determine the exact number of occupants. Counting Angela, at least five. Maybe six. Maybe more. I couldn't tell where they were. On this floor? Below? The third floor?

The important thing, no one had sounded the alarm. I had gotten this far undetected.

I readied my revolver. My talons extended midway.

The door was unlocked. When I opened it, a canine smell wafted out. I levitated, glided inside, and closed the door behind me.

Voices echoed down a hall from my right. Male voices. One woman's.

Angela. Her voice quaked with nervousness.

My skin prickled at the thought that she might be in danger. I brought the revolver up and crept down the hall in the direction of the voices. My feet slipped quietly above the floor. I hadn't yet been able to sneak up on a *were*, so I had to take it extra slow and careful. The hall continued past a stairwell and several rooms.

Some of the doors were closed. The open doors revealed rooms filled with more vintage junk.

My fingertips and the rims of my ears buzzed in alarm. My sixth sense wasn't alerting me to a specific threat, only that I was in danger. Like I wasn't aware of that already.

The voices echoed louder.

Angela. Sounding more nervous.

And Bourbon. His voice derisive and skeptical.

I halted at the corner. My shoulder hugged the wall.

The air was thick with adrenaline and male wolf musk.

Angela said, "You can't be that blind to the consequences."

Bourbon replied, "I expect consequences. You're talking to me like I haven't put much thought into this."

This *what?*

"If Calhoun wants to avoid a war, let him submit to me," Bourbon said. "When he rolls on his back at my feet, then I'll know he's sincere."

"He won't do that," Angela said.

"And you expect me to?" Bourbon asked, his voice gruff and mean. "Isn't that why you're here?"

I sprang from the corner, pistol raised, talons and fangs extended.

Angela was facing Bourbon, her back to me.

I recognized two *weres*, Sean Moultier and Jerry, the engineer I'd run into twice before. Four more *weres* stood about the room, which looked like a gaudy interpretation of Victorian fussiness. Lots of velvet, tassels, and more bric-a-brac.

Bourbon and his goons put their stares on me and growled. Their red and orange auras burned in fury.

My gun had six bullets, one each for the goons. I'd have to take care of Bourbon fang to fang.

But his *weres* were carrying guns. And they were transforming into werewolves. Coarse hair. Hulking muscles. Long claws. Fiery auras.

My ears picked up an intense buzz. More danger.

Behind me, three werewolves approached from the hall. From a door at the other side of the room, another three werewolves appeared. Two were dressed as groundskeepers and trained their leaf blowers on me. The blower nozzles hooded the muzzles of triple-barrel, rapid-fire shotguns.

Thirteen *weres*. One vampire. If I was a gambler, I'd lay odds against myself.

I stepped into the open, my revolver level, daring to see who would be the first werewolf to die.

Angela raised her hands, gesturing for me to take it easy. Take it very easy.

One shot from me and I could kill a werewolf. With Charleston bursting at the seams with them, that news would inflame the packs enough to ignite the trouble I was supposed to avoid. But I had no intention of letting them hurt Angela or me. I was neck-deep in bad choices.

I cocked the hammer of the Webley and fixed the sights on Bourbon's sternum. The big silver slug would blast the heart right out of his lupine chest. If there was a war, he wouldn't be part of it.

Bourbon grabbed Angela's shoulder and pulled her between him and me. Coward. She flinched, clearly nervous that a brash move by any of us might start the gunfight.

Sean and I made eye contact, a fleeting catch of each other's attention. In that brief exchange I didn't see anger or fear; I saw deceit. About what? He relaxed his grip on his pistol, a SIG Sauer, and the muzzle drooped to the floor.

Bourbon taunted, "Dumb move, you walking leech, coming here alone. I could kill you in self-defense and get away with it."

"I didn't come to fight, Eric. I came here to trade."

Bourbon tilted his head in puzzlement. Tufts of hair grew from his elongating ears as they jutted in my direction.

"I give you information," I said, "you give me Julius Paxton."

"Why should I know where he is?"

"Because one of the women who came after me admitted she worked for Paxton. She and her partner needed a *were* to get them into a party. You killed her partner. To shut her up. Because you knew what they were up to."

Bourbon scowled and took a step back like I'd cornered him with the truth.

The room suddenly got refrigerator cold. A breeze ruffled curtains, lampshade tassels, and the leaves of the dried flowers in the vases on the mantel and tables.

One of the werewolves looked about. "What the hell?"

I wondered the same thing.

Bourbon glanced about anxiously, at the windows and the

doors. A couple of the werewolves shivered and hunched their shoulders, auras pulsing.

Just as abruptly, the curtains went slack and the room was warm again.

The werewolves traded baffled looks. Bourbon gave them a chastising glare. They stood straighter and adjusted the aim of their pistols.

Bourbon asked, "Is Paxton this important to you?"

"The question is, how important is he to you?"

Carefully, slowly, deliberately, I reached into my trouser pocket and pulled out Wendy's talking ring. I held it by the rim for all to examine. Light gleamed across the golden hoop.

Bourbon leaned from behind Angela for a closer look.

I knelt on a section of bare wooden floor while I panned my Webley menacingly from *were* to *were*. I placed the ring on the floor and held it upright with my index finger. "You might want to clear the room," I said to Bourbon, "unless you want the world to know your dirty secret."

"Everybody stays," he barked. "Since when do we trust vampires?"

"Your call," I replied.

The *weres* kept their eyes fixed on the ring.

I extended a talon from my middle finger and gave the ring a hard flick. It made a loud *ping* and began spinning.

Angela, Bourbon, and his *weres* would soon learn the truth about the death of Inga Latrall.

CHAPTER 59

THE RING spun on the floor until it looked like a blurry golden sphere. The glowing center expanded until it was a grainy blue cloud around the ring. The pinging noise pulsed erratically.

The grainy cloud expanded and formed the head and shoulders of a woman. Her complexion and hair color looked washed out, like a color photo that had been left to fade in the sun. But there was no mistaking the face. Wendy Teagarden.

Her lips moved, but the pinging warble was incomprehensible. After a moment it sounded like a voice speaking at the far end of a distant tunnel.

Wendy's truncated image looked odd, but there was no denying the magic as everyone hushed and stared, eyes transfixed and wide in amazement.

No matter from what direction you looked at the ring, Wendy faced you directly. *Weres* on opposite sides of the room saw the same image.

By the time we could make out her voice, she was already in midsentence. ". . . in the early morning, one of my crows brought me this." She held up a thumb drive identical to one Gullah and I had buried under thermite powder before we torched her home. We might have destroyed that same thumb drive, but no matter.

The *weres* stared with their snouts open. Jerry's face sagged in distress.

Wendy said, "This thumb drive belonged to Jerry Dunlap."

He flinched as if the words had scorched him. His cheeks flushed red beneath the thinner patches of fur.

Wendy continued: "Jerry sabotaged Inga Latrall's Cessna Citation. He infected the onboard flight computer with a virus that shuts off the avionics and jams the controls. A coded radio message activated the virus and the jet crashed into the sea. Once the flight computer loses power, the virus is erased and undetectable." Wendy brandished the thumb drive. "This contains a copy of the virus, Jerry's notes planning the attack, and audio files he recorded of his discussions with Eric Bourbon, possibly to use as blackmail."

I reached through Wendy's image, put my hand on the ring, and stopped it. "We've heard enough for now." Her image and voice disappeared. "You can trust me to keep my mouth shut, but I don't know about the rest of your crew. I know shit about Lycanthrope Law, but I wouldn't want to be an accomplice in the murder of a top alpha."

Weres gaped at Bourbon and Jerry. Someone whispered, "They killed Inga Latrall."

"Lies," Jerry hissed. The hair on his face grew thick and his ears lay back. "Pure lies. Bullshit. Bourbon, do something."

Bourbon was seething. "Blackmail? You idiot. You've screwed us both."

Sean gave the *weres* on either side of him an elbow nudge. They stepped back.

Bourbon sensed the misgivings of his werewolves and he bellowed, "You've all known what I've wanted from the beginning. It's either the territory or war. No one is going to betray me." He glared at Jerry. "You rat. Sean, take him down."

Jerry hunched his shoulders and ruffled the hair on his neck. "So, this is how it ends, Eric? You, the great werewolf alpha, brought down by a dead dryad and a vampire." He dropped to a crouch and aimed his pistol. "Bring it on. Let's go down fighting like werewolves. None of us lives forever."

"Take him," Sean ordered.

The *were* to the left of Jerry faked a punch. Jerry parried the blow. The *were* to the right slapped the pistol from Jerry's hand and kicked his ankle. He spun around, claws slashing, his leg collapsing. The *were* to the left clubbed him on the back of the head with the butt of a pistol.

Jerry crumpled to the carpet, facedown.

The *weres* each grabbed one of Jerry's wrists and kicked him in the armpits, dislocating his shoulders. Jerry let loose a gruesome howl. The *were* on the left stomped his head, and Jerry lay quiet and limp. His aura dimmed.

These two were not simply *were* goons, they were *were* ninja goons. And I expected to fight them?

Sean stood above Jerry, aimed his SIG Sauer, and delivered the coup de grâce. Blood spurt from the back of Jerry's skull. Smoke curled from the bloody hole while the wound hissed. Silver bullet. His aura vanished. One of the goons picked up Jerry's pistol and stuck it in the back of his trousers.

Three nights ago, when Jerry and another *were* had attacked me, Sean had intervened to save me. Then he'd told me to keep the episode quiet. Was he planning a double cross of his own? Using me?

He shoved his pistol into a holster on his waist. His steely glance in my direction seemed to say: *Jerry knew you and I had talked before. But Jerry won't be talking.*

Mindful of Sean, I continued with my plan.

"Here's the trade." I placed the ring flat on the floor. "This ring for Paxton."

"Not so fast, bloodsucker." Bourbon grasped Angela's arm and spun her to face me. "How about I put this wrinkle in your plans." He shook her arm. "Tell him, bitch, why you are here."

Angela closed her eyes in shame.

I rose to my feet and put the front sights of the Webley on Bourbon's nose.

He slipped a finger under one strap of Angela's dress and gave a light tug. "Your friend offered herself to me. That's right—she came to me."

Angela opened her eyes and they begged me not to judge.

"She cited Lycanthrope Law," Bourbon explained. "In the case of a dispute between clans, a favored female from one clan could offer herself to the alpha of the other as a tribute of peace." He let go of the strap and ran a hand down her arm. "That's if I want her."

Angela shivered in loathing.

"Do you think she's worth it? Her body and passion, a gift. *Provided* I submit to the decision of Le Cercle. *Provided* I kiss Calhoun's ass."

His nose morphed into a dog's snout. Fur sprouted on his cheeks, neck, and the back of his hands. "You are a fine bitch, but what makes you think what you've got between your legs is worth more than the title of alpha of the territory? What makes you think I want you?"

He leered at me. "What is your problem, vampire? Does this bother you?" He ran his hand down Angela's arm. "She's not one of your kind."

She clenched her eyes in disgust, as if his fingers had been a tongue.

Every time he touched her, it was like a screw giving my *kundalini noir* another turn until the pressure of my rage made my hands shake.

Don't give in to anger. I needed a clear mind and steady hands to save her.

Suddenly all the werewolves, including Angela and Bourbon, straightened up. Their attention turned to the hall.

A door creaking echoed from the stairwell.

My ears buzzed.

Something thumped the floor, a rhythmic tapping that matched the cadence of a man walking.

The werewolves kept their claws and guns pointed at me, but they appeared confused by what was the bigger threat, me or whatever approached from the hall.

The thumping grew louder, an unhurried, ominous sound that neared the corner where the hall emptied into the room.

King Gullah entered.

CHAPTER 60

KING GULLAH measured his steps with the thumping of his crystal-topped cane against the floor.

The werewolves couldn't decide who to aim at, and their pistols moved back and forth between Gullah and me.

Gullah had changed into a cream-colored outfit and his dashiki had swirls of gold and white. He still wore his pork-pie hat and chewed the butt of an unlit cigar. In a new affectation, he wore a kidskin glove on his left hand.

He glanced at Jerry's corpse. "Looks like a work-related injury, am I right?"

Bourbon said, "Gullah, get out. This is not your concern."

Gullah took the cigar from his mouth and flicked it over his shoulder. "But it is—I need Felix to walk out of here."

"Old man, you might be the head vampire in Charleston, but I'll give you to the count of five before my wolves tear into you."

"I wouldn't be so sure of that," Gullah answered.

The windows exploded. Glass shards sprayed across the room.

A bomb? I raised an arm to cover my face. I thought about Angela and saw her and Bourbon turn their heads from the flying glass.

Yo-Yo and Rooster somersaulted through the windows and stuck their landings in Olympic perfection on either side of Gullah. Both vampires held MAC-10 submachine guns in each arm.

"Silver bullets, in case you're wondering," Gullah explained. "Nothing like automatic weapons to even the odds."

"I'm working a deal, Gullah," I said. "Bourbon's going to tell us where to find Paxton."

"There's no need," Gullah replied. "I got a lead on him. Let's go before things got too messed up."

A lead on Paxton? Another damn surprise in a day full of surprises. I could follow Gullah out of here. Find Paxton and finish him. Shake the Charleston dust from my shoes and go home.

Bourbon grasped Angela's hair and twisted. She didn't allow herself to show any pain and turned her neck only to relieve the discomfort.

I wanted to rip him apart. I couldn't leave Angela like this.

Gullah pulled my sleeve. "Come on. This is *were* business."

Bourbon licked his lips and brought his mouth to her ear. "And you—we'll discuss Calhoun's obituary in a kennel. While we're doing it doggie style. After that, you can slink home like a used dirty bitch."

Angela's expression changed from submissive to defiant like he'd tripped a switch. She'd come here on a mission of peace, offering herself, and he ridiculed her.

Her nose grew to a dark point. Fangs jutted from under the lip of her snout. Her fingernails curved into claws.

Bourbon yanked her hair. "Don't shift."

Angela's shoulders grew wider and thicker. The dress split open and barely covered her. She whipped about and broke free of his grip.

The smug look on Bourbon's face disappeared. "Shoot her. Shoot her."

Werewolves traded confused looks and turned to Sean.

"If you can't handle her," he said, "you don't deserve to be our alpha."

Angela scratched Bourbon's face and he staggered backward as she pressed the attack. Her skirt hiked up her legs and flashed her panties. Her calf muscles flexed into hard hairy knots.

I wanted to help, to jump in and hold Bourbon for Angela to take her vengeance on him.

Gullah warned me with a shake of his head. He waved his fingers. "Give me your pistol."

Outgunned as I was, I was in no position to refuse. I uncocked the hammer and handed him the revolver. Frustrated, I watched helpless as Angela and Bourbon fought.

They jostled against a wall table. Pictures and vases crashed to the floor.

Bourbon was in full werewolf mode now. His forearms had torn through his sleeves and his legs bulged with muscle. He and Angela snarled and bared fangs dripping with saliva.

My *kundalini noir* twitched, alternating between relief when she gained the advantage and dread when Bourbon scored a punch to her chin. Dazed, aura faltering, Angela stumbled backward and groped at the furniture as she fell to her knees.

Bourbon grabbed her hair. Angela tried twisting his fingers loose. He shook her head, hurting and humiliating her until she cried out in pain.

Doggie nostrils flaring and chest heaving, he touched the mangled flesh on his jaw and neck where she had slashed him. He swiped blood with a paw, grinned, and licked his claws.

Reaching around his waist, he pulled out the Vektor 9mm and pressed the pistol against her temple.

I could think of only one way to save Angela.

I yelled, "Me for her."

Bourbon's eyes cut to me in astonishment. A cruel smile

grew on his face. "Interesting. Tempting. You've been such a pain in my ass and I'd love to watch you drown in a vat of garlic oil."

"Keep the talking ring," I said. "Keep Paxton. Only let Angela go." I lowered my hands and retracted my talons. "You can kill me."

Gullah whispered, "Crazy bastard. What are you doing? What talking ring?"

I'd have to explain later.

"It's simple." I let my voice go Zen. "Take me. Let her go."

Bourbon looked at Gullah.

Gullah looked at me. "You sure about this?"

"Me for her."

Gullah sighed in resignation. Rooster and Yo-Yo lowered their MAC-10s.

Bourbon smiled triumphantly. "Very good." He trained the Vektor on me. "On your knees."

"Angela goes free, right?" My ears and fingertips buzzed in maximum alarm. I had no idea how to get out of this.

"On your knees."

I did as he said. Bourbon leveled the Vektor at my face. In prime shape, I might be able to dodge a bullet. But not now.

His smile turned sadistic. "I've changed my mind." He jammed the muzzle against Angela's temple. "You'll suffer more watching her die."

Time stopped. My vampire reflexes kicked to supervampire speed.

Bourbon blinked in slow motion. Every tooth shone with malevolent radiance. Every hair on his face and neck bristled with murderous intent. His clawed index finger tightened on the trigger.

My *kundalini noir* compressed like a spring and released. My arms outstretched, talons forward, I hurtled though the air like a rocket-propelled lance. I speared Bourbon in his left side. My talons slid deep into his rib cage, cutting meat and breaking bone. He shrieked and toppled over.

The Vektor fired once. A table lamp shattered.

The loud bang of the gunshot slapped me back to normal speed. I rolled on top of Bourbon and kept my talons locked in his torso. He elbowed me in the face, hard, and I fell away.

I scrambled to my hands and knees.

Bourbon sat up. Blood gushed from the rips in his shirt. The pistol lay by his side, between us. He struggled to keep upright. Blood pumped from his wounds, ran down his chest, and pooled on the floor. The wounds I'd inflicted could've killed a bear.

His eyes hooded in pain. His breath came in ragged labored gasps. His gaze swept the room and found me.

I expected his eyes to dull, but they lit up with hatred and renewed vigor. He wasn't going to die.

His eyes focused on the Vektor. He reached for the gun.

I sprang for the pistol. Bourbon's claws locked around the wrist of my right hand. My left hand seized the Vektor and I brought the gun under my right arm as my finger pumped the trigger.

This close, I couldn't miss. Bourbon jolted from the impact of each silver bullet. Dime-size holes peppered his chest. The ejected cartridge shells spun from the pistol and bounced off me.

A paw wrenched the Vektor from my hand. Sean. He put his other paw on my left shoulder while Gullah put a hand on my right. *Don't move.*

I had fired four times, five times, I didn't know. The blood seeping from the bullet holes merged into one crimson stain that covered Bourbon's chest. His wounds hissed and bubbled smoke. He relaxed and let go of my wrist.

He propped himself on his elbows and gazed at me with sad, dimming eyes. Beat by beat, the crimson stain spread down one sleeve and blood poured out the cuff. Beat by beat, smoke puffed from his chest. Beat by beat, his aura and complexion faded.

Bourbon gasped. His lower back pressed against the floor, then his shoulder blades, and finally, the back of his skull. His mouth stayed open. A rivulet of blood traced the outline of his body. His aura flickered and slowly vanished. Smoke feathered from his shirt.

The werewolves aimed guns at me. Yo-Yo and Rooster aimed guns at them.

Sean stepped close to Bourbon's corpse and studied the dead *were*'s face. He handed the Vektor to one of his goons and exhaled a troubled breath. He searched the floor and picked up Wendy's talking ring.

Angela had transformed back into a woman. The hair receded on her face and torso. Her nose flattened and turned back to a human color. She clutched the side of her dress to keep it from falling open and rocked from side to side to pull the hem to cover the tops of her legs.

I got to my feet, grabbed a cloth runner from a table, and wiped Bourbon's blood from my hands.

Sean ground his teeth and his sideburns churned. He slipped the ring into his pocket and looked at me, his eyes granite hard and cold. "I knew you'd find out who killed Inga Latrall. That's why I've kept you alive."

"So you used me to get rid of Bourbon?" All this so-called pride about *were* loyalty when it was actually a daisy chain of backstabbing.

"That's how it worked out. Now the Palmetto Clan belongs to me."

The *weres* tightened their grips on their pistols. Rooster and Yo-Yo kept their MAC-10s ready to spray the room.

No one wanted to back down, but no one wanted to be the first to die either.

"What do we do, Sean?" one of the werewolves asked. "The vampire killed Bourbon."

"This is shit," another *were* chimed in. "What happens to our cred when word gets out we let a bloodsucker kill a clan alpha?"

"That was fucked up that Bourbon and Jerry killed Inga Latrall," the first werewolf said, "but that was our punishment to give, not a vampire's."

"According to the law," one of the other werewolves said, "we're supposed to kill him."

"What do you morons know of the law?" Angela gathered her high heels. "Felix, Gullah, the rest of you vampires, go before someone farts and we're all shot to pieces."

Chapter 61

Gullah, Rooster, Yo-Yo, and I backtracked to the hall and down the stairs. We left the werewolves scratching the floor with their claws as they dragged Jerry's corpse next to Bourbon's. One of the goons injected them with the serum that shifted them back into human form.

We made it to the kitchen door and out to the side yard with the carport. At any moment, I expected the werewolves to rally and come after us.

Gullah's human gangsters had dispersed themselves in the garden and along the street. They left their sentry positions and congregated on the sidewalk in front of the house. Broken glass from the windows that Yo-Yo and Rooster had jumped through glittered on the hedges and trees.

Gullah halted beside his Impala, which was parked against the curb and sandwiched between the Escalades.

The tension had ebbed enough for him to speak. "Did you have to kill Bourbon?"

"Seemed like the right thing to do. Now give me my gun."

Gullah held the pistol like he was weighing his options. He slapped the Webley into my hand.

His forehead wrinkled in dismay. "You've put me in a jam. You killed a top alpha in front of his fellow *weres*."

"Why is that your problem? Calhoun ought to thank me for what I've done. Now he's got the territory all to himself. With Bourbon dead, that should end this talk of war."

Gullah handed his cane to Rooster and raised his gloved hand. "Let me explain how seriously the Araneum is taking this situation." He tugged at the glove, and when the cuff slipped past his knuckles, he revealed a stump instead of his little finger. The end of the stump was wrapped with electrical tape.

"It's called the *seiyakuyubi*, Japanese for 'finger oath.' After you and I talked in the hotel, a crow delivered a message from the Araneum, advising that I not let you fuck things up between us and the werewolves. They also said I've been flip in my attitude as head of the *nidus*. And to make sure I understood the message loud and clear, they suggested I reply by cutting off my finger. As down payment for the rest of my ass in case things go wrong."

Gullah winced as he replaced the glove. "You know those message capsules? My pinkie fit inside just perfect. How convenient for the Araneum."

"I'm sorry about your hand." I had a lot of ideas about the Araneum, but I never imagined them as a supernatural yakuza.

"You've put Calhoun on the hot seat." Gullah withdrew the rhinestone-decorated sunglasses from his shirt pocket and put them on. Rooster handed him the crystal-topped cane. "Had you killed a werewolf flunky, you might've been able to slide out of Charleston without more trouble. But a clan alpha? Doesn't matter that Bourbon was a rival and got what was coming to him, there's no way Calhoun can let you get away without satisfying werewolf justice."

"I'll deal with Calhoun the next time I see him." Which should be never. Still, I had the impression of being chained to an anchor that had been pitched overboard. Soon the chain would yank me to the bottom, where Calhoun would be waiting. Until then, I had other concerns.

Gullah asked, "What was that bullshit about a talking ring?"

I told him about the ring and how I'd discovered it.

"Where did Wendy get it?"

"Same place she gets the rest of her magic."

He tapped his cane hard on the sidewalk, not satisfied by my answer, but that's all I knew.

"If you had not showed up," I said, "Bourbon and his goons would've killed me and you wouldn't have these problems. So why did you show up?"

"You need to thank Deliah."

The ghost? "How so?"

"Remember that woman who attacked you at the costume ball? She dropped her cell phone when you jumped her and her partner. Deliah the haint told me where to find it."

"Deliah told you? How? What about that business with the haint cloth to keep ghosts away?"

"Come on. You know that's bullshit. I was in my kitchen taking care of this"—Gullah flexed his gloved hand—"when she came to see me because of you. Seems she's worried that if something happened, you might not be able to pay back her favor. Has to do with ice cream. Whatever that means. Deliah said that if I didn't help you, she'd go boo hag on my customers." Gullah frowned. "Wouldn't want to ruin my business model." He waved to the house. "And we showed up just in time. Like the buffalo soldier cavalry, only in this case, the Indians still got us by the short and curlies."

The cold breeze that had spun through Bourbon's house? Deliah. She had my thanks. If she asked, I'd eat my way through a freezer full of ice cream.

"What about the phone?" I asked.

"Yo-Yo sorted through its address book and found Paxton."

"Give me the number."

Gullah snapped his fingers. Yo-Yo recited the number from memory and I punched the digits into my cell phone.

I pressed send.

Okay, if Paxton answered, then what?

His number rang four times before voice mail picked up. There was no message, just a beep, followed by silence.

I hung up. "He didn't answer."

Yo-Yo had his iPhone out. His fingers traced across the screen and tapped the glass. He held the phone for me to see. "This app tracks his cell phone."

Impressive. I put an iPhone on my mental Christmas list. "Where is he?"

"To be more precise about it," Yo-Yo replied, "where is his phone?" He tapped the screen again. "Across the river. On the Savannah Highway."

"Which river? East or west?"

"You got GPS on your phone?" Yo-Yo asked.

"Yeah."

"I'll text you the address." His fingertips played on the screen again.

Seconds later my phone vibrated. I answered and loaded the address in my GPS function. A colored map filled the tiny screen of my phone.

At this scale, I couldn't tell where the address was in relation to where we were. I tapped buttons and reduced the scale to a map of the greater Charleston area.

Gullah kept rapping his cane against the concrete. The rapping stopped. He addressed Yo-Yo. "Let's add a little urgency to the proceedings. What's the address close to?"

"Between Wappoo and Oak Forest Drive."

By this time I'd gotten my bearings. I'd have to go over the Ashley River. Savannah Highway ran almost straight west from the other side of the bridge.

Gullah leaned on his cane. "What businesses are around that address?"

Yo-Yo played with his iPhone. He recited names and when he said, "The Stono River Architectural Modeling and Signworks Company," Gullah smiled in approval.

"That's it."

"How do you know?" I asked.

"That fiberglass crab that about flattened your ass? I'll bet they make those kinds of sculptures."

My *kundalini noir* trembled with anticipation. My fangs couldn't wait to taste blood.

"So what's the plan?" Gullah asked.

"Pay Julius Paxton a visit."

Gullah raised his cane and made a circle motion. "Mount up, kids."

I wanted Paxton to myself. Alone. For that I needed a car.

Angela limped out of the house and went to her Maserati. She sat sideways in the driver's seat with her legs extended to the ground. The torn seams on the side of her dress had worked farther apart. Her left breast was on the verge of popping out. She held a cell phone in her lap.

I approached. "Are you doing better?"

Her face was back to fully human. Sweat beaded on her forehead and trickled across her brow to her temples.

Her face was lined with strain. A yellow discoloration showed on her chin where Bourbon had punched her. "What are we going to do?"

"About what?"

"You." Angela massaged the bridge of her nose. "Sean's inside talking to Calhoun." She shook her cell phone. "He told him about the talking ring. All this time Sean's been working behind Bourbon's back. He wanted no part of Bourbon's schemes to start a war but couldn't turn against him without some advantage. Wendy's talking ring gave Sean what he needed to undermine Bourbon, but it's a moot point now."

"Calhoun should be relieved. The territory is his."

The frustration spilled from Angela. "You still don't get it. You've screwed everything by killing Bourbon. Calhoun's got to placate the werewolves and do it quick before Le Cercle de Sang et Crocs convenes tonight."

"I killed Bourbon because he attacked you."

Angela blinked uncomfortably. She wiped sweat from her eyes. Or were those tears? "You didn't have to offer yourself for me. That was stupid. And brave."

"I know. Stupid and brave are part of my business motto."

Angela's eyes crinkled and the corners of her mouth turned up. She was prettiest when she smiled like this. But the smile didn't last long. "I owe you my life."

"I'll take a rain check. Speaking of brave, I have to admire that you were going to give yourself to Bourbon to bring peace."

"If you knew the whole story"—she dropped her gaze—"you wouldn't think so highly of me."

"Which is?"

"If Bourbon turned me down, I was going to kill him."

"I kill an alpha and it's the end of the world. You kill an alpha and . . . ?"

"It's the end of my world. But what's one death if it prevents a war?"

"It would've been your death. That means a lot to me."

Angela brought her eyes back up. "Felix, why does this have to be so hard?"

Hold that thought. It's not over yet. I felt the pressure of hunting Paxton down before he got away again. I had the first confirmed location of where to get him. I couldn't wait much longer. "I need your car."

"To find Paxton?"

I didn't say anything. I felt low for thinking this, but if Angela didn't give me her car, I'd have to take it.

She pulled herself out of the Maserati and handed me the keys. "Calhoun's on his way here. I have to wait for him."

"What about the werewolves?" I nodded in the direction of the house.

"Sean?" Angela leaned against me like she was tired of the drama and the violence. Her body was alarmingly hot. "He's not wasting time taking over the Palmetto Clan. Once he gets his pack alphas in line, he'll pledge the clan to Calhoun."

"Sean's moving fast, like he's planned this."

"*Were* politics is like Thai kickboxing, Felix, but with fewer rules."

She sniffed the air, a quick nervous sniff as if catching the scent of a distant wildfire. "You better go."

I put my arm around her waist and pulled her close. She turned her head and offered her cheek. "When you come back and I've got your full attention, I'll give you a proper kiss." She slipped free and crossed her arms. "Do what you have to."

I sat in the car, suddenly unsure. A lot had gone wrong and a lot more could go wrong.

Angela reached for my hand but didn't touch me. "Take care of yourself. I'd hate to have nothing to show for all this trouble." She gave a quick squeeze and her fingers sent a reassuring warmth deep into me.

She stepped away.

I started the engine.

Angela stood by the kitchen door and gazed into the distance, looking lost and apprehensive.

I backed up the Maserati. King Gullah and his crew were lined up in their vehicles along the opposite side of the street.

Paxton was mine.

CHAPTER 62

IF KING Gullah and his goons were at my side when I found Paxton, I'd have to defer to Gullah unless I also wanted to take on his merry little band of gun-toting undead criminals. I had to think of a way to get to Paxton first and by myself.

The idea came. Gullah and company were in three vehicles. I rolled down my window and got my Webley.

I cruised to the first Escalade and aimed at the front right tire. *Bang. Bang.*

The tire hissed and went flat.

I drove alongside Gullah's Impala and did the same to his front right dub. I sped up and popped the tire of Rooster's Escalade.

I rolled my window up and gave the Maserati gas around the corner, throwing a quick look over my shoulder to watch Gullah and his posse spring out of their vehicles.

I got to Broad Street just as the light turned red. I checked the timing of cross traffic through the intersection and gunned the engine. I raced between a Toyota Camry and a delivery truck, narrowly missing an oncoming Buick to the screeching of tires and horns shrieking like curses.

I swerved around more cars, juking left and right over the center lane as I threaded my way through traffic. The next light was also red and I blasted through that intersection.

I was doing seventy on Lockwood Drive. My tires screamed on the ramp to the bridge over the Ashley River. Adrenaline fueled me, like my arteries and veins were full of burning gasoline.

I dodged near misses as I zoomed to the Savannah Highway. I pulled the Webley from my waistband and flicked it open. The spent casings spilled free of the cylinder. I dug into my pocket for extra ammo and reloaded.

I drove with vampire reflexes. At the edge of my peripheral vision, the world was a blur. In the center, everything was in microscopic detail.

My focus danced from traffic to the buildings and the street signs.

The address numbers approached those I was looking for. A sign on the left announced the Trinity Industrial Complex. Stono River was listed on the sign.

I rode the brakes. The speedometer dipped below one hundred, eighty, sixty. I took the turn into the complex at fifty miles per hour. I kept slowing, bounced up the entrance to the asphalt parking lot, and proceeded at a cautious walking pace.

A chain-link fence with diagonal privacy slats marked the property line. To my right sat warehouses and offices in identical prefab metal buildings. Two semitrailers were backed up to a loading dock at the first building. Inside the bay, a small forklift rolled against boxes stacked on pallets. The sign over the bay said: PIERSON MARINE SUPPLY COMPANY, LLC. A woman's voice squawked over a loudspeaker: "Marty, line two. Marty, line two."

Maybe a dozen cars were parked together, although this

part of the lot could've held a hundred. A row of Dumpsters perpendicular to the fence segmented the lot into more parking areas. Seagulls strutted along the tops of the Dumpsters.

About three hundred meters away, sheds and more Dumpsters delineated the southern boundary of the lot.

The warehouses ran one after another down my right. The address numbers progressed to the one I was searching for. For Lease signs on the buildings explained why the parking lots were empty.

I was next to a busy highway, more business complexes to my left and right, yet the farther I drove on the lot, the deeper the desolation. Empty warehouses with their dark windows stood mute as crypts. Creepy. Forbidding.

As a vampire, I enjoy the solitude of crypts. But these buildings should be teeming with activity. The tattered For Lease banners were like desperate prayers of hope, unheard and forgotten.

The Maserati advanced midway between the fence and the buildings. I wanted empty space around me, a buffer in case I was attacked. As I would be, I was sure.

Paxton wasn't alone. He had at least one assistant, the vampire who used the bat-wing suit to attack me.

I halted the car and craned my neck to see up through the windshield. I kept my eyes away from the sun. Without contacts, my retinas would be fried by direct sunlight. What I could see of the sky was as empty as the warehouses.

To my left, a shadow flitted on the ground. Seagull?

Definitely not a vampire, as he casts no shadow. Unless . . .

A vampire's aura is what prevents him from being seen in a mirror or casting a shadow. Anything inside the psychic envelope is affected. A cap tossed through the air casts a shadow. But once a vampire puts that cap on his head, then no more shadow, no more reflection.

What if something protruded beyond the aura? Something wide, like a pair of wings?

The shadow whisked across the hood of the Maserati.

Make that two shadows, a pair of matching triangles with scalloped edges. The tips of a pair of bat wings.

Circling closer.

Closer.

I pulled my Webley, pointed the muzzle right at the window in front of me, and cocked the hammer.

Chapter 63

THE TWIN shadows approaching over the asphalt shrank and grew, but I heard nothing.

Suddenly boot soles pounded the windshield.

My *kundalini noir* withdrew into a coil, compressing, clenching like a fist.

A submachine gun chattered and bullets raked across the windshield, spraying me with glass. Bullets chewed the leather upholstery. A bullet ricocheted off the rim of the steering wheel. Another bullet punched my chest, a white-hot stab of pain.

But I was ready. I absorbed the pain and pushed it deep, letting my *kundalini noir* smother the agony.

I expected worse, but the vampire had not used silver bullets. His mistake but not mine.

I fired once, right between the toes of the boots. At this angle, my bullet could hit only one target.

His balls.

An Uzi clattered against the windshield. The boots rotated on their heels. The vampire, clad in black, fell ass first on the car. The black wings beat on the hood and fenders in pangs of suffering.

I held still to see if anyone reacted to the submachine-gun fire, the blast from my Webley, and the clatter of the metal wings on the Maserati.

All I heard was a distant and muted echo from the first warehouse: "Marty, line one."

The beating of the wings slowed, as if to show the tortured fatigue of their owner. He lay with his back on the car. He cupped both hands over his groin. Blood seeped between his fingers.

He tried to sit up. He wore goggles with dark, circular lenses and a cloth helmet, black to match his overalls. I couldn't see much of his face except for a mouth gaping in agony. His fangs glistened like a pair of shiny nails.

He wore a metal vest buckled to his torso, the vest a crazy mess of cables, pipes, and articulated fittings. The wings were thin black material sewn to black struts. The helmet, the goggles, and the wing contraption looked like he was dressed for a steampunk costume contest.

"Here's first prize." I took aim through an area of clear glass between the pockmarks on the windshield. I fired once. Without the commotion of this guy dancing on the car and pounding bullets through the windshield, the Webley's heavy blast surprised me with its intensity.

The heavy silver bullet hammered the vampire's face. His nose disappeared behind a splash of blood and bone. A spasm rippled through his wings. He clutched at the air and fell flat on the hood.

I waited a moment.

Again, nothing but a distant "Marty, line two."

I put the Maserati in reverse and gave the gas pedal a quick stomp. The car surged backward. The vampire slid off the hood and crumpled to the asphalt.

The vampire? No aura.

Definitely dead.

I had little to celebrate. The pain of the bullet wound percolated from my *kundalini noir.* I extended a talon from my left index finger and dug into the hole in my shirt.

My talon sliding through my flesh was another stab of white-hot pain.

My vision shrank as misery and blackness wrapped around me like a tunnel. With each scratch of my talon, the tunnel shrank until my eyes saw nothing but a black wall.

I found the slug three inches inside my chest. The bullet had smashed through an upper rib and lodged itself in the dead mass of my useless heart. I used my talon to dig the bullet out of the wound. The bullet coming free felt like a great pressure suddenly released. The tunnel vision grew with every pulse of my *kundalini noir.*

The bullet rolled down the front of my shirt and left a trail of clumpy blood drops. I grasped the lead slug and held it to the light. The blood dried into maroon flakes and burned into ash and smoke.

I pushed the bullet into a trouser pocket. Might keep the slug as a souvenir. Yeah, it was free but had cost me plenty.

Blood flowed from the wound. I ripped a swatch from the tail of my shirt and jammed the cloth into the bullet hole.

I laid the Webley on my lap and rested for a moment to let the shock of the impromptu surgery pass.

I pressed my hand over the wound. The area was warm, not vampire cool, as my body heated up in the effort to rebuild tissue.

I guided the Maserati forward and veered to avoid the dead vampire. I stopped beside him, got out, and did a quick scan to make sure no one was approaching.

The vampire lay on his back, the broken and torn wings spread about him like an open shroud. Spent casings from the Uzi littered the vicinity.

Moving slowly—the bullet wound still hurt like hell—I picked up the Uzi; the extra firepower would come in handy. I ejected the magazine to check the ammo remaining. Empty. The dead vampire had no extra magazines. I tossed the Uzi and magazine aside.

Who was this vampire?

I knelt by his head. My bullet had made hash out of the

middle of his face. He looked Caucasian. Nothing remarkable. Maybe stood six feet. Athletic build.

Tiny cracks formed around the bullet wound. Now that he was dead, nature was hurrying to reclaim his corpse. We vampires exist on borrowed time. When the end comes, our flesh rapidly deteriorates in order to put the decay of our corpses back on their original mortal schedules.

I yanked off his goggles and helmet. Brown eyes gazed lifelessly from the bruised sockets. Still didn't recognize him.

Makeup and sunscreen protected his skin from the sun, but his eyes were vulnerable. They smoldered and shriveled into a pair of dried figs.

I parted his lips to let the sun go to work on the inside of his mouth. Smoke rolled from between his teeth.

Flames danced in his eye sockets. Fire shot from his wound and mouth. More smoke wafted from under his vest and his sleeve cuffs and through the bullet hole in his crotch.

I stood and backed away to keep his smell from funkifying my clothes.

Smoke jetted from the vampire's overalls. His head was a ball engulfed in fire, his fingers curling into black stubs. His vest popped, shooting sparks. Black smoke puffed from him and drifted over the parking lot.

Way at the front of the lot, at Pierson Marine Supply, LLC, the intercom called out: "Marty, line two. Marty, line two."

No one watched the vampire burn.

No one cared.

The vampire's flesh crumbled into dust, like the ash at the bottom of an outdoor grill. Smoke clung to his overalls. Tiny flames danced along the edges of his wings.

I paused for a second before getting back in the Maserati. My *kundalini noir* wilted as I inventoried the damage. The windshield had been chewed to pieces. The hood was dented and scratched. The leather interior was slashed by bullets. What a crime to damage the car like this. Hoped Angela forgave me.

I got in and drove to the end of the lot.

A colorful sign over the office of the last building in the complex said STONO RIVER ARCHITECTURAL MODELING AND SIGNWORKS COMPANY. The letters intertwined in a flowing Art Nouveau style. A pair of mermaids flanked the sign. There were two bay doors to the right of the glass office door.

Three cars and a van were parked together in front of the company. Somebody was at work?

Were they waiting for me?

I forced myself to relax. I cleared my mind to better read my sixth sense. The danger alarm hummed through my *kundalini noir.*

I studied the vehicles. All were older models. The van, a white Ford Econoline with a raised roof. The rest looked ready for the junkyard. Rust. Bald tires. Blotches of freshly leaked oil on the pavement. Holes in the doors where the locks had been pried out. Cracked windows. A Subaru coupe had red tape over a broken taillight.

I had no idea of Paxton's agenda other than to kill me. He could've lured me here to finish me with a car bomb.

My sixth sense remained at a hum.

No bomb here.

I parked to put the cars between the building and myself.

Another scan to make sure no one was watching. The roofline was clear. No auras in the windows.

I rubbed my wound. The hard scab felt like a coin had been grafted to my skin. Normal. The scab should fall off in an hour.

I topped off the Webley and carefully exited the Maserati.

I checked the cars up close. Empty. Inside, the vehicles looked as forlorn as they did on the outside. Cracked vinyl. Faded bath towels cinched with bungee cords over the seat backs. Drinking straws, artists' brushes, and scraps of paper trapped along the bottom of the windshield. Missing knobs on the dash. Fast-food bags and cups crushed along the floor. Flip-flops, rumpled clothes, tattered spiral sketchbooks on the seats.

The windows on the rear doors of the van were darkly tinted, almost opaque. The windows along the back of the cabin were blanked out, painted white to match the rest of the body. A Tommy Lift for a wheelchair had been attached to the cargo door on the right side. A quick glance through the front passenger's window didn't reveal much except for a handicapped-parking tag hanging from the rearview mirror.

Judging from the rain pattern on the dust of the windshields, none of the vehicles had been driven lately.

Except the van. The wiper smears on the windshield looked recent. We'd had rain yesterday.

The sixth-sense hum increased to a buzz.

I tried to piece the clues together. I was sure that whoever owned the cars worked here. The paintbrushes and sketchbooks belonged to artists, the kind of people you'd find working at a place like this. The condition of the vehicles meant they didn't have much money. Typical artists.

But the van? The wheelchair lift and the handicapped tag?

I looked back at the vampire's remains. Smoke lingered over the black lump of his corpse and the wing contraption.

I was after Paxton. So far I had this dead flying vampire. Plus the vampires that I'd killed my first day in Charleston. Add Paxton's arrangement with Eric Bourbon.

But what about these artists? And the van for the handicapped?

None of this fit together. It was like trying to make something out of a pile of Lego pieces, model airplane parts, and broken dolls.

I kept my pistol tight against my thigh and approached the building.

I wanted to sneak in. How?

A back door? Too obvious.

The roof? Unless there was an overlooked access hatch, which I doubted, the only way in was to bust through the ceiling. Nothing sneaky about that.

I checked my watch.

King Gullah and crew were due to arrive soon. I better hurry if I wanted Paxton to myself.

The front door, then.

CHAPTER 64

I DIDN'T CHECK if the door was locked. I simply kicked it hard, right on the dead bolt. The steel frame buckled. The glass shattered.

I pushed the frame and it twisted to the floor.

Granules of safety glass lay on the sidewalk outside and on the carpeted interior. There was a low counter to the left, stools and chairs scattered about, papers and posters randomly tacked to the wall. The phones and computers on the counter were silent.

I faced another door on the opposite wall.

I took a deep breath. The strongest smells came first.

Paint stripper. Mineral spirits. Epoxy. An odor of putrefying flesh. Feces. Urine.

From who?

The owners of the cars?

Another breath.

Alkyd paint. Welding flux. Latex paint.

A meaty aroma.

Human blood. Lots of it.

My sixth sense put the tingle in my ears and fingertips.

Whose blood?

I swiped a path through the shattered glass with my shoes and stepped over the threshold.

I stood to the side of the interior door and swung it open, thinking that if someone was waiting with a gun or a crossbow, they'd let fly right away.

Nothing happened.

I peeked around the corner.

The door opened into the shop area. Light filtered through a row of dingy windows high on the back wall. Fiberglass molds were stacked helter-skelter against shelves packed with cans, jars, and cartons. Drill presses, table saws, air compressors, arc welders sat randomly on the dirty floor. Hand tools, brushes, and spray guns lay everywhere.

The fiberglass crab that had almost flattened me must've been fabricated here.

Parallel marks crisscrossed the dusty floor. Could be from handcarts, dollies, or a wheelchair.

I crouched beside a plywood box containing lengths of black aluminum pipe, identical to the struts of the vampire's bat-wing suit. Black cloth spooled from a roll lying on a workbench. I compared the cloth to the tattered piece I'd found in my hotel room. Identical.

The lower shelf of the bench was piled with fittings, small electric motors, wires, circuit boards, and a duplicate of the bat-wing vest.

This puzzle started to make sense. The artists had made the crab and the bat-wing suit. Where were they?

I hoped the odor of rot and blood didn't answer that question.

The bay doors were to my right, the back wall and windows to my left. Shelves were behind me. Three doors to my front.

Door number one, at the right, was covered in marker graffiti and blots of sprayed paint. Somebody had written: MEN, which was crossed out and replaced with LIFE SUPPORT SYSTEM FOR A PENIS. Under that, the word WOMEN had also been crossed out and replaced with VAGINAL AMERICANS.

A shared bathroom, no doubt.

Door number two, in the middle, had placards for hazardous materials. Storeroom.

Door number three, on the left. More graffiti but no clue as to what lay on the other side.

I swiveled my head to home in on the smell of decay.

Door number three.

I approached the door, pistol at the ready.

My *kundalini noir* coiled like a snake ready to lash out. My fingertips buzzed hard. I swapped the revolver from hand to hand to wipe my fingers against my trousers as if to blot away the nervousness that infected them.

My hands again steady, I stood to one side of the door. The knob turned easily and I swung the door open.

CHAPTER 65

A NAUSEATING ODOR of rancid meat and excrement surged out the room. The place stank like someone had butchered a rotting cow in a Porta Potti. The smell left a greasy texture in the air.

My fangs and talons were at full combat length. I flexed my index finger over the trigger of the Webley.

Slowly, my reflexes on a razor's edge like I expected a bomb to go off, I peeked inside.

An orange aura blazed at the far end of a long and narrow room.

Vampire.

A head shaped like a stack of clay bricks. Nappy hair trimmed short.

Paxton.

No makeup. His complexion looked like brown wax. I remembered a full face; now his cheeks were drawn and his eyes sunken in deep, wrinkled pits. He sat in a motorized wheelchair.

Wheelchair? A vampire?

The last I'd seen of Paxton was him staggering away after I'd shot him in the back. Then a murderous psycho had run him down in her car. When I returned to get Paxton, he was gone. Hadn't heard from him since, until I got to Charleston.

The hit-and-run must have torn him up bad. A vampire can recover from most any injury but apparently not severe back trauma.

I didn't pity him. The opposite, actually. I wondered if he'd suffered enough.

His aura teemed with bumps of intrigue. Tendrils undulated from the envelope of his penumbra.

He could be faking. Throw me off guard.

But his complexion. The squalor in this room. He wore a dark baggy suit that fit like he was wasting away. Paxton was skimming close to rock bottom. Maybe his desire for revenge was what kept him going.

My impulse was to shoot him. Get this over with. Don't give him a chance to strike back or escape.

But I had questions. He better have answers.

I raised the pistol but kept my aim loose. I didn't want to focus so intently on him, tense up, and not be able to react fast enough in case of a surprise.

"You're somebody," his voice croaked, "I never wanted to see . . . alive."

"Don't blame you," I replied. "After all this time, to be found in this dump. Actually, it's a step up for you that I'm here."

Paxton pushed the control handle on the end of his armrest. The wheelchair eased forward with a whine.

I jabbed the muzzle at him. *That's far enough.*

He stopped. The tentacles retracted into his aura. He acted too confident, too sure of himself.

I stepped to the right, away from the doorway in case someone came in behind me. I tossed quick glances about the room.

Cubbies holding odd sizes of lumber and plywood lined the wall to my right. The far wall had one window, protected by bars. On the left, computers and printers sat on a counter, every surface covered in dust.

Dead crows hung upside down on the wall behind the counter. Wendy's crows? Paxton must have killed every crow that had come to spy on him except for the one he had poisoned and sent back to Wendy.

A red aura glowed faintly under the counter. A human. Male.

I swung my Webley from Paxton to the man and back to Paxton. He was the bigger threat.

The man crawled out from under the counter. His hair and beard were unkempt, giving him a hermitlike appearance. He wore jean cutoffs and a dingy T-shirt. A leather collar hung around his emaciated neck. The collar held a small box against his throat. It looked like a device used to discipline a dog against barking.

He had a mealy complexion like all of his blood had been wrung from his flesh. His eyes turned up to me. They shone dully from the bottom of black cavities. Vampire fang marks covered his body. An ugly purple rectangle filled with pus sores sat on his right shoulder blade. I guessed the dimensions of the rectangle. About the same as a playing card. His skin had been cut away to use as material for the note the poisoned crow had brought to Wendy's home.

The note sent by Paxton. I glared at him with loathing and anger.

The man tried to get closer, but one ankle remained chained to the counter. His shin and foot were green and purple with gangrene. His hands pawed tracks through the dusty floor. The fingers on one of his hands, the same color as his foot, flopped uselessly. Whoever had chained him here had broken these fingers and let them rot.

Something scratched inside one of the cubbies. I leaned close to look.

A young woman, brown hair frazzled and chopped to look like a broom that had been set fire, wearing a soiled T-shirt and even dirtier gym shorts, squirmed in the bottom of the cubbie. The sewer odor was strong enough to make my nose twitch. The floor under her looked like a used bed-pan. Dark, crusty stains covered her bare legs.

I faced Paxton and my voice was heavy with disgust. "These your minions?"

"What's left of them. Now they're mostly sustenance and even that won't last long."

"You should treat your chalices better. Not only is it good karma, but they'll be tastier."

Spikes of irritation churned from Paxton's aura.

"What about Orville Wright out there?" I nodded in the direction of the parking lot. "The one with the bat wings. He one of yours?"

"Was," Paxton growled, aware of what I'd done.

"What's this about?"

"Obvious, isn't it? Revenge."

"You should learn to let go. Grudges are never easy to carry."

Paxton ground his teeth. His hand tightened around the control handle.

I asked, "What about the vampires who dropped the crab on me? Who were they?"

"Acolytes."

"Fancy term for your incompetent help. Whose idea was it to murder Wendy Teagarden?"

Paxton's withered face relaxed. "Couldn't be helped. We were going after you."

Couldn't be helped? Paxton talked as if Wendy's death was a minor inconvenience. Anger pulsed through me in waves of painful shocks.

I'd lost Paxton once before. He wouldn't escape this time. This time I wasn't just going to kill him. He would know my visit was about justice and his death was going to be an execution.

"Why here?" I asked. "Charleston?"

Paxton wheezed, a rusty mechanical sound. "Because it's taken me this long to heal well enough to come after you."

"How did you and Bourbon find each other?"

"Where else in this wired age? The Internet."

Okay. "How?"

"He needed a supernatural private detective. I needed to find you. Eventually we connected. Do a Google search on 'people who hate Felix Gomez' and you'll be surprised by the number of hits you get."

"I'm flattered by the attention. And your plan?"

"Our plan was to destroy everything. Get you to kill Calhoun. Start a war between the werewolves. Pull in the vampires." Paxton wheezed like an old tractor motor. "Destroy the Great Secret. Destroy the Araneum. Free us vampires to live as undead kings instead of timid little serfs." He relaxed and fought for strength. "But as before in Los Angeles, you fucked everything up."

"It's a talent. But I don't see how this master plan of yours had much of a window of opportunity. Right after I refused Bourbon, you tried to kill me."

"It was those imbeciles at the garage jumping the gun. The crab was for after we had goaded you into starting trouble with the werewolves."

"And now you have no plan."

"I have the reason I came to Charleston. You."

The male chalice crawled toward me, his movements sluglike and repulsive. In the cubbie next to the one with the girl, something inside made a thump, then scratched on the plywood.

A hand gripped the edge of this cubbie. The fingernails were broken and dirty, the fingers caked with filth.

These poor chalices had been drained to the edge of life, starved, and kept in squalor. "What's your problem, Paxton?"

"I have to run a lean operation. Not much room for overhead."

"If you're counting on Bourbon for help," I said, "forget it. He's dead."

With a weak shrug, Paxton replied, "Then I'll get a day job. What's important is that you're here."

The female chalice struggled to get upright in the cubbie. Like the first chalice, she also wore a leather collar with a box against her throat. Her eyes were distant. Bite marks crisscrossed her neck and forearm. Her shirt was mottled with yellow stains and dried blood.

"What are the collars for?" I asked.

"To keep them under control."

"Maybe if you treated them right and used the pleasure enzymes, you wouldn't have to keep them in these pigsty conditions."

"I lost the pleasure enzymes." He answered bitterly and thumped his elbow against one armrest of his wheelchair. "The injury."

"What about the other vampires? You could've taken turns."

"Didn't work. The chalices wouldn't answer to me. But no matter. They are simply domesticated animals. We're mistaken to elevate humans above that."

The male chalice used his arms to pull himself across the floor toward me. His legs barely moved to push him along.

The third chalice propped herself upright in her cubbie. Her face was bright pink like the flesh of cooked salmon. Her blond hair lay in stringy bunches over her face and temples. Bite marks covered her neck, shoulders, and arms.

My sixth sense amped up the alarm. About what? These chalices were almost comatose. Zombies had more life to them.

The chalice closest to me leaned in her cubbie and tumbled over the front to the floor. Her face smacked the concrete and her body collapsed in a heap. She pushed her head off the floor, showing a nose that looked like smashed clay.

The third chalice did a similar move and also performed a face-plant on the concrete. She rolled to her butt and levered herself to her feet in awkward movements like she had forgotten how to stand. Skin hung from her lacerated cheek.

Something touched my ankle. The male chalice put a forearm and his rotted fingers over my foot.

I'd had enough. I'd shoot Paxton and then see what I could do to rescue the chalices.

The brunette chalice stood. She fell to one side, aiming her fall on me.

I tried stepping aside.

A sharp pain stung my left thigh. The male chalice held

a syringe in his good hand and pressed the needle against my leg.

I swatted the syringe away. A warm flush radiated from the puncture. My muscles became limp. My head swam in a growing daze.

The brunette snagged my right arm and grasped my pistol.

The world receded from me. Everything moved in slow motion.

Whatever caused this, fight it. *Fight it.*

The blond chalice opened her mouth and I think she shrieked, but her voice sounded distant and muted. She brandished another syringe and lurched for me.

CHAPTER 66

I HAD ALL three chalices after me, a trio of disgusting automatons.

Paxton gave an evil, triumphant leer. He held a video-game controller and manipulated the buttons. He set the controller into a bracket on the arm of the wheelchair. Lights on the front of the controller blinked and the chalices kept attacking on automatic remote control.

He reached behind the wheelchair and slowly withdrew the barbed shaft of an antique whaling harpoon. Reflections from the overhead lights sparkled across the polished edge. Sharp. Shiny. Silver.

Panic slashed through my *kundalini noir.* My throat tightened in terror.

Fight the drug. Keep alert.

I tried to pry the Webley from the brunette, but she held tight.

The gun went off. The bullet ricocheted with a whine off the concrete floor.

She tugged on the Webley. My brain sent the signal to wrestle the gun free and shoot her. By the time my fingers started to react, she'd pulled the gun away and let it drop to the floor.

Time began to speed up. The effect of the syringe ebbed. *Hold on a few more seconds.* I drew strength from a deep reserve within me.

The blond chalice raised her syringe to plunge the needle into my chest. I slapped the syringe out of her hand.

I flexed my right arm and lifted the brunette chalice off the ground. I snapped my arm and flung her to the floor.

Paxton's expression collapsed in dread. Every passing second, I grew more coherent.

He tapped the butt of the harpoon against the game controller. The chalices grabbed the front of their collars and yowled in pain. They let go of the collars and paused, shoulders stooped in relief. They turned their eyes back to me.

One of the female chalices lunged with a syringe. I leaned from her, too late, and the needle stuck me in the side. I grasped her hand and pushed it away. The syringe dangled from my shirt. I yanked it free and threw it on the ground. A wave of drowsiness dulled my mind and my eyelids grew heavy.

The three chalices swarmed over me. I tired to shake them loose, but my limbs were weak and numb.

My *kundalini noir* thrashed, futilely broadcasting signals for my body to fight.

Paxton cradled the harpoon in his lap. He grasped the control handle on the armrest. The wheelchair jerked forward and rolled straight at me.

I struggled to get away, but my body felt like it'd been packed with cotton wadding. As weak as they were, the chalices still overpowered me.

Paxton halted a few feet in front of me.

His frown deepened into a scowl. He wrapped his right hand around the harpoon. His left hand gripped under his left knee. He lifted the leg past the edge of the footrest and set his foot on the floor. His eyes never left me, as if he'd been rehearsing this movement for years. He lifted the right leg and set his right foot on the floor.

He adjusted his grip on the harpoon. His left hand grasped the end of the armrest. His eyebrows bunched. His muscles tightened and—legs quivering from the effort—he slowly raised himself from the wheelchair.

I tried to wrench my arms from the chalices.

His left arm reached for me. His fingers clasped a handful of my shirt. He pulled forward and leaned against me. A foul cadaver odor swirled from him.

Paxton's head shook as he struggled with the effort of standing. He raised the harpoon's barb to his face and pressed the silver edge against his cheek. His skin sizzled like meat dropped on a hot skillet and smoked and curled around the edge of the harpoon. He lowered the harpoon, revealing the shape of the barb branded into his cheek. His eyes stayed on mine, taunting: *You'll never be this strong or dedicated.*

He tucked the harpoon's shaft into his right armpit. He pressed the silver point against my sternum. The harpoon sliced through my shirt and the silver tip nicked my skin.

The touch of fire shot through the numbness. My fingers and toes curled from pain.

My *kundalini noir* hardened, defiant.

I wasn't going to die. Not now. Not here. Not by Paxton's dirty hand.

I pushed the veil of numbness out of my consciousness. Every detail—each wrinkle, each open pore, each scar—on Paxton's face came into sharp focus. The dull smell unraveled into distinct odors. My arms and legs, once heavy, became limber and vigorous.

Paxton was growing tired. His grip relaxed and the harpoon drew away. He steadied his grip, wrapped both hands around the shaft, and pushed into me.

My *kundalini noir* pulsed like a heart. Every beat sent new strength into my limbs. My bones felt like they were made of steel. My muscles like dynamos.

I shook my arms free of the chalices and grabbed the harpoon around the shaft.

The silver tip burned as it cut into my chest. My legs weakened. My blood oozed around the harpoon point. The tip touched bone. The pain burned like fire.

But I wouldn't give in.

We stared at each other in a test of wills. He pushed against me. I pushed against him. The harpoon trembled between us.

The acid burn from the silver sapped my power.

The chalices grabbed my legs and I kicked them away.

Paxton frowned and set his jaw. His muscles tightened even more. He put his weight against the shaft.

I would not let him kill me. With a grunt, I pushed against the harpoon.

Slowly, the shaft pulled from my chest. Tendrils of panic and alarm writhed from Paxton's aura like a halo of frightened snakes.

Inch by inch, as the harpoon drew back from me, I became stronger. With the harpoon free of my chest, I twisted the shaft and brought the sharp end against Paxton.

He let go and dropped back into the wheelchair. The tendrils withdrew into his penumbra and his aura bubbled with defeat and terror.

I grabbed Paxton by one shoulder. "Remember your boss in California? This is how I killed him."

Paxton grabbed my arms. The halo of snakes burst again from his aura.

I held Paxton steady to run him through with the harpoon. The point jammed against his sternum.

Smoke curled from the wound. Blood spurted and wet my arm. I twisted the blade to crack open his rib cage.

I gave the harpoon an extra shove, pushing hard enough for the blade to poke out the back of the wheelchair. He clenched his teeth, as if it were possible to absorb all this pain and survive.

His shoes kicked against the footrests. His hands let go and his arms flopped against the tires of the wheelchair.

Blood gurgled from his mouth and spilled down his chin

and neck, and into the collar of his shirt. His head fell forward, limp. His aura tightened like shrink-wrap.

I grabbed a two-by-four and shattered the dingy glass of the window. Sunlight, bright, searing, more deadly than garlic, bathed Paxton.

I tucked myself into the shadows along the wall.

Flames flitted over his body like orange moths. Smoke jetted from his collar and coat sleeves. His mouth opened into a maw of torment as smoke curled out and his body burst into fire.

Smoke splashed against the ceiling. The water sprinkler above him clicked. Water sprayed out, drenching us. A fire alarm screamed. More sprinklers kicked on. Torrents of water showered the room, soaking me.

The chalices lifted their faces to the spray. They cupped their hands under their mouths to funnel water through their lips.

Paxton's body smoldered as the spray sizzled on his burning flesh. His head began to disintegrate. First the scalp sloughed off. Then his skull collapsed. Water mixed with ash inside the bowl of his cranium and formed a gray mud. His eyeballs shriveled and rolled back into his head, leaving the sockets empty. With each passing second, his head softened into a doughy mass that melted off his shoulders.

Water pooled in the smoking cavity of his collar. Mud slopped out his jacket sleeves and trouser cuffs. His suit coat drooped around the harpoon holding up the disintegrating remains of his body.

The alarm went silent with a *be-boop*. The sprinklers sputtered, the sprays turning into drips, the drips turning dry.

Why had the alarm turned off? The fire department hadn't arrived. Was the system automatic?

The chalices crawled over each other and remained still, locked in a group hug.

Paxton was . . . nothing much. Muddy ash circled the wheelchair. His clothes settled into a grimy pile on the seat and footrests.

It was a ghastly spectacle, but the mood lifted when I heard from behind me, "I'm melting."

King Gullah walked into the room, swinging his cane, left hand still in the glove, and picked his way across the floor to avoid the deeper puddles. "Just like the Wicked Witch," he added.

I pressed my hand over the harpoon wound to stanch the blood. I felt embarrassed, shamed that I was sharing my pain and weakness.

Blood dripped from my hand, each drop flaking and smoking before reaching the floor. I'd survive the wound, but in the meantime, it burned like hell.

Gullah stepped on a board and shook the water off his shoes. His aura burned serenely like the flame of a candle.

He walked around me and stabbed the tip of his cane into the pile of clothes. He lifted a soggy pant leg and let it drop, then snapped his cane to fling away the wet ash. "You are thorough."

I started to bend over to pick the Webley out of a puddle. Gullah pressed the cane against my chest. "Leave it."

I grasped the cane. He pushed hard and levered me upright. I was still weak and slow from the drug.

"What's this about?"

Gullah kept the cane against my chest, making me shuffle backward until he pinned me against a wall.

"First of all, you owe me and my gang brand-new tires to replace the ones you shot out. But there's more."

Dan, Calhoun's bodyguard in werewolf form, came through the door. Two more werewolves followed. All muscles, hair, and fangs. They kept their stares fixed on me.

Gullah said, "Calhoun wants to talk with you."

"What are you talking about?"

"Charleston is my home. If I'm to live in peace among Calhoun's werewolves, I have to cooperate with him. Remember what the Araneum said? That you were expendable?"

Gullah's treachery buried me in rage. He pushed the cane harder. "Ironic, isn't it? You killed Bourbon and averted a werewolf war. Plus you left Calhoun as the uncontested alpha of the territory. But the rank-and-file werewolves don't see it that way. They only see that a vampire killed a clan alpha. The werewolves want werewolf justice and Calhoun has to give it to them."

"Traitor. It's about saving your ass."

"Keeping the peace, saving my ass, it's all the same thing."

Dan directed the other two werewolves to grab my arms.

If had my strength back, if I had my pistol, if I had my vampire speed . . . but I had nothing.

CHAPTER 67

CALHOUN'S GOONS dragged me outside. They wrenched my arms behind my back and secured my wrists with a length of steel cable. They shoved me into the backseat of one of Calhoun's ubiquitous black Mercedes limousines and morphed back to human form. They didn't care about my wet clothes staining the leather upholstery. Then we drove through Charleston to Latrall's estate in Mount Pleasant. A cordon of police cars kept public traffic from getting off the main road for the estate. A second cordon of werewolves guarded the perimeter.

We slowed for a checkpoint staffed by two female *weres* carrying automatic rifles. Dan rolled his window down; they recognized him and waved us through.

A dozen cars were parked in front of the estate. The limo passed a garage, drove off the pavement, and rolled over the grass to the grounds in back. We continued behind the terrace and stopped beside the concrete helicopter pad. The three *weres* got out. Dan gave the order for one to stand guard.

I was left in the car, still weak, still in pain. It was too much of an effort to remain sitting up, so I tipped over to lie on my side across the backseat.

I struggled to work free of the cable restraints, but they remained tight. With ordinary vampire strength, I might've torn free, but at the moment, it felt good to simply lie on the upholstery and rest. The dull ache of the harpoon wound in my chest smothered the outside world. I dozed off.

Someone yanking my feet woke me.

Dan and his two werewolf goons, auras glowing, were at the open door of the limo. They had changed into white shirts and blue jeans. They yelled at me, but all I heard was an intense mechanical clatter.

Groggy and nauseous, I couldn't stop them from pulling me from the car. A deafening thumping noise pounded the night air. Cool wind beat my face and rustled my clothes.

A werewolf gripped my head. Dan spread my right eyelid. I tried to squirm free, but these werewolves were too strong.

Dan brought his finger to my eye.

Overcome with terror, I fought as hard as I could. Threaten to disembowel, burn, behead me, just stay away from my eyes.

Dan pressed a contact over my eye. The contact was hard and made my eye itch. He started for the left eye. Now that I knew what to expect, I didn't struggle as much. Still, I was creeped out. The contact lenses eliminated my supernatural vision and the world looked dull.

The S-76 helicopter sat on the concrete pad, the spinning rotor a silver disk, the strobe lights flashing.

The *weres* dragged me along, and I stumbled to find my balance. They pushed me to the open cargo door and tipped me onto the deck. I was shoved face-first against seats. A *were* tied a strap to my wrist restraints and lashed me to the floor.

More *weres* hustled to the helicopter. They climbed aboard, stepped around me, and shoved crates against me. There was a rush to secure the crates to the floor, yelling, getting into seats, more yelling. The doors were kept open and grass and dust swirled through the compartment.

After a slight pause, the helicopter rose to a hover. I expected glare from the landing lights but realized there was none. The pilot and crew were all werewolves and had excellent night vision.

The helicopter banked and I got a panoramic view of the stars but no clue of where we were headed. I remained still, a trussed animal, afraid but waiting for the chance to escape.

The helicopter rolled level and I recognized the Cooper River, the wharf, the fleet of tall ships, the warehouses, and the Avenal Bridge as we swung in a circle heading northwest.

Water sparkled with the light of the full moon.

The full moon.

I was out of time.

CHAPTER 68

THE HELICOPTER turned off its strobe lights and descended to treetop level. We were far from Charleston and skimmed low over the gloom of strange terrain. I hadn't seen any ground lights for many minutes, which meant we were miles deep into the wilderness.

The nose pitched up and we turned to the left. The landing gear groaned as it extended. As we banked, I could see torches arranged in a large circle around a bonfire. Figures—of werewolves, I was certain—hurried across the circle and their shadows crisscrossed one another like the broken spokes of a wheel.

A circle.

Le Cercle de Sang et Crocs.

The Circle of Blood and Fangs. The gathering of werewolves to coronate Calhoun as their new territory alpha. The gathering of werewolves to pronounce judgment on me.

The helicopter slowed its descent, floated to a hover, then

sank against the ground. The werewolves in the cabin threw off their seat belts and scrambled out. Dan and another werewolf unfastened the strap around me and grabbed my arms. They dragged me from the helicopter and dropped me to the ground. I lay on the grass, confused, dizzy, filled with fear.

The other werewolf yanked me to my knees. Dan squeezed my jaw—my reaction was to clench tight—but he was too strong and I was too weak. He shoved an iron bar sideways into my mouth and cinched the bar in place with a cord that he wound across the back of my head.

I tried chewing on the bit but gave up. No sense breaking a tooth. Saliva welled in my mouth and slobbered down my chin.

The roar of helicopters surrounded us. I was pelted with dust and grass from all sides. A CH-47 Chinook landed close, a huge machine that looked like a school bus with rotors on its front and rear. It wore dark green camouflage with the markings of the South Carolina National Guard. The rear cargo ramp lowered and dozens of werewolves dismounted at a run.

The CH-47 leaped upward and another big helicopter took its place in the field, a gray H-3 Sea King with markings of the Naval Reserve. Once it landed, werewolves hopped from the side door and scurried in a crouch from under the rotor disk.

No kidding, this Cercle was a big deal. A half-dozen helicopters circled above, all big military machines carrying werewolves. The territory *weres* must've infiltrated all the local bases.

The S-76 helicopter took off in a storm of dust and grass. Scores of werewolves hustled around me. The air was electric with excitement. Every werewolf—male, female—seemed to be wearing a version of the same uniform: a white shirt over jeans. They'd snarl and flex their arms. The shirt would tear along the seams and show off hairy bulges of muscle.

The full moon beamed upon us, a perfect circle of white light.

Werewolves jostled one another like football players before a game. They assembled behind tall wooden staffs displaying cloth standards emblazoned with heraldic emblems and shields.

Dan and his assistant shoved me through the crowds in the direction of the circle of torches. The werewolves parted with growls and bared fangs.

Several raked me with their claws. I didn't give these shaggy mutts the satisfaction of seeing me wince. By the time we reached the perimeter of torches, my clothes were in shreds and my body covered in bloody scratches.

Inside the circle, the torchlights and bonfire gave everything an orange tint. A column of black smoke twisted upward from the bonfire and smudged across the full moon. The circle was a hundred meters in diameter and sloped upward from me. Formations of werewolves standing shoulder to shoulder packed the circumference.

Helicopters roared overhead with the frenzy of an air assault.

I was outnumbered by a thousand lycanthropes. Werewolf eyes, red as hot rivets, surrounded me. Terror prickled my skin. I worked my mouth to see if I could move the bit enough to chew on the restraining cord. Didn't work. Minute by minute I slipped deeper into desperation and hopelessness.

King Gullah's double cross had put me here. After I'd killed Bourbon and Paxton, I could've left Charleston and wiped my hands clean of these werewolves. But Gullah had turned me over to Calhoun. Gullah's betrayal had stung me to the core.

Werewolves carried logs as thick as telephone poles and tossed them into the bonfire. Each log landed with a puff of sparks that was sucked into the smoke.

The drumming of helicopters grew faint.

Dan and the other *were* led me around the fire to the upward slope of the circle. We faced a makeshift platform made of logs. Banners decorated with stylized wolf heads and paw prints hung from the front of the platform. The bonfire, the logs, the torches, and the banners gave the gathering the ambience of a summer camp with the theme of a fascist *Lord of the Flies*.

Seven folding chairs were on the platform. Six werewolves—two female, four male—occupied the chairs, leaving the middle one empty. Behind each chair stood werewolves holding standards. The center standard was identical to the one I'd seen before at Latrall's estate. A crescent moon rising above a howling wolf, superimposed over a palm tree. The emblem of the Lowcountry Territory.

I didn't recognize any of the werewolves except for Sean Moultier, Bourbon's surviving lieutenant, who sat to the immediate right of the middle chair.

At the end of the platform, a werewolf sat cross-legged and tapped at a laptop.

Where was Calhoun? Where was Angela?

I was pushed to my knees. The werewolves on the platform kept their eyes on the circle and ignored me.

A female werewolf appeared from behind the others on the platform. The murmurs of the crowd gave way to howls. Long excited howls. Howls from packs and packs of werewolves. Howls that chilled the air and made my *kundalini noir* turn into an icicle.

The female werewolf walked to the front edge of the platform. She carried a simple bowl in one paw and a necklace of fangs in the other. She was either a priestess of some kind or the emcee. She raised both paws. The howls faded to a reverential silence, disturbed only by the crackling of the bonfire and the torches.

She drew a breath, paused, and shouted, "Welcome, honored sisters and brothers." Her voice echoed in the darkness. This werewolf had lungs.

She bowed to the *weres* on the platform. "Honored council."

They nodded.

She faced the circle and drew another deep breath. "Welcome to Le Cercle de Sang"—she upturned the bowl and poured blood over the edge of the platform—"et Crocs." She shook the necklace.

The circle erupted in a fury of howls.

The werewolf at the laptop tapped furiously at the keyboard. Probably the secretary, taking minutes.

The emcee raised the bowl and fangs. The alphas on the platform stood. The howls softened. She shouted, "Le Cercle summons Randolph Calhoun."

Werewolves sang out, "Calhoun. Calhooon. Cal-hoooon."

The circle separated at the most downward slope. Calhoun marched through the gap. He was in full werewolf form, the first time I'd seen him like this. His snout was distended and fangs showed beneath his lip, but I still recognized him. His furry ears were up. Instead of a suit, he wore a simple white shirt over jeans like everyone else. His muscles bulged in his clothes. Tufts of hair sprouted through the torn seams of his shirt. The claws of his prosthetic clenched and unclenched.

He proceeded to the edge of the bonfire and stopped. Two werewolves used long iron rakes to pull the burning logs apart and clear a path through the hot coals. Calhoun kept his gaze on the emcee.

The packs of werewolves began to chant. "Huzzah. Huzzah. Huzzah."

The bed of coals before Calhoun glowed and pulsed with the menace of a demonic living thing, one made of freshly spewed lava. He set one furry hind paw in the coals.

He was going to walk through the fire. My *kundalini noir* shriveled until it twisted against my sphincter. I wanted no part of this ceremony.

Calhoun lifted his other hind paw and placed it in the hot coals.

"Huzzah. Huzzah. Huzzah."

I watched, transfixed, astounded by the pair he must have between his hairy legs. He walked resolutely across the coals. A corona of sparks swirled around his head.

When he reached the other end of the fire, the chanting became a chorus of wild howls.

Two werewolves placed steps at the front of the platform, center stage. Calhoun kept his stride. Smoke wafted from his feet and trouser cuffs. He climbed the steps and halted before the emcee, his back toward me and the audience. The emcee hesitated and waited for the circle to become quiet.

The emcee shouted, "Randolph Calhoun, are you prepared to assume your duties as alpha of the Lowcountry Territory?"

I assumed that walking through the bonfire had answered that question.

He replied with a confident "I am."

She offered him the bowl of blood. "Are you prepared to uphold the traditions of *were* family and administer Lycanthrope Law?"

He took the bowl in his good paw. "I am."

She offered him the necklace of fangs. "Are you prepared to guard the honor of your clans and packs?"

He raised his prosthetic arm. "I am."

She draped the necklace over his steel claws. Placing a paw on his shoulder, she turned him around. "Then, Randolph Calhoun, by the authority of Lycanthrope Law, I designate you alpha of the Lowcountry Territory."

Wolves howled, the noise so loud it was as if the skies had split apart and thunder from the next thousand years crashed at once.

The werewolf holding the standard of the Lowcountry Territory came forward. He stood behind Calhoun, who extended his arms, Sang in one paw, Crocs in the prosthesis.

With my contacts in place, I couldn't read auras, but if I could, I'd bet Calhoun's blazed in triumph and hubris. He had control over Latrall's estate. Bourbon, his only rival, was dead. Calhoun had the entire territory in his feral grip.

Calhoun handed the bowl and necklace back to the emcee. He gestured with his paw and the alphas on the stage took their seats. The emcee stepped to the side.

Quiet again settled over the circle.

The werewolf secretary kept up his tap-tap-tapping.

Calhoun stood rigid and proud at the front of the platform. "Fellow werewolves, I am humbled by this honor. I pledge to protect you all." He turned slowly to the left and right to acknowledge the entire circle.

"Together, we have averted a great tragedy. There were some among us who sold pack loyalty for selfish gain, family ties for perfidy, in a loathsome act of sedition. We were on the brink of war, a werewolf war, a war that threatened not only our clans and packs and families, but the Great Secret as well."

Hundreds of *weres* hissed and booed.

Calhoun raised his prosthesis and it shone in the light of the bonfire like a gladiator's weapon.

"Thanks to all of you, we have crushed the enemies of supernatural peace and *were* prosperity. We have brought the traitors to justice."

The far end of the circle opened again. A line of twenty werewolves marched through. Each carried a pole, but instead of a standard, every pole was topped with a were's head.

A procession of decapitated victims. I recognized two heads—those of Jerry Dunlap and Eric Bourbon. The rest must have been accomplices.

The beat of my *kundalini noir* stopped, paralyzed by yet another terror in this maelstrom of terrors. What had happened to the bodies? Was there a pole for my head?

The line of werewolves circled the bonfire, stopped, and angled the poles over the flames.

Calhoun leveled his prosthesis at the fire. "These traitors murdered our beloved Inga Latrall. Let us banish these criminals and no longer pollute our thoughts with their memory."

One by one, the werewolves tossed their poles into the fire. The circle of werewolves remained quiet, as if awed by this epic drama of werewolf justice.

I watched Bourbon's head lodge in a pile of burning logs. His hair disappeared in a quick flame and gush of smoke. His skull had settled facedown in the coals. After a moment I couldn't tell his head apart from anything else incinerating in the bonfire.

Calhoun took his place in the middle seat. He kept his face placid, yet—it might have been a trick of the shimmering light—I thought I saw a smile twist along his snout. What better revenge than to ruin your enemy and toss his head into the fire?

I had circles spinning and overlapping in my mind. This ceremony of Le Cercle. The circle of werewolves. The circle of the full moon. The circle of how I've known Eric Bourbon. In the beginning, he had showed me a decapitated *were*'s head. In the end, it was his decapitated head that I saw. I hoped this circle broke before it was my turn.

"Before we continue our celebration," the emcee shouted, "we have other business to attend to."

Dan pulled me to my feet. Hundreds of werewolves turned their snouts in my direction. The hundreds of werewolves in the circle.

CHAPTER 69

THE WEREWOLF emcee glared into the crowd from her spot on the edge of the platform. "Tonight, we must administer more justice."

The word *justice* brought a pressure that squeezed my head like a pair of torturer's tongs. The pressure relented when werewolves dragged a woman through the circle toward the bonfire. It wasn't yet my turn to suffer this macabre justice.

Where was Angela? Was she working a scheme to save me?

One werewolf yanked the woman's hair and pulled her head back in order for Calhoun, the emcee, and the council to identify her. She wore a white chef's coat, now grimy and frayed.

She was the blonde who had tried to assassinate me at the costume ball. Calhoun had said he would take care of her. What were they going to do? Tear her to pieces? Feed her to the mob? This was not justice—it was barbaric theater.

I chewed at the bit. I flexed my arms to see if the cable around my wrists had slackened. For all my huffing and straining, I remained as tightly bound as before.

The emcee beckoned and the werewolves brought the prisoner close. Her face was as white as her coat. Her eyes blinked in an unrelenting spasm of fear.

The emcee asked, "Are you Pamela Abedon?"

The woman said nothing.

A werewolf shook her hair. "Answer."

She sobbed and said, "Yes."

The emcee asked, "Were you a servant of Eric Bourbon?"

Silence. Another shaking of her hair. Another "Yes."

"Did you not collude with him to start a werewolf war?"

The woman whimpered and grew limp in the grip of her captors. "Yes."

Calhoun stood, took a deep breath, and shouted, "I've interrogated Pamela Abedon. The accused has confessed all her transgressions."

Werewolves howled in acknowledgment. Others growled in protest.

He shouted again, "Had she violated the Great Secret, her sentence would've been death."

"Death, death," chanted the werewolves. The mood turned black with the expectation of unleashed bloodlust.

The emcee raised her paw. Everyone went quiet.

Calhoun shouted, "Even though Abedon colluded with the vampire Julius Paxton . . ."

Werewolves hissed and whispered "vampire," like it was a disgusting thing to say.

". . . she acted as a trusted assistant to the late Eric Bourbon. She acted out of loyalty to him. As a human, she broke no Lycanthrope Law. I find her guilty of nothing."

Nothing? I squirmed against my restraints. "Nothing," I muttered to myself. "She tried to kill me," but the words slobbered over the bit in my mouth.

"Based on her loyal service and willingness to serve her chosen clan, I offer her the Turning."

Calhoun motioned with his prosthetic to Sean.

He stood and nodded. "As the newly chosen alpha of the Palmetto Clan, I agree." No mention that the former alpha had been the late Eric Bourbon, whose severed head now baked like a potato in the bonfire.

Calhoun returned to his chair. Sean waited for him to sit first. The emcee addressed Abedon. "Do you accept?"

Dan brought his mouth to my ear. "Not much of a choice—either she accepts or we kill her."

The woman's captors let her go. She staggered before the platform. She wrung her hands and panned the hundreds of red eyes fixed upon her.

She kept her head down and said in a faint voice, "I want to be one of you."

"Is it yes or no?" the emcee asked.

Abedon raised her head. "Yes."

The emcee lifted both paws. "She said yes."

Howls erupted. The stamping of feet shook the ground.

The emcee waited for the pandemonium to settle. "Now for the honor."

The circle became mysteriously quiet. A werewolf ran up from behind the emcee and handed her an envelope. She ripped it open.

Dan and the werewolf holding me reached into their pockets and pulled out red carnival ticket stubs. So did every werewolf except for the emcee and those on the council.

The emcee fished a red ticket stub from the envelope, gave it a turn, squinted, and bellowed, "Number 797166."

"Me. Me," shouted a squeaky voice far to my left.

Dozens of werewolves groaned and tossed their tickets to the ground.

A petite werewolf bitch sprinted from around the bonfire. She pranced and waved to the council. Her hind legs were midway between human and wolf. "My first Turning." She stopped before Abedon.

Flanked by the council and their standards, Calhoun looked like a Roman emperor at the Colosseum. He raised his good arm and werewolves barked and howled. He dropped his arm to signal the start of the Turning.

The werewolf sank to all four paws. Her snout drew into a canine muzzle. Thick fur covered her skin. The clothes drooped from her body. A shaggy tail sprang up when her jeans slid off her hips. She shook loose of her clothes and emerged no longer werewolf but a supernatural wolf.

Abedon recoiled in fright and turned to run away. Her captors snagged her. She cried out as they ripped off her clothes and pushed her naked to the ground.

One of her captors grabbed her hair and pulled her upright. "Make your Turning worthy of the honor we are bestowing on you. If not, then you die."

He pushed her away. She stumbled toward the crowd. Suddenly she stopped and whirled about. Fear had left her eyes and I saw the same cruel expression she wore when she had attacked me.

"You want me?" she shouted at the crowd. "You want me?" she shouted at the council. "You want me?" she shouted at the wolf. "Then come get me." She thumped her fist between her breasts. "Bitch to bitch." She dropped into a wrestler's crouch, extended her hands like a pair of claws, and growled.

The wolf growled back and bared her fangs. She sprang to initiate the attack.

Abedon connected with a roundhouse punch. The wolf's head snapped to the right.

Werewolves whooped and howled in glee.

The wolf and Abedon tangled on the ground, a blur of fur and naked human skin. Based on Abedon's first blow, I thought the fight would last several minutes. But it was over in less than ten seconds.

The wolf backed away, licking the shiny crimson stain on her snout. The crowd gave a collective disappointed "awww."

Abedon lay on her back, blood seeping from a bite mark on her left clavicle. The exact spot to induce the Turning.

Werewolves ran forward and grabbed Abedon by her ankles and wrists. They lifted her and jogged to the circle, which broke ranks and let them through.

The circle re-formed. Hundreds of eyes swiveled toward me. The night was quiet. The bonfire and the torches crackled.

The emcee stood in the center of the platform and stared at me. “Now for you, Felix Gomez, vampire. It is your turn to receive werewolf justice.”

CHAPTER 70

JUSTICE? I chewed at the metal bit. Clumps of spit flew from my lips. I managed to say, "What justice?" If it wasn't for me, Calhoun and Angela would be dead. At best, Eric Bourbon would be sitting up there on the platform. At worst, all these *weres* would be slaughtering one another in a prelude to the ultimate total war.

Dan wound a chain around my waist and fastened the chain to the cable securing my wrists. Another werewolf brought a long iron bar.

What did they plan to do?

I struggled against Dan, but he and his accomplice held me firm. The werewolves fit the bar between my back and the crook of my elbows. The cold iron scraped against my skin.

To my left, werewolves were sinking metal poles on opposite sides of the bonfire. The top of each pole was fashioned into a deep yoke. The iron bar on my back was long enough to reach across the bonfire and fit into the yokes.

They were going to cook me alive.

I thought I'd already hit the bottom floor of my fear, but now it felt like my insides had discovered yet a lower level and sank into greater terror. My *kundalini noir* withered into a tiny ball. I bucked from side to side, hoping to break loose.

Dan and the other werewolves had no trouble holding me in place. I gnashed my teeth against the bit, gagging on spit, cursing, damning the werewolves, damning Gullah, damning the Araneum for bringing me to this hellish end. I gnashed and cursed until my mouth went dry. The bit remained stuck to my tongue and a fierce thirst rasped my throat.

Werewolves tossed more logs onto the fire. Every spray of embers prompted cheers and joyous howls.

This couldn't be the end. I couldn't die like this, abandoned by everyone, forsaken by the Araneum.

I strained against the iron bar, feeling it give, doing to my best to channel Samson. But as soon as I relaxed, the bar flexed straight.

I was hoping for a miracle. Perhaps King Gullah and his posse would shoot up this place and rescue me. Perhaps the Araneum would parachute vampire enforcers to spring me free. Perhaps Deliah the haint would appear and go "Boo!" and all the werewolves would drop from heart attacks. Perhaps Angela—where the hell was she?—would miraculously show up and save me.

I stared at the moon hovering over us and realized I was alone. Beyond hope. Beyond mercy.

Calhoun nodded. Dan and the werewolves lifted the bar and jerked it into my armpits. I dangled on tiptoes, helpless as a gaffed fish.

"Burn. Burn. Burn," chanted the werewolves.

I was done, out of options, and about to be well done.

CHAPTER 71

A FEMALE VOICE shouted above the chanting. "Stop."

Angela Cyclone stepped into the circle. A white shirt and jeans clung tightly to her half-wolf, half-woman figure.

She was my miracle. A sudden rush of hope electrified my resolve and strengthened my *kundalini noir.*

Werewolves glowered and snarled, frustrated by the interruption of watching me turned into smoke and ash.

Angela marched close. The crowd grew more hushed. She exuded an authority that made Dan back off. Her right hand turned into a paw, extended the claws, and clipped the cord holding the bit in my mouth. She whispered, "I'm here to cash my rain check."

I spit the bit out and began working my tongue to bring the saliva back.

"I'm going to argue the nuances," she whispered again. "Remember what happened that night at the Blind Tiger Club?" Angela's paw shifted back into a hand. She faced the council and declared in a firm voice, "Spare him."

Werewolves cried out, "He must die."

Calhoun's eyes showed the thoughts worming through his mind. Surprise. Anger. Curiosity. Guile. That familiar opaque curtain fell across his face. Sean tipped his head to whisper, but Calhoun cut him off with a brisk wave of his paw.

I'd killed Bourbon, his rival, a powerful alpha. The fact that I'd prevented an idiotic war from breaking out had no bearing on the matter. Since I was a vampire, my actions had stained the reputation of the werewolves. My public execution would prove to Le Cercle that Calhoun protected them and preserved their honor.

The cries for my death grew louder. The werewolves shouted curses. The circle undulated as *weres* surged forward before the pack alphas scolded them back into formation.

The furry hearts and minds of the *were* masses had to be appeased. My pending death was intended to satisfy a twisted delusion.

The emcee's troubled gaze swung from Angela to Calhoun. She said, "The vampire must die for the murder of a clan alpha. That is the law."

Angela stood between the platform and me. "I invoke the rule of sacrifice as stipulated by Lycanthrope Law. One werewolf may accept the punishment of another."

"Of another *werewolf*," the emcee rebuked.

"No. No." The werewolves demanded my hide. The orderly circle threatened to disintegrate into a lynch mob.

All the panic and fear I'd let go of came flooding back. My bones turned to rubber. The iron bar I'd been lashed to seemed to weigh a thousand pounds. These werewolves would tear me to pieces. What was left of me wouldn't be more than vampiric hamburger.

Angela countered, "That's not what the law says. It doesn't define who may be the recipient of the sacrifice. Werewolf. Human." Angela pointed to me. "Vampire."

The emcee started to reply, but she faltered.

I whispered to Angela, "You don't have to do this Pocahontas routine for me. I'll find a way out. You go."

She spoke out the side of her mouth. "I know what I'm doing."

"Don't do it," I protested. "I won't let you burn for me."

"Felix"—Angela snipped the words—"shut the fuck up."

The council huddled around Calhoun and, after a moment, returned to their seats.

Calhoun rose and nodded to the emcee. She nodded in kind and, with a bow, stepped back.

He said, "Angela Cyclone, you've been a loyal assistant and trusted confidante. An expert in our law. I grant you the right of sacrifice." He gazed cruelly, Pontius Pilate before the Crucifixion. "You accept the vampire's guilt?"

"I accept his guilt." Angela walked forward.

"His guilt is now yours. Release the vampire."

The circle of werewolves howled and hollered in disapproval. The pack alphas barked for the *weres* to remain in place and respect Le Cercle. The dam was about to burst.

Angela turned left, right, and tossed an anxious look around, as if buffeted by the waves of anger.

Calhoun signaled to the council. They sprang from their seats and hurried down the steps to control their *weres.*

Dan unfastened the chain around my waist and the cable binding my arms. The iron bar clanged to the ground. I massaged my wrists.

"No hard feelings." Dan rested a paw on my shoulder. "I was only following orders."

"Don't mention it," I said. "If you ever get to Denver, I'll return the favor."

I was free? Relief buoyed me, but only for an instant. Werewolves kept their muzzles trained on me and hate spilled from their eyes. They weren't going to let me escape.

What about Angela? What did it mean that she accepted my guilt? If she had a plan, what was it?

She dropped to her knees on the grass before the platform.

Werewolves went crazy with howls. "No amnesty. No amnesty."

Calhoun glowered at his clan alphas as he waited for them to quiet their minions.

When silence returned, Angela lifted her head to Calhoun. "I petition you as the top alpha of Le Cercle to grant me amnesty."

Her request signaled another riotous outburst.

Dan whispered gruffly into my ear, "It's tradition to grant amnesty during this ceremony. He can't refuse without losing face."

This was her plan. Accept my guilt, then get amnesty. Ballsy. Clever.

Calhoun raised his prosthesis as if to give Angela a blessing. "As the alpha of the territory and Le Cercle, I grant you amnesty."

The howls faded to disappointed murmurs.

Angela's shoulders slumped in relief.

Calhoun lowered his arm but remained in place. He kept his eyes on the fire. Angela's gambit had robbed him of the chance of presiding over a great spectacle, watching his werewolves revel as a vampire roasted for the transgression of killing one of their own. With the fire reflecting off this shirt and face, he looked like a statue burning from within.

Angela waited for him to speak, and when he didn't, she glanced over her shoulder at me and flashed a victory grin.

Calhoun's snout wrinkled to give a sharp, calculating smile.

I recognized the expression. Powerful men rise to their station by outmaneuvering their opponents, either by force or by cunning. Whatever Angela planned, he was one step ahead.

Calhoun motioned that she stand. Angela hopped to her feet.

"Angela Cyclone," he said, his voice clear and confident, "did you offer yourself to the traitor Eric Bourbon?"

Angela straightened in shock. "I . . . I did. But—"

"And with that offer, you turned away from your clan, correct?"

"That's true, but . . ." Her voice cracked. "I did it to prevent a war. To stop Eric Bour—"

Calhoun raised his voice. "You left one clan for another without the permission of your clan alpha."

"The law," she shouted. "The law allows me to do that."

"Did Eric Bourbon accept your offer?"

Angela's posture began to wilt. "No."

I knew nothing of Lycanthrope Law but could see Calhoun's logic. Angela was in limbo between clans. She had spoiled his big show and this was his revenge.

Calhoun shouted, "Sean Moultier, alpha of the Palmetto Clan, do you accept Angela Cyclone?"

"No."

Calhoun turned his head. "Theresa Hogan, alpha of the Magnolia Clan, do you accept Angela Cyclone?"

"No."

Angela's shoulders trembled. Her head bowed. She began to cry.

Calhoun's eyes brimmed with revenge and satisfaction. "Angela Cyclone, you are without a clan. You are without a pack." His words pounded her. "You are without the family of your Turning. You are banished."

"Banished." The word rippled from *were* to *were*.

"No." She gasped and doubled over. She sank to her knees.

"Banished," I whispered as we began another spin on this carnival ride of horror.

"You are banished from this territory." Calhoun drove home the point like he was hammering a stake. "Your name will be forever chiseled into the Wall of Goness."

She clawed the grass and sobbed.

Calhoun climbed down from the platform. He hunched over Angela. His voice was low, his words barbed and stinging. "How dare you shame me? Tonight's Cercle was to be my celebration. Instead, what will be remembered about this gathering is that you came to save a vampire at the cost of avenging the death of an alpha werewolf. You snatched the laurels from my head. How dare you use the law against me."

Angela pressed her face to the ground and continued to cry.

Calhoun kept flailing her. "You robbed me. You shamed me."

Angela looked up at him. "Are you so vain?"

Calhoun tipped his head toward the platform. "You sit up there as a territory alpha and then tell me." He brought his snout close to her ear. "You chose to befriend that vampire. Then go. Let us be."

Angela lay prone in anguish. I wanted to get back at Calhoun. I was exhausted, but not too weary to take him on.

If I killed him, everything I'd fought to avoid would come to pass. There would be a war. Then so be it. Let a war start with me. Here. Now.

I tensed. My talons extended.

Two big paws seized my arms. Dan on my left. An even bigger werewolf on the right.

"Cool it, Felix. You rush Calhoun," Dan warned, "and you'll end up as undead rotisserie. Better that you and Angela cut your losses and get."

Angela pounded a fist into the dirt. Her gaze remained hooked on Calhoun as he returned to the platform. Her eyes were shiny, crimson welts of fury and pain. "Bastard. I've given him everything, and now that he's at the top, he throws me aside. His vanity is worth more than my loyalty. I'm left with nothing."

I gave her a hug. "You have me."

Angela sobbed harder.

The emcee walked to us. The flickering light from the bonfire animated the wrinkles on her face. Her expression was brittle with empathy and sorrow. "Calhoun won't enforce the banishment until dawn tomorrow. You have tonight to say good-bye to your family and pack."

The emcee cupped Angela's chin. "Several of us will soon return to Charleston. We'll see you in a few hours."

Angela wiped away tears. "Did I do the right thing?"

The emcee gave me the once-over. She let go of Angela's chin and walked off.

Angela started to get up. I grasped her arm. She leaned against me like a wounded soldier.

Werewolves hustled around the fire. They set up taiko drums and began dancing from drum to drum as they beat a rhythm that slapped the air.

The circle picked up the cadence by barking, "Roff, roff,

roff." They stamped their feet and turned to the right. The werewolves paraded in formation behind their pack standards, stamping their hind paws in rhythm with the drumming. One wolf within each group let out a long howl. Then another wolf. Then a third. Soon the night air thundered with the howling of hundreds of werewolves.

The circle parted to let us through, eyes averted, like Angela was unclean and not worthy to look at.

I had gained my life.

She had lost hers.

CHAPTER 72

THE S-76 helicopter shuttled us back to Latrall's estate. Angela found clothes and I changed out of the shirt and trousers the werewolves had shredded. She took a Lexus coupe from the garage and we zoomed back to Charleston. Destination, the Washington Arms. I had to pack and get ready to leave for Denver.

Angela's expression looked hard as glass and just as brittle. Headlamps shone in the rearview mirror and her dull dark eyes swallowed every bit of the reflected light.

My insides churned in joy and sorrow. Joy because I'd beaten the damning odds. I'd escaped being roasted by the werewolves. The enemies who had schemed to destroy me were themselves destroyed. Eric Bourbon. Julius Paxton. His vampire henchmen. There would be no werewolf war. The Great Secret remained intact. I was on my way home, safe.

Then my insides churned again, and sorrow welled through my *kundalini noir.* A viscous sorrow tainted with guilt. Guilt over those who had died by my coming here. Lemuel Cohen. His intern, Shantalya. And most of all, Wendy Teagarden.

And guilt because Angela had sacrificed herself in order to save me. She'd been ripped from her clan, her pack, and her family, and thrown out of the Lowcountry. Banished to live as a rogue.

We reached the bridge over the Cooper River. Angela relaxed her shoulders, like she was resigning herself to whatever fate awaited her.

This seemed like a good time to ask, "Why did you save me?" I hoped to hear something profound, something that would wipe away my guilt.

She kept her eyes on traffic. "Because letting you die would've been wrong."

"That's it?"

"What else do you want to hear?"

"I feel shitty about the way this has ended for you."

"So do I." Angela guided the car from lane to lane.

A CH-47 Chinook roared overhead, traveling south. Another followed. Their passengers had to be werewolves returning from Le Cercle.

The moon cast its glow across the pewter surface of the river. Dozens of ships—crammed with werewolves from outside the territory—crowded the wharf. Lights strung from the rigging gave the scene a festive glow.

A rocket shot from one of the tall ships and embroidered a trail of red sparks across the night sky.

My *kundalini noir* jumped in panic. The fear I thought I'd left behind suddenly caught up with me. Fireworks? Was this a signal? Perhaps not all the renegade *weres* had been captured, and the survivors were threatening a coup.

I sloughed off the fear. Calhoun had the territory in his supernatural grip.

More rockets launched from the ships. The first rocket burst into a cascade of gold and red sparks. The rest of the volley exploded and stabbed the velvet sky with sprays of glowing color. The blasts drummed the Lexus.

Another volley followed. Then another. In less than a

minute, Charleston along the Cooper River was lit up with a fireworks display bright as the sun.

Traffic backed up on the bridge. Angela slowed down. Colored lights from the fireworks whisked across her face and the interior of the car.

She didn't look up. "Calhoun must be very happy."

Angela kneaded the steering wheel. Hardness and brittleness returned to her face, and I thought she was about to break.

She said, "I need you to do me a favor."

Angela had given up everything for me; how could I say no? "Name it."

"Stay with me tonight."

"Absolutely."

"There's a catch," she said. "When I say good-bye to my family, you and I have to be in wolf form."

"I can do that."

Angela turned to look at me and smiled, the only time she'd done so since we left Le Cercle.

We turned off the bridge and headed south along Meeting Street. We turned left on Broad.

Pedestrians jammed the sidewalks and streets and gawked at the fireworks exploding above.

Angela tucked the Lexus into a no-parking zone between a minivan and a Dodge Charger. Keys in hand, she hustled out of the car. Together, we zigzagged through the crowds toward the Old Exchange and Provost Dungeon at the corner of Bay and Broad.

Dungeon? Didn't sound comforting, but I trusted her.

She bounded up the steps with me close behind. At the entrance, a guard in colonial dress waved us inside. One side of his upper lip curled to show a canine. Beneath the brim of his tricornered hat, his eyes shone werewolf red.

I followed Angela past the exhibits on the main floor and down the stairs to the dungeon, a large room of connected vaults made of bricks. Despite the dungeon being hundreds of years old, the extensive restorations made it seem recently built. The subterranean construction muffled the booms of the fireworks.

Mannequins in colonial-era costumes—one had a red parrot on his desk—occupied the vaults. The harbormaster. Guards. Clerks. And of course, the prisoners.

We walked to a jail cell at the back of one of the vaults. Except for Angela, me, and the mannequins, the dungeon was empty.

"Where's your family?" I asked her.

"On the way." She jiggled the cell door open and entered. She stood on the straw-covered floor next to a mannequin in a tattered pirate outfit. "We'll meet them outside."

"Outside?"

"It'll be my last night to enjoy my favorite spots. There's a network of tunnels that connects what's left of the original Charles Town. Werewolves use the tunnels to get around without being seen."

She shucked her blouse, bra, and jeans and shimmied out of her panties. Her shoulders and arms sprouted fur. Her nose darkened and her face distended into the beginnings of a snout. The sparkle returned to her eyes. She hid her folded clothes behind the mannequin.

"C'mon," she ordered. "Get undressed and turn."

I entered the cell, stripped naked, and lay in the straw.

The transformation came as it always did, in waves of pain. Afterward, I lay still for a moment. The air smelled of dank water, moldy straw, and dust.

Angela as wolf trotted around me.

I got to my paws.

She slipped out of the cell and ran down another vault. She jumped into a dirt pit and sprang toward an old wooden door. Rising on her hind legs, she smacked the door with her front paws and scooted to one side. The door popped open and revealed a dark tunnel. She disappeared into the opening and I chased after her.

The bricks of the tunnel walls were sometimes neat rows and sometimes crooked stacks that seemed ready to cave in. The loose dirt on the floor puffed beneath our paws. The tunnel cut side to side, past other doorways filled with piles of bricks and rocks.

Dim light illuminated the far end of the tunnel. The floor

sloped upward. A breeze heavy with the smells of water and plants drifted from an opening before us.

Angela scrambled up the slope. I stayed close. We climbed out of an exit disguised as an open sewer grate.

We were in a park near the ocean. I looked around to get my bearings—the southern tip of the peninsula. White Point Gardens.

Wolf musk tainted the air. I picked up the scent of five wolves slinking in the shadows, unseen by humans ooing and aahing at the fireworks.

Angela raised her tail and turned toward the other wolves.

A gush of cold air sliced through my fur. Angela didn't seem to notice. I looked in the direction of the breeze.

A bush to my right rustled. I lowered my head and advanced. I caught a new smell. Strawberry ice cream. A cup with one scoop rested at the base of a holly shrub.

The breeze circled me.

Deliah the ghost waited unseen. Because of her I'd survived two attempts on my life. I owed her almost as much as I owed Angela. Now Deliah wanted her reward.

She'd have to sleep for months to make up for the energy she'd used to bring the ice cream. I wondered where she got it. How did she know I was going to be here? More important, how was she going to know what the ice cream tasted like?

Angela scratched the dirt and gestured with her snout toward the other wolves.

I looked at the holly bush and back at her. I had one final task.

Angela lowered her tail and pressed her cold nose against mine. It was like a kiss, but it wasn't done out of desire—it was done with understanding. She turned in the direction of the wolf musk and waited for me. I continued to the holly.

A mist caressed on my face and I pictured Deliah as clearly as if I'd seen her. Gray ethereal smoke swirling into the shape of an attractive woman in her twenties. Her proud forehead. That pretty nose that kept shifting from pointed to rounded. Hair that curled from under her bandanna and trailed into vapor.

I opened my mouth and the cold wet mist swirled over my teeth and across my tongue. Deliah and her ghostly magic. My taste buds became sharper than ever before.

Now to eat the ice cream.

Deliah and I would share. This was going to be one of my better memories of Charleston.

Chapter 73

I WAS BACK where my adventures usually ended, in my office on the second floor of the Oriental Theater at the corner of Tennyson and Forty-fourth in Denver. The marquee on the front of the building was lit up and the neon bathed my office with an orange glow.

A new paperweight rested on my desk blotter. The paperweight was a deformed lead slug inside a dome of clear plastic resin. The bullet I'd clawed out of my chest. One souvenir of my trip to Charleston. Another souvenir, Wendy's key ring, rested in my top desk drawer.

I had one more souvenir of that trip. Angela.

At the moment, she wasn't in my office. She'd gone up to the roof, where, during the day, she'd sunbathe. But it was night, so she'd be looking at the moon—like the wolf she was—and sifting through her memories, her longings, her regrets.

Something tapped against the window and startled me.

But at this time of night and since I was on the second floor, the tapping could come from only one source.

A messenger crow.

The crow sat on the window. He tapped again impatiently, like I was delaying his rounds. Orange and blue highlights from the marquee and the corner streetlamp glistened across its shiny black feathers. It dug its beak into the edge of the window screen.

I opened the window sash and undid the bent nail securing the screen. The crow wiggled through the opening and hopped onto my desk. A message capsule glittered on one leg.

I unclipped the capsule and removed the cap. I turned my face to avoid the odor of rotting meat wafting out.

The crow strutted across my desk, its claws tick-ticking on the glass top.

I took the parchment note and unfolded it. The message said:

Our esteemed Felix Gomez,

Our condolences regarding the death of Wendy Teagarden. She will be missed.

You handled Julius Paxton and the impending werewolf war with your usual disregard for good sense. No one else could've succeeded considering the circumstances.

Prepare yourself for a new assignment.

Araneum

I crushed the parchment into a wad. This note was as close to an "attaboy" as I'd get from them.

Ingrates.

Assholes.

Standard procedure for destroying these notes was to expose them to sunlight. But I didn't have to wait until morning to get rid of this one.

I tossed it to the crow.

The wad of parchment landed between its feet. The crow looked at the wad and then at me with beady eyes that seemed to say: *The things I do for my job.*

The bird sighed and picked at the wad with its beak. It chewed the parchment until the entire wad disappeared into its mouth, and swallowed.

The crow shifted from foot to foot.

It burped a puff of stinky gray smoke.

I dispersed the smoke with a wave. After clipping the message capsule back on the crow's leg, I set the bird on the windowsill. It pushed against the screen, scrambled out, and leaped into the night sky. The crow fluttered past the marquee and disappeared.

I twisted the nail holding the screen in place and lowered the sash.

I left my office and took the stairs to the maintenance closet on the third floor, then climbed the ladder to the roof. I opened the access hatch and stepped out.

The roof was a flat rectangle surrounded by a low brick wall and cluttered with rusting swamp coolers, vent pipes, and discarded TV antennas. From up here I could see all over the Highlands neighborhood and to the east, the high rises of downtown Denver, the chaos of lights from the amusement rides at Elitch Gardens, and the red and white glow of traffic cruising north and south on Interstate 25.

Angela sat on a sheet of cardboard to avoid resting on the rough gravel and tar roofing. Her legs were scooped against her chest with her arms around her knees.

She was facing away from me, staring at the waning crescent moon. I knew she'd heard me, but she took no notice of my presence.

I leaned against one of the swamp coolers behind her. She wore a tank top, shorts, and flip-flops, a few of the clothes she'd bartered at the thrift store in exchange for her designer dresses and high heels.

"New tattoo?" I asked.

She touched the skin around the fresh tattoo on her upper right arm, a circle of wolf heads and broken hearts interlaced with a swirl of barbed wire.

A confusion of tattoos—more barbed wire, spines, thorns—covered her left arm from shoulder to wrist. Jagged red and blue flames flared across her shoulder blades. Her ponytail dangled over a Chinese character at the back of her neck. She had similar characters tattooed on the inside of her forearms and the backs of her calves. She wouldn't tell me what the characters meant. A full moon circled her navel and matching Carolina palm trees decorated the tops of her feet.

When we first arrived in Denver, sex had been carnal *lucha libre*. While there was vigor, the passion seemed forced, like she was trying to exorcise demons with her pelvis.

Then her thighs quit gripping me so tightly. Her bright eyes clouded with apathy. Her smile cooled. Her touch felt as though a membrane had grown between us.

If the words to warm her and bring her close to me existed, I had never found them.

She didn't have words to express herself either, as if the trauma of banishment had grown like a malignant tumor and choked her heart until it became mute. So she communicated her unhappiness with tattoos.

Angela surprised me when she waved and whispered, "Sit, I have something to tell you."

She scooted to make room on the cardboard. I sat. Our hips were close but didn't touch.

She kept her eyes on the moon. The tattoo of a star marked her neck below the earlobe. "I'm leaving."

The last pins of hope broke away, and I found myself tipping into a void of sadness.

"I'm going to Montana. Join a pack of rogue *weres*." She chuckled faintly. "That's an oxymoron. How can you have a pack of rogue werewolves?"

"I understand what you mean," I replied. She had tried to meet local *weres*, but they had shunned her.

"I'm going to miss you, Felix."

I wanted to believe her. "I'm sorry life in Denver"—I should have said *life with me*—"wasn't what you expected."

She bumped her shoulder against mine, the first gesture of affection we'd exchanged in weeks. She still didn't look at me. "Thanks for coming up. Now I need time alone."

I bumped her back. "You know where to find me."

I got up and returned to my office.

I counted the supernatural women that I'd gotten close to. Wendy was dead. Carmen remained in outer space, a prisoner of alien gangsters.

I'd lost them both and now I was losing another.

Angela.

My *kundalini noir* ached. I am an undead immortal bloodsucker. I have no heart. No soul. So where did this hurt come from?

Though I'd miss Angela, I had to let her go.

What business did I have with werewolves?